Detective Runewall
Uncut Gems

THANK you FOR YOUR SUPPORT

B.J Frost

Detective Runewall
Uncut Gems

B.T. Frost

COPYRIGHT

Acknowledgements

Foremost, I must thank my family and friends for all their support, encouragement, and patience. Years of my life have been spent talking their ears off with my grand ideas and lofty stories. Instead of talking, I got to writing.

I owe Grant MacEwan, and my instructors there, a great debt of thanks for turning me into a better writer. To McKenzie Spies, I thank you for turning my mess of a manuscript into something publishable.

To Marissa Puff, I must thank wholeheartedly for all your talent. Without your wonderful skills with the brush and pencil, my cover art would likely have been just another fantasy cover.

Last, but not least, I must thank Ansgar for taking the time to read every single chapter as I released it. His chuckle of enjoyment was the encouragement I needed; it fueled me throughout the entire first draft.

Chapter 1

Joe checked himself in the square mirror hanging on the back of the door, then adjusted his hair with a comb. Appearing untidy on the first day as a detective was not an acceptable impression he wanted to leave with the captain.

After assuring that his appearance was fit enough, he shrugged on his blue coat for – hopefully – the final time in his career. A snap of the fingers caused the wide-brim to bounce off the coat rack in the corner and lazily flip through the air to land on top of his ears. While technically forbidden from utilizing magic while in service as an officer of the law, he wasn't exactly on duty at that moment.

He checked the six-shooter in the holster under his left arm, then nodded to the reflection in the mirror. Joe unlocked the door and swung it open so that he might head out and begin the day.

The fates were unkind and heartless as The Crow stood on the other side of the door. She was tapping her foot in apparent impatience. Edith Bellcreaux was as warm-blooded as a bucket of ice. She was buttoned from neck to toe in a straight and outdated black wool dress like some eternal widow. As far as he was aware, she had never married.

The domicile in which he had taken residence seemed to emanate her persona with its drab and lifeless color palette. The wallpaper was a dull brown and gray stripe and it continued on without any hint of a whimsical pattern or desire for flair. The floorboards looked as though they hadn't been stained or oiled in decades, and the trim and cabinetry looked just as parched and lifeless.

Her fingers were entwined before her like some disapproving and grim superior. "Joseph," was said with such a sneer of vitriol; one would think he had just spat on her shoes. "Where are you going?" One ebony and silver eyebrow cocked in such a way as to suggest the question was rhetorical.

Joe didn't have time to play her mind games or subject himself to her abusive verbosities. "Excuse me, Ms. Bellcreaux, but I can't be late for work." In an attempted diplomatic gesture, he lifted his hat and lowered his eyes while attempting to sidestep her.

The overly strict landlady headed him off, and her leather boots clapped into his intended escape route. "You will stand your ground until you answer my question, Joseph." Again, she always seemed to spit his name out.

So we're going to spar again today, are we?

Joe straightened and rested his wide-brim back down on his head and squared his shoulders at his full height. He wasn't that much taller than the grave woman, only because she was a tall woman herself. "I'm attempting to head to work so that I may begin my shift as detective. You're impeding me. Why?"

Her cocked eyebrow lifted higher as she made a visible gesture of eyeing him up and down. "You're in a blue coat, you're *not* a detective." Her enunciations were like daggers.

He leaned in closer to her and glared with all the fire his young eyes could generate and ground through his teeth, "I said *begin* my shift as a detective."

She narrowed her eyes in turn, knowing that her attempted jab had not quite hit its mark. The implication hadn't been lost on her.

While she had missed the verbal technicality, the words had still dug into him. The lingering doubt as to whether he was good enough to be a detective still danced about the back of his mind, taunting.

Straightening again, he repeated the earlier unanswered question. "Why are you impeding me?"

The old crow simply stepped aside and maintained her stony disposition in answer.

Joe couldn't help but feel his eye twitch in irritation, and every corner of his mind railed for him to yell. There wasn't a single day that had gone by in the past two weeks that she hadn't tested him in one way or another. He swore she was put upon the mortal world to prick him with verbal needles until he cracked. Thankfully, two years of serving the city as an officer of the law had taught him how to maintain his outward cool in the face of outright infuriation.

The time-keeping partition he had set in his mind began to chime. The alarm snapped him back to his senses. He instinctively looked to his wristwatch and noted that if he didn't leave immediately, he would indeed be late.

Wasting no more daylight on his landlady, Joe took to the narrow stairs at the end of the hall and headed to the main floor. From there, he headed out the main door and down the steps to the street.

Residence in the brownstone walk-up had become a requirement after he received his official graduation papers. He had been a Blue Coat in the North East district, and was transferred to the South West. Traversing the entire city to get to his new precinct didn't appeal to him. The one-room occupancy, lorded by the detestable crone, was his only option with how little coin he had available.

The cobblestones were already alive with the bounce and traffic of footfalls. It was late Spring, and the rain was cool on the skin. Adjusting his hat, he made sure it wouldn't blow off with the quick pace he set. Tardiness was undeniably frowned upon for a first day.

After moving into his new lodgings, Joe had taken it upon himself to test the quickest route from home to the station. Sadly, the route to the station required quite a bit of crossing, as it was in a bit of a kitty-corner direction. Having timed the brisk walk, he was fairly certain there would still be a few minutes to spare.

It was only five minutes in and nearly halfway to the station when he stopped abruptly. Something had caught the attention of his partitioned mind.

A soft alarm was ringing out from somewhere down the alley between The Gnomish Cobbler and Pinkie's Powdered Pastries on the other side of the street. Nobody passing by seemed to notice the alarm at all. They walked on about their day as though there wasn't a sound. Some even cursed him in their passing as he blocked the walkway.

Reconnecting with the partition, he suddenly became aware that the alarm that had been triggered was magical in nature, and a barrier had been broken.

Intruders!

Joe couldn't ignore the crime taking place before him, but he wasn't on duty, and he didn't have the means to order backup.

Checking the street for any wagons or carts – self-propelled or otherwise – he quickly jogged across, ignoring any designated crossings. He was the law, after all. Once he reached the other side, he took a moment to let others pass in front of him before heading toward the mouth of the alley. Rushing forward would cause a scene. No point in alerting the perpetrators when he could catch them red-handed.

Joe waited until he had taken a few steps into the dimly lit alley before drawing his Sprocket & Iron six-shot from the holster under his coat. He wanted to catch the criminals in the act but didn't want to startle any passerby.

Taking a moment, Joe reached into the partitioned half of his mind and tasked it with homing in on the mystical disturbance. Once he was able to prioritize that to another part of his consciousness, he was free to focus on the physical world in front of him. He couldn't hear anything out of the ordinary. There wasn't any fussing or shuffling, as was common with typical ruffians. Whoever was at work was experienced enough to keep quiet.

Sidestepping closer to the outer wall of The Gnomish Cobbler, Joe slowly made his way to the intersection of back alleys. There still wasn't any unusual noise, but the portion of his mind focused on the mystical alarm told him that the building just opposite the shoe shop was the one experiencing the break-in.

The young officer lifted his hat from his head and pressed back up against the wall before peering around the corner. The back door of the opposite building was slightly ajar, and the lock looked to be busted with a few splinters of wood sticking out of the frame.

Looking to the plaque above the rear entryway, he noted that the building in question was a jeweler's shop. "Of course," he murmured his lack of surprise under his breath and stepped out, leveling his firearm at the doorway in preparation.

He adjusted his wide-brim to keep the rain from his head and shoulders, then took a few careful steps toward the breached back door.

Taking a moment, he steadied his breathing and strained his ears to listen for any noises. He could hear muffled whispering and hushing making its way toward him from the inside. A careful adjustment of the partition allowed him to focus his hearing to near fey-like sharpness. There was arguing coming from behind the door.

"Keep the gems out of sight, you numbskull!"

The admonishment came from a rather gruff individual. Based on the source they were likely of short stature. It was shortly followed by what sounded to be a meaty but non-debilitating cuff.

"Ow! S-sorry boss, I didn't mean to." The second voice seemed to come from a level height. It likely belonged to someone taller and younger than the first; by the nature of the footsteps and shuffling, they didn't seem to be all too hefty.

Noting that they were making their way to the door, Joe decided to refocus himself and bring his firearm to the ready. He shifted his weight, paused for the appropriate timing, then brought his foot up in a solid and thunderous kick to the door.

His foot and the door – as had been expected – met a great deal of resistance, as both assailants were struck squarely. Joe took the moment of chaos and panic to charge through.

Shouldering his way in, Joe leveled his firearm at the two individuals that had been knocked flat and bellowed with the aid of his finely-honed powers, "Freeze!" The thundering of his heart only fueled his door strike, barreling charge, and infused voice.

Both thieves let out a shout of surprise and threw up their arms. Intimidation magic tended to have an overpowering effect on those caught unaware, especially when the one throwing it about was fueled by the surge of the moment.

Joe noted that one of the two would-be thieves was a scrawny and ruddy-haired young man in suspenders. He didn't look to be of age, was as white as a clean sheet, and had likely been coerced by the smaller of the two. The more experienced one was an ashen-gray dark dwarf. They were commonly linked to criminal activities; much like a fox was likely to steal a chicken from the coop.

Joe looked to the scattered score littering the floorboards around his two culprits, and mentally noted the intended haul was uncut gems and bits of unfinished jewelry. A wise target, as they would be untraceable and easy to pawn on the black market. Not a bad ploy, had Joe not been nearby.

The young man shook free of the shock, then curled his knees up to his chest and began bawling like a child. The dwarf growled and began elbowing the young man in the side of the head, "Oi! Shut it!"

Joe cocked his gun with a pull of his thumb. The undeniably recognizable *click* put a deathly palpable silence on the back hallway of the jeweler's shop. The young man went wide-eyed. He simultaneously discovered and invoked the phrase 'silent as the grave'.

"Elbow him one more time," Joe shifted the aim of his barrel to the forehead of the dwarf. "I dare you."

The dark dwarf's arms shot straight up along the floorboards. "I give! I'm not touchin' the lad!" More uncut gems popped free from their improvised hiding spots as the stout man shifted on the floor. He cursed under his breath in his native tongue as he craned his head to see where the gems had fallen.

It never ceased to baffle Joe how culprits kept thinking the way they did, even when caught red-handed.

The young man on the floor continued to curl up tighter into a ball until Joe heard panicked, gasping breaths, followed by the stench of urine and sobbing. Both the dwarf and Joe had to turn their noses away and scoff at the unsightliness of it.

Not a moment afterwards, the partitioned portion of his mind informed him that the mystical alarm had been shut off. The soft yellow arcane lanterns hanging from the ceiling at the front of the store suddenly flickered to life

A half moment after the lights turned on, a fellow Blue Coat side-stepped into view with his piece raised. Joe lifted his free hand as a greeting. The white-mustached senior officer straightened out of the gun-ready stance he had entered in, then lifted a hand to scratch his temple under his hat. "How'd you get here so damn quick?" Johnson, if he remembered the name of the officer correctly, had a bit of a rasp to his voice.

Joe tilted and nodded his head to the door behind him. "Was heading in for my first shift when I caught wind of the alarm."

The elder officer seemed to beam with joviality and marched forth with his hand outstretched. "Right! You must be that new boy!"

"Uh…?" Joe looked to the outstretched hand, then to his own, holding the firearm at the two assailants at their feet.

Johnson seemed to remember himself and jumped to attention, "Right! Get up, you ol' scallywags!" He prodded the dwarf with the tip of his boot. His bushy white mustache twitched twice as he sniffed the air. "What's that smell?"

Joe nodded to the boy that was curled up on the floor, silently sobbing and shaking. "The young one had a bit of an accident."

The silent weeping ended as the young man covered his ears and shamelessly sobbed.

"Might want to find that one an advocate."

A slightly pitched voice rang out from the front of the shop. "What did those ruffians take!? Where are they? Lemme at 'em!"

Joe couldn't quite see who was producing the racket, but based on his time spent on the beat, he had a fairly good guess, "Halfling?"

Johnson snorted and nodded while stifling his own laughter and whispered loudly, "Ankle-biter could be carried off by a pigeon!" He pulled a pair of irons out from under his coat, hauled the dark dwarf up, and cuffed him.

The partition in Joe's mind was ringing loudly, and a panicked and unyielding dread overcame him as the reality that he was undeniably late for his meeting sank in. "By the stars, the captain will have my badge for breakfast. I'll be a Blue Coat till my dying days."

Johnson let out a barking fit of laughter. "HA! You'll do just fine, my boy. Not even your first day on the job, and you caught a pair of jewel thieves red-handed."

Joe felt only slightly relieved. He pulled out his notepad and stylus and began filling out his recollection of the events of the burglary so that he might pass them on to Johnson. "I'll believe it when I'm not fired this morning. If you hadn't shown up, I don't know what I would have done. I have no irons on me."

The dark dwarf must have heard their exchange, as he barked in astonishment. "What!"

An even darker thought struck him. He leaned closer to Johnson and nudged him with his elbow. "I don't have a badge…"

The old man's bushy eyebrows leapt up. "That is a bit sticky, I s'pose. But the captain will cover you; you did good, boy. Now finish your notes and hand 'em over so you can head on in for your first day!"

Joe looked down to his notes as his hand went about filling in the details. The professors at the Arcanum had told him repeatedly that learning how to divide one's mind was one of the greatest assets a caster could learn. It had proven to be an invaluable skill. Not one easily learned, but valuable beyond measure.

Johnson looked down at Joe's hand at work and whistled, "Fancy." He looked Joe in the eye, as if somehow doing so would gleam some important information he couldn't have had before. "One of them two-brainers, are ya?"

Joe didn't quite know how to respond to the inaccuracy of the question and simply left it at "Sure." He ripped out the corresponding pages, handed them over, and headed back out the door he'd burst in from. He only hoped that the captain was as kind and forgiving as mentioned.

~~

Fireballs!

Joe stood as wide-eyed and ramrod straight as a cadet on his first day at the Academy. A pair of real, electrically-charged blue dragon eyes dressed him down.

God-forsaken blasted fireballs! The captain is a dragon kin!

The captain standing before him was easily a head taller than Joe, was covered in cloudy storm-gray scales and had translucent electric-blue horns. Intimidating was about as much of an understatement as saying an active volcano was a bad choice for a campfire pit.

Joe had hoped that he would be given the chance to explain his tardiness, but the sudden and shocking realization that his precinct captain was a dragon kin was more than enough to leave him speechless. His lack of excuse was likely the reason for the painfully penetrating glare being fired at him.

The silence in the captain's office, by that point, had turned itself into an oppressive, palpable weight upon Joe's mind. He was so utterly terrified that he was afraid that any attempt to speak would turn into little more than a garbled bark or a rambling fountain of verbal incontinence.

He was so focused on trying not to fall to pieces that he developed a form of blind and deafened tunnel vision, in which the center of his entire world was a metal tack holding a piece of paper to the wall behind the captain's desk. So horrible was his focus that he didn't even realize that he had been asked a question until a pair of clawed and scaled hands clapped together directly in front of him, nearly causing him to jump out of his skin.

Captain 'Bolt' – it wasn't until that very moment that he understood the nature of the nickname – let out a brief grunt that Joe presumed to be a form of chuckle. "Ease yourself, soldier." His voice had vast depth and resonance. It was both soft and clear. He could almost feel the words vibrating inside his own chest.

Joe was uncertain as to whether Captain Bolt was calling him 'soldier' because of his service record, or because he was of the type to see all uniforms as a form of soldiering. Nonetheless, he didn't quite relax. He didn't think he'd ever know how to relax in the presence of one that was akin to a dragon. "S-s-sir." His heart continued to hammer like a drum at an execution sentence.

"Take a breath before you forget how."

Joe frowned in thought and decided to actively engage in some slow-breathing exercises he recalled from his days at the Arcanum. He honestly never thought he'd ever need to resort to such a simple basic form. "Yes, sir."

"Now stop panicking. Johnson informed me of your run-in over the Crystalline Network before you arrived." The Captain turned away from Joe and headed back around his desk to sit down.

Wait… What?

The thunderously chuckling dragon kin shuffled his way down to sit at his hilariously small desk and picked up a stylus to begin sifting through a pile of reports. "See your way down to the quartermaster to pick up your new armaments… you're dismissed."

"I… it… Johnson." His brain still hadn't quite caught up with what was happening.

Captain Bolt's head was amongst his papers when his powerful voice slowly rose to fill the room in its calming yet deep way. "Do you have trouble finding the door, Detective Runewall?" The massive lizard-like head slowly rose to pierce him with its electric gaze.

Joe was jolted into action and he quickly and embarrassingly bowed, saluted, and curtsied, then jumped out the door before he could think of some other means by which to prostrate himself before his superior.

With all that had happened that morning, he never thought he'd honestly see the day where his name was prefixed with 'detective'. Standing in the noise and hubbub of the bullpen, Joe couldn't help but feel a swell of pride.

He'd made it. Through all the turmoil and drudgery, he'd made it. Little did he realize how much he would then struggle to keep it.

Chapter 2

The quartermaster of any given precinct was located in the basement. Most of the basements in the precincts throughout the city of Stormbay were built upon the foundations of old guard barracks. The stonework dated back to an era when justice was dispersed from the tip of a spear, and a law officer's uniform was a helmet and shield.

Joe was rather glad that the world had advanced to a more civilized era. Some savage races still held to the old traditions, but they weren't ever likely to be seen roaming the city streets. Six-shooters and long-barrels were the new armaments of choice.

The descent into the quartermaster's domain was punctuated by the scent of gunpowder, polishing wax, oil, and rank dwarven sweat. The stone bunker was dimly lit with old and flickering sunstone lanterns. It gave the place a grungy tavern-like appearance.

A square metal cage took up much of the room, and an improvised firing range was at the far end.

Joe made his way down the stairs and stepped toward the large metal cage. There was a small window near the far end. He guessed that to be where he would pick up his new supplies. "Ahem…" He cleared his throat, then double checked his notepad for the proper spelling and pronunciation, "Dwobrom Grimstone?"

A bald-headed dwarf peered out from behind a weapons rack of long-barrels. He had what looked to be a gun barrel and an oil-stained rag in hand. "Aye!" His grin was full of gaps from missing teeth, and he had a wild look in his eye. "Boys call me Grimbomb!"

As the deranged-looking man stepped into the lamplight, Joe was unnerved to see that the dwarf's face looked as though it had been staring down the barrel of belching cannons. Soot was splattered in an explosive manner, and much of his ruddy beard and mustache looked to be singed black at the tips.

Joe put together enough evidence to simply nod in understanding. "With good reason, by the looks of it."

Grimbomb grinned wildly and laughed maniacally with a look of wide-eyed insanity as he stepped up to the small window. "What can I do ye' for?"

Joe leaned against the wooden countertop with his elbow and slid his official papers under the gate-framed window.

The long-barrel that the crazed dwarf had been holding simply dropped to the floor in a loud, clanging raucous. The attention-addled living powder keg scooped up the once pristine papers and soiled them with his grubby fingers.

Fireballs!

"Ahh! You're the green boy!" His eyebrows leapt up in excitement as his eyes darted across the page. "Yes, yes, yes! New things! New toys!" He turned and headed off down the aisles of armor and weaponry and began barking into the dark. "Vest! Coat! Badge! Boots! Hat!" he rattled off the list as he went.

Joe breathed out a sigh of exasperation as he felt that his time dealing with the quartermaster would be anything but uneventful.

As if to punctuate his thoughts, a belching bellow of flames suddenly erupted from somewhere far back amongst the stacks. Joe bolted upright and immediately began looking about for a bucket of water.

Grimbomb emerged from the darkness at a jog with a trail of black smoke curling off his body. "It's a'right!" I got it!" He had a pair of boots in one hand and the papers in the other. He made a quick stop at the gate and dropped off the boots and turned back to hurry on into the darkness once again.

Joe stared in disbelief for some time before deciding the dwarf wasn't going to return and explain himself. It took a moment more for him to trust that the boots wouldn't spontaneously combust before picking them up. He took them to a nearby chair with the same care one might give an incendiary device.

Before switching out his well-worn Blue Coat walkers, he gave the new boots a once over. They had the city seal of a cloud and bolt of lightning emblazoned on either side, just below the rim. They were well-tailored black leather and lifted to just above his ankles. They didn't smell of soot or explosive powder, and they actually looked clean.

There was a hint of magic trailing through the stitches and sole. They were undoubtedly enchanted to stay spotless, protect him from slips and falls, and likely any lightning strikes that were bound to occur. He stood up, and like anyone testing out shoes for the first time, paced back and forth to get a feel for them.

Comfy, sturdy, acceptable.

Joe approved. It was then that he noted that Grimbomb had dropped off another article while he was testing his shoes – a paper parcel wrapped in twine. A black wide-brim hat sat atop the parcel.

Fluttering overtook his heart as he slowly stepped toward the very thing he had worked so hard to achieve. It sat there in the light of the lantern like some grand relic on display at the museum.

It was almost tempting to simply let it sit there, basking in the light of his hard-won accomplishments. He paid no attention as Grimbomb returned in a huffing jog. It was several more moments before he heard the crazed man speak. "I've seen that look before, lad… take it."

He looked to the dwarf in slight confusion. "What look?"

Grimbomb let out a roaring belly-rolling laugh. He steadied himself and wiped a tear from his eye before answering with his half-toothed grin. "The look every dwarven boy gets when he receives his first hammer. The look every boy gets when he becomes a man… If you're here–" he lazily and momentarily lifted his hand and the paper in it "–with this paper, it means ye' earned it."

The crazed and explosive-happy quartermaster dropped off a small wooden box and turned to head back down amongst the aisles at a leisurely pace.

Joe took the advice and stepped toward the package. At first, he didn't want to rip the packaging out of fear he'd damage what was inside, but childish glee overtook him and he grinned as he tore the paper apart to get at what was within.

As soon as it was revealed to him, he loved it. The tan cotton was of high thread count and as smooth as the finest silk. Blue ribbons of arcane lettering were symmetrically stitched into the seams and down the button lining.

He took a step back and pulled the trench coat from the packaging and held it up into the light. It would easily reach to his shins, just as his blue coat did. It was lighter and in far better condition than the ratty coat he'd worn on the streets for the past two years.

Joe hung the coat on a nearby rack and shrugged off his old one, tossing it on the chair where he'd left his old shoes. He turned back to the packaging and un-wrapped the vibrant blue vest that had been included. It was similarly stitched with arcane lettering and would likely do a better job of protecting him than his current one.

A quick glance into the partitioned portion of his mind told him that all the necessary enchantments were in place: fire protection, shielding, magical resistances, deep pockets, and a handful of others.

Hesitation was lost in joy as he quickly swapped out the old for the new. Once he buttoned his new vest, he reached out to grab his gun and holster to throw them back on. That was when he remembered he'd be issued a new sidearm.

Frowning in thought, he turned to look to the cage, but didn't see Grimbomb or a gun case.

"Over here!"

God-blasted fireballs!

Joe nearly screamed in surprise, as the dwarf had somehow managed to get to the far side of the room without him noticing. "How did you–"

"Side door!" Grimbomb barked with a sly grin.

A quick glance of the layout of the stone-wrought foundations confirmed that a side door was indeed how the unnerving dwarf had managed to get by him.

Joe sighed in relief, checked his partitioned mind to be on high alert, then made his way to Grimbomb. "What are you–"

A frightening grin, a wooden gun crate, and a target at the far wall was all that was needed to answer the question he had begun to pose to the quartermaster "Never mind." The gun range had a small table for resting your arms or stationing ammunition. There was even a spyglass for eyeballing the targets after a shot was fired.

The wooden gun crate cradled in the quartermaster's arms was lined with hard-packed scraps of oil-stained rags. Nestled within was a well-polished six-shooter. The stock looked to be carved from dark-stained maple. Joe reached in and hefted the shining steel into his hand to test its weight. He was shocked to find it alarmingly light.

As if in answer to the thought that was just about to burst from his lips, Grimbomb explained, "High-grade gnomish stainless steel." He gingerly took the gun from Joe's hand, flicked the barrel out with his wrist and gave it a quick spin with his fingertips; it whirred for several long seconds. "Perfectly balanced cartridge barrel and alignment."

Grimbomb stuffed a round into one of the chambers of the barrel, flicked the cartridge into place, aligned the round with the barrel with a free finger, pulled back the hammer with his thumb, aimed along the sight to the target at the far end of the room, and fired.

So quick and smooth were the quartermaster's actions, Joe barely had enough time to stick his fingers into his ears before Grimbomb managed to fire off the round. The raucous eruption of gunpowder caused his ears to ring. It usually wasn't wise to fire a gun indoors, especially without the arcane audible muffling provided by his wide-brim.

The wood and straw target at the far end of the room leaped a smidge into the air upon being struck and settled in a cloud of dust.

Joe pulled his fingers from his ears and squinted at the target. He reached down, snatched up the spyglass and peered at the target. "You hit the bullseye!"

The mad dwarf chuckled triumphantly, "Aye! Ye' tend to get good at this sort of thing when ye' do it long enough."

Joe had an unnerving feeling that the dwarf was just as deadly in the streets if a quick draw was required.

Grimbomb was kind enough to hand the gun back to him with the barrel still smoking. "One more thing, lad." He stepped passed Joe and ushered him back toward the cage. "ye'll need yer ammunition." His firearm wasn't much good without bullets, so Joe followed.

The dwarf stopped at the countertop, reached inside, and picked up the small wooden box he had dropped off earlier. He pried it open, facing Joe.

Inside the box were a few rows of freshly pressed rounds. Some looked rather odd to him. "These," Grimbomb's meaty finger pointed to the top two rows, "are yer standards." He continued with his finger, tapping each row in turn. The next line of bullets was anti-magic, designed to penetrate arcane barriers. The next were tracers; the glass tips held a luminescent green liquid that bubbled about as they were shaken. The last row looked to be made from bone.

Joe pointed to the last with raised eyebrows. The 'bone' bullets looked as though they had been hollowed out and were carved in an odd fashion.

It was at that point that the dwarf's maddeningly joyful grin vanished and his brow furrowed in serious consternation. "Those be yer wailing banshees."

A very real chill ran down Joe's spine as he withdrew his finger. He'd heard of them but had never seen one before.

During his last day at the Academy, his Instructors warned him that he may one day require the aid of a wailing banshee. They didn't have any for demonstration purposes, and so had only explained what they were intended for.

Detectives in the arcane law enforcement were often targeted by organized criminal enterprises in an attempt to prevent any hindrances to business practices.

Due to that grisly reality, all detectives were required to carry a whistling bullet carved from bone. When a detective was in a jam that meant the difference between life and death, they would fire one of those bullets into the air to draw backup. It was said they could wake the neighborhood with a single shot. Few had ever been fired off before. He had never heard one himself.

Joe appreciated the explanations and took the small wooden case, "I understand."

His new firearm, thankfully, fit his old gun holster. His trench coat fit perfectly – not that he had doubted it, as he had been fitted for it a few moons earlier. The black wide-brim fit snug over his ears, and he felt all the more like a detective when he looked at himself in a banged-up metal sheet that Grimbomb had lying about.

Wait...

"Where is it?" Joe frowned at Grimbomb, then gestured with his hands as though he should be holding a broom.

The quartermaster waved his arm for Joe to follow. "That's not something I can give. Ye' have to find it yerself." The stout man headed to a door adjacent to the stairs heading back up to the main floor.

Joe thought it odd that he didn't notice it before, but figured it was simply due to the alarming and captivating nature of the quartermaster.

The dwarf stopped before the door and pulled out a keyring, mumbled something under his breath, unlocked the door with what appeared to be an antique white metal key and shuffled away from the door while avoiding looking at it.

"What do you–"

"Nope!" Grimbomb waved his arms frantically as he huffed and hurried past him to head back to his metal cage. "Find it yerself!" The dwarf skidded to a halt at the cage door and threw himself inside, slamming the door behind him.

Joe looked back to the door in question and tapped the partitioned portion of his mind.

Ah, that's why.

It was humming with energy, and the room beyond it was wrapped in layers of protective magic. He could feel the threads of alarms that strung out into the distance. No wonder the dwarf was frightened by it. He'd probably been stung by it in a moment of weakness and curiosity.

Joe lifted one hand and reached out to touch the door with his eyes closed. The door handle felt like any other door handle – simple, brass, round, cold. Just beneath that physical surface was a monstrous beast.

Anyone inexperienced in the flow and eddies of magic would undoubtedly sense a massive, snarling, gnashing, angry creature lurking just beneath the skin of the metal handle. In truth, it was merely a form of intimidation magic designed to deter people from even attempting to enter. Joe guessed that the magic was not designed to frighten him, as he was able to notice the magic immediately for what it was.

Time with the Royal Arcane Forces and years studying at the Arcanum had given him a sturdy understanding and experienced touch when it came to defensive barriers. The one surrounding the room he was about to enter was one high-caliber wall of power. "Color me impressed," he muttered to himself.

The part that unnerved him was that he could sense nothing other than the barriers. Not knowing what he was walking into, even within the confines of the precinct, didn't exactly calm the fairies in his stomach.

Turning the knob and pushing forward, Joe inexplicably found himself standing in a void of a room. There was no door behind him. There was no floor beneath him or anything surrounding him. It was just emptiness. Was it a trick? Had he been bamboozled?

Fireballs!

Joe shut his eyes, fully dropped the partition and opened his mind's eye to the energies of the room. Turning about, he found himself surrounded by nothingness. He could hear his feet shuffling across what sounded like standard stone and mortar, but he could feel nothing of it beneath him. There was no sensation of the walls or the magical barriers and alarms that should be infused throughout the walls. "What is this place?"

In immediate response to his words, an entity appeared to his left. Joe turned to it, only to find it little more than a free-floating vaporous construct of an idea. The color felt orange. He could not actually see it so much as feel it.

Curiosity?

He reached for the vaporous form, only for it to vanish in a trail of smoke.

Another entity appeared within his mind's eye – opposite of the first. It lasted for an even shorter period and vanished before he could even get a taste of what it was. Another appeared, then another, and another. Each entity felt like a form of thought; they all appeared and vanished in a shorter time than the one before it. "What–"

A wrenching pull in his gut yanked him nearly off his feet. Joe snapped open his eyes and wheeled his arms to catch himself from falling over. Thankfully, he was able to steady himself.

Somehow, he was back outside the door and facing the stony depths of the foundation. The quartermaster's cage and firing range were directly in front of him.

Grimbomb was hiding behind his counter with his eyes and nose peering up over the edge.

Turning about, he found the door he thought he'd just entered was shut. A quick test of the handle proved the door to be locked.

Thumping blue pixies... what the devils just happened?

"Oh my," the pitched voice rang out from the top of the stairs. Joe jumped and turned to look to the source. There, at the top step, a diminutive figure stood, silhouetted in the light of the doorway, "that hasn't happened in some time."

Joe couldn't help but dart his eyes from the door to the unnamed figure. "I – that – it – what?"

A bespectacled, white-bearded gnome casually bounced down the steps while Joe repeatedly attempted to jiggle the door open. "What happened?"

The elderly gnome turned his pinched-pink cheeks and a calmly polite grin toward Joe and declared in a delightfully pleasant tone, "You've been rejected."

C h a p t e r 3

A barrel of questions began bubbling to the surface. Joe was about to unleash them all when the mirthful gnome put up one finger as a signal for silence and chuckled pleasantly. "Calm yourself, Joseph. I will explain everything."

He turned back around and gestured up the steps. "Come, and do not fret, you haven't been rejected as a detective."

Joe opened his mouth when the gnome erected his small finger once more. "The panic-addled fear is plainly painted across your face, young man."

Despite the white hair and obvious wrinkles about the eyes, the gnome hopped up the steps with the ease and grace of a skipping child. He also bore the tan trench coat of a detective. "Come along!"

With his wits scattered about, Joe had no other option than to follow. Once they reached the main floor, the gnome proceeded to wave Joe onward. With the waist-high guide in the lead, they proceeded to walk past the Blue Coat desks and holding cells. Both the gem thieves were in holding from the morning's arrest.

After climbing a set of winding iron stairs, they made their way to the detectives' bull-pen. There didn't seem to be any attention given to the two of them. It was as if nothing that took place in the strange room had been apparent to anyone, or they simply didn't care.

The frustratingly jovial gnome waved Joe over to a squat desk that was half as tall as any of the others. With a snap of his tiny fingers, he summoned a chair from the corner of the room. It did not glide through the air or rub across the floor as he expected might happen. Instead, the chair simply vanished in a puff of bright blue, glittery smoke, and re-appeared in the same fashion, directly in front of the gnome's desk.

Joe had never seen magic implemented in that fashion before, nor could he sense any of it. There were no eddies in the flow of the natural world, nor were there any vacuums created by the sudden absence of the chair from where it had been pulled from.

He turned his attention to the grinning man and narrowed his eyes, "You're a trickster gnome, aren't you."

The pint-sized detective threw back his head and let out a gleeful fit of laughter, "Hahaha! Brilliant!" He clapped enthusiastically and let out a sigh of exultation.

Joe decided that he'd had far too many experiences with eccentric characters for the day. He tested the chair a few times by prodding it with his finger before daring to sit upon it. Trickster gnomes weren't named such without reason.

The moment he sat, the chair suddenly released a geyser of confetti with a loud pop. Joe naturally jumped from the sudden explosion, only to hang his head in his hands. "I'm not in the mood for this right now. Can you please just explain to me what is going on?" He looked to the gnome for answers, only to find the man kicked back in his chair with his fingers entwined behind his head and his feet up on his desk.

Joe seriously considered if this was some form of game that the gnome was playing with him. "Why couldn't I simply pick up my staff?"

He briefly reached out with his senses and felt that the room was still there – deep in the foundations – and it was just as ominous as when he first eyed it. "Did you do this?" Each question that bubbled to the surface made him angrier as the gnome simply sat and smiled. He did, however, note that the smile was fading.

Another thought suddenly emerged. "Are you even a detective here? Am I being pranked?" Joe bolted upright to a standing position and felt righteous anger rise within him, threatening to take over his reasoning.

A tiny snap of the fingers caused a brass plaque to suddenly pop into existence upon the desk, directly in front of Joe. It startled him slightly, just as anything the gnome did seemed to have that effect.

Tilting his head so that he might read what was etched upon it, Joe felt a sudden drop of his heart.

Oh… Fireballs…

He had just yelled at his training officer and accused him of being a fraud. He could feel the heated anger drain from his face.

The grin re-appeared. Senior Detective Wadnar Pettlebottom dropped his feet from the desk, leaned forward, and placed his elbows upon the polished wood. "Now, which question should I answer first?"

Joe flopped back down into his seat, his eyes unmoving from the small brass plaque. Party streamers of various colors erupted from the chair this time instead of confetti. He didn't jump or even notice them until they fell around him and disappeared in a shower of sparks.

While Joe admitted to himself that Pettlebottom was an unusual name, it wasn't impossible for it to belong to a human. He hadn't considered a trickster gnome as he had believed that most fey-born had retreated to their native realm following the War for Silvertree.

He lifted his gaze and opened his mouth to apologize when the grinning gnome lifted his hand to stop him. "Say nothing. You were well within your rights to question everything. That is our job now, isn't it?" His bushy white eyebrows were raised high as if imploring Joe to agree.

"Uh... yes." Joe panicked upon realization of his mistake and immediately corrected himself, "Yes, sir!"

"Pah!" Detective Pettlebottom waved it off. "No need to be so formal with me, boy. I also prefer 'Petals', if you don't mind." He turned his attention to his desk and snapped his fingers once again. With another puff of bright blue glittery smoke, Joe's file appeared on the gnome's desk, perfectly in front of him.

Petals swiped his finger through the air as if turning a page, and the folder flopped open of its own accord. "Ah... Joseph Runewall." He grinned as he adjusted the spectacles that were precariously balanced upon his nose and continued to read, "Approximately 22 years of age. You stand at six and an eighth steps; weight two stone and four pebbles. Orphaned and left on the doorsteps of the Temple of Light and raised in their care until the age of six. You were then in the dual care of the Arcanum and the Temple until you were of age." He looked up from his spectacles, "Correct so far?"

Joe simply nodded as his life was picked apart by the very man that would decide his performance as a first-year detective.

Petals continued grinning and returned to the document at hand. "You were conscripted at the age of fourteen." He took a moment to tsk and sigh. "Far too young." He returned to reading Joe's file. "You spent one and a half years as a Green Coat during the War for Silvertree, through the Royal Arcane Forces."

He looked up from the paperwork and squinted at Joe. "Tell me about that." He genuinely seemed to care and wasn't grinning, beaming, laughing, or prodding for a giggle.

With the same rigid practice that had been beaten into him as a cadet, he answered honestly and succinctly. "Stationed with the 47th platoon, Tertiary Defensive Unit, assigned with protecting the medical tents and supply trains, sir." He let loose with the formal ending as it had been drilled into him. "Uh, sorry, sir – I mean 'Petals'."

A soft chuckle escaped as he waved off the apology and returned to reading. "Upon returning to the Arcanum you turned the attention of your studies to arcane law enforcement… how interesting."

He couldn't help but raise his hand, as though he were once again a child in lecture. "Uh… Petals, sir, I understand your need to review my file, but what about what happened, in that room? My staff?"

The soft grin grew wider, "I'm in the process of answering the question. Pay attention."

"Yes, sir – I mean Petals." Joe placed an interceptive partition in his mind to stop calling Petals 'sir'. It was only a temporary solution; he couldn't waste that sort of effort on such a small issue. The partition had more important tasks than remembering a simple verbal flop.

"So something happened while you were a Green Coat that made you want to become an officer of the law."

He nodded again. "I saw the suffering of those in the medical tents."

Petals' bushy white eyebrows leapt up. "Oh? Why not join the medical corp then? Ease the suffering?"

Joe shook his head. "Doctors are all well and good, but they treat those that are already suffering. I wanted to stop the suffering from happening at all."

A wide, knowing grin spread across the gnome's face, causing his full white beard to shift slightly. "Some might argue with you, that your job is to discover the culprits behind a crime already committed."

Joe hardened his resolve and sat a bit straighter. He remembered well his instructors from his days back at the Academy, and the staunch ideology they preached. "A petty criminal today may be a hardened criminal tomorrow. Success breeds success and further suffering. Every scumbag I put away prevents further injury."

Petals applauded him and laughed heartily. "Hahaha! Excellent!"

Confusion overtook him once again and Joe was forced to re-ask. "What does this have to do with my staff?"

"Everything, my dear boy."

Joe simply sat staring at his superior in abject confusion.

Petals let out a deep sigh, "I suppose you're not that smart yet."

He changed his furrowed confusion to a scowl.

Another bout of laughter erupted from the detective. "Calm yourself, I shall explain."

He let out a small sigh of relief, as it had been an emotional roller-coaster of a day, and they hadn't even made it to the midday break.

"The room the quartermaster granted you access to was indeed the room you would enter to acquire your staff. Unfortunately for you, you're not able to pick from those staffs... or to be more precise, there were no available staffs that fit *you*."

Joe had never heard of such a thing. "Pardon?"

Petals lifted a finger and leaned closer while lowering his voice, "One of the many secrets they keep hidden from students of the Arcanum."

He continued to stare in bewilderment, "What secret?"

"As you are well aware, there are many different kinds of implements that a magic wielder might utilize to focus or strengthen their spell-craft."

Children were aware of such things. "Yes, but I used a staff while a Green Coat for the Royal Arcane Forces. Why did I get rejected if I could utilize that one?"

Petals pointed at him with fervor, "That is the rub! What is the difference between the one you were given, and the staffs in that room?"

Joe felt the weight of the scrutinizing mind being pressed upon him. He was being tested.

All right, I'm game.

The staff that had been given to him by the Royal Arcane Forces was a standard white oak with runes burned into the surface. As a youth, he couldn't quite sense the difference between that staff and a broomstick, but it did seem to allow him to respond more quickly and effectively when it came to setting out or holding mystical barriers. Had he looked at the same staff again, he was certain he'd notice more, as his senses were better attuned since that time. Joe felt that there was more to the answer than that.

He had been handed the staff by an army quartermaster. There was a significant difference between that man and Grimbomb. Not only were they distinctly different individuals, but Grimbomb was terrified of the door that the staffs were housed behind. The dwarf also refused to get the staff for him.

Solid clue, but that's not the whole picture.

Joe crossed his arms and leaned back in the chair as he chewed on what other information he had been given.

Petals said that Joe had been 'rejected' and that he had been deemed 'unable to pick', that no staff fit him. Such a thing implied that the staffs in the precinct were designed with highly specific requirements of ownership, if not sentience.

Joe shut his eyes and pinched his nose after having pieced the bits together. "The staffs provided by the army weren't real staffs, or they were of such poor quality that they barely counted as such. The ones held by the precinct's quartermaster are the real deal."

There was another round of jovial applause and praise. "Hope for you yet, my boy." Petals grunted as he hopped down from his chair and proceeded to the stairwell. "Come along, we have work to do."

What?

A tinge of worry pricked him to attention. "But don't I require a staff to be a proper detective?"

Petals turned back around to stand at the top of the spiraling iron stairs and adjusted a wide-brim hat that had not been in the small gnome's possession earlier. "You also require a few other things you failed to collect from the quartermaster in your haste, don't you?"

Fireballs!

~~

"Where are we going?" Joe had to maintain a brisk pace to keep up with the surprisingly quick-footed elderly gnome. They had returned to the street, and neither of them was carrying a staff. That thought unnerved him the most. The true mark of an arcane law enforcement detective was the wizard's staff.

A small finger lifted in exclamation, "To the scene of the crime, my boy!"

Joe took note of the direction they were headed in and realized they were heading down the path he had taken to work that morning.

Once they rounded the corner, Joe realized exactly what crime they were headed toward: Billburn's Brass and Gold. It was the very jewelry store that had been broken into that morning.

Instead of heading down the alley to enter through the back as he had done while following the thieves, they took the street down toward the main entrance.

The front entry was framed with glass cases and sparkling gems of various colors and qualities, set into gold. There were bracelets, rings, necklaces, broaches – none of which were anywhere within Joe's price range based on the tags he saw on some of the smaller items.

Petals stopped at the door, made a slight bow, and motioned with both of his hands. He was gesturing for Joe to step in first. He naturally questioned the courteous offering he had just been given and deemed it to be some sort of trick. After a moment's thought, he simply gave in and accepted whatever fate the prank-happy fey-born deemed appropriate for the moment.

The door glided open as if by some magical unseen command and the bell above the door jangled, announcing the arrival of a new customer. No trick... yet.

He knew that his senses weren't dulled or broken, as he still sensed the magical alarms and barriers around the jewelry store, and his enchanted armaments and clothing, but the gnome's magic might as well have been the workings of a ghost. That was the annoying part about trickster gnomes; their magic was near impossible to detect, and Joe detected absolutely nothing.

With a deep sigh, he followed his training officer's directions and stepped into the storefront and out of the gentle nip of the spring air. At the very least, it was starting to get brighter outside. Perhaps a sunnier day would bring about a sunnier mindset from all the chaos he had experienced that morning.

A sharp-eared halfling hurried to the front of the store, emerging from the hallway that lead to the broken back door that Joe had kicked in earlier. He huffed and greeted Joe with a worried smile, "Hello! Hello! Welcome! Nothing wrong here!"

For the very first time in his life, Joe pulled the crisp brass badge from his belt on his hip, held it aloft for the halfling to see, and introduced himself. "I'm Detective Runewall, and this–"

"PETALBOTTOM!" The halfling exclaimed, flying past him to hug the elder gnome.

Why do I bother saying words? Not like I won't be interrupted again... Why don't I get hugs?

Joe sighed, dropped his hand, and tucked his badge back onto his belt before turning to face the shopkeeper and the senior detective as they embraced. "Of course you know him; he's the senior detective in the neighborhood precinct."

Petals patted the back of the obviously distraught shopkeeper, "There-there, Billburn."

Billburn pushed himself away so that he might look to his friend and gave his shoulders a squeeze. "I know things will be well now that you're on the case."

Hey!

"Hey!" Joe couldn't help but feel a stab in the heart from the comment. He paused to think beyond his immediate insult. "Wait... case?"

Billburn turned and immediately apologized to him. "My apologies, young man, but..." He frowned as he looked Joe up and down. The man then pulled down a pair of jeweler's goggles that had been sitting atop his head and peered up at him through them. "You're new... who did you say you were again?"

Petals stepped between them and patted Joe on the arm, "There-there, my boy. No insult was intended, and no harm was done." He stepped onward to begin looking about the store with a critical eye. "And yes, there is a case still to resolve here."

"But I caught the culprits in the act this morning." Joe had even seen the ashen-skinned dark dwarf in the cells earlier when heading down and back up from the quartermaster.

Petals turned on the spot and grinned madly. "That may be true, but the case remains open, until we close it."

It dawned on him then. "Ah... what better first case to close than the one I opened this morning."

"Precisely!" Petals beamed. "Now, where was the third assailant?"

"Pardon?"

Please be joking.

Chapter 4

Petals guided both Billburn and Joe to the back door. He produced a silver cylindrical eyepiece with a luminescent lime-green lens from one of his vest pockets. "This," he declared while holding it for the both of them to see, "is a track-finding lens."

Joe reached out and picked up the small cylindrical silver spyglass, then peered through the indicated end with the other eye closed. The world around him was as black as a starless night sky. Footprints covering the ground, however, were as bright as the lime-green lens. "Huh!"

Footprints of varying sizes littered the ground like a forest. It didn't surprise him, as there had been quite the traffic in the past few hours surrounding the earlier break-in.

A lecture from several years prior popped to the front of his mind. It covered detective's tools and evidence gathering.

Right!

He took the lens from his eye and began examining it with his arcane senses. He immediately discovered that a metal outer ring could be turned. "Ah!" Joe stuck the spyglass back to his eye and began to twist the metal ring. With each *click*, a set of footprints was singled out and the others vanished. Once the footprints had all been accounted for, the visual returned to the mass of green treads. "Aha!"

Billburn began to jump up and down, expanding upon the green chaos that spread across the floor, "What is it? What is it?" To think most people considered halflings to be the calm and relaxed sort.

Joe hushed the store owner and waved him off with his hand, "Hold your horses, I'm in the process of learning and discovering." He returned to turning the dial and began counting. "Mr. Billburn?"

"Yes!" He seemed far too excitable.

"How many do you employ besides yourself?" He didn't know when or how, but Petals caught on to something that Joe would never have seen without the aid of the spyglass.

"None, it's just me!"

"Hmm…" Joe pulled the spyglass from his eye, looked about the room, and gazed upon the windows at the front of the store. "Too obvious," he said to himself. He turned to look to Petals, who stood in the alleyway.

The prankster threw his head back and burst out laughing while pointing at Joe.

Billburn snorted and turned his reddening face away from Joe so that he might stare into the back room and work area.

Joe quickly looked about the jeweler's shop, then stepped toward a glass display case to examine himself within the clean reflection. His dark brown hair was still neat and well-combed, his chin was smooth, but the eyelid and some of his eyebrow with which he had peered through the spyglass was painted in a swirling rainbow of colors.

"F–!"

~~

Joe sat on a crate in the alleyway behind the jewelry shop and seethed as he wiped at his eye with a wizard's handkerchief. It took a bit more time than was usual for an anti-magic cloth, but he eventually was able to remove the color that had 'mysteriously' found its way onto his face. "That wasn't funny."

Petals stood with one boot on an upended and discarded metal bucket with a look of absolute triumph slapped across his face. The angrier Joe got, the funnier it became for him. He laughed so hard that Joe thought the little man was going to die from asphyxiation.

Wanting to drop the subject and return to the matter at hand, Joe gestured toward his superior. "Mind informing me where you discovered the extra set of boot prints?"

Petals snapped his fingers and utilized magic that Joe couldn't sense to highlight a trail of footprints that started at one end of the alley and slowly revealed themselves one step at a time toward a steel storm grate at the far end.

Petals didn't need the spyglass.

I hate you.

As if sensing his enraged thoughts, Petals put his foot down and stepped over to Joe with his hands clasped behind his back. "It took me a great many years to learn these skills and the knowledge of when and where to use them. Don't be too hard on yourself."

"And my staff?" He had no more patience for games or half-answers. He felt the gaze of the gnome for a short while longer as Joe kept his eyes focused on the storm grate. He couldn't look his superior in the eye. He was simply too angry.

"How did you come to the attention of the Arcanum?" Petals turned and began walking down the alley, eyeing the sun that was rising higher in the sky.

The wizard's handkerchief came away clean from his face. After examining it and shaking it out, he stuffed it back into his left vest pocket, then wiped his face with his hand before covering his eyes and sighing, "What does that have to do with my staff?"

"Answer the question, young man." There was a touch of sternness to the order.

He lifted his head and looked to the gnome. His back was turned. Joe could read nothing of the emotional state, but the warning had been as clear as a ringing bell.

"I cast magic while at the orphanage." He didn't feel it necessary to go into more detail.

"Something you learned from a book?" The gnome kept his hands clasped behind his back as he looked up at the sky. The tone had returned to that of curiosity.

"No, I did it instinctively."

There was a long pause between the two of them before Petals turned back around with a soft, tight-lipped smile. "Do you know what separates humans from those of the fey realm?"

Almost everything.

"Much."

His eyebrows rose again in that way that suggested an implied answer Joe should have known. "Do we not all have eyes? Ears? Do we not all have fingers and toes?"

"Yes. But the eyes and ears of an elf are far superior to that of humans. You all live far longer than the rest of us. Gods! Some of you may even be immortal for all we know."

Petals continued to press the similarities with a pointed finger swirling about in the air, "But we all live and die."

"I suppose, yes. But wha–"

"Magic!" Petals barked it out with a look of agitation.

It was startling enough to cause Joe to jump a little. He hadn't yet seen the look of annoyance on the small man's face, and the fact that it suddenly emerged alarmed him. "All right, yes, magic. You all have magic that is beyond that of humans."

"And where did you get yours?"

Joe furrowed his brow in confusion. "What?"

"Where did you learn your magic?" Petals opened his arms wide as if begging for an answer.

He wanted to answer but feared it to be wrong. "I learned–"

"No!" Petals whipped his finger at him as if to strike the words from the air and admonish him for the thought.

Thundering pixies! How does he know what I'm thinking?

"Where did you learn to instinctively cast magic?"

His nose scrunched at the question as it failed to make any form of sense. "You can't."

"Precisely!" Petals threw up his arms in gleeful joy once again.

Many thoughts began to prick at the edges of his mind. Implications began bubbling to the surface. "What are you suggesting?"

The gnome began curling the corner of his white and bushy mustache with the tips of his fingers. "What do you think I'm suggesting?"

"If I'm following the chain of the conversation correctly, you're suggesting I may have some fey heritage, resulting in my having instinctual magical talents." He was an orphan, after all. He had no clue as to who his parents were, and he didn't exactly have any overly distinctive features to work backward from.

Petals pulled his fingers from his mustache, allowing the corners to curl perfectly. "Possibly fey, maybe something else."

Something else!?

He pointed a finger at Joe's nose. "The point I'm trying to make is that you, unlike every other human, did not need to learn to cast magic to use it. Had you not cast that magic as a boy, back at that orphanage, you likely would never have left to join the Arcanum. You would have remained an orphaned child that likely would have received dismal teaching at best and wound up a soldier on the front lines of the War for Silvertree. A much different outcome of your life, wouldn't you say?"

Joe didn't need to think very hard to follow that train of thought, as he had pondered it many times himself. "Yes, I'm well aware of what casting that magic meant for me. But what does–"

"Do you know how many humans can cast magic instinctively, my boy?" Petals was back to glowering at him.

He felt that any attempt to redirect the conversation back to his staff would be fruitless. "No... I don't."

Petals went back to pacing about the alley and gesticulated wildly with his hands, "Of all the years I have walked your mortal world, I could count on one hand, the number of humans I have met that bear no striking resemblance and yet had the innate ability to cast magic." He stopped mid-stride and turned his eyes toward Joe. "None of them were ever in arcane law enforcement."

Wait...

Years of schooling at the Arcanum came rushing back to him. Many students took grievance with Joe because he could pick up on things a bit faster than others. It didn't mean he was infallible – quite the opposite. He had just as much difficulty with some forms of magic as others. Any attempt he made to utilize clairvoyance or divination spells resulted in dizziness, nausea, and violent sneezing. He never understood the sneezing part, but he chalked it up to improper energy alignments.

It was then that another realization struck him like a lightning bolt. Joe stood up and began shuffling about the alley as his mind began piecing together the clues. He began realizing connections that before had been nothing more than mere memories.

His first class with the utilization of a wand had been disastrous. He caused a feather to burst into flames and a candle to transmute into wood when all he was attempting to do was make the feather float and the wick to light. The years following required more time and effort to get the damnable wand to do what he wanted it to; more time and effort than most of his classmates.

"I'm not a wizard... am I?" The question was rhetorical. Joe looked to his hands and found he was just as confused then as he was the day he had first cast magic. The fact was undeniably clear to him. It was as clear to him as it was jarring. He was not normal.

"No." Petals was surprisingly abrupt with his reply.

Joe looked to his superior and asked the only question that really mattered. "What am I?"

Petals patted the crate that Joe had been sitting on previously. Joe turned and walked to the crate with his hands before him, unable to shake the shock and confusion. He turned on the spot and sat down.

"You are what the magical community calls a sorcerer." Petals patted him on the shoulder, now that he could reach it. "You differ from a wizard in that you don't really need to learn the fundamentals of magic. The magic is inside of you and is as much a part of you as your blood is. Much of your power could be wielded purely by emotion and will."

Joe had heard the term sorcerer before, as any child did. He just never knew it was something different from a wizard. All his years at the Arcanum, he simply thought it was a preferred term and nothing more. "But... if that's true—"

"You can't pick up a staff from the precinct because your magic doesn't fit with the magic in those staffs. Those are wizards' staffs, created by wizard detectives of years past. You are a sorcerer, and there are no sorcerers' staffs available for you to choose from." The statement hit him as hard as a punch to the gut. It was also delivered with a sad smile of apology.

"I... but..." The words were nearly choked off by panic and tightness in his chest. He couldn't be a detective without a staff. His career would be short enough to be noteworthy in textbooks back at the Academy.

"Oh! No, my boy!" Petals backhanded him across the arm to discourage any fears. "Get that thought from your head. All this means is that you must go through the grueling task of building yourself a staff!"

The panic lightened significantly, not by the swat to the arm, but by the realization that not all was lost. "What? You mean I won't be kicked off the force?"

"Pah!" Petals barked at the absurdity. "They'd first have to go through the captain and I."

It was the first bit of good news he'd gotten that morning, and it lifted a massive weight off his shoulders "Thank you, Petals."

The elderly gnome cleared his throat, patted Joe on the back and nodded in the affirmative. "You're welcome, my boy."

Joe nodded, breathed deeply, and straightened himself out, before returning his mind to the task at hand.

It was at that moment that a thought dawned on him. "Petals?"

"Yes, my boy?"

"Did you put something on my back?"

"Fireballs!"

Chapter 5

A close examination told Joe a few things about the mystery third assailant. "He's human, or at least humanoid, based on the size of the shoe, and length of the stride."

Petals tapped a finger to his lips as he nodded along with Joe's observations, "Continue."

The footprints, as Petals had highlighted them, walked in an endlessly repeating loop. They started at the storm grate and traversed the alley to the back door of the jewelry shop, then returned to the storm grate. Joe kneeled at the storm grate and examined the locking mechanism. "They had a key, and they're familiar with the storm tunnels."

Petals said nothing and simply continued to observe Joe with a raised eyebrow.

Why this time of day?

The thought had been bothering him all morning. If the dark dwarf was smart enough to break into the shop, then he was smart enough to do it when he wouldn't draw any attention.

Unless he wasn't.

He had dragged along a rather unsteady youth; that wasn't a wise decision. If you're going to take the risk of robbing a jewelry store, then you take professionals with you. Joe knew full well that most crimes were a result of opportunity, not planning. This attempted theft felt like it was a mixed bag.

Criminals don't expect to get caught.

Joe turned on the spot and looked to the corner that he had rounded that morning. "They weren't expecting me."

For the first time that day, Petals looked to be the confused one – though his look of confusion was more of a narrowing of the eyes "Explain."

"I mean, no criminal ever expects a Blue Coat or detective to dance up on them in the middle of a crime." He stepped toward the alley, with his finger pointing at the other side of the road, and shook it excitedly, "They didn't expect someone with a talent for barriers and alarms to walk by at that exact moment."

Petals nodded in understanding. "Had it not been you in particular, they would likely have gotten away with it."

Joe lifted his wide-brim and ran his fingers through his hair to keep it combed back. "Exactly! They had no reason to fret, bringing a rookie in, because they thought they had good odds on getting away clean." He rested his hat back down on his head, turned back to the footprints leading to the storm grate and pointed at it. "They were probably the lookout and heard me coming."

What about the time of day?

He took to pacing the alley again in thought. "They didn't strike at night. Why didn't they strike at night? If they were good enough to get this far, then they were smart enough to strike under the cover of darkness instead of broad daylight."

Petals provided an answer he hadn't expected. "Noise. They didn't want to wake the neighborhood with their activities. Crowbars and crates tend to be common in alleyways during working hours but tend to be suspicious at night."

He'd never thought of it that way before, and a crowbar was the only tool they had found on the dark dwarf when he was apprehended. It stood to reason. "But what about the storm grate? They're not exactly quiet."

The storm grate in question suddenly swung up and open. It didn't scream in rusted defiance or make much noise at all. Petals stepped forward with a hand outstretched, as though his hand was what had lifted it. The sheer strength of will of the elderly gnome impressed Joe. "A valid question, my boy."

Petals looked down into the tunnel. "How often do you suppose the city workers inspect these and oil the hinges?" The question had been rhetorical in nature, and Joe had just been having the exact same thought. The hinges had been oiled, and likely not by city workers. There wasn't much need to oil a hinge on a storm grate when the storm tunnel didn't need any maintenance.

"They invested a lot of effort into this." Joe stepped up to the brim, looked down into the storm tunnel and peered through the newly cleaned spyglass. It revealed nothing. "Can your magic reveal any tracks?"

Petals squinted into the darkness, then snapped the fingers of his other hand as the first continued to hold the grate aloft. Nothing was revealed. "No, too much water."

Joe nodded and looked to his superior. "I suggest we take our findings back to the precinct and pull up storm tunnel blueprints to discern possible exits and warn other jewelry shops in the area."

The lid slowly lowered as the smiling gnome eased his hand back down to his side. "If you think that is the wise decision, my boy."

Wasn't it?

The confidence that he had been building over the past few minutes quickly deflated in a moment of uncertainty. It must have been visibly apparent, for his training officer tilted his head back and let loose a jovial fit of laughter.

"Why must you do this to me?"

Once the trickster had satisfied himself, he wiped a tear from his eye and smiled up at Joe, "Must keep you on your toes, my boy."

~~

The walk to the precinct was brief, but they used it to discuss proper documentation protocols and where Joe would find his desk, ink cartridges and arcane mechanical typesetter.

Before they reached the steps to the gray face of the precinct, Joe had one more question he had to ask. "When did you spot the tracks for the third assailant?"

The answer came in a roundabout fashion, as was seemingly the norm for his superior. "A few days ago, in the early hours, I noticed a young man standing outside the precinct. He didn't appear to be loitering in wait for a friend or acquaintance. He simply stood on the far side of the street and stared at the precinct."

I think that was me.

"I found it to be quite peculiar and alarming, as the intentions of such an individual could be limited to a few possibilities." Petals began lifting fingers as he counted them off, "Firstly, and most likely, the individual was merely admiring the architecture of the precinct and its grandeur."

It was me.

The precinct was, indeed, well designed both outside and within. It, and many of the other stations throughout the city, had been upgraded through the years. The most recent investments into the infrastructure resulted in a drastic exterior remodeling.

The street face was that of gray cement and featured grand shields emblazoned with the Stormbay crest. The windows had been sealed up to protect those on the inside, and to provide fewer means of escape for those imprisoned.

While wildly grand and argued to be frivolous in its expenditure, the design served dual purposes. Arcane energies had been infused into the shields to create an arcane barrier about the building. It wasn't uncommon for organized crime families to take shots at the precincts to tie them up in a siege while committing other high-stakes crimes.

Notability was the other purpose. Nobody could possibly miss the precinct while walking down a busy street. It was three stories tall and stood out against the surrounding red and brown square-brick architecture. It made it easier for panicked citizens to locate.

Petals raised the next finger. "Secondly, and also fairly likely, they had a crime to report and were afraid they would be singled out as the 'squealer'."

The pair of them met the steps of their precinct and climbed them. "Thirdly, and the least likely of all, they intended on lighting up the precinct while their friends went about collecting their fruits of the ill-gotten labors." – the aforementioned organized crime siege.

By the gods, I looked like a criminal!

He had been working on getting down the timing of his trips to the precinct in order to arrive before his shift started. On each occasion, he had stopped to admire the precinct and its architecture while also daydreaming about his first day and the hopefully good impression he would make. In all those trips, he'd never stopped to consider how he would appear to an observer.

A soft chuckle rose from the waist-high detective as he looked up at the undignified horror that must have been playing out across Joe's face. "I dismissed all possibilities when I noticed an innocent and childish grin spread widely across the face of a clean-cut man wearing Blue Coat walkers."

Joe dropped back his head and groaned, "Of course!" His superior was the senior detective of the precinct and obviously deduced the truth.

Despite appearing as a highly suspicious moron, there was more than ample visual evidence to suggest he was not a threat. Petals' 'counted' possibilities were exaggerations designed to make Joe sweat a bit. All intended to 'keep him on his toes'.

Were they exaggerations?

A moment of reflection resulted in a resounding no. The scenarios that Petals had proposed were all very probable and likely. It was a lesson within a lesson. The trickster seemed to enjoy multiple layers to his mental athletics.

"Never jump to conclusions until you have all the facts at hand." Joe voiced the lesson he felt was being subtly thrown at him. "I may have appeared suspicious at first, but my boots and my demeanor suggested the true answer."

"Bravo! Well done, my boy." Petals gave him a quick and soft applaud.

"And the footprints of the third assailant?" Joe felt he knew what the answer would be, but he couldn't be certain, not without all the facts.

"I followed you, of course."

Knew it.

Joe stopped on the main floor lobby and turned to face his superior with his hands on his hips. "And when you heard that there was a jewel thief caught in the act, and that the rookie detective was involved, you raced over to examine the crime scene to see what kind of a sloppy mess I had made in my rush to clock in."

The elderly trickster lifted his hands in a show of innocence. "I held no grievances with your actions." He lowered his hands and spoke in a respectful and calming tone. "You did exactly what was expected of a Blue Coat given the circumstances."

He narrowed his eyes at his superior and again went through a mental calculation of the events that had played out so far. "You already checked the storm grate, didn't you?"

A mirthful chuckle escaped the diminutive detective. "Hahaha!"

Joe shook his head, "I knew it. You wouldn't hold out on investigating, not a senior detective. All right, what did you find out?"

"Ah!" He shot up a miniscule finger in a signal for Joe to stop. "Documentation first. Let us not get ahead of ourselves. Details are important. The more details you try to remember, the more you tend to forget. Now, up! Go on!" Petals started shooing Joe up the stairs. "Get to your desk and start documenting what we have discovered!"

While mildly agitated by the dismissal and herding, Joe couldn't help but relent to his superior's orders. The man also had a valid point.

The two of them climbed the stairs and Petals headed to his desk, right next to the captain's office. Joe found his desk, in the far corner of the room, directly next to the radiator.

A brief examination of the layout of the room suggested that there were no alternatives for desk arrangement. As was customary for any new recruit, he was given the worst desk.

He hung up his coat and hat on the rack just behind his desk, sat in his chair and nearly jumped out of it as one of the legs tilted further than the others. A quick glance revealed that the leg had been broken at the tip and sanded down slightly to reduce any splinters.

Fantastic.

The pressure release regulator on the radiator would hiss and whistle. That wasn't unexpected, as it was the primary grievance most people had with a radiator. The greatest issue that Joe had with it was that the hissing and whistling occurred at odd times. There was no rhythm.

In addition, the top drawer of his desk only opened halfway. Something had to be jamming it. Unfortunately, Joe couldn't just stick his head inside the drawer and spot the issue; he'd have to use a mirror. Even worse, there wasn't even enough room to stick his hand inside. His belt knife proved to be just as useless; the metal wasn't polished enough to act as a mirror.

It can wait.

Joe sheathed his belt knife at the small of his back and went back to organizing himself. His arcane mechanical typesetter looked to be in working condition. A test of the moving parts proved that none of the rune keys or ink ports were jammed. Nothing was gunked up and no parts were missing, as far as he could tell. "At least there's that."

There were blank case file papers and two spare ink bottles in his second drawer, as well as a note pad and stylus. His desk also came with its own sun lantern. The bullpen had the limited natural light of some miniscule rooftop windows, so the desk lantern would have to do.

A calming breath enabled him to ignore the spontaneous and jarring hissing of the radiator. Joe turned inward and utilized the partition of his mind to shut out the noises of the room. He set a simple trigger that his name or any inclination of his attention being required would ring through the sound-fog like a lighthouse horn.

Everything around him suddenly turned distant and muffled. The radiator sounded like a soft blowing of the wind instead of a high-pitched tea kettle.

Thank the gods.

Joe had learned to muffle out noise while living at the Academy. The barracks were typically full of loud-mouthed knuckleheads.

Being able to focus on his studies was crucial to his goals of becoming a detective. He'd been ribbed and teased about it until he doled out a black eye or two. As much as the others had teased him about being a 'book-nose', none of them would ever have ratted on him for handing out a single helping of a knuckle sandwich. Being able to hold your own was probably the only thing they truly respected. They had also earned the strike by setting one of his texts aflame.

The boys looked out for one another. Besides, it gave them the opportunity to practice with their emergency medical kits to reduce the swelling and discoloration.

Fighting in the barracks resulted in grueling punishments, most of which were laps and push-ups. "If you have the energy to fight each other at the end of the day, then you weren't worked hard enough!"

Joe pulled a blank case file sheet from the pile, slid it between two pieces of glass so that it was aligned and settled, then touched the glass with the stylus to set his line. Once ready, he began tapping the rune keys.

The words began appearing in sequence, as if the glass had been stamped by the rune key that Joe had just tapped. He continued to use the stylus to re-set his line and fill in the necessary fields of information. Date, time, location, nature of the incident, etc.

He had spent enough time writing out his reports on notepads as a Blue Coat that it gave him the experience necessary to create succinct and detail-specific reports for the detectives. Joe included all his speculations and theories, as well as the next steps he intended on taking.

Once satisfied with the results – after re-reading the document twice, with brief corrections utilizing his stylus and smudger – he pressed down firmly on the imprint and watched as the glass struck the document. It left behind a perfectly aligned recounting of his notes. He lifted the parchment by the top, freeing it from the glass confines. He was careful not to touch the ink, as it still needed a moment to dry.

Joe stood, then turned to walk it over to his superior for review, when he nearly jumped out of his skin. A woman had been standing immediately behind him. He hadn't heard her or noticed her, nor had she said anything. She clearly hadn't attempted to get his attention, or was just about to.

Her sudden appearance was not the only thing that startled him. Her eyes were the kind of pale blue you'd see on a wolf, and she apparently liked the color so much that she colored herself to match it. Her lashes, hair, lips, and eyebrows were stark white. Her eyelids were slightly smoky, and she wore white slacks beneath her tan trench. Enchanted snowflake earrings slowly spun beneath her ears, trailing a froth of cold. The white color was by no means a result of age, as she looked far too youthful.

Most stunning of all was her staff. She gracefully and casually kept one hand at shoulder height as it gingerly balanced a length of what appeared to be diamond or crystal at her side. The number of facets in its many faces gave it the appearance of snow or ice glittering in the sunlight. Despite the fact that the woman standing before him was nearly a head shorter than him, her staff was just as tall as he was. Mindfully, most staffs stood at a standard length of six steps.

She had one hand on her hip, and the collar of her trench was flared out while her wide-brim hat – stitched in the woman's style with a rounder top and a greater span – was tilted askew and partially hid her right eye. Her boots were much smaller and the heel a little taller. Otherwise, she wore the full garb of a detective, and she stood with a confidence that dared him to dispute it.

Joe's ears popped and his eyebrows leapt up as he released the mental partition. "Ma'am?" He wanted to make sure he heard her clearly in case she had some order to give him. Being the rookie often meant you were on the receiving end of a lot of ribbing and menial tasks.

There was a long silence between the two of them. She continued to stare up at him, giving him the silent treatment.

Good gods, what is she staring at?! Those eyes are unnerving!

Joe dared not look away, out of fear that she wanted a reason to give him a dressing down. As far as he could tell, she was his superior and he couldn't outright ignore her.

Eventually, her eyes darted to the right of his chest. She finally spoke with a soft rasp before turning to leave, "You got ink on your shirt."

What?

Joe looked down, and only then realized that, in his startled state, he had hugged his freshly-inked document to his chest. "Fireballs!" He peeled the paper off his vest and shirt and groaned at the mess it left behind.

A roar of unified laughter filled the detectives' bullpen as everyone that had been nearby had paused to witness the silent exchange.

"Good job, rookie!"

"Way to not 'spill your ink'!"

Real original, buddy.

Joe sighed and calmed himself as he frustratingly slapped the smudged document back down onto his desk and pulled out his wizard's handkerchief for the second time that day.

It could be worse.

The soft clacking of the female detective's boots halted. Joe looked up to see where she was headed, only to find her looking straight back at him over her shoulder. "One more thing." Her eyebrow was raised to make sure he was listening.

"Yes, ma'am?"

She narrowed her eyes, which had turned pure white, and glared. The woman tilted her staff and the tip of it shimmered. Joe's partitioned mind immediately started screaming at him to duck or dive out of the way. A quick jump to the left was just enough for the mental alarm to quiet.

Joe felt a painfully bracing jet of wind shoot past his right side at hip height. A glance over his shoulder revealed that the very document that he had smudged was frozen in a sheet of crystal-clear ice.

"Call me anything but 'ma'am', stare at my backside or treat me as anything less than a detective, and that paper will only be an example of what I do to you." She launched another volley of wind and the paper on his desk exploded in a shower of confetti and ice bits, none of which caused him or the desk any harm. "Understood?"

Joe looked back to where she stood. Her eyes had returned to their pale blue, and she had turned to face him directly. The crystalline staff was still tilted and he could sense the power in her, ready to be released.

The precision required to drastically alter the core temperature of one object but not the surface it sat upon, was extraordinary. She was not a woman to be taken lightly. Joe had absolutely no desire to argue with her or treat her as anything less than capable. "Yes—"

"Amelia." The captain's low rumble filled the bullpen, but it never truly reached a height that made it sound like a yell as much as a stern warning. Their superior stood in the doorway to his enclosed glass office. His horns nearly brushed the top of the doorway and his massive, clawed hands were balled into fists on his hips. He looked like nothing less than the imposing figure that he was. Slacks, shirt, and suspenders did little to mute the level of intimidation that such a creature naturally radiated.

Detective Amelia turned on the spot and tilted her head up so that she might see eye-to-eye with the towering dragon kin from under her wide-brim hat. "Yes, Captain?"

"Don't kill the new recruit on his first day." That was all… No rebuke, no barked orders, nothing. The captain turned back to head into his office, and only paused briefly to await the subordinate's acceptance of the command given.

She nodded in understanding with a slight smirk painted across her face. "I never kill, Captain."

Bolt nodded in acceptance of the answer and closed the glass door behind him.

The chilly ice queen Amelia then turned and eyeballed Joe once more before heading for the stairs.

Joe shivered, despite the uncomfortably warm corner of the room. She somehow made death sound preferable.

"So!"

"Ah!" He couldn't help but jump and bark out in surprise. Petals had somehow managed to sidle up beside him during the chilly exchange.

By the gods, I'm going to die from fright!

Joe put a hand over his heart and simply slumped into the wobbly chair to find some semblance of calm.

"Finish the document?" Petals stepped closer to Joe's desk and tapped his little foot with his hands behind his back.

"No, sir," he said it with absolute frustrated exhaustion. After a moment to set his mind in order and muffle his ears to the noise of the radiator, he proceeded to right himself in the chair, pull out a new blank case file and start over. "I'll have it done shortly, sir."

Petals smiled politely, stepped closer, and patted him on the arm, "Petals will do fine, my boy."

...Fireballs...

Joe hung his head.

Petals patted his arm again. "Have it done in ten and I can guarantee you a warm meal."

Chapter 6

The wizard's handkerchief proved highly effective in removing the ink stains from his white shirt and the ink slid right off his vest without issue.

Petals sat with his chin tilted up so that he might peer through his spectacles and scrutinize the document Joe had rushed to finish.

The unnerving silence was spent trying to tidy himself back into a respectable appearance. The radiator had proved disastrously irritating when it came to keeping cool.

His superior cleared his throat, and Joe quickly snapped his head up from examining his shirt and vest. He wanted to make sure there were no more splotches of ink.

Petals gave him a polite smile. "Acceptable."

All he could feel to do at the moment was breathe a sigh of relief.

"Didn't expect your first day to be quite so eventful, did you?"

Joe shook his head and took another deep breath. "Also didn't expect to get so much hate." He pointed to the winding stairs and turned his thumb over at the captain's office.

Petals' soft smile quickly vanished. "Ah, yes." He didn't sound pleased in the slightest. "Ms. Iceheart has her own issues; none of which you are at fault for. I also highly disapprove of the captain's acceptance of her threats for equal treatment." He offered a tight-lipped smile that was devoid of any happiness. "But I am not the captain."

Joe understood and felt a bit better about it. "I take it she had an ugly run-in with a meathead?"

Petals partially returned to his chipper self and barked out a quick laugh, "To put it lightly, my boy." He wound down and sat silently while staring at his desk in thought. It didn't take long for the aging man to pipe in a bit of wisdom. "At most times, an action will trump the words we feel have meaning. I'm certain your actions will have you vindicated in her eyes in short order."

Joe heard his stomach interject with a rumble and gurgle. A hand placed over his stomach failed to stifle it, and only brought greater attention to its mournful cry.

The detective burst out in joyous laughter. "Rarely a moment that passes, my boy, that your thoughts aren't as loud as an obnoxious gull. Now your belly speaks for you!"

He couldn't help but chuckle as well. The comment stopped him and caused him to think about it. Turning to the gnome, he asked, "Can you read my thoughts?"

Petals shrugged off the question and waved it away as though it were of little consequence. "Sometimes."

Joe was about to persist when he heard a pitched voice ring out from the stairwell, "Pies and cakes!" It was slightly higher than that of Petals' and bore a feminine softness to it.

Turning himself in the chair, Joe was stunned to see an elderly gnome woman carrying a wicker picnic basket several sizes too large for someone of her stature to be able to lift. Yet she held it perfectly balanced in the crook of her arm as though it were empty.

A brief whiff of the air set Joe's stomach to roaring and his mouth to flooding.

By the gods, that smells delicious.

Petals jumped from his chair and hopped over. "Hello, dearest." She offered him a cheek and he planted a kiss upon it without hesitation. They grinned at each other in a way only happily married couples could.

She absolutely beamed and straightened her horn-rimmed wire spectacles and white hair bonnet. She was dressed in traditional housewife apparel. She wore a violet floral sundress and pastry print apron with off-white slippers.

After a moment of admiring one another, Petals' wife then set down the picnic basket and opened both sides of it.

The captain's office door swung open in a flourish, and the large and menacing draconic head peered round the corner. "Ah, Mrs. Pettlebottom, I thought I could smell your wondrous work."

It took only a few lumbering steps for the dragon kin to reach the stairs. He leaned down and placed his hands upon his knees and spoke softly to the senior detective's wife. "Did you find the one I asked about?"

Mrs. Pettlebottom absolutely beamed and nodded. "Of course, Adragan. Your directions were very specific and clear, I had no difficulties finding the shop." The tiny woman then reached down into the picnic basket, far further than the laws of reality could permit, then stood upright, producing a leg of something large enough to be ridden like a horse.

Good gods!

Whatever it was, it was large, and it smelled heavenly. He didn't know what spices or sauces it had been slathered with or how long it had been roasted or smoked or whatnot, but he could almost taste it from where he was sitting.

Most impressively, the elderly gnome woman held it aloft with the greatest of ease, as if that massive slab of meat weighed little more than paper.

The rumbling, storm-scaled dragon kin moaned deep in his throat before taking the offered piece of meat by the large bit of bare bone at the base, then dropped a coin in the tiny woman's hand.

Their captain thanked the detective's wife most sincerely, then turned around to lumber back into his office.

Joe watched in astonishment, captivated by the event that had just unfolded before him, then leaped from his chair to throw himself at the front of whatever line intended on forming following the captain's absence.

He leaned down and offered his hand while removing his hat so that he might introduce himself properly to his training officer's wife. "Mrs. Pettlebottom, it is a pleasure to meet you."

She took his hand and shook it while smiling broadly. "Such a nice young man." He could already tell she wasn't a trickster gnome like her husband. Joe could sense the flows of magic surrounding her and the basket. Best guess, from the nature of the smells wafting out of her seemingly bottomless picnic pit, she was a crafter gnome. They didn't all work with clay or stone or wood, some baked.

His stomach roared its displeasure and impatience.

She looked to jump slightly and turned her attention to his gut. "Oh my, well we're going to have to fix that, now aren't we."

Joe couldn't recall the last time he'd had a full and well-cooked meal. His landlady, Ms. Bellcreaux, was certainly not the nurturing type. At best, he would get raw carrots, a brick of a bun, and some lumpy gravy with a piece of meat so dry it could be considered leather. In fact, he wasn't entirely sold on it not being leather. That was if he was ever around at the appropriate hour, which she seemingly changed from one day to the next.

He sheepishly stood up and covered his stomach. "I apologize."

Mrs. Pettlebottom put her hands on her hips and pursed her lips at him, "Nonsense, a young man like you needs a good meal to keep him strong." Her pursed lips turned into a kindly and infectious smile. "Now, what can I get for you, dear?"

A quick partition of his mind and a mental tally of the available accounts suggested he didn't have the coin. "I don't know if I can afford anything, ma'am."

Her smile quickly vanished, and she turned on the stink-eye. "Now you listen here, mister. You are going to eat until I am satisfied, and you'll not hand me a copper penny or complain a single minute of it, you hear me?" She shook her finger up at him.

In all the years he'd lived, he'd never been threatened with a full stomach. "I... uh... yes, ma'am." He didn't feel threatened in the least, but he wasn't about to start an argument with her concerning food when his stomach was clearly begging him to take anything and everything she offered.

Her smile returned as quickly as it had vanished. "Good. Now, I have a bunch of pies already baked, what would you like?"

He sheepishly lowered himself and asked in a softer tone, "You don't happen to have any chicken pies, do you?"

Mrs. Pettlebottom absolutely beamed and reached down into the bottomless pit of salivation-inducing aromas and stood back up with a perfectly flaky pie.

I want the basket.

Joe tenderly offered his hands and she placed the warm mass of flaking crust within them. It felt like it weighed a few stones despite it being small enough to fit in one palm.

By the gods, I think I can taste it through my hand.

"Thank you, very much." Joe stood and looked to his superior. The trickster winked at him, produced a similar-sized pie of his own, and gestured with an arm that they sit at his desk.

The two of them sat, and Petals snapped his fingers, producing a pair of napkins between them. Joe nodded to his superior, picked up the napkin and used it as a plate as he bit heartily into the pie.

To say that the meal was divine was a discredit to Mrs. Pettlebottom. The chicken was tender, the carrots still had a little chew to them, and the gravy was silky. He devoured his pie and felt no need for a second. It weighed him down and re-invigorated him at the same time. Despite that fact, she came to him with a second pie wrapped in cloth.

Joe tried to refuse it, but she insisted, and even informed him that the cloth would keep it fresh and warm until he ate it for supper that night. He heartily thanked the woman and told her he would find a way to pay her back.

Her answer was that his service to the community was payment enough, and that if he attempted to repay her in coin, she would be insulted.

After a few more orders with some of the other men on the floor, she waved to her husband and Joe and headed off back down the steps.

Joe turned to his superior, "The hot meal you promised. She comes in often, doesn't she?"

Petals simply grinned as he chewed and brushed some crumbs from his white beard.

"You also knew she wouldn't accept me being hungry, regardless of whether I could afford it." He cleaned his face with the napkin and folded it on the table before clasping his hands before him.

Petals licked his lips free of any errant crumbs and gave Joe a small and polite round of applause.

Joe bowed his head in appreciation. A brief glance at his wristwatch informed him that it was only slightly past the lunch hour. "What is our next step?"

Petals finished clearing his palate and replied in kind, "We have to place a request with the city maintenance department to acquire the plans to the storm tunnels." He snapped his fingers, and their napkins vanished along with any crumbs that may have fallen astray.

The two of them then proceeded to a file cabinet, and Petals indicated to Joe what he was looking for. The requisition form required several fields to be filled out.

Oh lovely, back to my sweltering desk.

Joe sat down and placed the request form between the panes of glass on his arcane mechanical typesetter, when a door burst open off to the side. Grimbomb stood wide-eyed in the doorway with smoldering mustache tips and a blackened bald head. His apron was grease-smudged, and his shirt looked singed and burnt. "Where is she!?"

Nobody answered the mad dwarf. Everyone returned to their duties as though his question was insignificant.

Joe – being as naïve as he was – asked, "Who?"

Grimbomb gripped the air in despair as he looked skyward and yelled to the gods, "The pie lady!"

Good gods.

"You missed her, she left already." Joe lazily waved to the stairs before turning back around to focus all attention on the request form.

Grimbomb began barking in his dwarven tongue as he thumped off toward the stairs, tripped, fell, cursed, and rolled down the steps to the main lobby.

Nobody seemed to pay him any mind until an eruption of flames belched up the steps. A woman screamed and everyone jumped to their feet and looked to the stairs, awaiting some call for help. None came. After a few seconds they all heard the distant yell of the absurd dwarf, "I'm a'ight! I got it!" The room released a collective sigh of relief and returned to their tasks.

Joe turned to his superior to find the old man pinching the bridge of his nose and shaking his head.

He had to know. "Where does that fire come from?"

The trickster continued to shake his head. "I can bend the fabric of space and time with a snap of my fingers, but I have yet to discover the nature of his spontaneous conflagrations."

He looked back to his desk and refocused his efforts while attempting to keep his mind partitioned on two tasks – one on tuning out the radiator, and the other on keeping one ear open for the bungling menace. With everything Joe had experienced throughout his first day as a detective, he felt he'd need to expand his partitioning skills.

Over the next two hours, Petals spent a great deal of time going over the finer details of their paperwork and where those papers went for approval and archiving, during which they dropped off his requisition form with the outgoing mail.

Joe met with several of the support staff and learned their roles within the precinct. He met again with Officer Johnson, whose first name happened to be Bob. The white-mustached Blue Coat was a sailor in his youth and had the knot skills to prove it.

Other Blue Coats included Officers Redbell, Tanen, Anvilhearth, and Mountainbeard. The last two officers were a dwarf and half-giant, respectively.

During the guided tour around the precinct, Petals attempted and succeeded in two pranks. One involved sprouting orange polka-dot mushrooms from Joe's ears, the second involved turning Grimbomb's voice into that of a squeaking pixie. The first prank was annoying, the second was amusing.

Being a target of Petals' pranks only re-affirmed Joe's desire to strengthen his mental flexibility and arcane awareness.

It neared the end of the workday as their walk about the precinct concluded. "Joseph."

He stopped abruptly and turned to face his superior. "Yes?" The man had only utilized his full first name when they had first met, and his file had been present.

Petals waved him closer and clasped his hands behind his back in what appeared to be a more formal and serious stance.

Joe leaned closer and gave the gnome his full attention. "What is it?"

"We have some work to do in rectifying your current handicap amongst the detectives." Petals said in a much quieter tone. He obviously didn't intend for it to get out that Joe was without a mystical means of offence.

"Ah, yes." The lack of staff had been weighing on his mind, and he had absolutely no idea how he was going to afford the necessary tools and supplies to craft one. He had never had much in the way of funds.

His acceptance into the Arcanum was based on his inherent skill with magic. Without such, he wouldn't have passed registration without a hefty sack of coin.

The Academy where he studied arcane law was paid for in part by his veteran's allowance and the rest with loans. He hadn't paid off his loans yet, as a Blue Coat didn't exactly make a great deal of coin.

Joe chewed on the thought for a time as he contemplated possible alternatives.

"Joseph?"

He snapped out of his thoughts and turned to see that his superior was standing by the stairs to the detectives' bullpen. "Right, sorry." He hurried over to catch up to the light-footed gnome and followed him up the steps.

Again, Petals seemed to have an unnaturally youthful hop to his step as they climbed. Joe couldn't help but feel envious of the fey-born. He hadn't quite made it to the end of the day, and his feet were already screaming to be released from their confines. He felt mentally wiped.

Once they reached the top step, Petals pointed to Joe's desk. "Get your things, then meet me at the captain's door."

Joe didn't like the idea of having any other conversations with the Captain, but knew it was something he would have to grow accustomed to if he planned on staying a detective. He nodded in response and headed over to pick up his coat and hat before returning to the gnome's side.

Petals didn't hesitate and snapped his finger, causing the door latch to twitch and the smoked glass-pane door to swing open.

Joe very much did not feel like stepping into the captain's office without first knocking but felt himself being dragged along anyway. He took a deep breath and plunged in.

The door slowly closed behind Joe, by a snap of Petals' fingers. The captain didn't raise his head or even acknowledge their sudden intrusion into his office.

Petals slowly walked toward the other chair in the room – the one facing the Captain – and leapt up into it with little more grace than a single effortless hop. He stood upon the cushion instead of sitting in the chair and loudly cleared his throat.

The dragon kin rumbled deep in his chest in response. "Yes, Pettlebottom?"

"We have a disastrous issue."

Fireballs!

Joe felt his level of alarm jump several degrees as he clutched his coat tighter in his fist.

Bolt paused his writing, slowly lifted his draconic head and turned his gaze upon Petals, "Oh?"

Petals maintained a strict and serious posture as he held the gaze of his direct superior.

The stylus that the beastly fingers had been holding was gingerly placed back down upon the desk, and the fingers folded as the captain gave Petals his direct and undivided attention, "And what issue is that?"

Petals gesture broadly to Joe

Thundering fireballs!

Bolt turned his penetrating gaze to Joe, stunning him and rooting him to the floor. A twinge in the back of his mind warned him that he was being afflicted by magic. The realization spurred him into trying to discern what it was. It didn't take him very long, as he'd felt the very same thing earlier that day when touching the door to the locked room by the quartermaster. It was a chilling paralyses.

"You're—" Joe struggled to get the words out, "— using passive magic!" He understood then that his fear of the captain was because the man radiated intimidation magic. It was not just his presence, but his natural gift.

He had to find a means by which to break it. Shutting his eyes tight, Joe focused his mind on the image of a vault door slamming shut and threw all his will into it. A bell rang out in his mind and the oppressive force that had been nearly choking him with fear suddenly vanished. Exhaustion nearly overcame him, and he dropped to a knee as both the captain and his superior watched with little to no concern for him collapsing.

The dragon kin watched with no discernable emotions on his scaled face. "I was wondering when you'd finally break that."

"Fireballs!"

Both Bolt and Joe turned to Petals in surprise. At least, Joe presumed Bolt was surprised. The draconic head whipped about with a touch more speed and enthusiasm than Joe had seen in the past.

Petals stood on the chair with an irritated look on his face and his hands on his hips. "I had coin that you wouldn't figure it out for another day yet." He grumbled something about owing a coin.

Joe needed a moment before he pushed back to his feet. He was growing more tired by the minute. Holding off against the magic that the captain was emanating was proving taxing.

The captain lazily waved a finger at Joe. "That wasn't the issue then."

Petals shook his head before making a pinching motion with his fingers and drawing a wand from thin air. The captain didn't seem in any way shocked, surprised, or amused by the display, as he'd likely seen it before. "The boy doesn't have one of these."

A loud rumbling grunt came from the captain. He looked to the wand that Petals held aloft, then glanced at Joe. "Rejected?"

Joe disliked being talked about while he stood in the room and interjected himself into the conversation. "Sorcerer." He felt that was clarification enough.

Captain Bolt turned his full attention on Joe and seemed to give him another once over. He released a loud ascending rumbling grunt of understanding. "Papers?" His eyes flicked to Petals.

The trickster flicked his wand.

As a result, a piece of paper suddenly appeared in the captain's hands. The dragon kin turned his attention to what had been written. He nodded after a moment of reading, then lifted a free-standing stamp from an ink pad at the corner of his desk, set down the paper and gently tapped the paper with the stamp, 'Approved'. He handed the paper back to the senior detective.

The wand twitched once more at Petals' direction and the paper vanished in a puff of blue sparkles. With a great wild grin and a bow of his head, Petals excused himself and snapped his fingers at the office door.

Joe jumped to the side as the door nearly hit him in the back. He watched as the elderly gnome marched on out the door past him. He turned to the captain, thanked him, and pulled the door shut behind him on the way out.

He felt momentarily light-headed, then suddenly clear and vibrant again.

Good gods! How much was I focusing on keeping that aura at bay?

Joe shook his head and hurried after his superior. He stopped briefly as the elderly gnome continued toward the lobby. Turning about, he quickly ran back to Petals' desk, grabbed the cloth-wrapped pie, stuffed it into his coat pocket, and threw himself at the stairs.

Once he managed to catch up with the fleet-footed gnome, he proceeded to throw on his jacket and hat and straighten himself out.

"Mind explaining where we're going?"

"To the docks."

"For?"

"Parts."

Joe felt as though he knew what for. "And the approved document?" They both pushed open the wooden doors and began descending the steps of the precinct to the city streets.

"Acquisition of funds."

"For the parts?"

"Precisely."

Fantastic!

Chapter 7

The two of them hailed a gnome cart and hopped into the cramped carriage. Petals provided the necessary directions and deposited the required coinage into the brass tray that separated the driver from the passengers.

Their driver – a gnome – acknowledged the address, tapped a series of rune keys into the polished wooden dash, then handed Petals the slip of parchment that the dash spat out.

His superior pocketed the transaction parchment in his coat and turned to Joe. "Keep all your parchments and submit them for re-imbursement with Finance." He smiled with a raised eyebrow, "You remember Finance, don't you?"

Joe couldn't help but feel a bit red in the cheeks. "Penelope." She had a certain undeniably desirable quality to her. "Quite the lady."

Petals grinned broadly and wiggled his bushy eyebrows. "Will you ask her out?"

Joe waved him off. "We'll see if I make it to the end of the week."

His superior barked a laugh and reached forward to slide shut the small window that separated them from the driver. "Now," he gestured to the window, "Muffle us."

"Pardon?"

Petals gave him a sideways grin and repeated himself through an obviously faked smile. "Muffle us... now."

He didn't like being put on the spot but figured that there wouldn't be a repeat of the demand. Joe also felt that the gnome failed to do anything without valid reasoning, even if it wasn't always immediately apparent.

Glancing at the driver, he raised his left finger and eyeballed the windows while tracing their outline in the air. Simultaneously, he pulled on and rubbed his right ear between his finger and thumb. A softly whistled tune completed his ritual incantation.

Once he finished drawing out the framing of the window to his right, he released his ear and snapped those particular fingers. There was an immediate and painful pressure on his ears. All noise was significantly muffled as though his head had been dunked in water, and the only way to rectify the issue was by working his jaw and sticking his fingers in his ears and wiggling them vigorously.

The pop that finally came relieved a great deal of pressure and returned his hearing to normal. He looked down to Petals, only to find him glaring back with obvious agitation. "What?"

"That was hardly subtle." He stuck his pinkie in his ear and wiggled it just as vigorously as Joe had done his own.

"I'm not exactly an expert that can just snap their fingers and break the laws of the cosmos."

Petals didn't seem pleased by the answer and worked his jaw about before turning his attention back forward. "I didn't want the driver to over-hear us." He quickly turned his attention back to Joe and fired a finger at him. "Drivers talk, you know!"

Joe threw up his hands in innocent ignorance, "All right! I'll keep that in mind."

Petals settled back down with his arms crossed. "Best you do. They're good sources of gossip." He lifted one hand and tilted his wide-brim down over his eyes. "Now, no talk of this with anyone at the precinct."

Joe looked to the driver and back to his superior. "Chatty gnome cart drivers?"

Petals shot him a disapproving glare out the corner of his eye.

Joe caught on. "Right, my staff... it's not common for a detective to be rejected, is it?"

The gnome settled back into his seat and shook his head. "Not for quite a few years now. In the beginning, rejection was normal because new recruits were different from the detectives before them, so they had to go out and make their own. After a while, the rejections became few and far between as the number and variety of focuses became fairly sizable. Now it's unheard of, and either suggests you are truly unfit or there's something very truly unique about you."

Joe took some time to digest that as they sat in the cart and bounced on down the cobblestone streets. Joe partitioned his mind and directed the other half to take note of the storefronts they passed, as he was certainly going to need the information as a new detective on the streets.

While one half of his mind noted the buildings they passed, he focused on the primary puzzle placed before him. Eventually, he came to a conclusion. "If I'm truly unfit, then the others won't trust me to do my job; if I'm that unique, then they'll expect me to be more than I am. Both possibilities are dangerous."

The gnome grinned happily as he lifted the corner of his hat and peered out and up at him. "Excellent deductions." He lowered the hat again and returned to his rest. "Now, what do you know of focuses?"

Do you have a year?

Joe breathed out a deep sigh and began regurgitating everything he had learned at the Arcanum over a ten-minute period, over which they exited their designated patrol zone and entered the warehouse area near the docks. "In summary, most focuses are made from materials that sympathize or metaphorically represent the natural auras and energies of the magic intended by the caster."

Petals gave a dismissive sound. "Fah! Common tongue, my boy."

Really… you couldn't have said that ten minutes ago?

Joe shook his head after shooting a glance at the gnome. He took a moment to think about how it had been dumbed down for him. After some thought, he simply reiterated the same answer he had been given as a young student: "You don't use carved ice to throw fire."

There was a nod in the affirmative. "Indeed. Now, what do you know about staff crafting?"

Joe wasn't about to make the same mistake twice. "It's difficult."

Petals grinned. "How so?"

He sighed and considered how much detail he needed to go into. "A staff is typically made from wood, which is difficult to work with." He looked over to see Petals making a gentle gesture as if conducting Joe to continue the musical tidbits of information. "Wood has a mind of its own, it's alive. It has a grain to it and its own energy; trying to manipulate it to fit a specific mold is next to impossible." His superior slowly nodded along as though listening to some soft instrumentals. "A wizard usually has to 'find the wood that they are looking for and work with the natural energies and amplify them to the suited interests."

"Very good, my boy." Petals sat back up and peered out from under his hat to determine if they were close to their destination. "Now, why is it that your magic is so incompatible with that of a wizard?"

Damned good question.

"I've been pondering that myself."

Petals stretched a bit, then fixed his hat. "And what conclusions have you drawn?"

Joe couldn't speculate his way through it. "None... yet."

The trickster turned his head rather quickly about. "Truly? No thoughts at all?"

"I — no, of course I have thoughts on the subject, but nothing that I'd consider well-formed." He felt insulted by the insinuation.

The gnome cart pulled up to a large red brick warehouse with a wooden painted sign that read 'Goldfern's Antique Repairs'. Their driver lifted his hat in farewell and waved them out.

Joe was about to grab the handle when Petals stopped him. "Muffling first." A snap of the fingers released the spell-work that Joe had hastily thrown up, and he could suddenly hear the waves of the ocean rolling in the distance.

It was humbling and agitating how easy it was for the Trickster to undo what Joe had spent years practicing. After the spell dropped, he turned the brass handle and opened the door for both of them.

Joe stretched his legs once out of the cart, brushed off his coat, then waited for Petals to join him while he adjusted his hat. The driver turned about and drove off with his mechanical contraption puttering and growling as it rolled along, bouncing and swaying. Joe couldn't help but marvel at the ingenuity. "Not quite as fast as a galloping horse, but it gets you there."

The lack of answer caused Joe to turn about and see that his superior was halfway to the front door across the open stretch of cobblestone.

Fireballs!

He met the nimble old gnome at the front doors and let out an exhale from having jogged over. "How are you always so fast?"

Petals answered with a mischievous grin. "I put one foot in front of the other."

Joe looked about the entryway and noted that it was a very small wood-paneled waiting room. The front desk looked to be made from a large piece of wood, or many pieces of wood seamlessly fit together with an uninterrupted grain. There was a great deal of extensive filigree and accentuations to the curves and curls. Gold leaf and polish gave the desk a very expensive finished appearance. He doubted that any of it was real gold, as it would likely make an easy target for thieves.

The woman sitting behind the desk was the true treasure. She looked to have some fey ancestry, based on the almond-curve of her seafoam blue eyes, the gentle point of her ears, and the fairness of her skin.

Her smile was not only glamorous, but the partitioned portion of his mind warned him that she was charming him with a bit of a glamorous aura. Hers was nowhere near as strong as the captain's, and far more pleasant.

He was slapped on the leg behind his knee and it almost caused his leg to buckle under him, "Ah!" He caught himself on the desk, looked to the gnome that had swatted him, then righted himself and straightened out his vest. Thankfully, the sudden strike had snapped him out of the ogle-eyed drool he had fallen into. Joe cleared his throat and apologized.

A door behind the reception desk swung open, and the two of them were greeted by a young man in a well-tailored vest and trousers. "Afternoon... officers?" He first greeted them with a wide smile intended to draw in prospective clients, but his countenance quickly turned to one of worry. "Is there an issue?"

Petals waved off any concern. "No, my boy, just need to look at some wares." He reached into his coat and produced the approved parchment that Captain Bolt had stamped before they left the precinct.

The young man leaned down to look at it. "Oh! I... uh... I've never seen this before."

Joe wasn't surprised. Based on what Petals had said, it'd been some time since anyone had to make their own staff, and the young man looked no older than Joe.

Petals offered it to the young man. "Verify it with your superior, if you must."

He smiled in confusion, gingerly took it, and nodded. "Uh, yes, of course. Yes…" He trailed off as he eyed the documentation and turned back around to head through the same door he had entered from, reading it as he went.

Petals leaned closer and whispered, "What's your bet? Crafter gnome, dwarf, or human?"

Joe whispered back, "What?"

Petals elbowed him in the thigh. "Come on, guess!"

The door opened again, and a wiry middle-aged man appeared. He squinted at both of them through sawdust-caked spectacles as he scrubbed his hands with a dirty rag. Whenever he shifted or moved, he left a trail of powdered sawdust in his wake. He wore so much of it that his skin looked to be covered in a thin fur of oak. If the coating of wood wasn't an obvious clue as to his role in the warehouse, the man wore a dirtied cotton work shirt and a leather apron full of tools. "Who are you, and why are you disturbing my business?"

Petals stepped forth and tipped his hat. "We're detectives–"

"I can see that! Now, why are you disturbing my business?" The man finished 'cleaning' his hands and whipped the rag out in anger before giving them both the stink-eye with his hands on his hips.

A snap of the fingers brought forth Petals' wand, except it wasn't wand-sized. The wooden staff looked to be about nearly as tall as Joe – standard size – and was capped at half a step on either end with a bright stain. The core was deep and rich in color. The entire length was carved with swirling designs that doubled back upon themselves and twisted in odd ways that made it look like the entire staff was made from coiled knots and loops of rope. The more Joe looked at it, the more he felt himself being twisted in and folded.

Petals thumped his staff, snapping everyone to attention. "We, sir, *are* your business." The detective said it with great vitriol and enunciation, daring the man to interrupt him.

The woodworker – who had failed to introduce himself – didn't seem to notice the threat, as his eyes had been locked onto the staff the entire time. Petals even noticed the fixation. He smirked slightly and moved the tip of it back and forth, causing the man to shake his head back and forth to follow it.

It was Joe's turn to swat the gnome into focusing on the task at hand, but he felt it wiser to simply clear his throat loudly. "Ahem!"

Petals stopped, snapped his fingers, and made his staff vanish as quickly as it had appeared.

Shaking his head – causing a bloom of sawdust to rise into the air and coat the wood-paneled office – the woodworker turned his attention back to them. "Yes? What? What do you want?"

They both barked in reply.

"Wood!"

"Wood!"

~~

The woodworker was named Hilbert. He was the lead antique repairman at Goldfern's. There were others that worked in the warehouse, but Hilbert was the master of the shop. He had inherited it after his father had retired. Apparently, Petals hadn't visited the shop since Hilbert's grandfather was in charge.

The two of them were led through the warehouse to the scrap wood storage they had requested. Much to his surprise, a great deal of the warehouse was spotlessly clean.

Joe had expected there to be giant piles of sawdust and waste-wood littering the floor and tools everywhere.

He supposed a professional antique repair shop didn't stay in business for several generations with sloppy business practices or workspaces. He saw foot-pedaled saws, workbenches, sharpening stations, and all forms of tools and padded wedges and clamps. Hilbert knew his craft well.

They were guided to the far back wall, where the cantankerous woodworker huffed, "This good enough?"

Joe looked to the wall and gaped at the sheer number of cubbies. He guessed there to be at least fifty, if not more. Each boxed shelving unit had a label and a few pieces of wood sticking out the end. He saw a great many colors and diameters of wooden dowels.

Curiosity got the better of him, and he began reading the labels of the more curious colors. "Pixie-glow blue fir, phoenix-fire ash, alligator moss applewood… These can't be real, can they?"

Petals chuckled delightedly. "These are just types of trees that exist in your mortal world, my boy. You should see some of the marvelous plant-life that exists in the fey realm."

Hilbert barked, "Show-off!" then stormed off back to his work, or at least they presumed he did.

"So…" Joe eyed the plethora of options, turning his head as the shelving stretched from one end of the back wall to the other, "Where do I start?"

"Close your eyes."

He looked over to Petals, and the gnome nodded in the affirmative. Deferring to the wisdom of one that had done this sort of thing before, or possibly guided someone else through it, he did as he was told and shut his eyes.

"Open your mind."

Joe released the partition in his mind and fully opened himself to the cosmic energy of the universe. The trickster became invisible to him, the warehouse a soft hum of life surrounding him. He picked up a subtle and more concentrated line of energy winding its way through the walls. He presumed it to be the primary source of power for the arcane lanterns, transactional devices, and crystalline landline network.

The individual pieces of wood began to show off their personalities. Not that they moved or acted in any animated form, but they gave off unique auras that vibrated in unique ways.

"Good, now open yourself to your memories, your past; share who you are with them."

Joe didn't quite know what the elderly gnome meant by that, but he figured the only way to figure out was to begin with the first part of the instructions. Open himself to his memories.

The earliest memories he had were of the Temple. He had been orphaned as an infant and had no recollection of his parents at all. In fact, the only faces he associated with parents were those of the sisters of the cloth that raised him. He often felt a deep loneliness due to being told repeatedly that a sister was not his mother, and that he should never grow attached to any of them in case his mother ever returned, or someone claimed him. Nobody ever returned, and nobody ever wanted someone else's child.

Any fears of Joe turning into a heartless monster were quickly quashed by the fact that he embraced any other child that entered the Temple. It did not matter if their stay was temporary or as permanent as his own; he accepted them with open arms, and he protected them just as fiercely as he hoped any child would protect their blood relative.

Years passed in the orphanage, and he grew and learned his letters and numbers under the tutelage of the sisters. Then, the fateful day arrived.

Some older boys – that had been known to be troublesome and rough with the other children – were suspiciously quiet. When Joe pressed them for answers, he eventually discovered that they had managed to capture a fairy and were attempting to force it to do their bidding.

They had dumb ideas of grandeur and they thought a fairy could grant them wishes.

Joe demanded that they let the fairy go, and in turn, got a beating for it. He'd received a solid shiner, a bloodied lip, and multiple fist-sized bruises. Once they'd knocked him to the ground, they returned to mistreating the poor creature. The boys shook it, yelled at it, and demanded things that it couldn't give. The tiny woman cried. She cried as a child might, as any orphan might, as any of his *siblings* might.

The memory enveloped him so fully, that he could feel his heart hammering as loudly and as rhythmically as it did on that day, all those years ago. Joe ground his teeth and clenched his fists until he could hear and feel his knuckles popping.

He roared at the memory within him and demanded to go back and hit them harder than he had with what little magic he had conjured that day. He wanted them to rue the day they ever thought they could lord themselves over something so helpless and small. He reached out with all his fury and pulled, in the hopes that something would answer his call.

"JOSEPH RUNEWALL!"

Something cold and hard slapped into the palm of his outstretched hand. He woke in that moment. His eyes snapped open, and he was thrust from the darkness as Petals yelled his name.

He was not at the Temple. There was no fairy cradled in his hands with a bent wing. Instead, he stood in an antique repair warehouse close to the docks, and a length of wood was tightly gripped in his hand.

Shaking free of the past, Joe turned his head to look to his superior. The white-haired gnome was wide-eyed and ashen. His mouth was agape, and he stood in an open stance with his arms stretched wide.

He whipped his head back, looked to the length of wood gripped tightly in his hand and jumped with excited realization. "Oh! I did it!"

Joe whipped his head back around to Petals, turned and pointed at the finely-grained, oddly-reflective wood in his hand and smiled, "Look! I did it!"

Petals said nothing. He shut his mouth and slowly began moving his hands about in a gentle circular wave.

Frowning, Joe looked around him to try and see what it was that Petals was doing… he was cleaning.

Everything was scattered everywhere. Tools were floating in the air, the wooden dowels that had been neatly organized and shelved were littering the floor and sawdust had somehow appeared and was swirling the floor in oddly symmetrical patterns that he recognized as rune circles.

After turning full circle, he sheepishly looked back to Petals with what he hoped to be a look of apology. "Maybe I tried too hard?"

Petals said nothing.

Chapter 8

A great many apologies were uttered, and Petals reassured the workers and Hilbert that nothing had been broken and that they had acquired everything they had come to find. The workshop had been set to right without any incidents, and all the tools were exactly where they needed to be.

The fact that the trickster gnome was able to simply wave his hands about and set to order an entire workshop was overshadowed by the mess that Joe had made, and that he had made it in such spectacular fashion that rune circles had appeared through the sawdust. The Arcanum had taught him that such appearances were only generated by concentrated efforts or through traumatic outbursts. Joe chalked it up to a combination of the two.

Once the huff had settled, the workers had returned to their stations and Hilbert no longer looked like he was about to object, Joe dared to speak. "Um… what kind of wood is this?" He pointed to the dowel he had summoned and held in his hand.

Hilbert nervously shifted from one foot to the other while seeming confused about what to do with his hands. They moved from his hips to across his chest and back again. Eventually, the man leaned forward and squinted with one eye open as Joe presented the length between his open palms for examination. "That's uh…" He tilted his head in what Joe presumed was to examine the grain a bit better, "That's marbled iron maple."

Joe looked at it himself and peered at it with one open eye as Hilbert had. It honestly looked like the tree had grown with veins of mirror-finished silver in it. He turned to Petals and held it out, "What do you think?"

His superior failed to take the bait and simply gave him a tight-lipped, joy-less grin.

Fireballs.

Petals then turned to Hilbert, tipped his hat, and bid them a good day. Joe followed suit, and they left in a hurry. It turned out that the approved documentation was a form of voucher that businesses used to submit their own forms to the city for reimbursement of goods sold. It was simply a quicker and safer means for exchange of coin for officers and the City. No unnecessary trips to the banks, transactional tracking, or expense summary forms.

It wasn't until they had made it far out to the street that Petals rounded on him. "WHAT WERE YOU DOING?"

Joe halted and threw up his arms and the staff to defend himself from whatever the angered fey might throw at him. "I don't know! What you told me to do!"

Petals growled in frustration, yanked off his hat, and threw it on the ground before turning to yell at him again. "I didn't tell you to shake the building!"

He gaped at that revelation. "I *shook* the *building*?"

Petals raised a stern finger and growled with his reddened face. "I had to use charms to calm them into *not* calling the precinct!"

Joe got his hackles up and lowered into a wider stance so that he might be more on level with his superior. "Maybe I wouldn't have shaken the building if you had given me some better directions!"

"You're one mistake from getting yourself demoted back down to Blue Coat!" The small finger shook ferociously in the air as a signified axe hovering above the head that was his career. "One... more," the little man growled in warning.

The flood of emotions that overcame him was mixed with waves of anxiety, anger, and regret. Joe turned his back on his superior and took deep, calming breaths while looking upon his newly acquired staff.

What have you cost me?

Petals pulled out his crystalline network box and called in for a cart to take them back to the station. Dispatch confirmed the call, said that they would send one as soon as they could, and would inform them of the estimated arrival time.

Joe gripped tight the marbled iron maple and tried to steady himself. He needed to remain calm and not make any more mistakes. Citizens depended on him, and he needed to be as strong as the iron veins in the wood he was holding to be there when they needed him.

Many minutes passed in the dying light of the street before either of them spoke to the other. "What memory did you pull that from?" Petals sounded concerned, and his questioning was quiet.

He didn't exactly feel like sharing at the moment. "Couldn't you read my thoughts?"

The gnome snarled, "Don't get flippant with me!"

Joe rounded on the shorter man and shot back, "I wasn't! I was being *open*, just as you told me to do! If you're as capable as you suggest you are with reading my thoughts, then you should have had a full stage play dancing about inside of your mind when I pulled the memory that I did."

For a brief time, they eyed each other down. Joe couldn't help but notice a myriad of emotions play across the gnome's face. There was fear, anger, frustration, regret, sadness. He likely mirrored many of the same feelings on his own face.

After a time, Joe relaxed, and Petals visibly sighed. The network box echoed to life and startled them both into jumping. The voice of the woman from dispatch echoed into the evening light around them. The cart was on its way and would arrive in a few minutes.

Petals took a moment to calm down, then thanked dispatch and told them that they were both clocked out for the day and to take them off the call list. Dispatch confirmed and wished them a swell night.

Joe relented. "It was a memory of the orphanage… of the first time I used my power."

Petals slowly shook his head and lifted his hand to stop him. "It is none of my business, and I should never have asked."

He didn't care; he felt he needed to tell someone, and Petals was likely the only one he knew that would help him understand what had just happened in his 'material selection'. "Some older boys had kidnapped a fairy."

That seemed to catch his attention, as Petals' head whipped around in what looked to be a fresh swell of anger painted across his face.

"Yeah… I felt that too." Joe looked to the length of marbled iron maple in his hand and struck the butt end of it on the cobblestone before him, then continued his story. "I couldn't stand by and watch." He gripped the wood tighter and squeezed his anger into it. "I told them to let it go." A sneer was threatening to curl his lip as he ground his teeth. "They beat me into the dirt for daring to tell them what to do."

Petals barked, "Enough!"

Joe snapped out of it and looked to his superior.

Petals had a wide-eyed look on his face, and his hat was in his hands, being wrung in a fit of nervousness. He visibly shook himself and brushed off his hat before affixing it on his head. "You're going to go home and speak none of this to anyone." He glanced up at Joe with a stern glare, as if to say that it was an order and not a suggestion.

"Why? What is it that you're so scared of?"

The usually chipper and confident gnome looked about in a state of near panic. He glanced up at Joe, looked at Joe's staff, then shook his head. "I can't say, not here... and I'm not certain yet." He looked back up the road, toward the center of the city, and spoke over his shoulder, "Tell none, and get some rest. We'll discuss it in the morning when we can do so safely."

As much as he wanted to argue and know more, Joe also felt an overwhelming sense of exhaustion threatening to pull his legs out from under him. He'd expended far more of his will that day than he had in quite a long time.

The gnome cart rounded the corner up the hill and slowed to a stop before Petals. Joe trudged his way up the slope, then held out the length of wood in front of him and shrunk it with a simple compression spell and pressing his hands together.

It took a bit of work, but the marbled iron maple eventually shrunk to the size of a standard wand at a length of one step. He wasn't anywhere near as skilled as Petals, who could simply snap his fingers and do anything he wanted. The exhaustion was also catching up with him; magic was harder to do the more tired you were.

Joe stuffed the wand into his coat pocket, crammed himself into the wood-paneled cart, and pulled the door shut behind him. His superior didn't seem all too chipper or chatty, and he was in dire need of a decent night's sleep. So, they sat in silence for the entirety of the ride.

Once they arrived at the precinct, they exited the cart, waved their thanks to the driver, and turned to walk home. Petals turned back to Joe and pointed at him sternly, "Remember–"

"Say nothing! I got it." He didn't feel like making one more mistake today.

Petals lowered his hand and looked to him with a furrowed brow. "Be careful." He paused for a time, then lifted and tipped his hat before turning to head down the street and south of the precinct.

Joe watched as he left, then turned to head northeast toward his room and board. There weren't many people left on the street. Most everyone was heading home for the evening and some shops were starting to close up.

The night lanterns had already started lighting and began casting their yellow glow on the streets. The partition of his mind began to press upon him the urgency of removing his staff from his pocket – the compression was failing and wouldn't hold – Joe did so and released the compression, causing the wood to spring to full size. He caught it and began walking along, using it as a hiker's stick. It wasn't a long walk home, but it sure felt like one.

Fireballs, what a day.

His slow trudge up the few short steps to the door were cut abruptly short by a shadowed presence in the doorway.

Ms. Bellcreaux stood with her arms crossed and one finger gently tapping the sleeve of the other arm. "You're late."

Not. Today.

He hadn't the energy to spar with her and she hadn't directly said anything that wasn't untrue. His bed was calling him. "I apologize for the late hour of my arrival." It didn't seem to satisfy her, as she stood rooted to the spot. Joe decided to throw more of his pride on the fire. "Next time, I shall send a message to inform you if I am to be working late."

She still didn't budge.

Joe put one foot on the step, lifted himself up to tower over her, and looked over her head to the stairs just inside the door. He was near toe to toe with her and she still wasn't budging. "I'd like to head to bed, if you don't mind." His words brushed her forehead, he was so close.

"You're late, and you haven't eaten." She still didn't move, despite his discomforting proximity.

You would get along with Amelia.

Joe snapped his hand to her eye level. It held the bundle of cloth containing the devilishly delicious chicken pie. "My superior's wife was kind enough to supply me with a meal."

"Well…" she surprisingly stepped aside, "it appears as though you were prepared today." However, she kept her nose upturned and didn't bother to look him in the eye.

Joe glared at her out of the corner of his eye before proceeding for the stairs.

"And I see you *actually* made it to detective, Joseph."

He paused with his foot on the first step of the stairwell. Something snapped in him at that moment. He didn't know what it was, but he couldn't let the comment pass. Joe lowered his foot down and slowly turned to face his landlady.

"I am Detective Joseph Runewall." He punctuated his title and each of his names with a thump to the floor with the butt of his staff.

Ms. Bellcreaux furrowed her brow and turned her head slightly away as she watched him out the corner of her eye. She uncrossed her arms and looked to stand a bit straighter, if it was even possible for her posture to be any straighter.

Joe took a step toward her as he raised his voice just a touch. "I swore to uphold the law…" He wasn't certain, but he thought he heard his voice echo. He took another short step toward her; "I swore to protect the innocent…" He wasn't sure where it was coming from, but he thought that someone might have turned on a bright arcane lantern; "To shield them from suffering…"

Ms. Bellcreaux looked up at him with high eyebrows and wide eyes as she pressed herself back against the dark plaster wall. He'd never seen that look on her face before. He doubted it was fear, as the old crow seemed like the fearless type. If anything, she was exhibiting surprise.

Joe lowered his voice to a whisper, "And I swore to punish the wicked…"

After a long minute of silence, she responded with a whisper in kind, "I believe you."

Exhaustion finally took him as he let his arms sag and his head droop.

About damned time, you old crow.

He turned to head back to the stairs and quickly shut his eyes as the stairwell lantern flickered brightly.

Ah! That's where the light was coming from.

Joe made his way to the steps, reached up, and flicked the crystalline casing hanging from the wall. It kept flickering, and he gave up. He dragged his feet up the steps one at a time. Halfway to the top, she called out again.

"Joseph."

He stopped and shut his eyes, awaiting the second wave of the ceaseless assault upon his soul. "Yes, Ms. Bellcreaux?"

"Once you have finished eating, straight to bed and lanterns out. I don't want the neighbors complaining of nuisance lighting." She turned and headed her way to her main floor quarters and quietly shut the door behind her.

Joe nodded in understanding and whispered under his breath as he continued his way up the steps, "Love you too, old crow." From what he could tell, the other men that had taken up residence had already gone to bed. He could hear the low rumble of gentle snoring and heavy breathing at each of the doors he passed.

He pulled the key from his vest pocket and stuck it into the keyhole to unlock the door, only to realize that he had forgotten to lock it when he left.

Fireballs.

Joe opened the door, flicked on the lantern, and examined the damage. His law tomes had been arranged improperly on the shelf above his bed. The bed had been made incorrectly, as the ends were flipped around with the pillow facing the window instead of the wall.

The mirror he hung on the back of the door had been moved to the water closet, and his coat rack was nowhere to be found. He didn't have the energy or patience to rearrange or fix anything. He set his staff against the wall by the door, then leaned back against the nightstand that had been moved to the newly-arranged head of his bed.

Unwrapping the chicken pie, he couldn't help but smile to himself. He looked to the ceiling and thanked the gods for the good fortune and the simple pleasure he was about to indulge in.

The only warning he received was the prick at the back of his mind that told him the barrier had been breached. Joe threw himself toward the water closet and screamed as the window shattered and sent a shower of glass into his room and across his bed.

It wasn't until he landed on the white tile of the closet that he realized he'd been shot at. His left arm was numb, and the skin felt like it had been seared in fire. A quick glance told him that his tan trench coat had prevented the bullet from piercing through. Sadly, it didn't stop the impact force.

He opened his coat and yanked down the collar to expose his shoulder. His shirt had been torn and his skin looked like it had bad road rash. There weren't any bits of debris, but it looked heartily banged up, and there was blood. Based on the excruciating throbbing pain, he wouldn't be surprised if the arm was broken as well. At least he was alive.

Joe grunted, threw himself up to a seated position, and pulled his crystalline network box from his belt. He squeezed the button to activate it. "Detective Joseph Runewall, under fire!"

In response to his emergency call, three more shots ripped through the brick and mortar of the outer wall, then the wood and plaster of the inner wall, and slapped the opposing wall before coming to a full stop.

Frighteningly, the volley was fired with an equally-spaced spread. One after the other would strike at three-and-a-half-step distances from the first window shot. Whoever was firing at him knew what they were doing and attempted to shoot any space along the wall that he might be hiding behind.

The last bullet struck the tile of the wall just to the left of where Joe had been sitting. Upon realizing what the shooter was doing, Joe had thrown himself back down against the floor and prayed the bullet missed him. It did, but not by much.

Joe held his network box against his chest and let dispatch call out into the night. "Runewall, confirm your location... Runewall, can you confirm?"

He lay in silence as his housemates shouted and fumbled about in the dark. He tried to keep his breathing slow and let the panic pass him by. If he panicked, he'd die. It was one of the very first lessons they taught at the Academy.

One of the other men that lodged at Ms. Bellcreaux's began pounding on his door and yelled through it. "Joe! You hear us? What's going on in there? What's that racket?"

Dispatch called out from his chest, "All available detectives in South Western Village, converge on 97th and Old Oak Road. Detective under fire and unresponsive. Medical assistance is on its way."

There weren't any more shots being fired, but he didn't dare take the chance of moving. He lay there on the cold tile, accompanied by the pain of having been shot for the first time as a detective. He'd been shot before as a blue coat, and knew what to expect.

A partitioning of his mind helped him to handle the pain. Wisely, he didn't dump all the pain away, as his instructors had informed him that it could result in a shattering of the mind when the wall broke. He simply used the partition to help him manage it so that he could stay conscious and provide his report when backup arrived.

It didn't take long for Ms. Bellcreaux to arrive and unlock the door to his room. She marched in without a care in the world as to the mess. She stormed in with her hair hastily done in a loose bun and glared at him as he lay on the floor with his bleeding arm. "Why is the window shattered? Why are there holes in the walls?"

Joe sighed as he held the chicken pie handkerchief to his bleeding arm and let his head drop back down to the tile floor. "My heart is warmed by your caring nature."

A familiar feminine voice rang out over the network box lying on his chest, "Detective Amelia Iceheart on scene, entering the building."

Oh lovely, another heartless woman to criticize my efforts to stay alive.

~~

The Ice Queen – surprisingly – didn't insult him or berate him for getting shot. She went about her task with determined focus and proficiency. With her help, Joe had been moved to a chair in the lobby without any further incident. The shooter must have moved on.

Doctor Broom arrived shortly afterward and tended to his arm. The doctor was an ebony-haired, middle-aged man with nimble fingers and a gaunt frame. He had a long face and hooked nose with a pair of magnifying spectacles. His white trench coat bore the blood-red emblem of the medical corps, and it was charmed to resist any stains. His trousers, vest, and shirt were similarly enchanted and emblazoned.

The man had a soft touch and tenderly prodded Joe's numb arm with an investigative and discerning manner. "You're lucky, no breaks."

"Huh… Good thing I'm not a betting man."

The doctor scowled at Joe and narrowed his eyes. "Seriously? Jokes at a time like this?" He pulled tighter on the bandaging he had wrapped around Joe's arm.

"Ow!... Nice bedside manner there, Doc."

Doctor Broom clapped shut his black leather medical bag, stuffed the remaining bandaging into his white trench coat, then stood up and sighed heavily. "My advice is to get a full night's sleep and not subject yourself to any strenuous exercise. But what do I know, I'm just a doctor. You'll probably ignore my advice and go gallivanting about in the middle of the night with some hair-brained scheme of reclaiming your barbaric sense of honor and duty."

The man picked up his feet and took two steps to the door when Joe barked out a laugh. "Fireballs! I'd sooner toss myself into the ocean and the mouth of a mythical kraken than do something so brainless. I'm taking your orders and getting myself a full night's sleep as soon as I'm given permission to do so."

Doctor Broom looked back upon Joe and nodded in approval. "Good man." He tilted his head toward Joe's arm with his chin. "With a full night's rest, your arm should be healed by morning with the cream I applied to the wound. It may scar."

Joe nodded his appreciation, "Thanks, Doc. Sorry you got called out this late."

The gaunt man genuinely smiled. "It was truly no bother." He tipped his hat to Joe and headed back out, likely to home for the night.

Joe looked to his watch and groaned at the time. It was almost the middle of the night.

Fireballs.

Great heavy footfalls made their way down the steps, setting the wood to groaning loudly. Captain Bolt made his way down from Joe's room and turned to face him once he reached the bottom step. "Your arm?"

He didn't know if the captain had turned off his intimidation magic, or if Joe was just too damn tired to care about being scared, but he wasn't afraid, and answered simply, "Doc said I should be good once I've had a full sleep, may be some scarring."

The captain accepted that and gestured for Joe to go ahead. "All right, get your sleep and report to me in the morning."

Joe happily accepted his captain's orders, rested back in the chair, shut his eyes, and used the partition of his mind to force himself into an immediate sleep.

Chapter 9

Joe woke in a panic and bolted upright. He immediately regretted the decision, as every ounce of his body protested in pain – sharp, aching, and throbbing alike. He sucked on his teeth and squeezed his eyes shut as he attempted to grit his way through it.

The pins and needles running through his arm eased into a throbbing ache. "By the gods!"

"I leave you for one night and you almost get yourself killed. Dear boy, how do you plan on surviving the week?"

Joe blearily opened one eye and attempted to focus through the confusion. "Petals, that you?"

His superior stood at the foot of a bed cot that Joe had apparently been moved to. A quick glance informed him that he had been moved to the precinct... and had been set up beside his desk and the radiator.

So that's why I'm sweating. Fantastic.

Joe cradled his arm across his stomach and slowly began pushing himself to his feet with the support of his good arm.

Petals stepped forward with his hands outstretched, ready to catch him should he stagger and fall. It was an amusing thought, a tiny gnome attempting to catch a human from falling over.

Thanks, but I'd probably pancake you, little old man.

Standing up was painful at first, but a quick twist and stretch loosened up his back, neck, and shoulders. His arm was even feeling a bit better and less tingly. Wiggling his fingers and moving the arm in a circular rotation seemed to help as well. "I'm feeling a bit better thanks to the doc."

"I'm glad to hear it." Doctor Broom arrived and set his black leather bag on the cot before turning to the bandaging on Joe's arm.

It was only then that he realized he'd been sleeping in his trousers and cotton undershirt. "Uh… where're my things?"

Petals pointed to Joe's desk, where his shirt, coat, and vest were neatly folded. His hat and staff were also among his things, all of which sat atop his travelling trunk.

He couldn't help but frown and point at the trunk. "Why's that there?"

The doctor went about using a pair of snub-nosed scissors to cut away the bandaging, then used a cloth to clean the area.

Petals replied with a soft smile, "It wasn't deemed safe for you to remain where you usually lodge, so you were brought here with a trunk full of your things so that you might change and freshen up."

He couldn't argue with the reasoning and appreciated the gesture. "Thanks. I owe you."

Petals waved it off. "You owe me nothing." He failed to say it in his usual jovial manner.

Doctor Broom eyed Joe's arm and tested stretching the skin. At first, it pinched slightly, causing Joe to jump a little, but then the pain turned to dull warmth. "Looks like it healed well. You definitely have a bit of a scar, but it's better than the alternative."

"Am I clear?"

Broom nodded. "You're clear, but I highly recommend you get a full meal in you... and bathe. The cream leaves behind an unfortunate aroma." The man was crinkling his nose and breathing through his mouth.

Joe dared to turn his head and whiff. *WHOA!*

~~

Joe sank into the circular wooden tub of hot soapy water and groaned. It was exactly what he needed.

He'd have never thought it, but the men's washroom had full services, which included the tub.

"Ms. Amelia spent a fair amount of her night tracking down as much as she could on the shooter." Petals had followed Joe into the washroom and stood with his back to the tub curtain.

"What did she find?"

"Your attacker fired four rounds from a very powerful long-barrel, with frightening accuracy."

Joe couldn't help but rub his shoulder where he had been hit. "I'm well aware of that much."

"They fired from a rooftop two streets over."

Thundering fireballs!

"That's one hell of a shot! What was that, four hundred paces?"

Petals confirmed, "Four hundred and thirty-four, to be exact. They then descended the house by the downspout and retreated down a storm grate. That was where their trail went cold."

Joe took a moment to absorb that and vigorously rubbed his shoulder with a brush to clean his skin of any remaining cream. Whoever wanted him killed was a professional. "You thinking what I'm thinking?"

"Yes… the third assailant from the jewelry store."

He only had one case, and nothing came to mind that could have possibly followed him from being a Blue Coat that would warrant such a professional hit. "There's a great deal more to that jewelry theft than we're seeing."

Petals chuckled. "Clearly."

"Any word on those blueprints?"

"The captain contacted some officials on our behalf to expedite them."

Joe adjusted the tub mirror and quickly went to work with the straight razor, shaving and cleaning up. "What's our next move?"

"Your next move is to get some food in your belly before you collapse. Accelerated healing takes it out of you, and a hearty meal will do you some good."

He didn't want to ask, especially while dragging a razor around his chin, but he was eager to try some more of Mrs. Pettlebottom's baking. It didn't help that he never got the chance to eat the chicken pie from the night before. He had dropped it, and it had been stepped on by Ms. Bellcreaux.

Looking back, it was the most upsetting part of his entire night. Mrs. Pettlebottom made delicious pies, and he had desperately looked forward to eating the one she gave him for dinner. His stomach roared its agreement and even left him a touch lightheaded.

Joe finished with the straight razor, then splashed and rubbed his face before asking, "Any suggestions for a hearty meal on a budget of copper pennies?"

Petals chuckled and began walking to the door to leave Joe to freshen up. "Already taken care of."

He was suddenly stricken with hopeful urgency and hurried with scrubbing down, drying off and dressing himself.

Please be Mrs. Pettlebottom's baking!

~~

It wasn't her baking. At least, Joe didn't think it was her baking. A delivery box sat atop his desk. It bore a symbol he hadn't seen before, the outline of a whiskey bottle with a blue label set at an angle. Joe took a step closer to read it. "Blue Whiskey Grill?"

Amelia approached him from behind; he could tell it was her by the sound of her soft footsteps and the thinner heel. "Congratulations, rookie. It's your first bullet meal."

"What's a first bullet meal?" Joe pulled his belt knife from his lower back and carefully sliced through the paper packaging at the corners to preserve the symbol on top.

Amelia turned and sat herself on the corner of his desk, reached out, and tapped the box he was unwrapping with one of her white-painted fingernails. "Marcus, the owner, is a retired Blue Coat. He opened the Blue Whiskey Grill and honors officers with discounts and free meals when they reach milestones."

Joe was catching on. "Like getting shot for the first time?"

She confirmed it and slipped off his desk to head back out. "You did good, rook. Just try not to get shot again. Marcus only gives out so many meals."

He rolled his eyes and called out after her as he continued to unwrap the packaging. "I'll keep that in mind." The box felt warm on his hands, and upon lifting the lid, he delightedly discovered why.

There was a platter-sized plate loaded with all the fatty desirables a man could ever want. Large fried eggs on toast with butter; hearty, spiced, and smoked sausages; boiled beans; and thickly-sliced, bourbon-basted bacon with a hefty pile of hash browns.

Ohhhh, yes.

As soon as he lifted the lid, steam wafted up and filled his inhaling lungs with intoxicating aromas. The four corners of the delivery box easily broke away, leaving him with a clean eating surface. The lid of the box had a napkin and utensils wrapped in it.

Joe sat down and dived in. Doctor's orders, and he wasn't going to ignore them.

He could tell that there was some slight jealousy, as several of the other detectives around the bullpen kept taking long walks past his desk with their noses tilted up, breathing deep. Eventually, he spoke up for all to hear, "If you'd like your own plate, I'd be happy to spend some iron!"

A few of the men chuckled, but most just sneered and went back to their duties.

Lovely, I get shot at for doing my job, then get resentment for it.

It didn't take him long to polish off his plate and mop up the rest of it with the remaining toast. He felt full and satisfied once he was done and did his best to clean up his desk. He got as far as putting his utensils on the plate when the box began folding in on itself. Any bits that he had ripped off suddenly sprang to life and threw themselves back into the chaos of folding.

Joe watched in astonishment as the corners folded in only for new seams to appear and more folds to bend. It continued folding in on itself until it was almost as small as his fist, before it finally vanished in a puff of white smoke. "Huh." He figured it had to be some form of recall spell. It was simple and inexpensive enough for non-living materials that it actually made less sense to not use it for such delivery purposes.

In the wake of the white smoke, there was a calling card left on his desk. It was dark parchment that looked to be stamped with a leather-like print and a blue label with white lettering, reading 'Blue Whiskey Grill'. It also had an address. It wasn't far south from the precinct. He flipped it over and noticed something handwritten. 'Keep your head on a swivel. Marcus.'

While it was getting on his nerves a bit that people kept telling him "don't get shot" after getting shot, it was clearly advice he needed to take more seriously. Joe looked to his improvised wooden staff and thought about that very thing.

Petals stepped up to his desk and waited for Joe to turn his attention to him.

"Not going to make me jump today?" Joe looked from the staff to his superior.

Petals shook his head. "You were right yesterday."

Joe raised an eyebrow and turned his full attention to the short man.

This should be interesting.

"I haven't been very accommodating of your shortcomings."

Never mind.

Petals lifted his hand to halt Joe from protesting. "Allow me to finish."

He gave his superior the chance. Joe didn't feel like there was much else the man could say that wouldn't dig any deeper.

"The Arcanum fails its students in a great many ways."

You're full of sharp turns today.

"Come again?" Joe folded his arms and tilted his head as he tried to wrap his head around which direction Petals was taking the conversation.

Petals motioned for Joe to sit, then snapped his fingers and hopped into the air. The trickster gnome's office chair shot across the room in two puffs of sparkling blue smoke, only for him to land comfortably in a seated position.

Show off.

Once Joe seated himself on his own wobbly desk chair, Petals began again. "The Arcanum only teaches its students so much. There is much more that they could teach you, but they don't. They're selfish and petty."

Joe couldn't help but notice the little man getting worked up about it.

"You should have been well more aware of the selection process you were rejected from, but you weren't because nobody told you what it would be like. You probably had this idea in your head of a room full of racks where you just grab a staff, am I correct?"

He shrugged slightly. It hadn't been exactly like that in his head. Joe had figured there would be a large variety of different kinds available to choose from and someone to help him do so, but the idea was close enough. "A bit, yes."

"They also failed to recognize you for what you are." Petals said it in a softer tone to prevent eavesdropping.

Joe picked up on the subtlety to understand that he was referencing the fact that he was a sorcerer, not a wizard.

"You were also unfamiliar with the staff selection process or what many of the available types of wood were or their compatibilities."

He couldn't deny that part. Many of the available labels on the box cubbies were completely foreign to him. He still had no idea what purple dragon poplar was or why it was so damn expensive.

Petals then pointed to Joe's staff and wiggled his fingers.

Joe sat upright, turned, and looked back to the wood leaning against the wall beside his coat rack, then leaned over and picked it up to hand it to the gnome.

It was far larger than the small man could handle with one hand; his fingers simply couldn't encompass it as Joe's could. "Do you remember what the master woodworker called this?"

The question was rhetorical, but he answered anyway. "Yes, marbled iron maple." He was still uncertain as to why he called to that particular wood.

Petals nodded in affirmation, then offered it back to Joe. "This is not typically selected by anyone with arcane power."

Joe took the length, set the butt of it down on the ground between his legs, and held it close as he continued listening. "So–"

Petals lifted his hand to halt him. "It's typically not chosen because it's usually unavailable, and also because it's mostly used for martial weapons."

That had him stumped. Why would he select a wood typically utilized for gun stocks, sword handles, or spear shafts? Joe was about to ask when Petals lifted his hand once more.

At least you're not straight up interrupting me anymore.

Petals looked about the bullpen to make sure nobody was in earshot. "The reason you connected with that wood is the same reason for why you first cast magic that day. I'm certain of it."

That clears up absolutely nothing.

Petals sat upright. "You have a report to hand to the Captain."

Oh, fireballs.

Petals seemed to note the look of panic that struck Joe's face, and grinned all the wider. "Best get to work, my boy."

Having familiarized himself with the operation of his arcane mechanical typesetter, it did not take him long to produce the report in question. The fact that his incident with the shooter was so brief meant that the report had little details to provide; it only encompassed two pages.

Joe snatched the second page of parchment and set it aside to allow the ink a moment to dry. He quickly organized his desk, then checked himself in the reflection provided by the glass panes of the typesetter before picking up the documents and heading to the captain's office.

He'd just been reaching for the door handle when it opened inward. A tall and elegantly dressed man with a wire-thin mustache stood with his nose upturned. "Get out of my way."

Joe was about to bark at the man for his rudeness when the captain spoke. "Detective... step aside."

Having been given an order, he did as he was told and stepped back and to the side.

The discourteous gentleman – missing the gentle – marched on with his nose held high.

As was his occupation and custom, Joe gave the man an investigative once-over. Coin was clearly not an issue, as his three-piece suit looked to be of the finest stitch and was a rich and dark shade of violet. His cotton shirt was a soft pink, and his tie was jet black. As well-dressed of a stiff upper-class man as Joe had ever seen.

"Detective," the captain's deep rumble reverberated out to call him into the office.

Joe nodded, turned into the office, and shut the door behind him. The aura of intimidation that the captain seemed to naturally emanate was palpable. It took him a moment to steady himself and shake off the assault on his senses. "Let me guess, advocate?"

There was a deep rumbling huffing grunt from within the chest of the massive dragon kin. "What tipped you off?" The lizard-headed mythical creature snapped a stylus clean in half while glaring out the window of his office.

He had to steady himself again as he felt another wave of the captain's aura wash over him. "Well, sir, he was carrying a leather pouch under his right arm that was emblazoned with the seal of a private advocate firm. He was also dressed like a snob and likely doesn't live anywhere near here."

"Good eye." The captain turned his attention back to Joe and seemed to ease off the intimidation, as the oppressive weight lifted.

Thank the gods.

Joe took a deep breath and sighed with relief. After a moment of collecting himself, he straightened and stood at the ready.

The charged electric blue eyes of the dragon kin scanned the pages of Joe's report, then each page was placed on the desk with care. "Good report. Have you been cleared by Doctor Broom?"

"Yes, sir."

"Good. Return to your duties and find out everything you can from that boy you arrested at the jewelry store."

Wait, what? The boy? What about the dark dwarf?

"Sir? I can't speak with the boy when–" Realization struck him like a bell. "No! For the dwarf?"

The captain's head slowly bobbed up and down in the affirmative. "The advocate arrived to inform me that the charges against his client–" he reached over and lightly picked up a piece of parchment beside Joe's reports, "– Travok Blackfinger, was threatened into the illegal activities he allegedly committed yesterday."

Thundering hailstorms raining fireballs!

"Are you kidding me?" Joe was flabbergasted by the audacity of the claim.

The captain lifted one of his clawed hands and gestured for Joe to calm himself. "There's more."

Of course there is!

"The advocate has moved for a judicial ruling to dismiss the charges, as his client was under threat of death if he did not complete the task assigned. The crime was petty in nature and the necessary fines have been paid... he's being released."

Joe bolted from the captain's office and flew past his superior, who had his hand held up in an attempt to stop Joe. Upon reaching the winding stairs, he was able to look down into the lobby to watch as the ashen-skinned dark dwarf proudly paraded through the lobby to the exit with the stuffy advocate in toe. The smug, stout, and grimy thief waved up at Joe and laughed as he headed out the door.

He gripped and wrung the railing while standing at the top of the stairs. His teeth ground as he growled out his rage and focused every ounce of his mind on not acting in an unbecoming manner.

Captain Bolt's towering frame slowly thumped its way over to stand beside him, while Detective Petals stepped up to Joe's other side.

The captain spoke first. "This will not be the last time an advocate will ruin your day or your case."

Petals chimed in, "And you will come to learn which advocates work for which high-class criminals."

Anger was slowly being replaced by cold, hard determination and reason. "Travok Blackfinger is a grunt... with secrets to spill."

The captain grunted in the affirmative.

Joe stood straight, breathed deep, found his center, and calmly inquired, "You know which high-class criminal this advocate works for?"

Petals nodded. "Yes."

"You know the grunts that work for them?"

Petals chuckled delightedly. "I do, in fact."

Joe turned and began walking to his desk to collect his things. "After we question the boy, we're going to make some grunts squeal."

Chapter 10

Petals suggested that he be the one to question the boy, as Joe had caused the young man to wet himself during the initial arrest. As much as he wanted to be the one to spearhead the investigation and prove his worth by nailing that slimy dark dwarf to the wall, he couldn't argue with his superior's reasoning.

The two of them wound their way down the steps and headed to the Blue Coats' bullpen and the holding cells. None of the uniformed men that were present looked to be in a good mood. Releasing a red-handed criminal tended to hamper the morale.

Petals approached the cell in question, then spun on his heel to look about the bullpen. "Where is the young man that's supposed to be in this cell?"

Oh fireballs, don't tell me.

Joe halted and put his head on a swivel. It was then that he spotted the young man sitting in a chair before Bob Johnson's desk. It was also at that moment that he noticed the old man standing behind the shoulders of the youth that Joe had caught.

He couldn't help but step closer for a better look. "Wilbur?"

By the gods, it is him.

"Wilbur!" Joe threw up his arms in glee upon spotting the old man again.

Wilbur, on the other hand, ducked and cowered from the sudden outburst of his name. He had always been a mousy gentleman that was quick to twitch and cower away from anyone taller or even slightly louder than he. The old man was dressed as he always was, in near rags. His brown trousers had thick patches over the knees, and he wore an ill-fitting and well-worn gray cotton sweater with patches on the elbows. Despite his drab appearance, he always wore a bright orange bowtie and had a small stuffed teddy stuck in the front pocket of his gray vest.

Joe slowed to a stop before Wilbur and looked down at him with furrowed brows. "Don't you recognize me?"

The young man that Joe had arrested sat with his head between his knees, cowering.

Knowing he'd done the exact thing that Petals had asked him not to, Joe decided to right the wrong from earlier, dropped to a knee beside the young man, and offered him his hand. "My name's Joe."

Wilbur watched on with a slack jaw hanging from his push-broom gray mustache. He was supposed to be informing the young man not to talk, but there was honestly nothing wrong with providing his name, as he was technically required to do so.

"I... I'm Tim." He hesitated, but eventually straightened and took Joe's hand.

Joe gently squeezed Tim's hand. He let go of the hand before looking up at Wilbur. "You have a good advocate. He'll take care of you, like he took care of me when I was younger than you are now."

It was then that Wilbur's mouth clapped shut and his eyes narrowed in what looked to be an attempt to recognize Joe.

Tim seemed to ease a bit but continued to keep his head down.

Joe stood and offered his hand to Wilbur. "You were the advocate assigned to me when I was sent to enter the Arcanum from the Temple of Light. I was six years old and had a bit of a shiner on my left eye and a split lip. I've grown a bit since then."

The old man took Joe's hand and tilted his head before his soft and caring smile bubbled to the surface. "Oh, yes… hello, little Joseph. How are you?" His voice had a little bit of a whistle to it and he reached out to gently squeeze Joe's arm in a caring and grandfatherly sort of way. "Oh my," he chuckled and continued to squeeze Joe's arm, "You have grown quite a bit, haven't you?" His chuckle turned to a warm laugh.

The warmth was infectious and eased quite a bit of the tension in Tim. The youth had turned in his chair and was watching the exchange between the two of them.

"We should catch up some time; I'd like to hear how you've been."

Wilbur's laugh softened to a chuckle once more, and he agreed heartily. "That– that would be nice."

Joe then nodded to Tim. "Since we're here, is it okay if we chat?"

Wilbur's eyebrows furrowed in thought as he turned and placed his hands on Tim's shoulders in a protective gesture. "Oh… I– I– I don't know if that's a good idea." The old man tended to stutter a bit when flustered.

Not wanting to lose their chance, Joe gestured for them to step aside, "A moment?"

The old city-appointed advocate patted Tim on the shoulders, then shuffled along to follow Joe.

He's really getting old.

Joe kept his voice low and leaned down closer to Wilbur's height. "My initial arrest and report suggested that young Tim was subject to coercion by the dark dwarf, and I'm willing to swear by it in front of a judicial council and the gods themselves, if need be."

Wilbur's eyebrows shot up. "Truly?"

He nodded and tempted fate even further. "You know me, Wilbur. You helped me so that I could earn a name for myself, so I could become someone. You helped me become who I am today."

The elderly advocate wiggled his mustache in thought and eyed Joe up and down. Eventually, a soft smile spread across his face and he nodded. "You've grown into a fine young man. I can trust you." He slowly turned and shuffled back toward Tim and spoke with him in hushed tones.

Petals stepped up to Joe's right side but said nothing as he clasped his hands behind his back.

Wilbur returned with Tim in tow. The young man kept his eyes on his own feet and looked like he was trying to curl into a ball while still standing.

No wonder Travok chose you, you're a pushover.

Petals hopped and turned on the spot in his effortless way, then began guiding the rest of them to a private room. It only took a moment for them to wind their way past a few desks and step into a windowed room set with a table and chairs. The shades had been drawn to allow privacy while not instilling panic into whoever was taken in there. People tended to panic less when they could see multiple exits and didn't feel confined or imprisoned.

Once they all took a seat – Wilbur and Tim on one side and Joe and Petals on the other – Wilbur began informing Tim of his rights, that he didn't have to answer any questions he did not feel like answering, and that he would guide the young man through any troublesome waters if any were presented.

Tim said he understood in a barely audible whisper.

Joe pulled a notepad and stylus from the depths of one of his vest pockets, then partitioned his mind with the task of taking notes.

Petals began asking the questions first. "Tim, my boy, could you tell us how you got involved with the dark dwarf we found you with?" He asked the question with what Joe could only describe as the warmest smile he'd ever seen.

Laying on the charm pretty thick, aren't we?

Petals managed to kick him in the leg, as a sudden dull wallop struck him. "Ah!"

Wilbur and Tim darted a look at Joe as he clapped a hand to his leg and rubbed the sore spot. "Sorry... leg cramp."

Thundering mind reader!

The two of them ignored Joe, and Tim looked to Wilbur for permission. The kindly old man gestured for the boy to go on.

"I... worked at The Ruby Lounge... bussing tables." His drab cotton shirt and rough trousers attested to his simple job. He was also a very soft-spoken young man.

Joe attempted to partition his mind even further with the secondary task of training his ears on Tim's words. His hand freely scribbled notes across the notepad.

Petals pressed the young man for more. "Did he work there as well?"

Tim sat up straighter and looked a touch paler. "I– I– I don't know! There were lots of people that worked at the lounge. I'm sorry!"

Petals raised his hands to suggest that Tim calm and slow down. "No need to worry or apologize, my boy, simply tell us how you met."

Tim seemed to calm, then his eyes glazed over a bit as he recalled the events in question. "The night before the jewelry store, they cornered me in the alleyway when I was taking out the trash."

They?

"They?" Joe couldn't contain his excitement at the possibility that the young man might know the identity of the third assailant, the one who tried to kill him.

Tim's eyes darted from Petals to Joe and back again. "Yes. There were two of them."

Dragon's hoard! We got him!

Petals gestured for the young man to continue. "Keep going, my boy... you won't be interrupted again."

Sorry.

The kindly old gnome patted Joe on the shoulder as Joe's hand went about scribbling notes.

"The dark dwarf, what's his name?" Tim looked to be reviving and coming more alive as he told the story.

Petals answered, "Travok."

Tim nodded. "Him, he did all the talking; the other one stood in the shadows and smoked."

Fireballs!

Petals patted Joe on the shoulder again. "Keep going." It was encouragement for both of them. Details might still be revealed.

"He told me if I didn't help, that I'd..." He seemed to choke back sobs. Wilbur gently patted the young man on the back and whispered words of encouragement. Tim took a moment and gathered himself with a shuddering breath before continuing. "He said awful things."

Joe barely had a page of notes and nothing to work with.

Petals waved the young man on. "What can you tell us about the other one, the one in the shadows. Did they say anything at all?"

Tim shook his head.

"What about how they looked? You said they were smoking in the shadows? How tall were they?"

Joe's hand was itching and at the ready to jot down anything.

"He was about our height." Tim looked at Joe and gestured with his finger between them.

116

Joe's hand scribbled some notes across the page.

"Heavy? Thin? Broad-shouldered?" Petals fished for more.

"He was thin, like me."

"Bearded?" Petals stood tall upon the chair and stroked his well-groomed mass of chin hair.

A smile cracked the corner of Tim's mouth. "Uh, no, he was stubbly though, from what I could see from the light of his smoke."

Joe's hand furiously scribbled more notes as he began piecing together details.

"Did they have any distinguishing features? Anything that looked odd?" Petals curled the tips of his mustache with a grand gesture and broad grin.

More of a smile began to slowly emerge on Tim's face. He looked down in thought, and the color drained as he began nodding. "Yeah... his eyes."

Joe's hand twitched.

Petals shrugged and gestured with his hands for more. "What about them?"

Tim shook his head in confusion. "I don't know; they looked off. It was like they weren't people eyes, you know?"

Joe's hand took brief notes.

"What color were they?" Petals stroked his long beard with the tips of his fingers, drawing the hairs downward in gentle tugs. The man knew how to be humorously distracting.

The young man continued to shake his head. "They... were like gold or something. Bright yellow," he shivered from the memory, "and penetrating."

Joe flipped the page in his notepad and started anew, creating an image in his mind as he jotted down notes.

"Did you ever see this man again after that night?"

Tim shook his head. "No."

"The morning of the jewelry store, who all did you see that day?"

"Just Travok, that dark dwarf."

The third assailant was a professional, didn't get their hands dirty or show their face unless they absolutely needed to. They also had the ear of a high-end private sector advocate. Joe thought for a moment, then inquired, "What did his smoke smell like? Did you get a whiff of it?"

The young man nodded and looked down in furrow-browed thought. "It didn't smell like the usual stuff people smoke; lots of smokers in The Ruby Lounge. It was..." He seemed lost trying to find the words. "Sweeter, I guess. Kind of like a flower."

Petals and Joe turned to one another and exclaimed at the same time.

"Sweet leaf!"
"Sweet leaf!"

~~

Joe and Petals marched along the street with Tim between them and Wilbur huffing to keep up from behind.

"Why am I coming along?" the young man whined as Joe pulled him along with his arm wrapped in his.

"You're here to tell us which brand it is."

"But I only smelled it for a second! How am I supposed to know?"

Joe made a quick turn, and the lot of them stepped to the front doors of a brick storefront painted bright green. They'd only walked a block from the precinct. The storefront in question had a strong, sweet smell of flowers billowing out as the door opened. Tim was pushed forward as they made their way through the double set of doors one at a time. The inside of the establishment was a humid jungle of potted plants and chirping crickets and frogs.

Straightening up onto his toes, Joe looked about the store to see if he could spot anyone. Eventually, a low and drawn out crackling noise called from the far end of the store before a grandmotherly, shaky voice echoed about them from all sides, "Helloooo?"

Joe peered down one of the rows of metal racks and lifted a length of leafy vines to spot a red-scuted shael wearing a green sash and botanist's leather apron. The leathery and wrinkly old creature slowly waddled their way toward them with arms outstretched, crackling loudly.

The grandmotherly voice echoed about them once again, "Come in! Come in! So lovely to see you!"

Tim peered through the vines that Joe had lifted. "What.... What is that? Where is that voice coming from?"

Joe couldn't help but chuckle and moved out from around the racks to approach the elderly reptilian. "This is a shael; her species are effectively giant turtles or tortoises."

As was customary for one of her species, she reached up to touch Joe's face. Understanding the custom, Joe bent down low so that she might cup his face with her stubby clawed hands. Her people didn't have the best eyesight or hearing, but their sense of touch was extraordinary. She also wasn't very nimble, and despite being as tall as a dwarf, her arms didn't reach very far.

Joe lifted a hand and pointed to the ceiling. "The voice is coming from the store itself. She likely has some form of translation box set up. The crackling sounds she makes get translated into the common tongue."

Tim, for the first time since he knew the boy, gave off an arrogant, irritated retort. "She should just learn Common then." He proceeded to cross his arms and shake his head. "I don't know why we're wasting our time here."

Joe turned a glaring eye at the young man, who was looking uninterestedly about the store, and answered for the shopkeeper "She can understand you, you know."

Tim looked back at Joe, stuffed his hands in his pockets and lowered his eyes. "Sorry."

He had the feeling the boy wasn't actually sorry. He likely grew up in an environment that was intolerant of other races and picked up some of the same flawed ideologies.

Education would hopefully help him. "She can't speak Common because she doesn't have the ability to. Her species doesn't have the same vocal cords, mouth shape, or tongue that we do."

The crackling began again, and the grandmotherly voice echoed all about them. "It's all right, he's a young man. How can I help you?"

Joe turned to the elderly shael. "Yes, when I passed your shop the other day, I saw that you sell smokes. Do you carry all the popular brands and types?"

The reptilian creature put her scaly, clawed hand on his and made a soft groaning in her throat. "Oh, dear, don't go putting that awfulness inside of you, it will take years from your life."

Tim barked from the far end of the store, "Then why do you sell it?"

Joe straightened and turned a disapproving glare on the young man, who ducked his head. He turned his attention back to the storekeeper and shook his head. "No, I don't wish to smoke any, its part of an investigation. We're trying to identify a culprit based on the type of smoke they use."

The elderly shael patted his hand, then gently grabbed it and guided him through the chaos of leaves and shrubbery to the back, as she crackled and groaned on. "I have all the popular leaves and weeds and roots and papers to go with them. I even have a few pipes."

Petals did the honor of pushing Tim to the back of the store, where a glass case was set up and a transactional device sat atop it. All sorts of wraps and leaves were on display.

Joe gently squeezed the shael's hand and inquired, "Do you sell sweet leaf, and how is it wrapped? What kinds are there?"

The green-skinned head turned to him, and the orange and black beady eyes steadied on him. The grandmotherly voice sounded greatly disappointed in him.

"That is a vile leaf, and I will never sell it. It is as addictive as it is damaging."

Joe was familiar with its addictive and mentally corrosive properties, but that was not the nature of his question. "Are there different kinds, different smells?"

She shook her small head and answered the very question he had been hoping to hear. "There's only one sweet leaf, and I refuse to sell it in my store."

"Who does sell it? And have you seen a man that fits this description that has asked for it in the past?" Joe pulled a series of artist sketches from his vest pocket and unfolded the parchment on the glass countertop.

The elderly shael near stuck her head against the parchment in order to see the paper. A loud screeching crackle escaped the shael as she stepped back from the presented likeness. "HIM!"

I'm on to you now.

She looked to Joe and back to the drawing before taking a step forward and pointing at it with her long claws. "The face is wrong… but the eyes. Those yellow eyes, I will never forget them – eyes of a predator. Eagle's eyes."

Chapter 11

Prior to leaving the precinct, they released young Tim into Wilbur's care. Fortunately, there was only the one type of sweet leaf smoke, and according to Lin – the shael owner of The Blooming Jasmine – those particular smokes were only rolled in one kind of paper. With that revelation, they no longer had need of the boy, and parted ways.

While they had caught the young man in the act of stealing gems, there was sufficient evidence to suggest that he had been threatened into doing so. It was up to the judicial council to determine sentencing. In the meantime, he would be held by the city, since he was a juvenile.

Joe and Petals waved their goodbyes to Wilbur and Tim, then turned to head back to the precinct.

"While you completely ignored my orders for you to stay back and allow me to handle the young man, you admittedly pulled quite the rabbit from your hat. Well done, my boy." Petals chuckled heartily with that familiar joviality.

Joe took the compliment with a slight chagrin, but then refocused himself. "Thanks. Have you ever heard of a man with eagle eyes?"

His superior continued to chuckle heartily as they walked along. "Yes, but only in rumors. This is certainly a dangerous person we're dealing with." He let out a hearty laugh as he looked up at Joe.

The reason behind the trickster gnome's amusement was obvious to Joe almost immediately. Sighing to himself, he took a few steps toward a storefront window and examined his reflection. "Oh, c'mon!"

Great big pink fluffy bunny ears sprouted from atop his hat. Joe reached up to grab them, only for them to disappear in a snap of Petals' fingers and a puff of blue sparkly smoke.

Joe let out an aggravated sigh and looked down at the triumphantly beaming gnome, "Satisfied?"

"Wholly."

"Good, can we get back to work now?"

"Certainly!"

"Good. First things first. Who owns The Ruby Lounge, and does that private advocate work for them?"

Petals continued to chuckle in his self-satisfied way. "The Ruby Lounge is run by an individual with a dubious past, and yes, they employ that particular private advocate."

"Okay, he officially has my attention. Second, we need to check the archives for any information relating to a man with eagle eyes and put out a city-wide watch for anyone fitting that description. They can't hide forever."

"No!"

Joe ground to a halt and turned to his superior. He was about to question the objection when he saw the look of worry on his face. "What is it?"

Petals looked up and down the street and watched a few pedestrians go about their day, then stepped closer to Joe. "I think this conversation requires some confidentiality."

He thought about it for a second, then grinned. "I think I have a destination in mind." He pulled his crystalline network box from his belt and gave it a wiggle for Petals to see. "Care to do some shopping?"

Petals returned with a slightly less worried grin.

~~

The two of them hurried back to the station and informed the captain of their plans. Joe made a quick stop to generate an updated report for the captain and grab his staff.

By the time they returned to the front steps of the precinct, a gnome cart was waiting. The driver gave them the typical greeting, punched in the destination, and gave them the slip of parchment once the coin tray was filled.

It wasn't long before they were off and Petals had snapped his fingers, creating a muffled bubble around them both. Joe asked, "All right, so what's the big issue with using the archives to hunt down Eagle Eyes?"

Petals stroked his chin in thought and shook his head. "I kept asking myself why you had been targeted when I'm clearly the senior detective and was the one to spot the footprints of the third assailant."

Joe paused and processed that for a minute. The older gnome was right. Joe had been fated to be in the right place at the right time. If it wasn't for Petals, he would never have known about the third assailant – or would he? He surely would have thought to gather all the evidence before closing the case. That was his hope, at least. "You're right. Something definitely doesn't add up there."

There was a great deal to speculate about. Joe backtracked and offered a theory. "It's possible they targeted me because I was simply the weaker of the two of us." He wasn't afraid to admit it; he wasn't anywhere near as skilled as Petals was.

Petals shook his little head in disagreement. "No, targeting either of us would have only brought more suspicion down on the entire case altogether."

Right... Fireballs, what am I missing?

It was Petals' turn to offer a theory. "You were targeted for a reason. And there is only one of two possible answers for how the shooter knew where you lived and which window to shoot through. Either you'd been followed for several days and they were very good at staying hidden, or they had your records from the station."

Thundering fireballs! A mole!

There would have been absolutely no reason to follow him for several days, as he was just a rookie and had no connection to the jewelry theft prior to that morning. The only clear answer was that they had gotten the records from inside the precinct.

Joe couldn't believe it. He had to take a moment to soak it all in and removed his hat to run his hand through his hair. "Jumping blue pixies, this is a mess."

Petals patted his arm, "There-there, my boy. It's only a theory."

"A thumping good one."

They both let out deep sighs. It felt too real to be anything less.

He then understood the gnome's earlier rejection of the archival search and the city-wide watch. They would only alert their target to the very fact that they were looking for him. "Good catch."

The gnome cart bumped along the cobblestone streets and eventually came to a rumbling, puttering stop in front of an old arcane supply store named Runelore's Refuse.

Petals snapped his fingers and released the charm that had muffled their conversation. They both piled out of the cramped little cart, then brushed themselves off before heading to the store.

"This is your grand idea?" Petals raised an eyebrow in something mixed between disapproval and disgust.

Joe pulled his compressed staff from his pocket and released it from its wand-sized state to full length. "Hey! I used the discount castoffs from this place to work on my Arcanum assignments. Don't knock the very thing that got me through to the Academy." It looked bigger back then... and less sad and dingy.

He lifted one hand and touched the door in a semicircle-patterned sequence, then recited the password for entry, "Boogers, candies, and childish delights. Grant me access to your wondrous insights."

The door released its arcane lock and slowly opened while firing party streamers into the air. The grand trumpet that was supposed to announce his arrival wailed off tune, then died in what sounded like a drowning vermin kind gargling for life. "Oh... that sounds bad."

Joe glanced back to find that Petals was standing far from the door with a look of absolute mortification.

We could do worse.

Acknowledging the lackluster first impression, Joe headed inside and looked about the shop that had been his grand savior. It was a neighborhood hot spot for children – or it had been. Dust covered everything. The lights were dull and animated knick-knacks were dead. The candy bins on the right-hand wall were either empty or had large red signs that read 'Out of Circulation'.

The rack that once housed imitation wands for children to fire colorful sparkles from was near empty. The only ones remaining were broken or bent wildly out of shape.

Joe went walking up and down each aisle with sadness in his heart. "What happened here?"

"I got old."

He turned to find Jacobs standing at the door to the storage room. He had a hunched frame and walked with a cane. His knit cotton sweater was beaten and torn, and his balding head was haloed by wisps of dark gray hair.

"By the gods, Jacobs, what happened to you?" The man looked as though he had aged twenty years in the few short ones since last Joe saw him.

Jacobs McMillan was the owner and founder of Runelore's Refuse. He had always been fascinated by the stories of wizards as a child and wanted to pass that wonder and joy onto the next generation. He opened his shop and began selling toys and candies and collected whatever bits and pieces he could find from the arcane community.

He chuckled and repeated himself, "I got old, Joseph." He was then struck by a coughing fit that shook him from head to toe with the violence of it.

Joe rushed to Jacobs' aid and quickly helped him over to a chair behind the counter. "The years have not been kind to you."

The store owner let out a few more lung-rattling exhales before clearing his throat and nodding that he was all right. Once he was steadied, he looked to Joe and gave him a once-over. It was then that his eyebrows lifted, and he got a bit of a tear in his eye. "You did it!" His voice was choked and ragged from the coughing. Tears streamed down his cheeks. "You became a detective!" His voice was almost an inaudible whisper.

Jacobs started teetering and fell off his chair.

Joe threw aside his staff and lunged forward, catching the old shop owner. "Jacobs!"

~~

Doctor Broom descended the steps from the residence above the shop and sighed heavily. "I'm sorry, Joe, he may have a few weeks left. Bad lungs."

The hammer dropped hard on Joe's heart. He had known the man for several years and they had shared a great many joyful stories together. He had told Jacobs all about his time at the Arcanum in exchange for supplies for his studies. "There's nothing you can do?"

The doctor shook his head. "I'm sorry, no. All we can do is keep him comfortable for now. I'll submit a request when I get back to the office. The city should send someone by to check on him after that."

Joe nodded his thanks and looked up the steps. "Can I see him?"

Again, the doctor shook his head. "He's resting, but he did say something about her being yours now. Do you know what he means?"

He couldn't help but blink in eerie surprise. "Holy Fates, I do."

"All right then." He tipped his hat and headed for the door.

Joe raised an eyebrow. "Not curious?"

The doctor turned back and shook his head, then proceeded on out the door while waving goodbye.

Petals stepped up to his side. "You all right, my boy?"

It took him a minute. He'd sadly been tasked with breaking bad news to relatives of victims in the past. Those had touched him, but none of them had been as close to his heart as Jacobs was. He eventually nodded, looked up the stairs behind the storage room door, and whispered a prayer that the Sisters of the Temple of Light had taught him. "Rest well, Jacobs."

Picking his staff up from the corner where he had thrown it earlier, he proceeded into the back. The cobwebs were disastrously thick. Dust covered everything in a fuzzy gray blanket. Boxes littered the floor and were piled up the walls in a haphazard system of organization. Even the mop bucket was dry as bone.

By the gods, Jacobs... how close are you to bankruptcy? Maybe it's a blessing your time is nearing.

The thought sickened him, but the alternative seemed even worse. Life on the streets would have suited him ill; he was too gentle a man to survive.

After examining the back room, he turned, headed to the far wall, and pushed aside some boxes to reveal the door leading to the basement. The lock, unsurprisingly, was unchanged.

Joe decided there was no better time to test out his new staff. He pointed the head – or the end he deemed to be the head, seeing as how it was rounded out with a few knots in the wood, and the other end had a clean-cut bottom – at the thick, dwarven-iron padlock and shut his eyes. He whispered a prayer under his breath and released the energy he had balled up inside.

The arcane forces that he had gathered travelled along his arm, flawlessly through the staff, and jumped into the padlock. There, he was able to visualize the internal mechanisms and manipulate them with ease as he used the partition in his mind to organize the pins and cogs into alignment.

A loud click announced his success. Joe snapped opened his eyes and grinned at the simple accomplishment. "Well, test one complete."

Petals gave him a gentleman's applause of a soft clap. "Well done."

Don't jinx me.

Joe twisted the padlock free and opened the door. The stairwell leading down was dimly lit. Having visited often enough as a young man, he reached his hand inside the doorframe and blindly found the switch that lit the arcane lantern hanging above the landing below.

They descended the rickety stairs that led to the cellar and Jacobs' true store. Rows of metal racks filled the floor space, each with its own clipboard and labels. Baskets, boxes, cupboards, and tin cans, all filled with wondrous items.

A secondary transactional station was set up just to the side of the stairs.

Petals began walking down the rows, examining everything present. He undoubtedly saw the raw ingredients that had been tossed aside or deemed insufficient by the arcane community. "Oh my, these items were for sale?"

Joe nodded and shrugged. "If it worked, he sold it – dried dragon's breath vine, broken sticks of infused chalk, less-than-perfect crystalline arcane sources. It didn't matter to Jacobs; he liked magic, and he wanted to give others that same sense of wonder." He turned and headed to the transactional station as he spoke, then headed to the safe hidden behind a painting of a grand wizard.

He loved that painting. It depicted a purple-robed, white-bearded wizard with a pointed hat throwing a grand bolt of lightning at a horned demonic beast with magmatic skin and fiery wings.

With the painting safely set aside, Joe lifted his staff and did as before with the padlock. He could see the inner workings, and he was able to manipulate them with the gentlest of touches. He could hear the dial whirring and clicking madly as he went about his business. In less time than three shakes of a stiff drink, there was a loud clunk as the safe released and opened.

Petals cleared his throat before interjecting into Joe's thoughts. "Wouldn't your friend have given you the safe combination if he wanted you to have whatever was inside?"

It was a valid question, but one with a simple answer. "Jacobs routinely changed the lock and challenged me to open it. He loved watching me work."

"Fair enough."

Joe looked to his improvised mystical focus – that would hopefully soon be a true staff – and nodded in approval. Setting it aside, he pulled open the door to the miniature wall-safe and reached inside to pull free the leather-wrapped bundle that Jacobs had gifted to him. Once free, he closed the door, enclosing the other rare valuables that the store owner had managed to miraculously find and squirrel away.

He turned to find that Petals was standing on a chair, observing Joe from the other side of the table. It was unnerving how quiet the gnome was at times.

His superior eyed the bundle of leather with raised eyebrows, as if demanding it be unwrapped immediately.

Joe obliged, setting it down on the tabletop and untying the leather thongs before unfolding the bundle. In the middle of the leather sat the very thing he'd desired the most from Jacobs' shop.

Inside the bundle was a dark iron cloak pin in the shape of a kite shield. There was an emblem of a knight bearing a shield at the ready. The knight's shield was centered within the cloak pin, and in the center of the shield was a small rivet of metal that gleamed and shined as brightly as a polished bit of silver.

The thing itself looked no more special than a well-polished relic, but it held a much more powerful nature – it was an enchanted pin. It was designed to protect and empower any cloak it held pinned. To the modern world, it acted as little more than a downgraded blue coat or detective's trench coat; it could be worn on any article of clothing. It likely couldn't stop a bullet, however.

Petals gasped, looking wide-eyed at the pin. "How!" He snatched it up and examined it in the light with one eye squinting.

Joe flinched at the elder gnome picking it up so carelessly. In truth, he could have gone at it with a hammer and not left a scratch, but he still felt reverence for it and what it meant to him as a child. "What do you mean, 'how'? Please don't drop it!"

The gnome looked to him, aghast. "I would NEVER! Do you have any idea what this is?" He pointed at it with one hand while the other held it aloft.

Joe nodded quite enthusiastically. "Why do you think I'm here? I want to use the pin to enhance this!" He grabbed his staff and pointed to it in much the same fashion that Petals had been pointing at the pin.

Petals squeezed shut his eyes and made a face of absolute irritation. "No... This!" He pointed more specifically to the well-polished metal core.

The exact metal composition had remained an enigma, especially since he was not a smith or metallurgist. He shrugged while trying to pull the answer from any corner of his brain that might be able to suddenly discover what years of research had not. Sadly, he couldn't answer, and stuttered and sputtered, "I– it– you just– it's– well..." until he was forced to drop his shoulders in defeat and admit, "No."

Petals hopped from the chair to the countertop so that they stood eye-to-eye. Joe leaned back at the suddenly aggressive step forward.

His superior went into a lecture of ascending gravitas. "This, my dear boy, is the eternal fey metal, the silver of silvers, Luna's tear and the great Lycan's bane!" He dropped the revelation on Joe and nearly knocked him off his feet. "This is Mithril!"

WHAT!

Joe jumped and snatched the pin from Petals' hand and near stuck it in his eye, he was so desperate to examine it more closely. "No!"

It fit part of the profile with a silvery coloring and high polish. He couldn't test its weight, as it was imbedded in with the darker iron, but he figured the best person to recognize fey metal was a fey-born.

"Seriously?"

Petals simply glared at him.

Joe raised his hands in apology, then returned to studying the treasure he held in his hands. "All these years... I had no idea."

"You're not selling it!"

It was Joe's turn to glare as he snapped his head up and gave Petals a hot look. He would never think of such a thing. "I already told you what I was going to do with it. This changes nothing. If anything, it now makes all the more sense."

Petals narrowed his eyes and placed his hands on his hips. "Explain."

Joe sighed and gathered his thoughts as he watched his superior tap his foot on the wooden countertop. "All right... but first, get back on the chair."

Petals hopped backward and landed in the dead-center of the chair without so much as blinking or looking where he was going.

Show off.

He lifted his staff and set it down on the counter between them, placed the pin back into the center of the leather wrappings, before leaning forward, putting his hands on the countertop and nodding to the two items. "I need to put these together, because of what you told me."

Petals remained as silent as the grave and continued to eyeball Joe. He didn't interrupt or gesture for more; he simply waited in silence.

Joe lifted one hand and pointed to the length of wood. "You said that I 'selected' this particular wood because of that memory – that day – and that it is almost never selected because of its common use in martial weapons."

Petals stood eerily still and watched in silence.

Joe's finger pointed to the pin next. "I've always wanted this, ever since Jacobs first showed it to me. I never knew why I wanted it, until today." He calmed himself and went into the story of that first day. "I don't care if you don't want or need to hear it. I need to say it, so that you understand why."

Petals eyebrows lifted slightly.

"The boys that day, I hit them with magic, all of them." Joe had stood and simply yelled. He didn't know you could cast magic by angrily yelling, but he did. The bullies had been hit by a wave of rippled air. It looked like the distortion hot cobblestones gave off in the summer.

"I smashed them against a stone wall like a toddler throwing their toys in a tantrum." He had only hit them once, as the act had taken a great deal out of Joe. He'd never cast magic before, and it utilized much of a person's will and reserves.

"I did it to protect that little fairy, to save them from being abused." He had failed. Joe had not only swatted the boys, but he had also hurt the fairy. He had bent its little wing in the process of hurtling the bullies. "But I also hurt the fairy."

Petals flinched in that moment, but Joe raised a hand in a gesture of restraint. "She was all right, just a bent wing." He'd still never forgiven himself for it.

The older gnome settled and seemed to relax and ease a bit from his statuesque posture.

"Since that day, I promised I wouldn't lash out ever again. Instead, I promised myself that I would become stronger, and I'd protect everyone smaller than me. I swore to become a guardian." Joe picked up his staff and gripped it tight. "I needed to be unbending. I needed to be incorruptible." He needed to be like the marbled iron maple. "Years passed, and I eventually joined the Royal Arcane Forces."

Petals interjected, "Tertiary Defensive Unit."

Joe nodded and finished, "47th platoon, assigned with protecting the medical tents and supply trains." He took a moment to remember those horrible days. He was forced to listen as young men screamed in pain and others went eternally silent. "Hearing those men suffer made me stronger. It made me want to become a better protector. As a result, I took to arcane barriers like a duckling to water."

It was then that he picked up the pin and eyed it. He looked to his staff, thumped it, and said "Unshakable iron," then held aloft the pin at eye level, "Will to protect."

Petals suddenly beamed at him in approval. "Bravo, my boy."

Joe gracefully accepted the approval and looked to the pin, and eyed the Mithril core. "Knowing more of what this is only makes it more valuable to my goals and explains a lot as to why I desired it all those years. The Fates wanted me to have this."

Petals hopped down from the chair and turned to eye the rows of shelves. "You're most certainly correct, my boy; now, how about we clear some space."

Joe had the same thought in mind. "I'll collect what we need."

Time to turn this improvised staff into the real thing.

Chapter 12

Joe went about the cellar store and collected what he felt to be the necessary components: infused chalk, iron shavings, shield pendants, and parchment and ink. Once collected, he sorted out all the components on the wooden countertop and began working out the spell-work on his notepad.

Petals did what he did best – anything he wanted with a snap of his fingers. The mischievous gnome animated the metal shelves and set about waving his hands as though directing an orchestra and had the shelves march themselves about in synchronized choreography until they were comfortably spread about the room in a horseshoe pattern, providing ample floor space.

A broom and dustpan glided out of the corner and began sweeping away the dust and bits from under where the shelves had once resided.

Joe utilized the partition in his mind to keep and maintain his focus on writing out the necessary runic sequences and balanced trigonometric symbols. He found himself frustrated at certain crossroads, then decided to leave the space blank and fill it in once he figured out the problem.

Petals eventually finished his cleaning act and hopped up onto the chair by the countertop that Joe was working on.

Once he had filled a page, he ripped it from his notepad and set it out in order.

His superior leaned over and peered at Joe's work, nodding along and frowning at points. It made him uneasy that his work was being criticized while in such a rough draft. Eventually, Joe reached a point in his notetaking where he couldn't continue without finishing the pieces he'd earlier left blank.

"Looks as though you're ready."

Joe cocked his head at the trickster gnome with a slightly raised eyebrow.

You must be joking.

"Seriously." Petals nodded with a look of absolute confidence and deadpan seriousness.

Stop reading my damn thoughts.

He grinned smugly. "Stop having such loud thoughts then."

Joe stood straight. "Fireballs! You really can read minds!"

Petals shrugged, "I said I could," then backpedaled, scrunched his nose a bit and waved his hand as if to suggest unsteadiness, "sometimes."

"Right." Joe looked back down at his notes and shook his head, "There's no way that this is ready. It's wholly incomplete."

Petals nodded in understanding. "On paper it's incomplete, but there's nothing more you can write down that would make it complete." He pointed to the pages that outlined the foundational circles. "This is all good. It's fundamentally stable and correctly drawn."

Again, he couldn't believe what he was hearing. "But I left pieces out! There are no symbols on the intersectionals. If I were to draw this right now and attempt to infuse it, it would fall apart and blow up in my face!"

Petals lifted his hands to suggest that Joe calm himself. "I didn't say that you should leave them empty. I'm simply saying that you won't know what to fill them with until you fill them."

What?

"What?"

His superior took a deep breath, clasped his hands behind his back, and looked off in thought before turning back to Joe. "You studied at the Arcanum and learned all the methods that wizards utilize to understand the functionality of the cosmos and how to bend, if not break, the rules governing the physical realm, correct?"

It was precisely correct. Joe had to learn everything from the ground up, just as any other did. He gestured in the affirmative, still uncertain as to where his superior was trying to lead him.

Petals narrowed his eyes and leaned forward. "A true wizard would take days to formulate a proper sequence for imbuing one magical item into a receptacle such as a staff due to the complexities involved... but a sorcerer doesn't need to follow the same ABCs that a wizard does."

He felt a tingling in the back of his mind. "Instinctive magic."

The trickster gnome grinned from ear to ear and gestured for Joe to carry on.

Another thought bubbled to the surface. "Hold on... does that mean I could have skipped entire lessons at the Arcanum purely on the fact that I can instinctively call magic when others can't?"

Petals made a maybe gesture by shrugging his shoulders and tilting his head from one side to the other.

"Yes and no. In truth, you could have skipped a great many classes if another sorcerer had taught you how to feel your way through the magic. Sadly, you didn't have any such instructor. In all honesty, it's actually better to understand the fundamentals anyway."

Joe didn't know if he agreed with having to know the fundamentals if he could just feel his way through magic, but he couldn't really argue with the fact that there wasn't anyone to teach him anyway.

His superior pulled up his sleeve to check his wristwatch and tapped it. "We have a criminal to catch and my dear wife is expecting me for dinner."

"Right!" Joe pulled the stopper on the ink bottle and set to marking the parchment as he had indicated in his notes. The partition in his mind assisted with making short work of the preparations. Once the parchment was finished, he sprinkled it with iron shavings and infused chalk dust. The ink lines flashed briefly, suggesting that the magic took.

Huh!

Joe set down the parchment and grabbed all the broken infused chalk and compressed it with a bit of magic. It quickly turned into a free-floating ball of glittering white powder. Once crushed, he adjusted the compression he applied to it and formed it all into several whole pieces of chalk so that he could draw with it.

Once done, he set the chalk down on the countertop, pulled his silk gloves from one of his belt pouches and slipped them on.

Petals watched on with the usual grin.

Joe picked up his staff, set it in the middle of the cleared space, then picked up the metal Mithril-core pin and set it down adjacent. Once he had the arrangement right, he picked up the pieces of chalk and began drawing out the necessary circles and intersectional lines.

Once he got to the intersections, he found himself dropping a piece of chalk, as he still had no other idea what to draw. The bent-over work broke him into a bit of a sweat, and he nearly dripped onto the chalk lines a few times.

With all completed, Joe took a step back and examined everything spread out on the floor. Looking back to the countertop, he realized that the shield pendants wouldn't be required.

He still didn't have anything for the intersections, but he supposed he'd just have to wing it with instinct and intuition.

Joe took off his hat and trench coat and set them on the other side of the countertop, then took up position in the apex circle as was required.

Please don't blow up in my face.

Petals darted a look at Joe, looked at the circle, then leaped over to the other side of the countertop.

Thanks for the confidence.

A little hand shot up and gave Joe a thumbs up.

He rolled his eyes, rolled up his sleeves, and tried to ignore the hammering in his heart. It was his first time crafting anything magical and he wasn't entirely sure he could do it.

There had been multiple projects that he had completed while at the Arcanum that required crafting a simple magical potion or imbuing an item with power. All of that had been done under an instructor's supervision in sterile conditions. Joe was in the cellar of a children's toy and candy shop, utilizing sub-par materials with spell-work he had thrown together in less than an hour.

Despite his hesitations, he had to try. Time was working against him. He was the one detective on the force that didn't have a standard staff. It was a necessary tool to help guide him through cases. It could also be used for combative measures, if required.

Not wanting to let down those that counted on him to be their protector, he dove on in. Joe released the partition in his mind, closed his eyes, and opened himself up to the energies of the cosmos.

He started by breathing deeply and allowing the power to flow through him and into the prepared spell-work drawn onto the cellar floor.

It took no time at all for the winds to pick up as the vortex of energies coalesced. Joe opened his eyes and watched as the lines of chalk turned into sources of bright light.

By the gods, it's working.

Bits of paper and dust began billowing about the cellar and swatted him as it all circled the room. He rooted himself and opened the floodgates. The lines that ran about the cellar floor grew brighter.

Frighteningly, he didn't know what came next. He hadn't completed the intersections. The only thing he could think to do was follow his instructor's guidance from the Academy: stay calm.

Joe let out a deep breath and shut his eyes as he steadied. The flow of energy eventually came to a balance. A gentle partition of the mind allowed him to regulate that while he tried to think of what came next.

He needed to combine the power of the pin with that of his staff. Some of the less educated would think it would be simple enough to hammer a nail into the wood and hang the pin, but it was far more complex than that.

The power needed to flow from the pin into the staff; they needed to be one and the same, yet have their own identities and purposes… not unlike the knots in the wood.

Joe was suddenly very aware of the knots that riddled the head of his staff. A knot in a bit of wood simply signified where a tree branch had been. It was a different form of structure that interrupted the flow of the grain and often irritated woodworkers. It wasn't like a parasite or a disease. It was a part of the wood. It was interruptive in design if taken as a piece, like a plank, but it was still part of the initial whole.

He lifted one hand and let it move of its own accord. He could hear the dancing of chalk over the whirring of the wind cyclone in the room.

His intention was to meld the pin with one of the knots at the head of his staff. It would allow him to both separate and combine the two. It didn't hurt that the knot was marbled with rings of polished metal like the rest of the wood. He wanted to meld them, but not through heat, as it would burn and damage the wood.

His other hand lifted and began moving of its own accord. He could hear more chalk beginning to dance. It felt like a soft harmony of music playing in his heart and head as he began to meld layer after layer of the knot rings to the back of the pin.

The other knots would function wonderfully as placeholders for other upgrades and advancements to his staff as he gained the necessary supplies and skills.

He could hear the chalk dance about the room, and it sounded as though it was moving in tune with the music. He felt thrumming through the core of his being. Each layer of metal rings that connected to the pin felt like a layer of orchestral music.

The winds began dying down and his hands started slowing in their movements as he felt the music rise to a high-note crescendo, then end with a thundering finish.

Joe snapped open his eyes after a gust of wind burst past him. It had originated from the epicenter of the room. He breathed heavily as the energy of the cosmos slowly left him. He felt drained and empty and nearly collapsed when the magic released.

The staff clattered to the floor and smoldered with white power through the metal veins. A closer look revealed the pin melded perfectly into the wooden knot he had intended it for.

"Huh… I did it."

Blackness overtook him.

~ ~

He awoke with a start and slammed his head into some wood. The sharp pain fired through his skull, causing him to scream out in pain, "HAAAAH!"

Blasted thundering fireballs!

Joe kicked his feet into the air only to find they were dangling off the edge of what he thought might be a very short bed. He didn't know why it was a smart idea, but he attempted to lift his head again and try and see why his feet were kicking freely. His mindless idea only caused him to slam his fingers into the same wood he had struck his head against.

He dropped his head back onto what he was certain was a gnome's bed and shook out his hands. "Ow!"

A quick glance about the room answered the obvious question. He was in a child's room... a gnome child's room. The ceiling was dropped significantly from that of a human household, and the architecture and pictures scattered about depicted a gnomish family.

"What in the thundering blue pixies?" He tilted his head to the side and noted that the bed was a bunkbed.

"Why *blue* pixies?"

Joe jumped and slammed his head into the bottom of the bunk again. "Doh!" He vigorously rubbed his head to make the pain go away. He peered out the corner of his eye to spot a white-haired gnome child in blue nautical-themed pajamas, hugging a green teddy bear. "What?"

"You said 'thundering blue pixies.' Why blue pixies? Are blue pixies bad?" The little boy was missing several teeth and spoke with the appropriate whistle to match. He stood with his belly poking out from under his shirt while shoving a stubby finger up his nose. The green teddy was held by his other arm.

Joe crawled himself free from the bunkbed out of fear the death trap would suddenly spring to life and begin swatting him with the wood-lattice he had familiarized himself with twice. "I… No. I don't think blue pixies in particular are bad. I don't know why I said blue, it's just what I heard when I was a boy." He righted himself and sat upright on the soft rug floor while continuing to rub his head.

The diminutive child shrugged his shoulders in acceptance. "Okay," he proceeded to walk across the room to the bunkbed Joe had escaped from. He climbed the rope ladder to the top bunk to crawl in for the night.

Joe looked back to the door and almost jumped again as a white-haired little gnome girl stood there.

She wore a pink nautical-themed nightgown and looked at him with a tilted head. She was hugging a purple teddy bear that looked identical to the green one the boy had been hugging. "Gram-Gram said you needed to sleep in my bed." She was similarly missing teeth and had an appropriate whistle to match. "Can I sleep now?"

He looked to the bottom bunk and noticed the bed sheets were the same pink pattern as her nautical dress. Joe looked back to the little girl and nodded. She pitter-pattered past him as silently as she had arrived, hopped onto her bed, and crawled under the covers.

Not wanting to disturb either of the children, Joe got to his knees and crawled to the bedroom exit.

Petals!

The white-haired old detective came hurrying down the cramped hallway, hushing him. "Shhh… You'll wake the children!" He rebuked him in hushed tones.

Joe looked up and down the hallway, noted the simple yet brilliantly-lit gnome domicile he had been brought to, then whispered back, "I yelled it in my head so only you would hear me!"

Petals stood upright and peered into the bedroom to check on the children. "Oh… really?"

Joe pulled his feet free from the children's room as Petals flicked off the lantern light and closed the door. "Yes, really. Couldn't you tell?"

The trickster gnome shrugged. "Not always."

He couldn't help but feel that hearing words and not knowing if it was spoken aloud or in thought could prove slightly irritating.

The old gnome wasn't wearing his coat, hat, or vest, and to his own surprise, neither was he. "Where are my things?"

Petals pointed down the hall to what Joe could only guess to be the den. He didn't dare stand up and slowly crawled across the rug to poke his head around the corner.

He was undeniably delighted to see a full-sized kitchen with a regular-height ceiling and a delightfully grinning older woman with her hands on her hips and a wooden spoon in one hand. "Uh... hello, Mrs. Pettlebottom. I'm terribly sorry for intruding like this."

"Nonsense, come out of that hallway and get yourself a bowl of stew."

Yes!

Joe scrambled to get to the edge of the low ceiling and brought his feet around.

Petals, unfortunately, had horrible news. "Terribly sorry, my love, but the boy can't stay."

Noooooo!

"There's been another break-in, and we've been called to investigate." He said so while hanging his head in mock shame.

Mrs. Pettlebottom scowled at her husband, took the obvious bait, whipped out her spoon, and swatted him on top of the head. "Nonsense! He'll take a bowl to go. He can eat it in the gnome cart, and I'll make sure to pack him some biscuits to go with it."

Yeeessssss!

Chapter 13

As Mrs. Pettlebottom had suggested, Joe took the stew to go. Fortunately, the gnome cart was a bit late, and he was able to finish it while waiting curbside.

It had been a hearty and thick stew, with tender pieces of meat, potatoes, carrots, and spices. The biscuits were light and fluffy and had proved to be the perfect medium by which to wipe clean the bowl.

Once he had stuffed himself, the bowl and napkin vanished in a bit of sparkly blue smoke. Presumably another recall spell like the one that had been utilized with the care package from the Blue Whiskey Grill.

A glance at his watch told him it was already ten at night. He wouldn't likely get to bed anytime soon. "I was out for quite a while... is that normal with the spell-craft I completed this afternoon?"

"Quite. There's rarely a time when it doesn't sap the caster into a spell sleep."

Noted.

"Why were we called for a break-in? Shouldn't we be off duty by now?" Joe pulled his staff from his pocket and released it from the compression so that it sprang to full size. He proceeded to examine the melding as he awaited the answer he felt was coming.

"Billburn's Brass and Gold was struck an hour ago."

He'd figured as much. "Any details?"

Petals shook his head. "We usually don't discuss such things over the network box."

Joe understood. He compressed his staff to the size of a wand, then slipped it into his vest pocket once again. The staff was surprisingly more responsive since last he utilized it.

When the gnome cart finally arrived, they both clambered in and provided the address of the crime scene.

"So... Grandkids?"

Petals chuckled. "I was wondering when you would ask."

Joe watched his superior as the trickster gnome seemed to occupy himself with staring out the window.

"... And?"

Petals glanced back to him with a sly grin before returning his attention to the window. "Of a sort."

He couldn't help but sigh. "You just love this whole mystery thing, don't you?"

Petals shrugged. "It is part of my nature; I can no more change my mind about it than a blade of grass can change itself into a tree."

It didn't feel like an acceptable answer, but he also wasn't a mystical fey creature that was bound by rules and laws of another realm. He chose to accept the answer and move on.

Halfway through their ride, which only lasted twenty minutes, the rain started. Their driver, thankfully, turned on the lanterns and flicked a switch that set a pair of arms wiping the front cart window.

"The rain won't do us any good when it comes to footprints."

Petals looked out the window and up at the sky. "It will prove quite the hindrance. And it looks like it will last for a few days as well."

Joe peered out at the sky and came to the same conclusion. He had lived long enough to recognize the different sorts and weights of rain clouds. The clouds hanging above were low, heavily concentrated, and barely moving.

They eventually came to the only storefront down the street that still had its lanterns on. The 'Billburn's Brass and Gold' sign was unlit and the 'closed' sign was facing out.

The gnome cart pulled up to the curb, and they piled out with Petals in the lead. He had his wand out and was pointing it skyward. It created a bubble of protection from the downpour and gave Joe a dry spot upon which to step onto the curb.

He stepped out, drew his wand as well, and pointed it skyward. The deluge of rain that had been striking Petals' umbrella suddenly burst into the air as Joe released the magic he felt was necessary to deflect the rain. "Oops."

Petals raised an eyebrow at him.

"Sorry... not used to the magic being this responsive and powerful." Joe was accustomed to a certain amount of 'spillage' or magical loss when casting directly from his hands or non-magical mediums. That was no longer an issue since he had imbued his staff.

The rainwater that had been launched into the air dumped back down around them in a giant wallop.

A familiar feminine voice called out to them from the storefront awning. "You boys done playing in the water?"

Joe adjusted the flow of magic and reduced the canopy of protection until it fit a suitable area around them both, then closed the gnome cart door behind him. "Mind telling us what happened here?"

Amelia gestured over her shoulder, "Inside."

Petals and Joe looked to each other, then headed into the shop through the door that Ms. Iceheart kept propped open with the tip of her shoe. The bell above the door jangled as they entered.

Joe couldn't help but notice her lingering and scanning the street. She eventually stepped back inside, closed the door behind her, and locked it by flicking the latch at the top of the doorframe.

"You think they're watching?"

Amelia turned around and breezed past him as she headed to the back. "Maybe."

Petals was already consoling poor Billburn. The halfling sat on a comfortable chair in the corner and looked absolutely distraught. His shoulders were shaking as he sobbed into a wizard's handkerchief that presumably had been handed to him by Amelia.

He followed the detective into the back room and poked his head in through the doorway leading to the craft station. The room had been furnished with hundreds of tiny cupboards and drawers. He presumed that most of them contained some arrangement or organization of gems and precious metals. It looked like every single drawer had been ransacked, as many of the small wooden drawers littered the floor.

Ms. Iceheart crouched amongst the chaos while peering through a spyglass at some overturned drawers.

Joe looked about at the chaos, then looked to the back door. The frame was brand new. Billburn had it replaced after it had been broken and splintered by the crowbar that the dark dwarf Travok had used the day before. He pulled the spyglass from his pocket that Petals had given him and examined the carpet.

The footprints he spotted were identical to the ones that Joe and Petals had seen the day before when examining the alleyway. He put away the spyglass and released his staff from its wand confines, then tipped the head to the handle on the back door and shut his eyes.

His mind was immediately struck with an image of the barrier surrounding the store and the complexity of the locks that encompassed the doors. He could move about the frame as freely as a bird might fly. The doors had triggered alarms designed to respond to a key. The craftsmanship of the barriers, alarms, triggers, and the key itself was of general quality that he had seen before, but it was sufficient enough to deter criminals of a lesser standard.

Pressing deeper into the inner workings of the back-door lock, he found that it had been opened with a key, but not the same one the door had been initially triggered to respond to.

Joe popped open his eyes and turned to find Amelia standing in the doorway to the workroom with a raised eyebrow.

She kindly gestured for him to go first.

He quickly hurried back to the front of the shop to where Petals consoled the poor store owner. "Mr. Billburn, I need to know something. Who did you hire to fix your back door and reset the barriers and alarms in your shop?"

"I– uh– what?" The thin little man looked ragged, with heavy red bags under his eyes and his hair all in a frazzle.

Joe dropped to a knee to get closer to him and impress upon the halfling the importance of the question. "Who did you hire for the door and barriers?"

The small man shook his head a little to clear the tears and sorrowful thoughts before looking up in answer. "That would be… um… Ironwall… Ironwall Locks and Alarms on 102nd, but why?"

Joe thanked the store owner, stood back up and headed toward the back while pulling his crystalline network box from his belt. He squeezed the button on the side of the box to activate it and called in, "Runewall to dispatch. Dispatch, come in."

Amelia narrowed her eyes at him as he returned. "What did you find out? Share with everyone and stop being a lone wolf."

Dispatch came through, "Dispatch. Go ahead, Runewall."

Joe lifted a finger, suggesting she wait for him to finish. "Can we please send a unit to check on Ironwall Locks and Alarms on 102nd?"

Dispatch confirmed his request and said that they would send someone out as soon as they could.

Amelia tapped her foot and crossed her arms in impatience.

Joe stuffed his network box back onto his belt and pointed to the back door. "Only one key was assigned to this building, and that door was opened by a different key that bypassed the barrier."

She unfolded her arms and looked to the back door, then back to Joe. "You can tell that from spending a whole of two minutes with the door?"

Joe seemed confused by the question. "What... you can't?"

"No!"

That simple answer helped to connect a few dots that had been swirling about in the back of his mind.

"Anyway, there's only one of two ways that can happen. One, you have a really expensive skeleton key that's capable of mimicking and beating most barriers. Or..."

She gestured for him to go on. "...Or?"

Joe glanced to the front and kept his voice down, "You force the original crafter to make a second key."

~~

Petals joined them once they had gotten poor Billburn to settle with a cup of tea. "So, where are we?"

Joe gestured to Amelia, "Ladies first."

She narrowed her eyes at him, but proceeded anyway. "Whoever broke in was quick and efficient. They mostly targeted the drawers containing uncut gems. There were no fingerprints to trace."

Joe picked up where she left off. "The footprints at the back door match the ones we found in the alley from the initial attempt two days ago. They also either used a skeleton key, or they targeted Ironwall Locks and Alarms prior to coming here to have a second key crafted for this particular store." He patted his network box on his belt. "We'll know soon enough."

Petals chimed in as he stroked his beard. "It appears as though our unknown friend *needed* you out of the way. Your talents may have given us a clue we might have otherwise missed."

He couldn't help but shiver at the prospect. "Barely two days into the job and I already have a target on my back."

Amelia smirked and slapped him on the arm. "Good job, rook. You know you're doing a good job when the criminals hate you and want you dead."

He couldn't help but frown. "How reassuring. I feel so much better now."

Not.

Dispatch rang. "Speaking of." He pulled his network box from his belt and called in, "Go ahead, dispatch."

The feminine voice that was dispatch informed them, "Blue Coats on scene at 102nd, multiple bodies found."

The three of them looked to one another with a sense of dread.

Amelia was the first to say it. "None of us is getting any sleep tonight, are we."

Petals and Joe both shook their heads. It didn't matter whether other detectives took up the murder investigation; it was directly tied into their investigation.

Joe looked to his superior and asked, "Protocol?"

Petals sighed, removed his spectacles, and rubbed the bridge of his nose. "First things first, you need to wrap up this scene and combine notes."

Amelia grumbled, "'You need to wrap up this scene' meaning you're going to?" She left the question in the air for their superior to fill in.

Petals stood a bit taller and raised an eyebrow at her. "Would you like to escort poor Billburn home in the rain?"

She quickly turned on the spot and flicked out her notepad. "Nope, busy doing my job." Joe watched her return to the workroom and the task of cataloging all the details.

And that's why she's called Iceheart.

A sudden strike to his shin caused Joe to bark out in pain and grip his leg. "Ah!" He turned his attention on the only person close enough to strike him, only to find Petals two paces too far to have kicked him.

How?

Petals glared at him and whispered while grinning devilishly, "I have my ways." He turned away and headed back to the front.

Joe was left standing on one foot. He leaned against the wall and vigorously rubbed his shin. The pain quickly subsided, and he was left with the task of taking down his notes as instructed.

After grumbling a curse under his breath, Joe pulled his notepad out, glanced at his watch, and began utilizing the wonderful partition in his brain. Petals announced his departure a few moments later, followed by the chime of the doorbell.

Thanks to his partition, Joe was able to breeze through his notetaking. He'd lost only ten minutes of his night at most, and as suspected, he finished long before Amelia had even managed to get halfway through hers. She had the task of cataloging all the drawers that had been opened or tossed aside, and there was a mess of them.

Peering inside, Joe offered his assistance. "Want me to start at this end?" Joe pointed to the doorway.

Amelia paused, stood up from her bent-over scribblings, and flicked her hair out of her face. She was at the far end of the room and working her way to him in what appeared to be systematic order. "I'd rather do it myself. I don't want it getting screwed up."

Joe lifted his notepad to eye level with a raised eyebrow and pointed to it. It had all his notes in perfectly legible and aesthetically pleasing shorthand. "I can partition."

She sighed and hung her shoulders. "Please."

He noted the time on his wristwatch.

Middle of the night… fireballs.

Joe bent over and got to work. Eventually, he could only stand so much silence and dared to ask the question, "What made you want to become a detective?"

Amelia stood up straight again and blew hair out of her face before putting her hands on her hips and cocking her head at him. "We going to gossip like little old ladies, or get this work done?"

He threw up his arms in defense and went back to work.

The front door opened, and the bell rang. Joe sighed in relief, as he believed that Petals had returned. A second after the front door closed, he heard the unmistakable sound of a gun hammer being pulled back.

Instinct overtook him. Joe simultaneously dropped the notepad, released the partition, and drew his six-shooter from its holster. He did so while throwing himself on his back out the workroom door.

The front end of the jewelry store had its lights out, as the intruder must have turned them off while entering. A tall figure stood in the shadows of the doorway and looked to have been startled mid-stride, as he was in the process of stumbling back with a long-barrel tucked under his arm.

Joe didn't hesitate. He took the fraction of a second of surprise that he had gained and fired. His ears were thankfully muffled from the thunderous release by his enchanted wide-brim.

The man that had tried to get the jump on them grunted from the dull impact.

A muzzle flash burst from the end of the long-barrel, and the display case at the front of the store erupted in a shower of glass.

Joe began pulling back the hammer on his six-shooter as the would-be attacker grunted again and threw themselves at the front door. They dropped their long-barrel on the way out.

Joe scrambled to his feet and pulled free his wand, released the wand into a staff, then barreled forward.

They both had the rarest of moments to exchange a glance with one another as lightning lit the sky outside.

It was Eagle Eyes. The man was rail-thin and slightly taller than Joe. He wore a wide-brim and a bandana over his face. One hand was clutching his side over his dark vest while he ran out the door.

He didn't want to shoot through the glass, mostly because it was covered by a barrier, but also because he didn't want to do any more damage to the poor halfling owner's shop.

Seconds felt like minutes as they both dug deep into their reservoirs of will and tried to outpace the other. Eagle Eyes was wounded, and that gave the advantage to Joe.

Striking the front door, Joe burst into the pouring rain, allowing him to start gaining ground. He felt as though he'd caught a break in the case, and the sudden surge of excitement spurred him on.

Eagle Eyes made the corner of the store and turned on a dime to hit the alleyway while still clutching his side.

No! Not the storm drain!

Thunder roared and lightning split the sky as Joe put everything he had into making the corner in time to catch his prey. Knowing full well that the man could be waiting to jump him, he ran wide of the corner to prevent any surprises and kept his gun and staff level and at the ready.

Nothing!

He was nowhere to be seen around the first corner. There was no logical means by which Eagle Eyes could have gained that much ground in that short of time.

He pushed on toward the alleyway intersection that lead to the back of the shop and swung wide again with his six-shooter and staff leveled and drawn.

FIREBALLS!

Amelia was the only person in the alleyway. The back door to the shop was open and she stood atop the storm grate with her six-shooter leveled and her staff at the ready, as he had been. "Where is he?"

Joe had no clue. He holstered his weapon and threw up his arms as he marched about in the rain. Turning about in a circle, he took out his frustration on a box and punted it down the alleyway while yelling out his aggravations in the thundering rain.

Chapter 14

Joe pinched the bridge of his nose and tried to breathe past the infuriating headache pounding behind his eyes as Petals examined every line of his notes. "Did you check the rooftops?"

He dropped his hand and slightly nodded. "First thing; no sign of any tracks being washed away in the rain." His first guess had been a teleportation spell of some sort, but there were no visible arcane circles, and there had been limited time. Second guess was some form of lift boots, hence the rooftop examinations.

Petals paced the storefront of the jewelry shop as he examined their combined notes. "No blood trail?"

Joe shook his head and kept his eyes shut, as the light of the storefront was only aggravating the headache. "Nope, must have been wearing a vest like us."

The little gnome returned to pacing the storefront for a few moments, then stopped and asked of the room in general, "Footprints?"

Amelia answered that time, "Stopped dead in the alleyway shortly after the first corner."

Petals grunted in acceptance and stood in thought for a while. Eventually, their superior turned and looked to the blown-apart glass display case, then looked to them both. "You're very lucky."

They nodded their heads in understanding of the situation. It wasn't as though it hadn't played through their heads already.

Being the senior detective, it was up to Petals to determine their performances, given the situation. "Otherwise, you acted accordingly."

Amelia let out a sigh.

Joe didn't feel any more relieved and didn't seem to even care that he'd been given approval. The only thing running through his head was that he had failed to catch Eagle Eyes.

Petals tapped him on the knee with his wand and raised his eyebrows when Joe opened his eyes. "Hm, what?"

Petals smiled sadly. "I said, 'Go home.' You need the rest."

"But—"

Petals waved it off. "No buts."

Joe stood from leaning against the wall and looked about the store. Amelia was already heading out the door with long strides. She seemed unbothered by it all.

He wished he knew how to let it go like she did.

A poke to the ribs told him to get going. Joe flinched and proceeded for the door.

Petals did as he always did and fixed everything in a snap. Or at least, he fixed the display case. The glass shards lifted from the hardwood floor and floated across the room to seamlessly meld back into place, boxing in the jewelry that had been contained within.

Joe was familiar with repair and mending spells, but he'd never seen it done on such a scale with so many moving parts. His superior had a seemingly never-ending bag of tricks.

Not wanting to get wet, he pulled his wand from his pocket and pointed it skyward. His hand was on the door when a thought came to mind, and he changed his tactic. Joe changed his wand to a staff, then surrounded himself in a bubble of protection. He didn't feel like being shot from a distance again.

The walk home was cold and dreary, as it often was during a downpour. He was uncertain as to whether it was any colder than any other stormy night, but the wind that passed through his barrier felt bitterly cold. His thoughts weren't exactly the warmest of company either.

Much of his time was spent toiling over those few brief seconds that he had Eagle Eyes in his sights. Scenarios ran through his mind as he tried his best to figure out where the man had gone.

Invisibility was unlikely, as the rain would have exposed him immediately. Illusion was a possibility, but he hadn't seen any objects in the alley large enough to hide his frame behind or inside of.

Joe found himself standing at the door to Ms. Bellcreaux's brownstone walk-up but unable to bring himself to enter. The key was in his pocket, but the thought of bringing more trouble to the residence put a pit in his stomach.

He turned, only to get a sudden burst of powder blown into his face by someone he hadn't the time to identify. So powerful was the need to sleep that he couldn't even get out a word or thought before finding himself drifting to the hard stone at the foot of Ms. Bellcreaux's door.

~~

He bolted upright with a start, only to find himself in his own bed.

"Mornin', mate!" Joe looked to the door to find a man sitting in a chair beside his bed.

The stranger had a self-satisfied grin on his face and tousles of blonde locks peering out from beneath a detective's wide-brim. His eyes were as bright as silver, and he had a darker tone to his skin.

Joe let out a groaning sigh and closed his eyes while pressing the sides of his skull. "Oh, fireballs; what did you do to me?" His mind felt like it was muffled in cotton that happened to be dipped in acid and set on fire.

"Might need a bit o' this to set you right."

Joe recoiled and gagged as something ungodly and pungent was stuck beneath his nose. "Hngh!" He threw himself back onto the bed and covered his face. Unfortunately, it did nothing to stop the smell from crawling further up his nostrils. It invaded like a brushfire rampaging across a field.

He gripped his pillow and shoved it against his face as he screamed at the agony of it and tried desperately to recoil from it, writhing and twisting in the bed.

Amazingly, once the smell burrowed deep enough into his skull, the pain vanished. His mind cleared as quickly as a lantern light erased the darkness. He inhaled deeply through his nose and smelled only his sweaty pillow.

"Thought that ought to do the trick."

Joe lifted the pillow from his face and looked to the man that had drugged him into a sleep, then alleviated him from the morning-after effects. "Who are you... and *why*?"

The man chuckled heartily and politely tipped his hat with one hand while reaching out to shake with the other. "Name's William Windwalker. Detective. Pleasure to meet you, rook! I'm on the night shift." He winked and kept grinning like it somehow excused the behavior.

Joe looked about his room out the corner of his eye. The window was shut and bordered, the holes in the walls had been repaired, and his clothes – all of his clothes – were hung up for him.

He peered under his sheets and set them back down before clearing his throat, "Did you–"

William threw up his hands and looked the other way. "Not me, mate. Cheery old ma'am downstairs did that bit."

Oh, fantastic.

"And why did you drug me?"

He scrunched his nose. "Well, you see there, you were about to turn away from heading to bed, which was what ol' Pettlebottom told you to do." He shrugged apologetically. "So it really looks as though you did this to yourself there, mate."

Joe glowered at the man. "Petals had you follow me."

William winked and pointed at Joe with both fingers. "Catch on quick!"

Hurray for me... I still hate you.

Despite William's pleasant charm, Joe didn't like being ambushed with sleeping powder or whatever it was the man had hit him with.

He gestured to his clothes. "Can I get dressed, or must you supervise me doing that as well?"

William waved it off and got up from his chair. "Aw, no worries, mate. You go ahead and get yourself ready, I'll wait outside."

He got up from the chair he had been sitting in, gently picked it up, and set it down where Joe had liked it most. He waved goodbye and crept out the door to allow him privacy.

A quick partition of the mind and sharpening of his hearing told him that the overly friendly detective was still standing on the other side of the door. He was undoubtedly given orders to make sure he made it to work the next morning as well.

Not having much of a choice, he went about getting himself ready for the day. A quick scrub in the tub and shave was all he really needed to clean up.

After he pulled on his watch, he checked the time and noted that he had enough for a quick bite before work.

At least the man woke me up at a decent enough hour.

Joe buttoned up his vest, checked all the pockets to make sure nothing was missing from his required toolset, then buckled on his belt and gun holster before throwing on his trench coat and grabbing his staff.

He yanked open the door and nearly sent the detective sprawling to the floor. "Oi!" William caught himself before he could fully topple, then stood straight at half a head shorter than Joe. "Sorry, mate. A bit sleepy myself. It's my time to clock out, you know."

The feeling was fully understandable. Since becoming a detective, he hadn't exactly gotten a regular schedule.

"How did you manage to follow me, let alone get through my barrier without me noticing?" The thought had been driving him nuts as he had been getting ready.

William threw up his arms, shrugging. "Names Windwalker, mate. My specialty is not being noticed and passing through barriers."

Fantastic. Add another theory to the pile as to how Eagle Eyes got away.

The detective slapped him on the arm. "Get yerself a big brekky, then head straight to work, right, mate?"

Joe breathed deep and sighed in resignation. "Not like I have a choice."

The charming night detective nodded, smiled, tipped his hat, and took a step into what Joe could only describe as a smoke state. His form looked vaporous and ethereal. Within two or three steps, he vanished completely.

Holy fireballs... Windwalker indeed.

He craned his neck and turned his ear to the steps, to hear nothing. The man was either playing games, or he was able to truly pass without making a noise. "I've got to learn how he does that."

The ghostly voice of William called back to him from near the stairs. "Like it if you didn't, mate."

That's not unnerving at all.

Ms. Bellcreaux began climbing the stairs as Joe waved his arms about while approaching them, hoping he wouldn't bump into the invisible detective. She stopped midway and looked up at him with her typical straight-laced raised eyebrow and inquired, "Blinded yourself?"

Joe put his hands back down as he realized what he must have looked like. "No, ma'am."

She gave him a once-over and narrowed her eyes. "Breakfast will be ready soon."

Joe nodded as he stopped partway down the steps. "Yes, ma'am."

She held his gaze, then peered around him to the top of the steps. "Your *friend* isn't joining us?" Her emphasis on 'friend' made it feel like his favorite curse had been dropped, and not so subtly.

He couldn't stop himself from smiling at the thought of Ms. Bellcreaux using such language. "No, ma'am. He's already left by the looks of it." Joe descended a few more steps with the intention of heading to breakfast.

The Crow threw up her arm as a signal for him to stop. She turned her eye on him. "I didn't see or hear him leave."

Joe nodded in understanding. "I know. He's one of those kinds of people." He turned his attention back on her. "If you'd like to examine my—"

"No!" she turned on the spot and descended the stairs in a hurry.

Room... I was going to say room... oh, fireballs, this is going to be an awkward meal.

~~

Joe sat down for breakfast for the first time in what felt like a week. The dining room was a bit cramped with the four of them sitting down to eat around a single table length. The cabinetry that lined the walls was filled with finer dishes and utensils; those also made the room a bit cramped.

Ms. Bellcreaux went around the table, dishing out for each man. Hash browns, scrambled eggs, strips of bacon, and toast were all passed about. The other men that resided in the building went about reading the paper or barking about one thing or another as they were served their breakfast.

George was the eldest of the lot and had a roundness to him. He worked in finances a district over. His hair was thinning on top and his brown mustache was starting to get peppered with silver. He also thoroughly enjoyed his sausage links and bacon.

Hamlin was a young dwarf with a short beard. He wasn't much older than Joe and was as driven as anyone he'd ever met. Not quite yet a full man, he was apprenticing for a fireworks master and constantly smelled of explosive powders.

Dodge was a thin man that worked for the city licensing department. He liked to talk, endlessly. It was no wonder he was so thin; he barely stopped talking to get food in. Joe often wondered if he ever needed to stop and inhale vast amounts to refuel or if he just took micro-breaths between words.

The lot of them greeted him with a quick 'hello' before returning to their discussion at hand. He didn't know what the topic was, as he was too busy trying not to look their landlady in the eye.

Thankfully, Ms. Bellcreaux never stopped near him long enough or looked in his direction for any length of time to even consider his existence. It was typical of her to show him such lack of warmth.

Once enough food had amassed on his plate, Joe put up his hand to halt Ms. Bellcreaux and began to dig in.

He didn't realize how hungry he'd been until he started inhaling one bite after the next. For once, The Crow hadn't burned anything into a blackened leathery state.

He sipped from his tea and stopped mid sip, as the others were staring at him, including Ms. Bellcreaux. Pausing to swallow, he put down his mug and apologized.

"Haven't seen you since the shooting. How are you, Joseph?" George had a genuine look of concern on his face. "We also didn't hear you come in last night."

Joe couldn't help but glance at Ms. Bellcreaux. The woman immediately collected a handful of plates to take into the kitchen. "Well... the last few days have been quite something, as I'm sure you understand some of it."

Hamlin nodded and pointed upstairs. "Some, yeah."

Checking his watch, he saw that he still had time to sit and let his stomach settle while he socialized. He hadn't exactly had much of a life since he started as a detective and felt it couldn't hurt to talk to normal, non-magical people for a minute or two.

So, with certain sensitive details omitted, he told them what he could, and even inquired as to whether any of them had heard or seen any men with eagle-like eyes walking about.

The lot of them sat in complete awe and shook their heads.

Sure enough, Dodge piped up after about four seconds of silence. Clearly, the lack of noise bothered him. The man started telling some off-topic story about a time he saw the circus that came through town while Joe continued polishing off his plate.

"What you think, Joe?"

Joe tuned in and shook his head. "Sorry, I wasn't paying attention, what was the question?"

Dodge gave him a frown.

He shook his head again. "Work is always on the mind; I apologize."

Dodge seemed to accept the answer, and repeated his question. "I asked if you heard anything about those black market doctors... you know... the kinds that do weird experiments and stuff?"

He'd clearly missed a great deal of the circus story. "Sorry, what?"

"C'mon! You know, the freak doctors that put animal parts in people."

Wait...

Joe bolted upright as a realization struck him. "Fireballs!"

Ms. Bellcreaux sternly objected from the kitchen. "Language, Joseph!"

"Lovely breakfast! Late for work!" He threw his napkin down on his plate, picked up his hat and trench coat, and bolted out of the dining room. He skidded to a halt, short of slamming into the wall, then turned on one foot and bee-lined it for the main door.

Once he made it street-side, Joe put all the panicked energy he could muster into hoofing it to the precinct.

~~

Doctor Alexander Broom looked up at Joe over the top of his glasses and repeated the question. "Black market surgeries?" The man was sitting at his desk in his cramped little office and had been scribbling notes into the margins of a medical report.

Joe was standing before the desk, gasping for every bit of air he could find. He could only nod in reply. Winded from running, he was afraid to attempt to say anything more, as his breakfast would likely follow the words.

The gaunt man harrumphed and shook his head. "It's more than just likely, my friend. It's almost certain that there must be some form of learned medical professional keeping the injured crooks alive."

Joe shook a finger and his head, then took several more moments to calm his thundering heart before expanding on his original gasping question. "Experimental... surgeries."

The doctor raised an eyebrow. "Continue."

Joe slumped into a chair and put a hand over his heart before clarifying. "What if... someone wanted another creature's attributes... Another animal's eyes... for example."

Both eyebrows raised as Doctor Broom looked off in genuine thought. "Possible. Difficult, but possible."

Joe closed his eyes and prayed for strength, then hauled himself up out of the chair to continue on. "Thanks, Doc... Got to go."

He made his way back up through the precinct and to the detective's bullpen while dragging his feet up the last few steps.

Petals stood at the top of the steps, tapping his foot with his hands on his hips. "Where have you been?"

All the other detectives in the bullpen were gathered in front of the captain's office. The captain was standing in the doorway with a clipboard in hand. All of them were looking to Joe as he crawled his way up the stairs.

Ah, Fireballs.

After pulling himself to his feet, Joe straightened himself out and joined the rest.

Amelia leaned closer and tsked him in hushed tones.

Petals swatted him in the shin as punishment for his tardiness.

Joe had to stifle a yelp and grit his teeth through the pain as their captain made his announcements.

"As of last night, a second murder attempt was made on the detectives of our precinct. It followed a double murder and robbery." As always, the captain's voice carried like rolling thunder across the room. "Following standard protocol, as of this morning, all detectives are to be partnered until the suspect has been apprehended or there have been no further attempts for a period of thirty days. That is all." The captain stuffed his clipboard under his arm and turned to return to his office.

Grumbling and curses rose from the gathered men.

Bolt paused and turned to glance over his shoulder with one hand on the door handle. It resulted in immediate silence and a dispersal of the crowd. The only noise heard was the hurried shuffling of papers and feet.

Joe, Petals, and Amelia were left standing together after the others had turned to resume their daily duties and individual cases. Before any of them could speak, someone from the lobby below barked out his name. "JOSEPH!"

Stepping to the railing and looking over the side, he spotted the old advocate Wilbur bent over and huffing. "Fantastic, my shift just starts and there's already bad news."

Chapter 15

They sat old Wilbur down on Joe's wobbly office chair and handed him a cup of tea. "All right, start from the beginning, what happened after you left us at the flower shop the other day?"

Wilbur took a sip of the tea and shut his eyes to savor its calming effect before putting the cup down on Joe's desk and answering. "We headed back to my office, closer to the central district."

Joe noted that it was quite the distance to walk. "How did you get back?"

Wilbur shook his head and grumbled, "One of those confounded death traps." He was referencing the city-operated mechanical carts. They were in far worse shape than the private business carts and rattled themselves nearly to pieces as they sputtered, coughed, barked, and exploded along the road.

"Ah. I presume you made it back in one piece?"

The old advocate snorted, "My bones may have been rearranged in the process, but I made it back well enough."

Amelia piped up, "Why didn't you take a gnome cart? They're by far the best in the city."

Why are you still here? Shouldn't you be with your partner?

Wilbur smiled politely up at her while pulling a stiff card from his pocket. "I'm a city advocate." She took the card from his outstretched hand and noted it as his identification and expense card before returning it. Joe was already aware of it, as he had spent enough time walking about the city with the old man several years prior.

"My rides are expensed, but only on city-operated carts." He leaned to the side, stretched out one leg, and reached into his trouser pocket to pull out his coin-purse and gave it a near-hollow jangle. "Did I mention I'm a city advocate?"

Amelia guiltily apologized under her breath for having asked what she perceived to be a bit of an insensitive question.

Wilbur, as always, smiled broadly with his kind eyes and waved off the thought that any offense had been given. "Nonsense, dear, it's your job to ask questions." He looked to Joe. "Where were we?"

"Headed back to your office?"

The old man jumped a little as he got back into the flow of the story. "Right! We made the trip without any issue or incident. Young Tim looked distracted, so I let him work out his own thoughts for the trip."

Joe had always appreciated the fact that Wilbur never pressed for answers or demanded to know what he was thinking at all hours.

"Once we made it to my office, I sat Tim down and gave him a sandwich from the kitchens and a cup of sweet tea. Once he was settled, I got to work on my papers. There was a lot of documentation to fill out concerning the young man. He apparently has no living relatives." Wilbur looked to Joe in that moment, knowing how he had a kinship with orphans.

He nodded in understanding and gestured for the old man to continue.

"After all my papers were filled and submitted, I took the young man back to my apartment and set him up in the spare room, as I do with all my cases prior to their relocation." The old man shook his head. "I don't know when, but sometime during the night he must have ran out."

Joe understood. "He likely lives with other orphans in an abandoned house or has his own bed under a fake name. It wouldn't do him any good to suddenly break routine. Either the other orphans would grow suspicious of him, or the landowners would question him up and down for his odd absence."

Petals followed the conversation and added his thoughts to the theory. "He likely wants to keep his job as well."

That's right!

Joe snapped his fingers and pointed at Petals. "He worked at The Ruby Lounge!"

Wilbur looked back and forth between them, then interjected so he might finish his story. "Once I realized the boy was missing, I went to the office and told my superiors and amended the boy's file before coming here to inform you that he'd run off."

Joe couldn't help but reach out and shake Wilbur's hand. "Thank you again. Your help is always appreciated. Sit for a while, finish your tea, and rest before heading back out again for another bumpy ride to central."

Wilbur squeezed Joe's hand and smiled broadly. "I'll do that. Thank you, my boy."

Joe nodded and stood straight again before turning to his superior and gesturing toward the gnome's desk. The three of them turned and left Wilbur to relax with his tea.

They began speaking in hushed tones. Joe was first, "That kid is in danger; we need to find him and get him back here."

Petals was second, "Blueprints of the storm drains from the city finally arrived and need review."

Amelia was next, "Grimbomb said that there were oddities he wanted us to see concerning the long-barrel we collected from Eagle Eyes."

Joe added to the list, "Doctor Broom said he needed to speak with us concerning the bodies found at Ironwall Locks and Alarms."

They all stopped at Petals' desk and eyed one another in a long awkward silence. Joe eventually asked the question none of them wanted to touch. "All right... who talks to Grimbomb?"

~~

Joe grumbled and cursed under his breath as he descended the stairs into the cellar. "Stupid pulling rank! Tankard of goblin piss is what that is!"

Once he was low enough to view the lower depths of the precinct, Joe sought out the partition in his mind and set it at the highest alert he could think of.

His mind immediately jumped to full alarm as a thunderous eruption of noise filled the stone bunker that was the quartermaster's den. Thankfully, Joe's hat blunted the ear-destroying cacophony and turned it into a muffled wallop.

Good gods... not even three seconds down the steps!

Joe finished descending the stairs and turned to face the quartermaster's cage and improvised firing range. Grimbomb was standing at the firing range with what looked to be Eagle Eyes' long-barrel tucked under his arm with the end trailing smoke.

"Couldn't resist, could you?" He held his staff at the ready, just in case any spontaneous plumes of fire or explosions decided to appear.

Grimbomb enthusiastically spun on his heel and whipped the smoking barrel around to point in Joe's direction.

Not wanting to take the chances that the Fates would decide to frown upon him, he threw himself to the ground and covered his head with his hands.

Grimbomb barked with his arms open wide and the smoking barrel pointed at the wall. "Boyo! Oi! What you doin' down there?" He tilted the long-barrel so the tip was up in the air in a very casual manner.

The dwarf's casual handling of the destructive weapon made Joe very uneasy. Grimbomb used the non-barrel-holding hand to wave Joe over. "Come! Get up off that floor and see this wonderfully destructive device!"

Good gods, I'm going to die at the hands of a mad dwarf.

He pushed up off the floor, picked up his staff, and brushed himself off. With a strong barrier conjured into place to help block out the smell and any stray bullets, Joe shuffled his way closer. He was afraid if he took too heavy of a step, it might somehow trigger an explosion. Once he was close enough to eye the barrel from a distance, he nodded the lunatic onward. "All right, what did you want to show me, Grimbomb?"

The weapon-crazed dwarf side-stepped closer to Joe and pointed at the walnut stock and the engravings in it. "See this here?"

As much as he didn't want to get any closer to a device that detonated gunpowder while in the hands of a man whose nickname included the word 'bomb', he had no choice but to lean in and squint in order to see better. "Somewhat. What is it?"

The dwarf chuckled maniacally and looked up to Joe with his singed eyebrows wiggling. "Rune work!"

Joe stood up straight for a moment to reach into a vest pocket and pulled out one of his detective's tools. The violet-shaded tint of the magnifying glass that he pulled from his pocket helped to reveal arcane energies.

A brief examination proved that the pyro-obsessed bearded menace was correct, the only exception being that there was a break in the runes. "Bring this over into the light; I want to examine it better."

Grimbomb, while endlessly eccentric, was undeniably reliable and quick to take an order. He secured the long-barrel in his hands and hurried for the side door leading into the cage.

Joe headed to the cage window and waited for the dwarf to come around. As he presumed might happen, a bright belch of fire suddenly lit up the far and dark end of the cage. Grimbomb yelped and ran free of the fire with the hems of his clothing and the ends of his whiskers smoldering.

He had sensed nothing. His partition had given him no warning at all. Petals' earlier statement came to mind: "I can bend the fabric of space and time with a snap of my fingers, but I have yet to discover the nature of his spontaneous conflagrations."

The only thing Joe could think to ask was, "Are you cursed?"

Grimbomb swatted at his rear end to put out what Joe could only surmise to be burning fabric. He shrugged after having put himself out, "Not that I can think of."

"Why is there always fire around you?"

The dwarf chuckled maniacally and admitted to the most frightening thing Joe had heard that morning, "I have no idea, but I like it. Keeps life interestin'."

Joe gave up. He threw out his arms in a gesture for Grimbomb to put down the long-barrel. "Please!"

The dwarf took great care in placing the device down between them on a stretch of oil-stained cloth. He leaned in and began pointing out specific details on the metal barrel. "Ye see this?"

Joe didn't dare speak, out of fear he would say something highly sarcastic, and opted for a simple nod.

Grimbomb pointed to his rack of long-barrels. "It don't match any of those."

Joe gave up. He shook his head and asked, "And? There are lots of different models of long-barrels, Grimbomb. Why would you compare this one to those ones?"

"'Cause those ones fire this!" Grimbomb slapped a long, pointed bullet down on the countertop. He pointed to the long-barrel between them, "And this one fires these." He lifted a tin bowl from a nearby counter and gingerly set it down. It was filled with iron pellets.

He felt a cold chill run up his spine as he stood straight. Joe hadn't bothered examining where the bullet had gone in the jewelry store, as he had been more focused on trying to figure out how Eagle Eyes had gotten away. It was only then that he realized and recalled that there had been no bullet hole in the wall behind the counter.

"He modified a long-barrel into a shock barrel?"

"Aye!" The maniacal grin returned.

Shock barrels were used during the War for Silvertree in close combat whenever the green-skins stormed the trenches. They found that the widespread distribution of iron pellets did a better job of shredding the attacking forces than long-range armor-piercing bullets did.

A myriad of questions inundated him as he stood in thought. "Why did he use a long-range against me one night and then switch tactics to something as risky as the shock barrel the next?"

Grimbomb was quick to answer, "That's easy lad, he figured it was too risky to use long-range 'cause he couldn't penetrate yer coat. One or two shots and ye have his position."

It was a technically correct answer, but it didn't feel like the right one.

"And the rune work?" Grimbomb gestured to the stock.

Right.

Joe leaned back in and brought his magnifying glass back up to read the spell-work a bit better. "It looks like some kind of muffling, not unlike the runes used in my hat." He reached up and took his hat off as he kept his eye on the lettering engraved into the stock. A quick-glance comparison confirmed it.

He took his time examining the break in the spell-work. It wasn't so much a line-break as one of the runes wasn't emitting energy. "Odd." Joe put his hat back on and stuck his magnifying glass back in his pocket before pulling his gloves from his belt pouch.

Once he slid on the silk gloves, he placed a hand on the wooden stock and shut his eyes. A gentle probe showed a defect in the wood. He popped his eyes open, pulled his knife from his belt, and leaned in closer.

Grimbomb let out a gasping screech and grabbed his beard as Joe stuck the very tip of his spear-point utility knife into a bit of the grain and twisted. A small chunk of wood lifted free with little prying. The broken rune lifted in one solid square piece.

The panicked dwarf let go of his beard and scowled at the piece that Joe had so easily pried free. He looked to the stock, stuck his finger on the exposed wood, and rubbed his fingers together. "Glue."

Joe nodded and answered the very thought that had just bubbled into the dwarf's mind. "Sabotage."

Another chill ran up his spine, as he realized that he was never meant to hear the hammer pull back that night. Nobody was meant to hear the explosive power of the shock barrel.

~~

Joe regrouped with Amelia as she emerged from the doctor's section of the cellar; they both headed up to report to Petals. He quickly informed her of what he'd discovered with Grimbomb, and how neither of them would likely have survived the sneak attack that had been coming for them.

Unsurprisingly, she got defensive and insisted, "You might have died, rook, but I would have been ready for the second shot." They climbed the stairs in chilly silence as the unspoken understanding of how close they'd both been to death struck home.

Once they got to the top step, they found Petals standing on his desk with a sea of old parchment documents surrounding the floor around it.

"Make any progress?" Joe was hopeful.

Petals smiled enthusiastically, "Nope. What did you two find?"

Joe motioned for Amelia to go first, as he'd already shared with her what he'd discovered with Grimbomb.

She flicked out her notepad and started reading from it. "Galen and Ursa Ironwall were discovered dead in the back workshop of Ironwall Locks and Alarms. By the looks of it, they died due to an industrial accident of improperly mixed chemicals, creating toxic fumes."

"They were a couple? Were there any kids left behind?" He couldn't help but interject.

She lifted her hand and waved him off. "They were siblings, new to the city and establishing their business. No kids. Can I continue or do you need a tissue?"

Joe leveled a serious scowl at her and motioned for her to keep going. He didn't take kindly to anyone making light of the fact that there could have been orphaned children.

"If it wasn't for the rook's suspicions, the doctor might have written their deaths off as an accident, but he was smart and gave them both a thorough going over. Puncture marks behind their ears on both of them."

Petals stroked his white beard in thought. "Dead before the fumes?"

Amelia nodded in confirmation. "Doc thinks they got hit with some sort of poison that mimicked the symptoms, but their lungs were clean. They were dead before the 'accident' was staged."

Joe had a few theories. "Either Eagle Eyes was sloppy, or smart."

Petals motioned for Joe to continue.

"He was sloppy in that he didn't have the two dwarves build the second key to deactivate the alarm. Or he was smart and wanted the key to only deactivate the barrier and not the alarm. Through one method, he would be able to get away with the theft and there wouldn't be any investigation until the morning. Or he knew that I would have to answer the call and waited for me to arrive to finish me off." He glanced to Amelia, who seemed to be staring off into the void of despair as she hugged her arms, "And by the looks of the shock barrel he brought along to do the deed, he was aiming for option two."

Petals narrowed his eyes. "Explain."

Joe provided his superior with the same details he had summarized for Amelia. "We weren't meant to make it out alive last night. Someone sabotaged Eagle Eyes' weapon of choice. Someone wants him out of the picture. There's double-crossing taking place."

Their superior went about pacing the tightly confined space of his desk for a minute, then looked to the two of them and gave a wicked grin. "Looks like the both of you have an underage youth to find."

Fireballs!

Joe let out a groan and an exasperated sigh and pointed to Amelia. "I'm her partner, aren't I?"

The mischievous little man grinned even wider. "Wondering when you'd pick up on that. Yes, until Eagle Eyes is caught, that is."

Amelia turned, headed to her desk to pick up her trench coat, and fired her disagreement back over her shoulder in turn. "Don't think for a second I'm enjoying this either, rook."

Chapter 16

The ride in the gnome cart was so eerily silent that the driver kept peering into his rear-view mirror at them. Joe tried to keep his attention forward on the road. Eventually, it was too much for the driver. "The two of you off to a funeral or are you getting divorced?"

Amelia turned her attention to the driver and glared well enough for him to throw up a hand in apology. "Not my business, ma'am."

Joe found himself wishing for the company of his superior, pranks and all. The trip lasted a whole of twenty minutes, but it felt like an hour.

The Ruby Lounge was situated north of the precinct and in an entertainment-heavy district of the city. The men and women walking down the street were in a higher class of fashion, and there seemed to be larger and more extravagant privately-owned carts rolling past.

Joe couldn't keep silent. "We're going to stick out like sore thumbs."

"Speak for yourself, rook."

He whipped his head back and shook his head in disbelief, as Amelia sat in completely different clothes than when they had left the station. "When– that– you– HOW?"

Amelia was wearing a long white coat over a silvery-blue strapless sequined dress. Her shoes had been switched with white open-toed heels. The hat, made from a finely woven black silk, was easily twice as wide as his hat and covered both her shoulders. Her detective uniform was nowhere to be seen, and her wand was balanced delicately between the gloved fingers of her right hand like some sort of diamond smoke holder.

The driver did a double take in the rear-view, then whistled. "Looking good, ma'am."

Amelia turned her glare back upon the driver, who promptly set his eyes back on the road. After a few seconds of glancing out the window, she informed the driver to pull over.

"Yes, ma'am."

She turned back to Joe, smirked, and waved him out the door. "A girl has to have her secrets. Now, play the part of a gentleman and help me out?"

Joe glared at her for a moment more before turning to open the cart door and hauling himself out. He turned on the spot and offered his hand while drawing his wand and tilting it skyward to deflect the downpour of rain.

She scooted to his side of the cart, took his hand with a few of her fingers, and acted the part of a true noble lady as she stepped out of the gnome cart and hopped up onto the curb. "Keep an eye out for the little brat." She whispered it under her breath as he shut the door and held his wand by her side to act the part of her gentleman.

"Yes, ma'am." Joe turned back to offer his arm, and she took it without hesitation as they both walked down the street toward The Ruby Lounge. "Mind answering why we got out of the cart before the doors?"

She muttered under her breath while keeping her attention on everything but him, "We don't want to pull up to a ritzy joint in a gnome cart. If we want to look the part, we'd be better off pulling up in a private cart."

Smart.

He nodded in understanding and turned his attention to the surrounding buildings. Many of them were larger than what he was used to, as they were designed to house a great many more patrons and entertainers than the typical joints he could afford.

The Silver Curtain Stage was on the other side of the street, and, based on the billboard, they were currently presenting the famous play *Seven Dragons and Seven Seas*. Next door to the stage was the infamous restaurant Witches' Cauldron Marshland Delicacies. It was known for its eccentric menu and the myriad of licenses it was known to have acquired to serve such foods. He'd never had the chance to check for himself, but he'd heard lizard-kind eggs were on the menu.

The Ruby Lounge fit its name, as the front pillars that marked the entrance were made from red glass etched to look like cut gems. The rest of the brick building had been painted black with red stripes.

There didn't look to be too many people walking in and out of the establishment, but that wasn't too much of a surprise, seeing as how it was barely middle of the morning.

Amelia spoke softly as to not be heard by anyone else around them. "You seriously don't have a suit and tie for formal occasions?"

Joe replied, "I'm an orphan. I don't have any friends or family to invite me to special occasions. The only formal event I ever attended was my graduation from the Academy, and as you know, they provide the uniform. So no, I don't have any formal attire."

She patted his arm and smiled as if she were having a friendly conversation; all part of the act, he supposed.

"You'll need to fix that if you wish to be a good detective. You need to adapt to situations."

He dared to inquire, "Mind telling me how you managed to slip into that without me noticing, all while sitting in a cramped cart together?"

Her smile widened and she gave a brief shake of her head. "Nope."

Of course not.

As they drew closer to The Ruby Lounge's main entrance, he couldn't help but notice that the doorman was very large. His shoulders were almost as wide as the doors, and he easily stood a head taller than Joe, and Joe wasn't, by any means, a short man.

Another oddity that he noted was the man looked to be far hairier than any other man he'd ever seen, and he'd seen dwarves with eyebrows that could be classified as full-grown sewer rats.

Amelia pinched his arm and harshly whispered through her smile, "Keep walking!"

Joe glanced at her and did as he was told. They continued past as he did his best to act as though that had been their plan all along. A quick glance at the man at the door told him much more than earlier.

Amelia whispered again at him through clenched, smiling teeth, "Those were bear claws!"

Joe couldn't help but squeeze her arm. "Keep it down or you'll get us caught."

She turned to look at him and gave him a warm smile, but glanced back over her shoulder before facing forward again. "They're not watching us."

"Now what?" They needed a new plan, and soon.

"Go around the corner." Amelia picked up the pace a little bit and even hiked up the front of her dress so she could move quicker without worrying about tripping and falling.

Joe kept pace with her. At best, it simply looked like they were hurrying to escape the rain. The next building over from The Ruby Lounge was a restaurant called The Diamond Swan.

They hurried past the front entry of that building as well and eventually made it to the corner. As soon as they rounded it, Amelia pointed to a network booth. "There!"

"What? I have a—"

"Shush!" Amelia quickly tiptoed her way into the black windowed box and shut the folding door behind her.

He was genuinely confused, as he had his crystalline network box if she needed to contact dispatch.

Joe felt an odd sensation prickling the back of his mind, and he could tell she was busy utilizing magic while in the booth. After a few brief moments, the sliding door opened and she emerged with her wand in hand, pointed skyward, and her regular detective garb on. "HOW?"

She smirked and adjusted her hat before stepping over to him and peering around the corner. "Get yourself some nice clothes there, rook, and I might just show you how."

He threw up his one available arm as a show of defeat. "Yeah, sure, where am I going to find the coin to afford nice clothes?"

Amelia looked back to him, eyed him up and down, and raised an eyebrow. "Who said you had to buy it nice?"

Joe gave her an exasperated look. "I don't know how to sew either."

"Sounds like you need to learn or find yourself a woman willing to stitch you up nice."

The thought of Ms. Bellcreaux sizing him up for clothing made him shudder.

Amelia gave him a strange look. "What was that for? Are you not into women?"

Joe shook his head, "No, it's— look, I had an awkward encounter with my landlady this morning, so the thought of her helping me with a suit just threw me off."

Amelia turned her full attention to him and put one hand on her hip while smirking. "Now I'm really curious."

"Focus! Why did you have us run past the doorman with the bear claws?"

She gave him a look. "You serious? I didn't feel like getting clawed up today. Besides, that was a werebear."

Joe made a broad gesture. "And?"

"By the gods, you really are an inexperienced rookie. Have you never heard of the Brown Claws?" She raised her eyebrows in genuine surprise.

He kept his frustration to a simmer and pointed at her. "No, I have no idea who the Brown Claws are, because I spent my two years as a Blue Coat on the north end dealing with the Viper Tails." He presumed that the Brown Claws were some sort of gang.

Amelia sighed and gestured to the corner. "Werebears... Brown Claws."

Joe pinched the bridge of his nose. "Wow, life was easier as a Blue Coat when the gang members got themselves venom tats to become part of a gang."

Amelia raised an eyebrow. "Venom tats?"

He waved it off, "Another time. How do we get into the lounge and back out in one piece?" They stood in their bubbles for a time while the rain fell around them and they contemplated their options. "I think disguise is a bad idea."

She agreed, "Especially since you don't have one. I can't count on you for backup if you're out here."

Joe agreed, "Fair enough. I also don't think we should try and sneak in, as that would be considered a criminal charge against us for breaking into a private establishment."

She nodded again and looked off in thought. "Our only option is to walk up to the front door and show our badges."

He nodded. "We are looking for one of their employees, after all, and have more questions for him."

Amelia shut her eyes and muttered something under her breath. She gave him a hot glare and pointed her finger in his face. "I swear, if the eagle-eyed man is in there and we go swimming with the fishes because of you..." She continued shaking her finger with the unspoken threat.

Joe released his wand to a full staff and checked his six-shooter in his holster. "Eagle Eyes has made two attempts on my life, and I'm still here."

"What's that saying about the third time?"

Don't jinx me, woman!

~~

The two of them stepped up to the hair-suit doorman and raised their brass badges for him to see. "We'd like to speak with management concerning a young bus boy in his employ by the name of Tim."

Now that they'd gotten even closer, Joe was surprised to see that the doorman did indeed have ursine features. His nose was black and wet, and his ears were tufted higher up on his head and flicked whenever some noise caught his attention. Otherwise, he looked mostly human. He didn't have the typical muzzle and snout of a bear. His hands, however, were massive, meaty, and clawed paws that were surprisingly still dexterous enough to operate door handles and fix his suit when it needed a straightening.

The werebear doorman stood staring at the two of them, unmoving.

Joe leaned slightly to Amelia. "Did he understand us?"

Amelia nudged him in the ribs with her elbow, causing him to jump slightly.

Eventually, a great lumbering figure filled the entire doorway. His face was far more bear-like in appearance, and his snout more pronounced. His frame was far more muscular, and he waddled a bit like an upright bear.

By the gods, that's a big man.

Amelia seemed to be thinking the same thing, as she stood rooted to the spot and stared up at the behemoth, wide-eyed, with a pale complexion. Joe nudged her and made her jump slightly.

They waited as the massive brute of a werebear spoke, "Management would like to speak with you." The massive figure slowly turned on the spot, taking several steps to do so, and slowly lumbered back inside. The doorman looked to them both and waved them through.

Amelia reached out and snatched Joe's forearm and gripped it tight in her small hand.

Easy… we'll make it out so long as we don't say or do the wrong thing.

Joe picked up his staff and started forward, careful not to step out ahead or too close to the great lumbering creature guiding them.

The interior of The Ruby Lounge was as luxurious as the outside. The carpets were black with sparkling streaks of red, and the tables were lit with faceted red lanterns. Immediately to the right of the entrance was a dining hall and sit-down restaurant. To the left of the door was a bar and a set of stairs. The stairs lead to the stage seating, and in the stage spotlight, a young woman in a blue dress breathily sang of betrayal and heartbreak. He could tell that she wasn't a bard, as he couldn't feel her magical fingers entwining their way through his ears to his heart.

Amelia released his forearm as they picked up the pace, and she focused on looking as tough as she could. Her jaw was tense, and he could feel her anxiety through the partition in his mind.

Stay calm; we're not in trouble yet.

The two of them were led down a walkway that overlooked the stage to the left and a wall separating the kitchens and dining area on their right.

Eventually, the lumbering werebear guided them to a door that was hidden in the wall, as it was painted to blend in.

Joe's ears perked as he heard keys jangling, and the massive shoulders and head looked down at the narrow door. A quick partitioning of his mind allowed him to enter that quiet calm of the void where no music or chatter could reach him.

His mind was immediately struck with an image of the layers of barriers that protected the wall before them and the door the giant werebear was in the process of unlocking.

To say that there was some serious coin put into the security of the back office was a great understatement. Even with his natural talents, it would take him some time to work through the barriers based on the level of complexity he was witnessing.

All right, we're in trouble.

He snapped open his eyes as the door latch clicked, and the hidden door swung open. Beyond was a dimly lit hallway. The brute of a werebear turned to look down upon them before slightly tilting his head for them to go first.

Joe didn't like it, but he wasn't about to start arguing over it. Tipping his hat respectfully, he stepped forward and shuffled sideways past the massive man, who took up most of the walkway. The Brown Claws were so big that they would absolutely have to travel down the walkway single file.

Amelia was quick to follow and kept her eyes down to the ground. Once inside, the door slammed shut behind them and locked. It was more than enough to cause them to jump and draw their weapons to the ready.

"Damn you, Joseph!" She really was scared if she wasn't calling him 'rook'. Amelia turned and kept her back to Joe's as they made their way down the hall, covering one another. There had to be another exit.

As they made their way down the hall, they checked each door they came across. They were all locked, physically and magically. It would probably take him an hour or two just to break through one of them. As such, they kept going. It wasn't like they had any other option.

Halfway down the hallway, which seemed to be a great deal longer than it first appeared, a door swung open of its own accord.

Right, like I'm going to step through the beckoning murder-door. No thanks.

A wheezing and muffled voice called to them from inside, "Detectives."

Joe shook his head.

The voice called again. "I have questions about this Tim you mentioned." Whoever it was, they sounded old. "I swear to you upon my mother's grave, that no harm will come to you should you sit and break bread with me."

Fireballs.

Joe cursed himself and holstered his firearm. Amelia near lost her mind and started to shove him with her elbow. He dared to take the risk and put his back to the wall, then shuffled his way over to the doorframe. He had to pause for a moment to steady his heart while Amelia fully panicked.

The woman spun on the spot while aiming her six-shooter and staff at each door they had passed and those they had yet to. She slowly spun her way to him with her head on a swivel.

Eventually, she flattened her back to the wall beside him and glared at him with maddeningly wide eyes. "If we don't die in here, I'll kill you myself!"

Joe accepted that fate and darted his head around the corner for a quick peek. The room in question looked surprisingly cozy. It was well lit with several bright lantern lights, and the flooring and walls were a rich, warm hardwood. Bookshelves lined the back wall and a large desk sat in the middle of the room. Behind the desk sat a large and graying werebear in a trim and clean blue suit. The suit was fit for a giant.

He straightened back up and nodded the all-clear to Amelia before turning the corner and stepping inside. As foolish as his decision was to holster his firearm, he kept his staff at the ready.

Once he was standing in the doorway, he was able to get a clearer picture of the room. It looked to be a manager's main office. There was even a large metal safe in the far corner of the room beside one of the bookshelves.

The great big graying werebear lifted a hefty paw and gestured to one of the two seats situated before his desk. "Welcome, detectives. Welcome to my place of business. I'm the manager, Mr. Marcano. Please, sit."

Joe looked to the rotund man sitting at the desk and dared to step closer. He looked back to see Amelia peering into the room with her weapons still drawn and pointed into the hall. "I apologize for our state of alarm, but the door was shut rather... forcefully... behind us."

The old man lifted a hand and made a slow shake of his head. "Excuse my son, he has a temper."

Amelia eventually holstered her weapon and straightened herself before stepping into the office to join Joe. The glare of icy murder in her eyes told him he'd likely get it when they left the lounge.

The great big man made a gesture with both his hands toward the chairs. "I feel like a terrible host, please." He made a soft shrug and another gesture toward the chairs.

Joe glanced at Amelia, then dared to sit in the right chair. She glowered at him and made a point of sitting rather detestably in the chair on the left.

"So," the old and wheezing werebear leaned forward in his chair, "I hear you have a problem with an eagle-eyed man."

The simple statement caught the attention of them both.

Amelia got the words out first, "How did you hear about that?"

Mr. Marcano seemed to smile, but it was hard to tell with his sagging jowls and elongated muzzle. "I have ears." He pointed to his actual ears, and they flicked like those of an actual animal would. A grand shaking of his shoulders was followed by a wheezing laugh that carried for several minutes.

When neither of them laughed, the old man settled into a deep sigh, "I take it you want to talk about this Tim?"

Joe nodded. "That's why we came, yes. We would like to speak with him."

The werebear slowly nodded his head. "So would I." He lifted a small ledger from his desk and dropped it in front of Joe, "Because I have no Tim on my books."

... *Fireballs.*

Chapter 17

They stood and took turns scanning through the ledger: first Joe, then Amelia. It was well-organized, and the penmanship was near impeccable. They had names, addresses, dates, times, and even wages for each individual that operated in The Ruby Lounge. As the werebear before them had said, 'Tim' was nowhere in the books.

Seeing as how The Ruby Lounge looked to be the base of operations of an organized crime syndicate, Joe had no doubt in his mind that the books before him weren't the actual dollar figures running through the lounge. He just didn't have the means to argue or deny them without proof.

"How do we know you didn't pay him under the table?"

The well-groomed and graying grizzly sitting before him released a rather displeased grumbling growl, "That's quite the impolite accusation, Mr. Runewall."

Amelia continued scanning through the pages, one at a time.

Joe didn't like the idea of making a bear angry, but he had to do his duty. "While I understand your distaste for the question, it remains one that I must ask."

Mr. Marcano held Joe's gaze for a while before he finally raised his raspy voice. "Thumbs!"

A miniscule man – no taller than a hand – suddenly appeared in a showering puff of white sparks upon the wooden desk. It was startling enough to make Joe jump a bit, but Amelia was so wound up that she tripped over the chair leg and fell to the floor in a belted scream of surprise and panic.

Flaming fireballs! A fairy!

The miniscule man had a pale complexion, wore a well-tailored brown suit, had spectacles balanced on a thin little nose, pointed ears, and blue hair. Insect-like wings protruded from his suit and flicked every once in a while.

Thumbs, as Mr. Marcano had called him, turned on the spot to face the great and lumbering werebear and lifted his head. "You rang, sir?" The fairy's voice was surprisingly deep and clear.

Mr. Marcano shook violently in the shoulders and began wheezing again as he laughed.

Joe couldn't help but chuckle slightly and looked down at the little fairy in amazement. "Huh. Mr. Thumbs, do you mind if I ask what your specialty is?"

Fairies could be summoned from the fey realm, given certain conditions were met. The knowledge of what each fairy liked was typically a well-guarded secret to prevent the summoning from being abused.

The little man slowly turned on the spot and placed both hands behind his back as he looked up at Joe. He narrowed his eyes and peered up at him for a time before deciding on answering. "I am particularly experienced with codexes, cryptic cyphers, and cross-reference organizational paradigms. In the case of Mr. Marcano, I 'keep his books'." The well-spoken fairy bowed his head.

Joe couldn't help but nod in awe and approval. He pointed back to the hallway with his staff in hand. "I take it the barrier and lock-work around the back area here is something of your design?"

Amelia quickly darted her eyes back and forth between Joe and the tiny fairy. It was at that moment that he pondered whether she'd ever met one before. Fairies were extremely rare since the exodus following the War for Silvertree, so he presumed she hadn't.

Thumbs lifted his head and stood a bit taller. "Why yes, indeed, it is. You have a keen eye, Mr. Runewall."

Joe smiled and nodded in appreciation of the returned compliment. He pointed to the books. "I must now apologize and request an accounting of the books. Do you have any knowledge of one 'Tim' being employed at this establishment?"

Thumbs looked to the book in question that Amelia had been riffing through, then looked to Joe before shaking his head in reply. "I am afraid not, my good sir."

Mr. Marcano piped up, "Sir? Thumbs, my friend, you have never called anyone 'sir' but me." He gestured to Joe, "Why now do you give this stranger the same courtesy?"

Thumbs turned on the spot and bowed deeply to the suspected gang leader. "My deepest apologies, good sir, but it is a matter of fairy custom and law."

Joe interjected with a raised finger, "Fairy law dictates that any compliment given and returned bestows a status of respect unto that which is not fairy. That respect can be revoked or broken according to the actions of the non-fairy." He put down his hand and stuffed it back into his trench coat pocket. "There's a great deal more to it, but I fear if I continue, we'll be here all afternoon."

Thumbs slowly lifted from his deep bow and looked to the werebear. "Mr. Runewall is quite correct."

Joe shrugged and suggested it wasn't so big of an offense. "Your contract with Thumbs is untouched."

The great and massive werebear wheezed out a cough, then a chuckle. He threw his head back and let loose a great belly-clutching fit of wheezing laughter that lasted for several moments.

Amelia slowly clambered back into the chair beside Joe. She had a confused blank stare and didn't seem to be coping well with the situation.

Eventually, Mr. Marcano settled and wiped his beady eyes with the palms of his paws as he continued to wheeze and cough. "Oh my, I haven't had a laugh like that in some time. I like you, kid. I like you." He gently waved Thumbs away, and the tiny fairy turned to glittering dust in the air as he returned to the fey realm.

Joe didn't know what it was that the werebear found so funny, but he accepted the fact that it put him in the good books, so to speak, and didn't get them thrown in with the fishes. "All right, 'Tim' doesn't exist on your books; is it possible he is going by a different name?"

The great lumbering man waved Joe to sit down, so he sat. "Enough business for the moment, we need to break bread. The kitchens are always running. What can I get the two of you?" He leaned forward in his chair and opened his paws as a sign of offering what he could.

Joe compressed his staff to a wand, then stuck it in his vest pocket. Glancing at his watch, he noted that it was indeed lunch time. Not that he was that hungry, but he could do for a quick break. Seeing the fairy had set his mind to ease of being poisoned or killed. "I could use a cup of tea, with honey and lemon, if you don't mind?"

Amelia seemed to snap free of her mind-fog and glared at Joe.

He smiled kindly to her, "We are discussing a troublesome 'employee' with a citizen that has offered us a meal at lunch time. It would be discourteous to refuse."

The waiter came and left, and Amelia abstained. She said she wished to watch her figure. Mr. Marcano accepted her answer and made nothing more of it. If the great big man-beast was a criminal, he was a high-class one.

While they waited for their dishes to arrive, the great husky werebear entwined his fingers and rested his hands on his desk. "So, what does this young man look like?"

Joe provided as accurate a description as he could, even describing how the young man stood and dressed himself. Daring to go a bit further, he described the incident involving the eagle-eyed man and Travok Blackfinger in the alleyway, as told by 'Tim'.

"Hmm… I have no recollection of the young man you describe. I don't hire mousy little men, especially ones that aren't of age."

Joe doubted the man held to every single law, but the spontaneous arrival of the fairy cast doubts upon his doubts. Fairies had strict codes of conduct and often had contracts that included villainous clauses. Such moralities didn't always include the mortal realm, however. It was fully possible that the arrangement between Thumbs and Mr. Marcano was strictly about the books and nothing else.

"However."

Joe lifted his eyes from the desk to the great werebear.

"I am familiar with this Blackfinger fellow."

That caught both of their attention, and they sat forward in their chairs. Joe pulled his notepad from his pocket and partitioned his mind.

Mr. Marcano pointed to his ears, and they flicked again. "Like I said, I hear things."

Sure.

"I kicked a dark dwarf out of the gambling lounge the other day for trying to pass off fake tokens. Naturally, I asked around to see if any of the other establishments have had similar problems. The Blue Oyster, down by the docks, says they've had issues with him before, and they gave me his name."

Joe's hand scribbled as he listened.

"Then, last week, one of my boys is heading home and spots this despicable dwarf talking in the alley with a man with golden eyes."

"Did your man say where this alley was?" If he scooted any closer to the edge of his seat, he would fall off of it.

"Yeah, Cinderbeard's Smokes and Pipes off Red Lightning Boulevard."

Of course.

Red Lightning Boulevard was popular with dark dwarves and bloodlings. Very few Blue Coats or detectives went to that road without good cause and their weapons at the ready. The fact that Eagle Eyes was able to survive the alleys only contributed to the reputation of being a dangerous criminal.

"What else can you tell us?" Amelia finally joined the conversation instead of glowering at him.

"This man with the golden eyes, he concluded his business, and then headed down into the storm tunnels."

Joe looked to Amelia out of the corner of his eye and saw her giving him the same look.

"Have you ever heard of him before?"

Mr. Marcano leaned forward and lowered his voice, "Twenty-three years ago, there was a series of murders around town." Thunder rumbled the building as the werebear began his tale.

Great timing on the drama there, gods.

"Detectives like yourselves were left scratching their heads and running circles as body after body dropped."

Amelia put a hand on Joe's arm.

He turned his attention away from the werebear to see her eyes widen and focus. She'd clearly heard of the events as well. Joe looked back to the old lumbering man as he continued the story.

"Eventually, one man got lucky, and caught a glimpse of the killer, and he thought he saw golden eyes."

"The Noble Killings." Amelia whispered in reverence and fear.

It was only then that Joe remembered a case study at the Academy about a series of nobles being killed in a mysterious murder spree two decades previous. The killer had never been found.

The old werebear eased back on his creaking chair as the door to the kitchens opened again and the waiter returned with a cup of tea for Joe and a platter of salmon and eggs for the salivating manager.

The three of them sat back in silence and absorbed what they'd just learned from one another. Joe lifted the teacup and dish and sipped slowly, savoring the invigorating warmth. Mr. Marcano used a spoon nearly as big as a ladle to shovel orange fish eggs into his mouth while using a grill-sized fork to swallow baked salmon as well.

Amelia said nothing, ate nothing, and shot her loathing at Joe with a glance. He'd have to take her to get some food or she'd probably bite his head off.

Once he'd finished his tea, he set down the cup and saucer and thanked the gorging werebear with a nod of his head and tip of his hat. "The tea was wonderful, but we must be going. We have a criminal to remove from the streets that I'm sure will help you sleep better at night."

Mr. Marcano used a small white napkin to dab at his muzzle, then swallowed before answering in kind, "It was a pleasure to meet the both of you."

Amelia continued to act as stony and transfixed as ever. She needed a better game face.

The two of them stood and turned to the door. It was then that Petals stepped into the office in his calm and quick near-skipping manner.

The weight-strained chair that the werebear had been sitting in suddenly sighed and creaked from the weight being lifted. There was a loud noise from the chair rubbing against the hardwood floor as it was pushed away.

Petals looked to Amelia and Joe. "I was wondering what was taking you two so long, so I decided to come and visit." He looked to the suspected crime boss and smiled wickedly. "Hello, Gino."

Petals... I swear by all that is holy.

"You!" Mr. Marcano was standing and almost yelling.

What did you do?

"You stand there, like you did on the day of my daughter's wedding."

His daughter's wedding!

"You smile at me now, like you did on that day..."

Joe was uncertain if it was possible, but he thought he could hear his own rear clenching.

The wheezing laugh slowly started filling the room until eventually Petals joined in and threw back his head and laughed delightfully. Joe looked back over his shoulder to find the massive werebear holding his gut with laughter. "What?"

Petals imitated the massive bear and placed both hands on his stomach as they both laughed heartily. Mr. Marcano pointed at Petals and managed to get out between wheezing, "He... my fur... pink!"

Petals waved it off. "Your daughter loved it!"

He couldn't handle any more, and by the looks of it, neither could Amelia. She was as pale as her white hair and she was hanging on with both hands to the back of the chair she had been sitting in, and her legs looked like they were about to give out.

Joe simply slumped to the floor and sat there behind the chair for a while, holding his hand over his heart. "Your pranks will be the death of me."

~~

Joe stumbled out the door while his hat sailed out to the curb. He managed to stay on his feet, but his jaw felt like it'd been knocked loose.

Amelia quickly followed while shaking out the pain in her hand, "That was for being a lunatic and nearly getting us killed!" She'd punched him. She rounded on Petals and stuck a finger in his face, right between his eyes. "And YOU!" She made a frustrated growl before storming off into the rain with her wand raised. Her footsteps left ice prints on the street as she headed back to, Joe presumed, the station.

He couldn't help but throw up his arms after having collected his hat. "Thanks for letting me explain!" He slapped his hat against his pant leg to knock off any muddy water, then fixed it atop his head before lifting his own wand.

Petals simply watched and smiled before pulling his wand and stepping out from the doorframe. "Learn much?"

Joe grumbled and rubbed his cheek as he watched Amelia march off into the distance.

"Ah. Much."

He handed his notepad to his superior and didn't feel like talking, especially with such a sore cheek and jaw. He only hoped she hadn't knocked any teeth loose.

Petals updated him on what he'd found out. "The storm tunnels beneath the city streets have multiple junctions and cross-connections that would make it a nightmare to navigate unless you already know where you're going."

Nodding in understanding, he worked his jaw around and probed the teeth on that side of his mouth with his tongue. Nothing was wiggling, thankfully.

Petals began walking in the same direction that Amelia had stormed off in and waved for Joe to follow. "We best follow, or she'll be in violation of direct orders by the captain."

Fireballs... the partner system.

Petals looked back over his shoulder and smirked. "Yes, that system."

"Stop reading my..." He glared at the gnome. "Wait... where's *your* partner?"

He smugly grinned. "Senior detective."

Of course.

A grunting shout rang out from down the block and around the corner, and it was quickly followed by a woman's blood-curdling scream.

Joe set the partition in his mind and turned his wand to a full staff before barreling down the street. Petals was, somehow, ahead of him and had his wand at the ready.

They both reached the corner and Joe drew his six-piece as well-dressed men and women ran round the corner toward them, screaming about a dwarf being shot.

Thank the gods it wasn't Amelia.

Petals nodded his head at the corner. "Joseph, shield!"

Joe gripped his staff tight, envisioned the heartiest dwarf-iron kite shield and then rounded the corner. He held up his staff like it was a shield itself, then released the energy he had balled up inside.

There was a thump to the air and a hearty thrumming hum as a translucent silver barrier appeared in front of him. It was rounded to suggest he was contained within a bubble. He could see a thick wavering shimmer to the air as well, and it moved with him as he made a quick and orderly advance down the street.

A stout form lay on the ground ahead, a dark puddle growing beneath it. Whoever it was, they were close to an alley.

Joe halted and grit his teeth as something struck the shield he had conjured, rippled the air, and shook his will. A crumpled bit of iron and brass fell to the ground and bounced to the side.

A bullet with no bang! Strike three!

He looked up and flexed his arm and tightened his control over the shield. The hum grew louder and steadier. He continued to push forward. That time, he kept his eyes focused on the buildings in the distance.

A flash from a second story rooftop on the far side of the street – at a distance of three hundred paces – was the only warning he received. The barrier that was protecting him at eye level shook violently, like a pebble hitting the surface of a pond. The barrier didn't break or shatter.

He watched closely and saw something metallic shift and pull away from the ledge of the rooftop. The second bullet fell to the street in front of him, and it had red sparks of shimmering light sputtering from the iron and brass. He didn't have the time to examine it.

Petals ran past him and hurried to the alley corner where Amelia appeared with her staff and firearm drawn. Petals looked to them both and nodded them to go on as he knelt to check the dwarf that was bleeding out onto the street. "Go!"

"Yes, sir!"

Spurred by a hungering need, Joe dropped the shield and threw himself into a straight dash for the other side of the road, and the building he had picked out as the shooter's nest.

Amelia was surprisingly just as quick as he was and darted across the road along with him. She looked to be as focused as him, as they both set off down the street at a full sprint.

I'm coming for you!

Chapter 18

Joe took the lead as they both reached the corner to the alley. He brought his staff to the ready and brought up the shield again. Once prepared, he signaled to Amelia, turned the corner, and barreled his way down the alley with her on his heels.

The shooter had ample time to descend the rooftop ladder, and they didn't have any time to waste catching them. Most two-story brownstones had a rooftop access in the alleyway, mostly intended for maintenance and repairs, but the odd hooligan used it for nefarious purposes.

Joe stepped into the alley with his firearm drawn. He made a steady advance and eyed the windows and garbage bins, ready for any sudden movements.

There was a sudden rattling clang of a knocked-over trash bin and the angry meowling of a cat several buildings over. Joe didn't bother questioning it and went with his gut. Amelia was of a similar mind, as she didn't object to continuing their chase.

The two of them sprinted down the back alley and skidded across the soaked cobblestone upon reaching the corner. Joe felt a renewed rush of energy as he spotted a figure in a dark trench coat running away from them with a long carrying case in hand. The figure was across the street and almost at the end of the next alley, but he was visible.

Amelia pulled her crystalline network box and began directing dispatch to the shooter's location and direction. Joe diverted the partition in his mind to help him focus his senses.

He lowered the shield to reserve his strength, holstered his firearm, pulled his brass badge, and roared as he set out at a dead run. "Freeze!" He knew the man wouldn't hear him from such a distance, but it got civilians out of the way. The sight of a detective running with a badge in the air and yelling for someone to freeze tended to cause everyone to stop moving, at least momentarily. It made things easier.

Amelia was right on his heels and continued directing dispatch as they made their pursuit.

You're not getting away today!

The street was clear of any carts as they both made the mad dash across and to the next alley. Their suspect looked back, jumped at the sight of being pursued, and bolted to the right. Amelia made the appropriate correction with dispatch between puffing breaths.

Despite his rigorous studying, Joe didn't finish top of his class when it came to legal theory or case studies, but he was certainly one of the best athletes they had. Two years as a Blue Coat had helped him stay in shape as well.

As soon as he saw the man bolt right, Joe took the first alleyway to match and soon started pulling ahead of Amelia. He pocketed his badge and drew his firearm once more, glancing at it repeatedly as he turned the barrel. He kept rotating until he saw the luminescent ammunition aligned, then locked it back into place.

Joe saw pedestrians walking past, completely unaware that he was coming out of the alley, and yelled at them, "Out of the way! Detective coming! Out of the way!"

An older couple that had been walking by turned their heads to spot Joe and quickly hurried forward to follow his shouted order.

The moment he burst from the alleyway and into the open street, he felt every hair and nerve in his body tighten. The shooter was across the street at the corner of the intersection; they had their case in hand and knelt on one knee. They were aiming at Joe with their case hiding their long-barrel. The older couple were behind him and potential collateral if he didn't do something.

Seconds could mean the difference between life and death. Joe balled up all the fury he could conjure, focused his will, and slammed the butt of his staff onto the cobblestone. Joe noted a flash that ripped apart the end of the shooter's case at the same time his staff struck.

Thunder rippled around him, and the cobblestones beneath his staff cracked violently. Chips of stone burst into the air, and there was a blinding flash of light as Joe felt something rip past his leg and send searing hot pain up his spine and down to his toes.

Drawing his six-shooter up to eye-level, he took the rush of sudden pain to steady himself, partitioned his mind, and aimed down the barrel as the shooter stood from where they had been kneeling and turned to run.

He could count the thumps of his heart with each agonizing half-second as the shooter gained every step of distance.

Panic was beginning to strike innocent civilians as the realization of what just took place was settling in. Soon, they would be running in every direction, causing a screen of people that he could never shoot through.

His window was growing smaller by the moment. With one last hardening of his will and his arm, he brought the point of the barrel of his firearm in line and squeezed the trigger.

The muffled thunder reached his ears as the end of his six-shooter flashed and recoiled. The shooter jolted, threw their arms up, and arched their back as they fell to the wet cobblestones face first.

Time seemed to release its grasp as Joe crumpled to the ground, his right leg giving out beneath him. Hot searing pain thundered through his leg as blood stained his trouser. Blowing out the smoke from the barrel of his firearm, he holstered his weapon.

"Someone call a doctor, the boy's been shot!" The old man had run to his side and knelt down to aid him.

With assistance, he pulled himself up to sit and tried to get an eye on where the shooter was. Amelia emerged from the other side of the building that Joe had run around, and she crossed the street with her staff and firearm drawn. Once she reached the other side, she began spinning on the spot. Eventually, a pedestrian grabbed her by the arm and pointed down the road to where the tracer trail had likely started

You're marked now!

She looked back to Joe and looked like she was about to come after him when he waved her off. "Go!"

Amelia nodded and turned her attention to the trail and started following it. He watched from a distance as she turned down another alley and out of sight.

The old man began taking off his belt when Joe put out his hand. "No, I have something better."

He shifted, flinched from the pain, and pulled a small tin box from a pouch on his belt. It bore the bright red droplet insignia and white crest of the medical corps. Joe used his thumb to flick open the lid, reached in, pulled out a cotton bandage and slapped the cloth on his leg.

To say the pain was excruciating was a great understatement. Thankfully, the bandage was treated with a numbing agent that would start to work quickly. He didn't have any more energy or will to partition his mind to help him handle the pain. After applying pressure to the wound on the side of his thigh, he rummaged around inside his little tin box once more and pulled free a glass finger-jar with a wax and cork stopper.

Joe gestured to the old man to take the cloth. "Press hard." Thankfully, the gentleman didn't faint at the sight of blood as he knew some were prone to do. He grabbed the cloth and held it tight to the side of Joe's leg. It stung like a red lightning wasp, but it quickly started to numb with each thrumming of his heart.

Another thing to be grateful for was that the wound wasn't too deep; it looked to have grazed him. Joe used his teeth to crack the wax seal and yank the stopper free. The tiny jar, no larger than his longest finger, released a satisfying pop.

He spared no time, as he knew Amelia would likely need his assistance. Having opened the finger-jar, he waved off the old man's hand, lifted the bandaging on his leg, and poured some of the fine white powder onto his open wound through the tear in his trousers.

The blinding, searing pain was immediate. Joe gripped tight the jar and used his thumb to stopper it as he twitched, curled his toes, gripped his leg tightly, and roared incoherent babble as he swore up a storm inside his own mind. The sisters at the orphanage would have gladly taken an hour from their day to cane him until he was blistered and raw for the words if they ever crossed his lips. Joe sucked on his teeth and gripped his leg with both hands until the fire subsided.

"Blimey, my boy, that's some awful stuff!" The old pedestrian put a steadying hand on his back to keep him sitting upright.

Joe couldn't help but chuckle his way through the unforgiving stress, anger, and pain. "This is only... my third day... on the job."

"Forgive me saying so, young man, but I think you need a new job."

The two of them quickly set to work tying off the bandage against his leg and setting it tight.

"Joseph?" The rumbling voice came from behind, and it sounded like it came from a mouth full of pebbles and cotton.

That must be Henry Mountainbeard.

The squared-faced half-giant quickly appeared by Joe's other side and was easily two heads taller than Joe, with massive meaty fingers and a frame like a brick house to match. The Blue Coat must have been dispatched to the area.

"Help me up."

Henry reached down and picked up Joe by the back of his trench coat like he was nothing more than a sack of potatoes. Joe wobbled as he landed on his feet and grabbed his leg as he felt the searing powder still doing its work of stopping the bleeding.

Looking out in the direction that Amelia had ventured, he reached out and grabbed his free-standing staff and yanked it from the cracked cobblestone. Despite his best efforts, he had simply exhausted too much energy deflecting the earlier shots.

A quick glance told him that nobody else was injured or required medical assistance. There were quite a few spooked onlookers though.

Thunderous shots rang out in the distance and Joe could tell it came from the direction that Amelia had followed the shooter.

"Henry!" Joe pointed in the direction of the shots. "Go help Detective Iceheart!"

The great lumbering oaf took off in the assigned direction while bellowing in his slowed speech, "Okay!" He easily covered a great deal of ground with his long thumping strides.

Joe used his staff to steady himself as he took after the half-giant in hopes of catching up. He didn't last very long, as exhaustion overtook him and the pain in his leg was far too great. Digging as deep as he could, he managed to make it as far as the street corner where the shooter had been kneeling.

Something about their appearance had been off to Joe. He hadn't been able to cover as much distance or get anywhere as near as he did the night before, but something about the way they moved told him it wasn't Eagle Eyes.

More thundering shots fired in the distance. Every shot set him more on edge. He didn't know if Amelia or Henry were injured, or if any pedestrians were caught in the crossfire. Unfortunately, he could do no more until he was checked out by the doctor.

One last shot rang out, bringing Joe's count to twelve.

More Blue Coats arrived on scene, the majority of which immediately ran toward where he figured Amelia to be. It was only then that he realized he could have been listening to his network box and had forgotten to switch it back on after leaving The Ruby Lounge.

Idiot.

Joe let out a great sigh, leaned back against the corner wall, pulled the box from his belt, and flicked the necessary dial to listen in.

"Target escaped via port; tracking their destination." Amelia was still alive and sounded uninjured, and angry.

Thank the gods.

The target having the chance to use a port to escape was undeniably annoying, as it would take time to trace them and dispatch appropriate personnel to search the area. However, he felt as though they'd gained crucial information that day.

Blue Coat Bob Johnson showed up, looked down on Joe, and whistled, "You look like a dead fish on deck there, son."

Joe nodded and waved it off. "All right, help me up."

~~

After twenty minutes, the two of them managed to make it all the way to where Amelia had cornered the shooter. Thankfully, Joe's tracer shot had left them a bright glowing-green line of droplets to follow.

"Smart thinkin', kid."

Joe shrugged it off as they followed the winding path through the back alleys to a warehouse nearly a block away. The other Blue Coats had already set up a perimeter and were keeping nosey citizens at bay.

The brick building had a large sheet metal door for loading and unloading and a small man-door for workers. The man-door had been kicked in.

Once inside, Joe noted that the only other exits were through windows on the second story. There was no second floor by which to reach the windows; they were likely intended for ventilation only. Looking about, he spotted some ladders that were probably used to open and close the windows. He guessed that the shooter didn't quite have the chance to get to any ladders while being shot at and cornered.

There were several bits and chunks of brick that were shattered or cracked on either side of the room. It made it quite easy to tell where the shots landed.

Amelia sat on a nearby chair someone had managed to find, likely from the nearby manager's office. She sat with her head in her hands, and Petals stood near to her, taking notes.

Bob helped him hop and hobble over to his superior, then helped ease him down onto a wooden crate before heading off to help the others contain and collect evidence.

"Nice of you to join us," Amelia sounded as snide as she did when leaving The Ruby Lounge.

Petals came to his defense before Joe could start barking back. "He's bleeding."

Amelia's head snapped up and she turned to eyeball him with a furrowed brow. A great many thoughts flowed through his mind. He wasn't certain as to whether he should be glad that she was concerned for his well-being or angry for the earlier punch. He eventually settled on spiteful indifference. "What happened to Travok?"

Petals snapped his head back around to Joe and quickly turned his expression of surprise to one of prideful glee. "Well deduced, my boy!" He then declared in a flat tone, "He's dead."

Amelia didn't seem at all surprised by the fact, as she had been the one to watch the dark dwarf get shot. At least, that was what he had presumed had happened.

He focused his attention on Amelia. "It wasn't Eagle Eyes; did you recognize who it was?"

Petals again snapped his head back to Joe. "What do you mean?"

He recounted his doubts and comparisons from the night before. "He didn't move the same, and while I couldn't see his eyes, I'm almost certain they weren't golden. A gut feeling, I guess you could say."

Amelia confirmed. "I saw his eyes, and they weren't golden. They're likely trying to frame Eagle Eyes."

No… this was an act of desperation. Travok knew something.

The trickster gnome approached Joe, placed a hand on his leg, and looked to the blood-stained bandaging while raising an eyebrow. "You'll likely get a scar from this one as well."

Yay for me.

He lowered his voice so that only Joe could hear, "Speak privately with Amelia. You both have pieces to the puzzle."

Joe didn't dare make any obvious moves and simply flicked his eyes over to glance at the frosty woman. She was frowning at him as Petals examined his wound.

Did you tell her the same?

Petals subtly responded, "Of course, if you give our dear doctor the time of day, he might be able to patch you up with no scars at all."

I take it back; your mind reading can be useful.

Petals grinned and smacked him on the thigh, causing Joe to flinch and scream as the pain fired through his leg.

Chapter 19

Petals ordered Joe and Amelia back to the precinct. She needed to restock on ammunition and Joe needed to see the doctor to get patched up. They would both also have a great many reports to complete and submit.

Joe wondered and salivated over the thought of the Blue Whiskey Grill giving out another free meal for being shot a second time but doubted it.

"What are you grinning about?" Detective Iceheart was glaring at him with her arms crossed. The two of them had been sent back to the precinct in a gnome cart and were bouncing along when Joe had the thought of stuffing himself with a hearty meal.

He frowned, remembering what it was he was supposed to be doing. "I was thinking of food, but that has to wait."

"You think?"

Joe shot her a hot glare back in turn. Not wanting to get snippy or testy with her, he decided to point to his ear, then the driver.

Her scowl eased, slightly. With a wave of her crystal-like wand, she created a pane of clear air between them and the driver; it reminded him of ice with its mirror-like sheen. "Now, start talking."

As much as he approved of her quick spell-work, he couldn't help but feel it wasn't enough. "What about the windows? Aren't you going to bubble us?"

She rolled her eyes and made a frustrated growling noise in her throat. "To what end? The driver can't hear us, and the windows are shut!"

"Someone might be trying to listen in on us, find out how much we know."

"WHO?" She was growing less and less patient with him.

He didn't want to say it aloud, but he felt there was no other choice. Joe lowered his voice and brought her in on his suspicions: "A mole in the precinct."

She sat for a long minute, staring at him with her arms still raised in their exaggerated gesture of confusion from the earlier question she yelled. Her eyes eventually darted away from his as she stared off at nothing in particular and absorbed the words that Joe had dealt her.

Her brow furrowed as she glared at him again. "That's a serious accusation to level against another officer."

Joe threw up his hands to deflect. "No, I didn't say an officer. This person could be anyone in the precinct with access to our records. It could just as easily be an archivist or receptionist."

She looked all the more confused. "Records?"

He nodded and proceeded to walk her through the evidence he and Petals had gathered and the theory they had formulated. "That first night where I was shot, they were either guided by the hand of fate, or they had someone on the inside pull my record from the precinct. I'm betting odds on records. How else would they have been able to set up for that shot in such a limited amount of time?"

Amelia sat in silence for a moment before she lifted her wand and spun the tip about her head. Joe felt a chill run down his spine as all the glass panes in the back of the cart suddenly frosted over. Amelia looked to him, "We're covered now. Keep talking. We have another few minutes before we reach the station."

Joe nodded in appreciation, then first apologized for his behavior in The Ruby Lounge and explained his trust in the werebear due to the sudden appearance of Thumbs the fairy.

"Where did you learn all of this about fairies?"

He didn't feel like talking about it and waved it off. "Another time. Did Travok say anything to you before he died? What direction was he heading?"

Amelia shook her head and focused on the topic at hand. "Right, Travok was heading toward me, toward The Ruby Lounge. I don't think he expected to see me, as he seemed to jump at the sight of me. That was when he jerked and fell over. Only reason I knew it was a bullet is because it passed through him and hit the brick to the right of me." She angrily scowled. "I managed to take cover in the alley before that prick took a shot at me."

Joe cursed at the Fates and slumped back in the seat.

Amelia put her hand on his shoulder. "He did say something though."

He jolted back to sitting upright and thumped the top of his head on the short roof of the gnome cart. "What did he say?"

She slowly shook her head in thought. "It was hard to make out between coughing up blood, but it sounded like he said 'Nathaniel Grimthorn'. Wasn't that one of the victims–"

Joe felt a bell ring through his mind at the mention. "Yes! Nathaniel Grimthorn was one of the nine victims of the Noble Killings. I remember reading over the case file several times. I tried desperately to spot anything that the detectives had missed, like some naïve rookie."

She chortled, "You're still a naïve rookie."

Ha ha ha, ice queen.

After shooting her a momentary spiteful glare, he returned his thoughts to the case at hand. "I'm starting to think that the golden eyes from then and Eagle Eyes of today aren't related."

"Or," she raised a finger as she gathered her thoughts, "today's shooter and the one that hit your arm the other night are one and the same."

Fireballs! That puts a twist on things.

He couldn't help but agree with her assessment. "You're right. The Noble Killings were flawlessly executed. The detectives working those cases had nothing to work on. Whoever shot me that night left a glaringly obvious set of footprints, and the shooter of today was just as sloppy."

They reached the precinct, and the two of them looked to one another in silent understanding. "We talk to Petals about this and only him. He was the one that brought forth the possibility of a mole in the precinct."

Amelia scrunched her nose and looked to him. "How are we going to write up our reports?"

Double fireballs!

"First, leave out this entire conversation."

She raised a disapproving eyebrow, "Obviously."

"Second, don't mention Nathaniel Grimthorn. You weren't entirely certain you heard it, and the less they think we're on to them, the better." She took a moment to think about that one before accepting and breaking the silence spell covering the windows.

Sparkles of glittering snow fell from the glass windows and the barrier separating them from the driver. She opened her side's door and stepped out, leaving the door open for Joe.

Once he made it to the curb, he drew his wand and released it into a staff, using it for balance as he hobbled toward the precinct's steps. He then spoke normally, as though they'd been having a regular conversation the entire ride over. "I'll head to the doc first, you start on your report and then we'll switch; you restock on ammunition, and I'll write up mine. We'll double check each other's for errors or any notes the other might have missed before we submit. Sound good?"

She played the part well and scowled at him. "Just because I'm a woman, you suddenly think you can give me orders there, rook?" She balled up her fist at her side.

He found himself pulling back and flinching slightly. "All right! I'm sorry!" Her earlier hook had caught him off guard and was well-thrown.

She smirked, then delightedly fixed her hat and hair before heading up the stairs. "That's better."

Great job, nobody could possibly believe we get along...

~~

Joe hopped up onto the metal examining table and turned to the left to let his right leg dangle freely.

The ebony-haired doctor lowered his spectacles down his nose and peered up at Joe over top of them, then shook his head. "I'm not working around your trousers young man. Off with them." He gestured with his hands when he said "off with them."

He wasn't exactly comfortable with examinations, especially with recently discovering the fact that he was a sorcerer, not a wizard. Not that he had anatomically changed since the discovery, but the vulnerability made him uneasy. "Oh, all right."

No sooner had he unbuckled, unbuttoned, and dropped his trousers did the door to the doctor's office suddenly swing open.

Joe barked a panicked scream as Amelia marched in and used one hand to push him over onto the examining table, then swiped his trousers from the floor. "Don't worry, rook. I'll have these mended and cleaned of blood in no time." She winked at him and headed out the door with his only pair of pants.

He barely had time to object or even sputter a curse before she was gone, while he was busy fumbling and trying to cover his boxers.

The doctor did nothing to stop her or even yell at her after her entry. The man simply lifted his hands and said, "Sorry, kiddo, I don't mess with wizards."

"Seriously!"

The thin and frail-looking man simply sighed in exasperation and shrugged his shoulders. "What would you have me do? There's already a sign on my door that says 'knock before entering'."

He adjusted his spectacles and ripped off the crusted layer of searing powder that had formed over the wound on Joe's leg. The immediate and sudden shock nearly caused him to pass out. "Besides, you weren't the first and won't be the last to be pants-snatched in this precinct with a trickster gnome as senior detective."

Joe's head swam as he dropped back onto the examining table, and the doctor probed the wound with his finger. Cold sweats broke out over him as the pain and exhaustion was so overwhelming that he couldn't even bring himself to scream or use words.

Blackness took him for a brief moment. The irritating and alarming smell of salts brought him to his senses, and he flailed his arms about as he jolted upright. He immediately regretted the action as his head began spinning. "Ugh, doc, I need to eat something, or I'll pass out."

The gaunt man slapped something heavy and thick down upon the examination table.

Joe dared to open one eye and look down upon the mysterious meal. Something had been given to him wrapped in cloth. "What is that?"

The doctor crinkled his nose and frowned as he glanced at it while filling out notes in Joe's medical file.

"That is something I could never imagine to stomach; it's a military ration."

Ooo!

He reached down and gladly picked up the thick, weighty slab of cured food. He never really learned exactly what was put into the ration, but it had kept him alive for a year and a half on the battlefield while tending to the barriers. He unceremoniously un-wrapped the cloth bundle and took a hearty bite out of the dark brown solid mass.

The ration was savory, sweet, salty, and chewy. The brick was so dense that he figured it would take him a solid three minutes just to finish the first bite. Each swallow felt like a lead weight dropped into his gut, and it started warming him immediately.

Memories of the warfront rushed back to him. Days of sitting beneath a tree with his commander or some of the other boys in his unit. The military ration was one of the few good memories he had from his days as a Green Coat. Joe sighed heavily and melted into the warmth that filled him again.

"Ugh!"

Joe opened one eye and looked to the doctor.

The doctor gaped at him with sheer repulsion and horror. "You actually enjoy those things?"

He merely shrugged and nodded while taking another big bite from the solid brick of... something.

"Do you have any idea what's—"

Joe shot up a hand and waved his finger at the man. "Mm-mm!" He didn't want to know; he never wanted to know. So long as it tasted like it did all those years ago and got him back on his feet, he didn't care.

Looking to his leg, he noted the doctor's work. Solid bandaging had been wrapped around his leg. Kicking his leg out from the examination table told him that the painkillers, whatever they were, had kicked in already.

Wonderful!

The door swung open once again, and Joe jumped in surprise as his trousers struck him in the face. "Congrats, rook. I salvaged your–"

Joe pulled his trousers from his face and swallowed before sticking the weighty bar of food into his mouth to hold it while he examined his trousers.

"What are you eating?"

Joe looked to Amelia to find her just as horrifically repulsed, if not more so, than the doctor. She was covering her mouth and pinching her nose.

He dropped his trousers to the table and took the solid slab from his mouth. "Ration," he said, then took another bite.

She turned her eyes away, shivered, and quickly retreated through the door while closing it. "No wonder you don't have a woman."

Thanks for the dating advice, Ms. Iceheart!

He merely sneered in mock appreciation and went back to examining the repair job. Joe nearly spat out the full mouthful when he spotted the giant patch of dancing pink ducklings on white satin. His glare was quickly fired back at the closed door.

Ohhhhh, I'm gonna get you for this.

Doctor Broom chuckled heartily and patted Joe on the knee. "Get yourself some rest and another full meal, and you'll be good by tomorrow morning. That means put your feet up and rest. I'd say there's a good chance you'll get away without any scarring."

Joe looked to his watch and noted it was getting close to the end of the day. If he spent the rest of his shift on reports, he could head home and be there in time for dinner.

He eased himself off the table and looked to the small mess of bloodied cloths and bandaging, then to the doc. After swallowing the last mouthful, he asked, "Was it really that bad?"

"No," he turned back around, casually shaking his head, then pointed to Joe's leg. "Minimize the amount of walking you do, though; don't want the work I did to come undone."

He tested the doctor's work and put some weight on the foot. It pinched slightly, but it didn't seem to hurt too much. Nodding, Joe went about balancing himself and pulling on his trousers and boots. "Thanks, doc. You've patched me up more in these past three days than my first three months as a Blue Coat."

The doctor set down his stylus and spun in his chair to look up at Joe. "In the years that I've worked for this precinct, your first three days as detective have been some of the most exciting first few days of any rookie I've seen." He shrugged to tell Joe to take the information however he wished, then turned back to his paperwork.

Joe didn't quite hear any of what was said, as he was too busy glaring at the patch on his leg. "Uh-huh." He took another big bite of his ration and chewed on it as he waved goodbye to the doc and headed back to his desk, one limping step at a time. Each set of stairs he approached became the subject of his intense hatred and loathing, but there was little that could be done about it. He simply hopped his way up on one foot.

By the time he'd reached the top step and the bullpen, he was nearly gassed and ready for bed. He rolled over onto his back upon reaching the top step and lay there for a minute with his eyes shut while catching his breath.

"Detective Runewall." The floor-rumbling voice of his captain woke him from what he could only hope was a brief nap. Joe popped open his eyes, then grunted as he heaved himself to roll over, pushed himself to his feet, and stood at attention while leaning on his staff for support. "Yes, Captain?"

"You can imagine my confusion when I suddenly heard the mating call of the great growling boar coming from my bullpen."

Oh, fireballs, I was snoring!

"Greater yet was my confusion when I spotted one of my newest detectives practicing said mating call while lying upon the floor." The grand and imposing posture of the dragon kin standing before him remained unwavering as he turned to look out over the precinct proper below. "I take it you're a hunting man?"

"Uh... No, sir."

"No?" The dark-scaled captain turned his horned head to glare down upon Joe, and he could feel the intimidation magic that slapped him along with that gaze.

"I mean... yes, sir... practicing for... hunting season."

The oppressive and will-destroying magic released and vanished as quickly as it had appeared. "I see. I suggest you reserve such practice for your off hours and return to your regular duties. Am I understood?" The captain turned and stood facing his office, awaiting Joe's reply.

He wavered where he stood, then swallowed before answering, "Yes, sir!"

"Good. Dismissed."

Joe dipped and nearly nose-dived into the floorboards as he scooped up the remnants of his ration, stuck it into his mouth, and hobbled to his desk in the corner.

The captain slowly lumbered back to his office, having left Joe with what he believed to be a very thinly veiled warning.

I can make it... just a few reports to fill, and then home to bed.

"And, detective?"

Joe rounded on the spot and nearly threw himself to the floor from the dizziness of having done so. "Yes, Captain?"

"Nice patch." If he'd never seen a dragon kin smile before, he then knew what it looked like — toothy and frightening.

Amelia snorted while she tried desperately to stifle her laughing in the corner.

I SHALL HAVE VENGEANCE, WOMAN!

Chapter 20

Filling out reports while exhausted proved to be problematic. His first draft was full of errors and mistakes. Amelia even went so far as to ask him whether he wanted her to type it up for him. Naturally, he refused. Joe had just as much to prove as she did.

She walked away and left him to his own devices. It took him an hour longer than he intended, but he managed to produce a legible and detailed report of the day's events.

Captain Bolt scanned over the documents at an aggravatingly slow rate, but he eventually accepted and gave the report his stamp of approval. Once he filed, he was free to head home. A glance at his watch suggested he might even make it in time for dinner.

Gods, please let it be palatable.

Ms. Iceheart followed him out the front doors of the precinct and silently waved to him before turning to leave the opposite direction. A brief moment of concern bubbled to the surface, only for it to quickly vanish as he noted a detective from the night shift standing by the corner. He waited for Amelia, then turned to walk her home.

Joe turned on the spot only to jump then crumple to the ground while clutching his chest. William Windwalker had been standing behind him.

"Evenin', mate! Headin' home for dinnah?" William leaned over Joe and offered a hand to help him up.

I still hate you.

"Next time, call out my name, and don't just creep up on me, okay?" He took the offered hand, hauled himself to his feet, and leaned heavily on his staff.

"Gotcha!" William clapped Joe on the back, nearly sending him over to land on his face. The man looked down at Joe's trousers and beamed. "Beauty patchwork!"

He let out a long and deep sigh. "Just get me home, William. I'm tired, injured, and hungry."

The man beamed and stood proud as he pointed to a waiting gnome cart. "No worries, mate! I'll have you home in no time."

Okay, I hate you slightly less right now.

The ride only took a minute or two, then William was kind enough to help him out of the cramped cab and up the steps to the front door of the brownstone.

Ms. Bellcreaux opened the door before Joe could even reach into his pocket for his keys. She stood as straight as ever and eyed him up and down once before commenting, "You're late." She then looked at his trousers. "And–"

He interrupted her, "And you want me to take off my pants?" Foolishly, he believed that she thought he had attempted to fix them and failed miserably, and she wanted to correct his mistake to prove to him how useless he was.

Those thoughts were clearly not on her mind, as he had forgotten about the awkwardness from much earlier in the day; his ill-chosen words merely reignited that awkwardness.

Never before had he seen such color liven her face. Her eyes widened and a furious anger looked to be boiling up inside of her. She made an irritated sound in her throat and swung the door as violently as she could, slamming it in his face. He could hear her stomping in her heels away from the door in a mad flourish.

"Oi!" William clapped him upside the back of the head, causing his forehead to bounce off the door. "Not the way to talk to a lady, mate!"

"Ow! What?" Joe shook his head from the impact and from confusion. It was only after repeating the words in his head that he finally realized what he had said and done.

Wait… oh… ohhh nooo…

Joe slapped his free hand to his face and groaned. "I meant for her to fix them… I should have added 'for you to fix them'."

"Ohhhh… that's what you meant… yeah, you should have said that, mate."

He lifted his hand and knocked on the door, then began scrubbing his face with his hand, hoping to wipe away the embarrassment. There was nothing. He dared to knock again. After a few moments, he heard heavier footfalls and the door swung open.

"Joseph?" George stood in the doorway, filling it with his rotund frame. He stood there with a perplexed look upon his face. "The door was unlocked. Why didn't you just walk in?"

Joe waved off the question and simply turned and thanked William for the escort. The night shift detective saluted happily and chuckled as he headed on down the steps, then vanished as quickly as a puff of smoke in a high wind.

"Blimey!" George took another step out the door and squinted. "Where'd he go?"

He waved off that question as well. "Is there any food left? I'm starving."

George turned on the spot and looked around inside. "Where did Ms. Bellcreaux go?"

"George!"

The large man turned on the spot and looked over his shoulder with his eyebrows raised.

"Food?"

"Right!" George headed inside and waved Joe in. "Chowder and bread tonight to help fight off the rainy weather." Like he had predicted, the rain still hadn't quit.

Joe took small steps on his way into the dining room, then sat himself where he had that morning as Dodge chatted Hamlin's ear off about whatever it was that caught his fancy for the moment.

Thankfully, there was still a fair amount of chowder left in the pot and half a loaf of bread.

The lot of them greeted him as they usually did and inquired as to his sudden departure earlier in the day. He went about dishing up a hearty helping of chowder as he answered. "Something you said about black market doctors and surgeries gave me a thought about a case I'm working on."

"Really? Blimey." George gently tapped Dodge on the arm. "Here that, good man? Helped a detective with his case!"

That's not even close to what I said.

Joe was about to interject, then decided against it, as it would require him to divulge too much info about an ongoing case. Instead, he opted to fill his gullet.

It was a bit under-seasoned, but the taters and carrots were on point, and the clams were fresh and cooked properly. The bread was hard as a brick, but the remnant chowder helped to soften it up. Overall, it filled him, and that was all it needed to do.

Once he was finished, he felt as though he might pass out where he sat. Ms. Bellcreaux didn't appear to be anywhere. Though, he didn't quite blame her for it. He felt bad for what he said, and he wished to apologize and explain, but maybe he could let it wait until the morning when she wasn't quite as angry about it.

"George?"

"Yes, Joseph?" The chair creaked as he turned and shifted in it.

"Mind giving me a hand up the steps?" He grabbed his staff from the corner and used it to gently tap the patch on his leg.

"Blimey, what's that nonsense about?"

Joe didn't want to say too much, so he simply opted for the generic answer, "I was injured on duty."

The men all seemed to jump in their seats and raised their eyebrows in genuine concern.

"What now?"

"How did that happen?"

"Injured? I hope you get compensated for such things!"

Joe waved off all their comments. "It's nothing, it's nothing. I've already been patched up, and there won't even be a scratch by morning. I'm just a bit stiff and I don't want to undo the doctor's good work."

That seemed to deflate the huff from the lot of them, as they all went back to grumbling and nodding and clearing their throats.

"All right then, you take the lead."

Joe nodded and groaned as he pushed himself up from his seat. He took a moment to stretch his leg out and wiggle his foot about. The patchwork still felt a little pinched and tight on the side of his thigh, but there didn't seem to be any pain that followed.

His staff took the brunt of his weight as he hobbled his way to the stairs. Looking back, he instructed George to simply follow him up the steps and make sure he didn't teeter backwards.

The large man wiggled his mustache and cleared his throat before nodding and putting his hands out in front of him in preparation to stop Joe from falling back.

He severely doubted the man had done any physical work his entire life, and the baby-soft fat fingers on his hands attested to that possibility. Joe thought then that young Hamlin would probably have been a better choice.

Too late to change his mind, Joe made his way up the steps one hop at a time. The chowder sloshing in his belly made it a bit of a nauseating affair, but he managed to make it in one piece.

He bid George and the others, watching from the base of the stairs, a good night and good sleep. He headed to his door at the end and pulled out his key. It was when he was looking at his keys and eyeing the doorknob that he noticed a slip of paper poking out from under his door.

Joe quickly unlocked the door and opened it wide. There – sitting on the threshold on the floor of his room – was a letter sealed with red wax. Red wax was only ever used on documents of utter importance requiring immediate attention.

He hobbled into his room, shut the door, then leaned against it to balance himself as he miniaturized his staff into a wand and used the slightest of will and power to cause the letter to float up from off the ground and into his open hand.

Snatching the letter, he turned and dropped onto his bed, bouncing upon it as he flicked his wand at the door. The lock flicked and Joe was left in the quiet privacy of his room to examine the letter he held in his hand.

His name and address had been posted on the front of the letter in a polished looping script. There was no postage. That made him wonder whether it had been hand-delivered and left with Ms. Bellcreaux.

If he hadn't agitated her earlier, she probably would have told him. Ignoring that problem for the moment, he returned to examining the letter and looked to the wax stamp.

The wax had been pressed with an odd stamp that he was unfamiliar with. It looked to be some form of rune and circle seal. A brief partitioning of his mind informed him that it was designed to be opened by Joe and only Joe. If any other had attempted to snap the wax seal, they would have caused the letter to self-ignite to protect what had been written.

He couldn't imagine anyone sending him such an archaic method of communication but figured there had to be a reason for it. Taking the chance, Joe held the seal in both his hands and bent it. The wax snapped and released the magic within. There was a brief flourish of red light that swirled around his hands, then it all vanished as quickly as it emerged.

So far, so good.

He folded open the parchment and looked to the penmanship that began appearing within.

Mr. Runewall,

Your visit was most pleasant this afternoon. I felt a sense of comradery as we conversed. In an effort to keep our common streets safe from violence and theft, I feel it is necessary that we speak once more. I may have information crucial to your case.

Tomorrow night at midnight, meet me at the abandoned warehouse of the most recent incident. I ask that you come alone and make sure you're not followed. I'd like not to face any retaliatory offenses.

Your acquaintance,
Gino Marcano

Joe read the letter a second time and committed it to memory. He then gripped the broken wax seal and triggered the spell built into it. The paper suddenly flashed and vanished in a red flare of fire. So efficient was the spell that not an ounce of ash or wax remained.

Despite the warning, he felt it necessary to inform Petals of the letter he'd received. It was always possible that he was running into a trap, especially since he was being called to an abandoned warehouse.

Not wanting to waste any more time, Joe went about his nightly routine of preparing for bed. He set the partition in his mind, and he started moving about his little room in a practiced fashion. He changed into his night cap and pajamas, set out clothes for the morning, and placed his day's clothes in the hamper.

All the while he hobbled and moved about, he thought about the letter. He contemplated whether the abandoned warehouse was the trap he feared it to be, but he needed to reason it out to be sure. The mention of retaliation suggested that it wasn't. If Joe was spotted entering The Ruby Lounge and the suspects in question were pursued, they'd likely assume the information that lead to their pursuit came from the great big werebear.

There was no telling how connected the culprits were, or what sort of retaliation might result. Similarly, if a great lumbering werebear was spotted entering the precinct, the same problem arose.

That then brought him to the question of utilizing the crystalline network. Surely a direct line would be far more secure and discreet.

The mole. Can't risk the mole finding out.

Joe determined that any form of direct communication between Mr. Marcano and the precinct was simply too risky. As much as he disliked the idea of utilizing cloak and dagger spy craft, it appeared to be the safest means for the time being.

He would discuss it with Petals in the morning, and they would determine the safest course of action.

Joe released his mind from the partition and examined his room for any missed chores. Once he determined that there was nothing left to do, he set to turning in for the night.

He flicked off the light switch and plunged the room into calming darkness. Crawling into bed, he utilized the partition in his mind to set an alarm and willed himself into a deep and restful sleep.

Chapter 21

It was a far brighter morning than it had been the past few days. Rays of sunlight pierced through the cracks of his boarded-up window, and no strangers were in his room. On top of those small victories, his leg looked to be as good as new. It felt a little stiff, but he could bend and flex it without any issues. Removing the bandaging revealed that the skin had healed over nicely, and there was nothing to suggest any injury besides a fresh patch of hairless skin.

Joe went about his morning routine and readied himself for the morning. All the while, he tried to fathom what words he could provide to his landlady so that she might understand his intentions the evening before.

As soon as he opened his door, he was a little surprised to find Ms. Bellcreaux standing with her hand raised. She looked as though she were about to knock.

She kept her stony disposition and didn't even blink as she lowered her hand and clasped her other while staring him down.

Wanting to get off on the right foot for once, Joe brought his patched trousers up and opened his mouth to speak when she swiftly snatched them from his hands.

"I will have them ready by dinner." She turned and marched off to head down the stairs to serve breakfast for the others.

Joe was left standing in the doorway of his room with his mouth slightly agape. He hadn't the chance to say anything. Letting out a sigh of frustration, he simply muttered "Fireballs" under his breath before heading down for his morning meal.

As before, George, Dodge, and Hamlin were already seated and stuffing their faces while gossiping about the latest news. They all turned as Joe approached and greeted him with the summary "Morning" before turning back to their conversations.

It wasn't until Joe sat down that George quickly turned his head back around. "Joseph, did you walk down the stairs unimpeded?"

He nodded and shrugged. "Yes, of course. I told you I would be good by morning."

The portly man beamed and clapped his hands. "Splendid! That medicine is absolutely splendid. The marvels of today's medicines, I tell you!"

Dodge piped up while holding aloft a sheet of the *Stormbay Nautical*. "Not good enough for that Blackfellow!"

Hamlin growled in correction, "Blackfinger."

"Right-right, him."

Joe, stricken by a bout of curiosity, gestured for the paper as he shoveled egg into his mouth. "May I?"

Dodge handed it down to George and George to Joe. He thanked them and quickly held it aloft in one hand so that he might read it while using the other to eat.

The front page featured a grand article titled "Murder on the Diamond Streets!" Blackfinger was the only name mentioned, as he had been the victim. Amelia, Joe, and Petals were only described as 'detectives on scene'. While he wished he'd been given a bit more credit, it was likely for the best that the news didn't glorify the officers for doing their jobs. The last thing any precinct needed was an officer with a tragic hero complex.

He finished reading the article in short order, as he had been present and knew far more than the article could provide. Joe returned the paper to Dodge via George and thanked him for the read. The man barely seemed to notice, as his focus and drive to continue talking had superseded any possible need to wait for Joe to finish reading. They'd moved on from medicine and murder to politics and power.

Joe had his mind stuck inside the letter he'd received. It still bothered him, but there was little else he could do until he spoke with Petals about it. He finished his plate by swiping up whatever was left with his toast, and then summarily devoured it as the partition in his mind began chiming that he would need to leave soon. He cleaned his plate and gulped down his tea before piling all his dishes and bidding the gentleman a good day.

They summarily waved him off with the same short departure that seemed to be common amongst men. "Good day."

Joe picked up his staff, compressed it into a wand, and stuck it into his vest pocket. He walked over and opened the front door, only to be greeted by a bag-eyed William leaning against the railing to the steps. "Mornin', mate." The detective yawned and stretched before crossing his arms again.

Joe greeted him in turn and stepped to exit the building when William halted him.

"Wait… somethin' I was supposed to tell you." The man looked as though he genuinely couldn't remember. He even shut his eyes and murmured something. He eventually popped open his eyes and smiled half-heartedly. "Right, Petals said you'll need a spare change of clothes. Manhunt in the storm tunnels today, mate."

Oh, fun.

Joe frowned, sighed, and headed back up to his room to grab a change of clothes. He quickly returned after locking up and headed out the front door with his escort shuffling in tow.

~~

He managed to make it to work with a few minutes to spare. With the time, he stored his spare clothes in one of the deeper drawers of his desk. He even took the time to lock it with a set of complex and interconnected layers of barriers. Nobody was going to tamper with his spare clothes. Or so he hoped nobody would. It was more than possible that Petals could just snap his fingers and take them.

Once he was finished locking those away, he turned his attention to his superior. He was about to throw a mental message the short man's way when the captain's door opened. The massive dragon kin thundered in his low rumbling way, "Gather 'round."

Joe came to attention as the others in the bullpen did. Amelia stepped up to his right while Petals hopped up to his left.

The electric gaze of the captain fell on Joe. "Well enough for some work today, Detective Runewall?"

Joe nodded in the affirmative. "Yes, sir, good as new."

"Good to hear." He turned his attention to the rest of the officers. "We have been given special permission by the city to enter the storm tunnels now that the rain has abated and the water levels have dropped." The massive dragon kin pointed to the stairs. "We have also been given guides to help us navigate."

Joe went up a bit on his toes to peer over the heads and hats of his colleagues to note a handful of men in leather overalls, boots, and maintenance hats standing off to the side.

"Each pair of detectives will be given a guide to help them through the sewers." Captain Bolt turned and touched a finger to a large roll of paper.

The partition in his mind alerted him to the fact that magic was at play. It was the first time he'd ever seen the captain do anything but intimidate. There was very little to be registered, but he picked up on it.

A single static pop transferred from the dragon kin's clawed finger into the roll. It immediately snapped to attention and unfurled vertically to create a perfectly flat wall map. The fact that the map didn't immediately ignite into flames was by far the most impressive part of the magical display.

He pointed to several spots on the map and turned back to the bullpen. "We will be entering at multiple intersections and sweeping the storm tunnels in a coordinated effort to flush out whomever may be hiding within them."

Joe had several thoughts that immediately came to mind but figured it best to ask them of the city maintenance crew, as they would likely know better than the captain would.

"Are there any questions?"

Nobody raised any concerns. Everyone knew who and what they were after.

"Good. Get to work, detectives."

Joe turned to Petals only to find that little man wasn't there.

Fireballs! Where did he go?

Amelia jabbed him in the ribs, causing Joe to jump slightly. "Let's get going, rook. I want to get this over with."

"I– just– wait!" Joe spun on the spot, turned his head about, and went up on his toes to see if he could see over the dispersing crowd. "I need to talk to Petals first!"

"Can't it wait?"

"No, it's rather urgent." Joe frustratingly searched about as the detectives met with their corresponding city worker and started heading down the steps. "Where is he?"

"Where's who?"

Joe barked and jumped at the pitched voice had come from behind him. "STOP DOING THAT!"

Petals grinned triumphantly. "All to keep you on your toes, my boy."

"I need to speak with you, urgently."

The little gnome's eyebrows shot up in curiosity. "Oh? Out with it then."

"Privately?" Joe gestured pleadingly.

I received a letter from Gino Marcano.

He willed his thought as hard as he could throw it at the little man.

Petals frowned in thought. "Ah." He looked about them and nodded before lowering his voice. "We'll discuss your payroll issue tonight over supper."

Nice cover.

Joe let out a deep shoulder-sagging sigh and thanked him.

The little man grinned broadly and gestured over to the city workers. "Best get to it then."

Right.

Joe turned and made his way over to Amelia and the only remaining city worker and introduced himself.

The leather-faced old man looked at Joe's outstretched hand, then looked back up and said, "People call me Bill." His voice was dull and lifeless, and his face looked unemotional.

Joe glanced at his own hand, looked at the man, then lowered his hand. "All right, Bill–"

"My name's not Bill, it's Frank." The man continued to speak in his lifeless monotone way.

"I– all right… why did you tell us people call you Bill?"

"'Cause that's what people call me."

Joe let out a deep sigh and started over. "All right, Frank—"

"You can call me Bill."

A growing need to strangle the man bubbled to the surface. He asked through slightly gritted teeth, "Then why did you tell me your name was Frank?"

"Just wanted to make sure there was no confusion. People seem to get confused easily with my name."

Oh, I bet they do, Frank.

Amelia piped in, "How about you lead us to our storm tunnel entrance, Bill."

The monotone man gave the smallest of shrugs. "Okay." He turned and shuffled his way to the stairs.

Joe shut his eyes and let out a deep breath to calm himself. He shook his head before following Amelia as she followed their guide.

~~

The sun beat down on the three of them; it left the air around them muggy and thick. It came with the territory of living in a seaside city. Heavy storms were followed by muggy days while the rainwater evaporated. The sun could be a bit merciless even in the Spring.

Bill, or Frank, knelt over a storm grate with his keys in hand. Amelia and Joe stood at the ready with their staffs. They had made their way from the precinct to the back of Billburn's Brass and Gold. They hadn't requested the spot; they had just been fated that their guide had been assigned to it.

Having grown up in an orphanage, Joe had been taught that luck was how a poor man understood the will of the Fates. His involvement from day one with the jewelry store had been the work of the Fates.

Amelia voiced her own opinions, "Did you pay the man off?"

Joe scowled at her. "With what, my pocket lint?"

She scrunched her nose slightly and shrugged. "You have a point."

The storm-grate swung up and opened with little to no noise and great ease. The old city worker watched it open, then tested it by lifting and shutting the grate several times. "Huh."

"Freshly oiled hinges." Joe had already noted that several days ago.

Bill shrugged, un-wavered by the oddity. "Guess so." He put his hands on either side of the opening and lowered himself into the dark tunnel below.

Joe and Amelia both peered in as he went down, then looked to each other with similar frowns of disgust.

He took it upon himself to make a quick wisecrack, "Ladies first?" while gesturing to the darkness between them.

Joe went first. Unfortunately, the tunnel wasn't very tall, and he was stuck in a hunched posture as they waded through the lazy stream of refuse. It smelled of rotten foliage and gods knew what else.

Amelia took up the rear as Bill led. The man's maintenance helmet came equipped with a miniature lantern light that he had flicked on to light the way ahead.

A quick glance back revealed that Amelia had tied a handkerchief around her face and was breathing freely. Joe frowned back at her as he pinched his nose and covered his mouth with his hand.

Fireballs, woman! Couldn't have given me that suggestion?

She'd clearly been in some sort of life-lesson scenario that prompted her to take along a handkerchief. It was likely scented as well. He couldn't tell, but he was almost certain she was smiling smugly again.

Joe whipped his wizard's handkerchief from his pocket and growled as he noted that it was too small to wrap around his head. He quickly stuffed it back into his pocket, then partitioned his mind to ignore the smell. It would only work for so long and only so well, but it muffled enough of it to be bearable.

Bill didn't say much of anything the entire drudge through the tunnel except to point out what access hatch they were traversing under or what street intersection they passed. He pointed out other entrances and noted how well kept and greased the hinges were.

"Is it possible that one of the other workers did this?"

The leathery old man continued wading along and shook his head, shaking the beam of light that came from his helmet. "Nope."

Joe waited several moments for an explanation before asking, "Why not?"

"Only grease them when they stick. Otherwise it's a waste of grease."

Amelia piped up from the rear, "Waste of grease?"

Bill grunted in what Joe could only assume was his form of a chuckle. "City budget, city grease."

"Right." She then kicked something off the end of her boot and watched in disgust as it hit the curved tunnel wall.

He kept his sanity by simply not looking at his feet, despite whatever it was that hit his leg or tugged on his foot.

The lot of them kept trudging through the storm tunnel for what felt like hours as they made their way from one intersection to the next, then backtracked and zig-zagged. He'd sworn they'd passed the same tunnel entrance a dozen times before he finally asked, "What are we looking for down here? There's no possible way of finding tracks or evidence, it would all be washed away by now."

Bill paused and turned to tell him, "We're looking for false walls."

Amelia peered around Joe to ask at the same time as he did.

"What?"
"What?"

Joe looked back at Amelia, and she glanced at him as well. Apparently neither of them had heard of such a thing existing in a storm tunnel.

"Yep, false walls." He kept walking as though it didn't need any explanation.

Joe hurried to catch up to the man and Amelia followed while dodging and avoiding whatever was floating about. "Wait! What do you mean 'false walls'?"

Bill shrugged. "False walls," he repeated, then continued shuffling through the foul water.

Amelia made an attempt while speaking around Joe, "We're asking for you to explain what you call a false wall. Shouldn't these tunnels be solid to contain the storm runoff?"

The leathery city worker shrugged again. "False walls can be solid. They're still walls." He didn't even break stride.

Joe felt a great struggle rising within him whether to strangle the man. "What's behind a false wall?"

"Hideout. Vermin kind den. Stuff." Each suggested answer was punctuated with a small shrug.

He couldn't help but rub his face with his hand and mumble over his shoulder to Amelia, "Getting answers from him is like visiting a dwarven tooth doctor. You walk away in greater pain than when you first visited."

She snorted and smacked him on the back.

The smack caused him to jump slightly and smash the top of his skull on the roof of the tunnel. Joe groaned and gripped his head while squatting in the slimy waters as the teary-eyed pain fired down from the top of his head to his toes. "HAAA!"

Bill continued to shuffle on without even glancing back. "Watch your head."

Ms. Iceheart patted him on the back and turned away to stifle her giggles.

A sudden static filled the air, then it was cut by the sound of chatter. "Hey, Bill?" The voice was muffled and echoed through the tunnel, making it hard to make out.

Joe took off his hat to vigorously rub the top of his head and watched as the old city worker pulled a variant of the crystalline network box from his leather trousers.

Bill gripped a metal ball near the top of the little wooden box and pulled it up, extending it like a retractable antenna. He pressed a button on the side of the box and spoke into the metal mesh, "Hey?"

Amelia and Joe exchanged a look before turning back to watch. He'd never known that any department other than enforcement had mobile network boxes.

The muffled voice came back, "Found something under Sprocketweaver's."

Bill looked back at them both, blinding them with the sudden beam of the lantern light shining in their eyes. "Do we go?"

Joe and Amelia both barked at him at the same time.

"YES!"

"YES!"

The light turned away from them and left them temporarily blinded and seeing spots.

Bill replied in his monotone voice, "On our way."

Chapter 22

Bill led them through a winding zig-zag of storm tunnels that took them further North. Eventually, they started hearing voices echoing off the stone.

Joe guessed that they had spent the better part of half an hour down in the tunnels when they finally caught up with the others. A final turn led them to a stretch of storm tunnel that was filled with detectives and two other city workers.

By the looks of things, it was getting cramped. He turned back to Amelia and nodded his head. "We should go topside. No more room down here." His neck and shoulders were killing him with all the hunched-over walking, and he would have appreciated some fresh air.

Unfortunately, one of the detectives piped up, "Hold on there, Runewall."

So close.

"Yes?" Joe turned back to find a man even more hunched over and cramped than he.

The man must have been from the Scorched Sands, as his skin was quite dark, and his eyes were a deep brown. He was built like a brawler, and carried a staff that looked like it was made from raw ore and stone. Similar to Amelia's, it had facets to it, but it was far rougher in nature. His head was shaved clean, and he bore a thick black mustache.

He offered Joe a hand. "We haven't been formally introduced." His voice was pitched a bit lower, but he spoke with clarity and distinction. "My name is John Stonehand."

Joe took the offered hand and found the man had cold and rough hands like sandpaper and gravel. John smirked and kindly shook his hand while making no physical show of strength by squeezing. He took his hand back and made a fist for Joe to see.

Joe could feel the vibrations in the air and sense the magic flowing through the man and into his fist. The skin suddenly turned ashen gray and the fist near doubled in size and began flaking bits of dust. As if to demonstrate, John gently knocked the stone wall of the storm tunnel with his ashen hand. It sounded as if two pieces of rock had been *clacked* against each other.

Stonehand. Got it.

Joe nodded, impressed by the display of magic. He'd rarely seen anyone exhibit transformative or polymorphic abilities while at the Arcanum.

John gestured back into the throng of detectives that were crowding the tunnel. "We have a problem I think you would be better suited to resolve."

That made Joe's eyebrows climb in curiosity. "Oh?"

John nodded and turned back to the rest. "All right, let's clear some space. The rest of you go back to your regular sweeps in case this turns out to be nothing."

There was some grumbling, splashing, and sloppy shuffling as the men began making their way topside or turned a corner to head in a different direction.

After a few moments, Amelia and Bill were able to follow John to the source of the call. He led them to a segment of brick that was slightly off in color from the rest. "I found this while exploring with my guide." He pointed a thumb over his shoulder to a short little man with a gap-toothed grin that was enthusiastically waving his hand.

Why couldn't we get the lively one?

John demonstrated the oddity by tapping his stone-like hand on a regular-colored brick, then on to the slightly discolored one. It sounded different.

"Hmm…" Joe stepped closer and eyed the shape of the discolored brick. It was entirely possible that there was simply a section of brick that needed to be replaced or patched up due to a crack or break.

After a moment of thought, he figured it best to test it. He pulled his staff closer and carefully tipped it to touch the head against the brick, then probed it with his mind.

At first, he felt nothing. It just felt like regular wall. Like any material of the cosmos, it had its own unique peppering of magic. It reflected light and heat like stone would. The stone would erode over time, just like water eroded most things. It didn't seem to be anything special. For good measure, and to put his own thoughts at ease, he tested it for something else and pressed his staff a bit harder. That was when the magic itself changed. The wall suddenly lit up with a glowing framework of lines and layers of spell-work.

Joe pulled back and bumped his head again. "Ouch!" He quickly rubbed his head through the top of his hat, "You found something all right."

John gestured for Joe to keep at it. "As much as I would love to knock down whatever spell-work is in place, this is a city tunnel." He pointed above their heads. "And there are people living above us. Do what you do best."

Joe went back to prodding the wall with his staff and closed his eyes. Once he figured out that the face value of the spell-work was mostly illusionary, he was able to ignore it and press further into its design and structure.

It was there that he had to take a step back and breathe out a long whistle. "There are some layers of fuse spells here designed to set off and destroy whatever is inside... and potentially outside as well."

John raised his eyebrows in alarm. "Fuse spells?"

Joe nodded.

The man turned to the city workers and Amelia and gestured for them to get out. John then took several long steps back toward the storm tunnel grate entrance and asked, "Can you disarm them safely?"

He had done the necessary training while at the Arcanum and the Academy, but he'd never done it outside of a training scenario. Joe shook his head and breathed out hard. "I don't know. Best get people out of the area to be safe."

John pulled his crystalline network box from his belt and started issuing commands to dispatch while waving people out of the way and climbing out of the storm tunnel.

Joe suddenly felt very alone in the quiet of the tunnel, and a rising tide of panic threatened to overtake him.

Rule one: don't panic.

After several deep calming breaths, he steadied himself and prepared to dive back into the framework of the magic in front of him.

"Rook!" Amelia's voice rippled and echoed through the tunnel and up Joe's spine. It startled him and caused him to jump once again and crack his skull on the roof of the tunnel.

He didn't bother stifling himself and simply cried out in pain, "Fireballs!" His vision swam momentarily as he squatted in the tunnel and gripped the top of his head through his hat.

"Oops... sorry... uh, good luck and don't die."

It wasn't until Joe squinted through one eye at the tunnel entrance that he spotted her head retreating through the storm grate entrance. He continued to mutter swears under his breath while rubbing his head and whimpering.

Once he'd settled the firing pain into a gentle throb, he decided it was better to take precautions, looked back to the entrance and yelled, "Someone get me a helmet!"

~~

Joe shifted and adjusted how he sat on the tiny footstool as he wore his trench coat backward and tilted the helmet forward to help cover his face.

After requesting the helmet, he decided it would also help his back if he could sit and not worry about suddenly standing and clapping his helmet against the roof. His feet were out of the water and pressed against the wall as he leaned forward with his staff in both gloved hands. He felt a great deal safer than he had a few minutes before.

All settled in, he took a moment to calm himself, despite the awkward angle he was working with, and pressed his mind back into the framework.

The illusion magic covered how the door looked, smelled, and acted like stone. Beneath that was a series of fuse spells designed to set off something if certain triggers were met.

One of the triggers was obvious. If anyone attempted to smash their way through the magic, they'd set off the fuse.

Good thing you're a smart man, John.

Detective Stonehand wasn't just smart enough to transform his physical body into other elements; he was also smart enough to know when not to use it.

One fuse identified, Joe continued to examine the others. The second fuse looked to be triggered to anti-magic. If they attempted to shut down the barrier using an anti-magic incendiary, then it would set off the fuse. Two fuses identified. The third looked to be associated with brute-force magic of any sort. Three fuses identified. The fourth fuse was the final fuse. It was designed to prevent tampering. If someone tried to sneak their way in, as Joe was about to attempt, then they would set off the fuse.

Thankfully, there were no fuses for probing the nature of the magic at play. That would have been the first that Joe would have set, but he didn't have anything he'd blow up to prevent others from getting.

The nature of the fuse spells made him question the purpose of the barrier. He couldn't think of any reason to destroy a building or harm people if all you wanted to do was destroy the contents of a secret room. A simple Inferno spell would quickly erase whatever was inside, and then choke itself out from lack of oxygen.

Whoever was talented enough to set the illusion work and the fuses was smart enough to know that as well. That thought in mind, he still wasn't taking any chances.

Joe opened his eyes and lifted his head to eye the brick. "It's probably a hideout."

"It's a what? Speak up!"

Joe jumped again and nearly teetered over into the flowing water but was thankfully able to right himself. He threw a glare over at Amelia as she hung her head down into the tunnel. Her hand came down and gestured in apology as her head slowly retreated again.

He exhaled in frustration, calmed himself, turned his focus back to the brick wall, and pushed his mind back into the framework.

Beyond the fuses was a simple trigger spell. The entire purpose of which looked to be to disarm the fuses and release the illusion. It was effectively the keyhole. Joe just needed to figure out what key fit to it.

Another thought struck him in the moment. He pulled free, turned his head back to the hole, and barked, "Does Sprocketweaver's sell keys?"

~~

The owner of the shop, Fallston Sprocketweaver, had selected ten of the most common key types and placed them on an iron keyring at Joe's request and thrown it down to him. As requested, none of the keys had been cut. They were all blank slates.

Joe smartly partitioned his mind and muffled out any unwanted noise. He didn't want to get startled again while in the middle of picking a lock attached to a fuse. He couldn't be absolutely certain that the fuse led to something small and localized; for all he knew, the contents could be capable of leveling the city block.

With the keyring balanced on the head of his staff, Joe went back into pressing his way into the framework. His hope was to test each key and probe ahead to see how the magic responded to the key. If he felt something would trigger the fuse, he could pull the key away and try the next.

Joe took several deep breaths and held it as he leaned into the magic and tested the first key. He immediately felt something pressing back, and it set the hairs on the back of his neck standing on end.

Nope!

He pulled back quickly, hauled his staff from the stonework, and curled his toes, awaiting some horrific event.

Nothing happened.

Joe let out a gasping sigh of relief and nearly fell from his seat, causing him to stiffen again. With a few more calming breaths, he flipped the key over on the keyring and examined the next in line. He memorized it and created an image of it in his head.

Once he was reset, he pointed the tip of his staff at the barrier, shut his eyes, and tested it once again, but far more gently. He could see the 'keyhole' glowing slightly red instead of calm and neutral blue.

Nope.

Joe pulled back and flipped to the next key on the ring. He reset his mind and focused on the new key type, then dipped again into the framework. The new key made it further than the last before the 'keyhole' started to change.

Not quite, but closer.

He pulled out once more, examined all the keys on the keyring and selected the option similar enough to the third. He reset and tested again. It nearly made it all the way to the end before the 'keyhole' began giving its warning.

Joe pulled back and examined the remaining keys. There were no others that matched it. He shut his eyes once more and shaved off a little bit of the key in his mind and tried again. It turned red even quicker. He reset and instead added instead of subtracted.

It took him several long minutes of probing and resetting, but he eventually got to a point where the key fit and the 'keyhole' gave no indication of rejecting it.

Joe paused and felt his entire body break out in a cold sweat of anxiety. The moment of truth had arrived, and he wasn't sure if he was ready for it.

Don't panic.

"Great holy father of light and life, grant me the strength to survive the coming night." He jerked his staff and subsequently turned the key.

There was no explosion, roaring flame, or blinding light. Joe dared to peek out one eye.

In what he could only describe as a moment of earth-moving relief, the barrier of bricks slowly melted away in a shower of blue sparks as the barrier descended. Joe slumped back against the slime-covered storm tunnel wall and laughed giddily.

After adjusting his helmet so that it sat straight, he peered into the darkness beyond the false wall, only to spot an iron door. Shutting his eyes and prodding it with his staff revealed a similar barrier protecting the door.

He dropped his staff in frustration and sighed out through his nose as he rested his elbows on his knees and scrubbed his face with his hands.

A shadow filled the square sunbeam that penetrated the depths of the tunnel. Joe released the partition muffling his ears and looked to the source. Amelia hung her head back inside again. "You dead yet?" It was clearly a rhetorical question intended to lighten the mood and keep him sane.

He rested his head on one of his open hands and picked up his staff with the other. "Nope."

"Need anything?"

Joe glanced at the iron door, glanced at his watch, and decided he needed to reward himself and think for a bit before continuing. "Yep."

"What you need?"

"Iced cream."

He couldn't see her face, but he was certain she was frowning at him in confusion. "What?"

"You heard me."

"I did, but why do you think you deserve iced cream?"

"I unlocked an arcane barrier riddled with fuses without it exploding in my face."

"Ah… fair enough… what flavor?"

He hadn't thought that far ahead. He'd never actually had iced cream before. "I don't know… orange."

She scoffed in disgust. "Seriously, orange? What's wrong with you, everyone knows the obvious answer is chocolate and raspberry."

Joe frowned in turn. "Well, I like oranges, and you weren't the one to put their life on the line, so I want orange iced cream."

"Fine." Her head vanished from the hole.

He turned his attention back to the iron door and poked it with his staff again. He lazily probed it and saw much of the same as with the first barrier.

Iced cream first; dumb door second.

"Hey!"

Joe was too tired to jump and simply turned his attention back to Amelia's head hanging into the tunnel. "Yeah?"

"You want orange juice iced cream, orange chunk iced cream, or orange juice iced cream with orange chunks?"

He raised an eyebrow in absolute confusion. "There's a difference?"

She shook her head in disappointment. "Oh... you have so much to learn, rook."

Chapter 23

After some much needed education in iced cream, Joe opted for the orange chunk. Apparently, the mixture of orange juice and orange chunks would have been too overwhelming, according to the self-proclaimed 'Queen of Iced Cream'.

Joe sat on the curb with a wax parchment wrapped bar of vanilla iced cream with orange chunks. The first bite had proven a bit chilly, as it stuck to his tongue for a second, and had him blowing froths of cold air.

Once he'd worked it around inside his mouth a little and chewed on the small frozen orange bits, it had proven to be the exact thing he had needed at that moment.

The cream was silky, the orange chunks retained their strong citrus flavor, and the frozen dessert helped cool him down as the sun beat down on him. "Oh, by the gods."

Amelia sat beside him on the curb and smacked him on the arm. "What did I tell you?" She took a bite of her own brown and red treat before sighing in joy and relief.

It wasn't long before Joe felt an authoritative presence towering behind him. He turned his head to find Petals had arrived and was looking down upon him with straight-faced disapproval. The little man was barely a hand taller than the sitting Joe, but was still looking down upon him.

"I'm being levied some serious questions by a city noble."

Joe slowly nodded his head. "What's he asking?"

Petals scowled slightly. "He's demanding to know why we have evacuated the block and have shut down several well-to-do businesses during peak hours, while two detectives sit on the corner eating a treat."

He took the moment to contemplate his answer and decided honesty was the best course of action. "I just spent," he stopped and glanced at his watch for accuracy, "a quarter of an hour cramped inside a storm tunnel identifying and deactivating a four-fuse, multi-layer, incendiary spell that could very well have left me a vaporized smudge on the wall… or leveled the block… still not sure which."

Joe thought about that for a moment and felt a sudden flutter in his heart upon the implications of it, then took a deep breath and calmed himself again before continuing. "I then discovered a second barrier behind that one, and felt it wise to recollect my thoughts before making any further attempts."

The dread of it suddenly struck him even harder as he looked at the storm tunnel entrance. He held aloft his treat. "This could be my last meal…"

Petals cocked an eyebrow at Joe, then turned his attention to Amelia. "And you?"

She slapped Joe on the arm and gestured with her treat in hand. "I'm showing my partner emotional support in this trying time. It could very well be his last hour in mortal flesh."

Joe looked down upon his treat with dread and a nervous sickness, then looked to her with disapproval. "Thanks."

Petals cheerily accepted their explanations. "Wonderful! I shall explain it to the nobleman."

Joe looked back down at the iced cream melting in his hand and offered it to Amelia. "I don't think I can stomach any more food right now."

"Nonsense! This is iced cream! It is the most delicious thing, and you will finish it, mister!"

Joe turned his scowl upon her. "Seriously? This isn't a time for games!"

She nodded while scowling back. "Seriously! It's delicious! And you will need the energy if you're to sit back down in that dinginess and fiddle with things that could blow up in your face and kill you."

Please stop mentioning the killing me part. You're going to make me sick.

"If you intend on surviving, you'll need all the strength you can get, and the instant you crawl back into that," she pointed at the storm tunnel entrance, "you'll wish you finished your iced cream 'cause it's far better than the rotten smelling stuff that's in there."

Joe shut his eyes and felt a burp rise to the surface. "Ugh… and what if I get nauseous from the nerves and the smell?"

"Oh… easy." He heard the snap of cloth and opened his eyes to see her holding up the cloth that she had wrapped around her head earlier. "It doesn't just smell nice, it's spelled to help keep food down. Great for murder cases where the body has been around for a while."

He reached out, touched the fabric, and smelled it. His stomach immediately settled and felt as solid as it had that morning before he stepped into the sewer. "Huh." Joe looked to his treat in hand and took a bite. It wasn't anywhere near as cold, but still cool. It also filled a void inside he hadn't realized was there until he took that bite. His will was strengthening again.

Magic drew from many places – mental and physical will were the most obvious. Sometimes the emotional will of an individual could affect spell-work. His dread over possibly being turned to bones and ash had messed with him.

After getting another fat and silky bite of iced cream into him, he could feel his nerves steadying.

It was at that moment that a large shadow approached alongside Petals. Joe turned to see a tall man in bronze robes bending down to shake his hand, "Hello, detective."

Joe wiped his hand clean on the front of his vest and shook the man's hand. "Hello, sir."

The man stood back up, blocking out the sun over Joe. He had a bit of a hooked nose and a balding head. His vest beneath his robe was a deep bronze, and he nervously glanced about. "I understand that you're dealing with some very dangerous spell-work, young man."

Joe glanced to Petals, who absolutely beamed. "Indeed, I am, sir."

"Well then, I wish you the best of luck in your efforts and ask that you take all the time you need to prepare yourself and feel no rush or pressure." The man was smiling nervously and seemed highly uncertain what to do with his hands as he stared down at Joe for entirely too long.

He broke the awkward silence and nodded in understanding. "Absolutely, sir, I will get to it as soon as I've had a moment to enjoy a frozen dessert on a hot spring day."

"Good-good… excellent. Yes, you do that." He turned on the spot and headed off in the direction he had come from.

Amelia nearly spat out her iced cream as she spotted the giant twitching rainbow rabbit-tail attached to the back of the man's robe. Joe didn't quite find it as funny as she did, having been the target of Petals' pranks in the past, but he couldn't deny the fact that it was rather amusing. He turned back around to prevent any attention from being drawn to the rabbit tail and tried to keep his focus on finishing his iced cream before it melted in his hand.

Petals patted Joe on the shoulder and whispered words of encouragement. "You've done well so far, I trust you will do just fine with the rest, my boy."

Thanks, I needed to hear that.

He couldn't quite say the words aloud as his mouth was full of delicious fruit and cream. It didn't take him long to devour the last of his treat and lick his hands clean.

Amelia was far more delicate with her meal and wiped her hands clean with her wizard's handkerchief. Eventually, Joe did the same with his own cloth, but he wanted to savor every bit of the sticky remnants of his dessert.

Midday struck, and Joe found himself eager to get back into the water, despite the smell; it was at least cooler in the shade. Joe got to his feet, dusted off his hands, and headed over to the dingy storm tunnel entrance. He whipped out the enchanted cloth that Amelia had given him and wrapped it about his face before lowering himself back down inside.

A quick examination of the space behind the false wall proved that he had enough room to sit down on the stool and work his magic against the iron door. It wasn't a lot of room, but it was enough that he no longer had to deal with the water.

He took several minutes to position himself into a place of comfort and adjusted all his clothing again so that it provided him the most protection it could. The backwards trench coat offered him the most protection from a blast, but he doubted it would save him from being engulfed in flames.

With his staff in hand, he calmed his mind and breathed deep and slow. Once settled, he pressed into the new framework. He was immediately alarmed by the number of fuses connected to it. Much like the first barrier, there were fuses designed to prevent brute-force penetration. Unlike the first barrier, there were two additional fuses. The first prevented scrying of the inner workings of the door lock. The second prevented scrying whatever was on the other side of the door. He swore under his breath and kept prying.

By the looks of it all, there were six fuses total. There was also another trigger spell like the one before it. The only problem was that this time the trigger spell was requiring a physical key.

Joe sat back, took off his helmet, and scratched his head before combing his hair back and contemplating the issue at hand. He could easily pull the same trick as before and figure out what key he needed to activate the trigger spell, but he'd need to get the physical key cut to match it.

A thought occurred to him. The trigger 'key' could be anything. It could be a phrase, a word, or a type of metal the key was made from. The only reason he was able to utilize the 'mind key' from earlier was because he had manipulated the magic into mimicking the shape of the 'keyhole'. His twisting of the key in the lock was simply his successful mimicking the trigger in a mystical sense.

He exhaled in an attempt to rid himself of doubts and attacked the problem anew. With his staff to the door, he pressed back into the framework, pulled his 'mind key' to the ready, and gingerly tested it into the 'keyhole'. Unsurprisingly, it didn't fit.

Fireballs.

Joe retreated from the framework and looked back to the opening in the brick and stone that shaped the storm tunnel, then turned the head of his staff back to that framework and pressed his mind into it. The barriers were down, the fuses were untouched, and the 'key' was still active, as he had left it.

That was when he noticed something. There was a string of the frame that connected from one keyhole to the next. A brief struggle allowed him to bring up both frames at the same time. A probing of that thread of the framework revealed that triggering the iron door would shut the brick illusion barrier.

Makes sense.

He figured he didn't notice it earlier because he was on the other side of the barrier and couldn't see the trigger spell-work from that end. Daring to test fate, he plucked at that bit of framework and found it be flimsy and unprotected.

Hello.

Joe pressed down hard upon that bit of spell-work and found that the very answer to the iron door was inlaid within it. It read "Gold is better." Another quick bit of backwards magic revealed that the answer to the first barrier was "Greed is good".

Aha!

Working backwards yet again, Joe was able to create the 'mind key' around the wording. He gingerly tested it, and found that it started to fit, but it required the slightest and most subtle of adjustments to prevent it from turning the 'keyhole' red. Once it fit, he set the magic forward again and played it in his mind. The phrase hadn't changed at all, but the voice was no longer his own. It was deeper, and far more sinister and eloquent in its enunciation. It was the voice of the one that owned the hideout and set the spell.

Double aha!

Having resolved the issue of the mystical part of the lock, Joe turned and snapped the framework connecting the iron door to the brick wall. He didn't want to get locked inside once he broke through. It would also grant the remaining detectives access.

He just had to figure out the key at that point. Unfortunately, his mastery of barriers and locks was regulated to the meta-physical and mystical.

A new thought occurred to him. He leaned back and looked to the entrance. Amelia's head was peering in while her fingers gripped the edge.

Joe yelled to her, "Get Stonehand!"

~~

The two of them crouched in the darkness and tented themselves with their jackets as John used the length of his staff to hold one of the ten keys to the keyhole of the iron door.

Joe had the head of his staff touching the iron door just above the keyhole. "All right, so the plan is to 'pick' the lock. I'm going to be your eyes and sense your way through this and tell you if you're about to set off the fuse. I'll give you a thumbs up or thumbs down whether to back up or go further. As we figure out what works, you adjust the key to fit. Got it?"

John stared at Joe for a long minute before asking, "You're deadly serious? This is your brilliant plan?"

Joe took a moment to rethink his words. "Well, it sounds stupid when you question it, but there's not exactly a manual for doing this sort of thing."

"How have you survived this long?"

Joe shrugged. "Idiots call it luck. I call it fate."

John continued to stare at him for a long minute before taking a deep calming breath and shutting his eyes. "Okay, but I'm taking this *really* slow, because I don't feel like dying today."

Joe nodded in complete agreement. "I don't feel like it either."

They both turned to the iron door and John muttered under his breath, "I get an iced cream after this."

Joe shut out all other distractions and focused his will and thoughts into the framework around the physical keyhole. He lifted his hand up for John to see and gave a thumbs up.

There was a long moment where nothing happened, and the key didn't move. Joe took it as John simply psyching himself up to embark on the insane plan. Eventually, he felt the key moving, and it immediately started turning the framework around the keyhole red. Joe threw open his hand and yelled, "STOP!"

John inhaled sharply and froze.

Neither of them moved, and the framework remained a glaring red in his mind's eyes.

Joe gently gestured with his hand for John to pull the key back. Neither of them breathed, as the iron key gently scraped against the metal as it retreated.

The framework immediately returned to blue, and Joe let out his breath, sighing heavily, "Thank the gods!"

John similarly sighed in relief and muttered something under his breath before asking, "Was that supposed to happen?"

Joe shook his head. "The key didn't get anywhere close to the first pin. Something else is wrong. Maybe it's the material composition."

John sat upright on his little stool. "NOW you tell me?"

He threw up his arms in surrender. "How am I supposed to know? Not like I've done this before!"

The bigger man let out a deep sigh and wiped his face with his hand. "All right, I have an idea."

They reset themselves and took deep breaths, calming their nerves as John went about sticking a heavy keyring on the end of his staff. It seemed to stick there without the need for any grips or grooves. It just stuck.

On the keyring was a series of thin metal rods barely wider than a needle. Each bit of metal had a different color to it. To Joe's senses, some of the metals were mystical in nature.

John turned and pointed the keyring at the keyhole, then looked to Joe. "You ready?"

Not knowing exactly what the man was attempting to do, Joe simply put his staff in the appropriate position, closed his eyes, and prepared his mind. He looked to the framework and nodded. "Ready, I guess."

"All right." The bigger man released some of his own magic, and Joe could see some of it through his mind's eye. "This one is copper."

Ah... smart.

The framework around the keyhole started turning orange as soon as the copper started nearing the keyhole. "Nope."

John pulled back and started again. "All right; silver."

The testing process continued for quite some time, until John eventually sighed out of frustration. "All right then."

Joe grumbled, "How many have we done now?"

"Twenty-one. This one is obsidian."

He watched, awaiting the orange alarm to trigger again — except it didn't. "You doing it yet?"

"I am."

Joe sat up straight and opened his eyes. The twig of obsidian was stuck in the keyhole and there was no alarm. "About time!"

John pulled the sample metal from the keyhole and gripped it and the key they had tested earlier. The man shut his eyes and released his magic from one hand and through to the other. The key transformed before Joe's eyes and changed from a dull iron gray to a shiny obsidian black.

Alchemical transformation magic... most impressive.

The big man teetered on the spot and breathed out a heavy sigh. "I'm not too great at that part and can only do a tiny bit at a time. It's super illegal too, so don't tell anyone I did that."

Joe nodded in understanding. "Right." He made a gesture of turning a key beside his mouth. The black market would love to get a hold of someone that could turn copper to gold.

The two of them set themselves back up for the long haul, and Joe began the tedious processes of eyeing the framework while directing John to alter the key. Keeping an eye on his watch, they finished the entirety of the key in seventeen minutes. Joe noted the time when John told him that the key wouldn't go any further into the lock, and Joe couldn't sense any resistance.

"Uh... I think you can go have that iced cream now."

John sat in silence as his staff held the key in the iron door. "You sure?"

Joe thought about it and nodded. "Yeah... no point in us both turning into smudges on the wall."

John sat for a little longer, then eventually nodded. "Probably right." He slowly clambered out of the hole in the wall and pulled his trench coat back on before offering his hand to Joe. "In case you turn into a smudge on the wall, it was a pleasure meeting you."

He shook the big man's hand and nodded in appreciation. "Thank you." He waited a bit longer for John to exit the storm tunnel before turning his attention back to the iron door.

Gritting his teeth, Joe stood up, gripped the key, infused it with the 'mind key' that was previously prepared, and jerked the key in the lock.

Chapter 24

The key turned in the lock without issue and the iron door clanged as the lock gave way to the key. There was a long silence as Joe stood with his eyes shut tight, breath held, and hand holding the key.

His watch ticked on in the silence. Exhaling slowly and cautiously, he eventually opened one eye and peered at the door.

There was no smell of smoke or char, and there wasn't any audible or physical *thumps* to the air. Daring to test his fate, Joe pressed against the door with his fingers and it opened a touch.

Uncertain as to the nature of what was on the other side of the door, Joe pulled his six-shooter and tipped the head of his staff toward the shadows beyond. A quick glance into the framework informed him that the room was small, not much larger than Ms. Bellcreaux's dining room. There didn't appear to be any more traps, triggers, or fuses that could potentially endanger any of their lives.

Satisfied with the initial probe, he backed up with his firearm drawn and aimed at the door. Peering out the corner of his eye, he could spot Amelia's nose and eyes peering into the darkness of the storm tunnel.

A wave of his hand and a gesture for silence was all she needed to pass the message along. Mr. Stonehand eased his way down into the tunnel and tip-toed his way over to Joe. Ms. Iceheart followed immediately after.

Another series of gestures communicated the plan. They were going to kick in the door and storm the room with their weapons drawn. John, being the bigger man with the ability to turn his body to stone, took the lead. Joe was second, and Amelia took up the rear.

John lifted his meaty hand and began counting down with his fingers.

Three... two... one!

The massive boot made the door screech in resentment as it swung wide and struck the wall. John took two large steps into the room and roared with an infused bit of intimidation magic, "FREEZE!"

Joe jumped through the doorway and raised his six-shooter and scanned the room starting at the opposite end as John.

Something was clearly wrong, as John and Amelia both started cursing and coughing while throwing their arm up to cover their faces.

"What is it? What's wrong?"

The cloth that had been wrapped around his mouth and nose was suddenly untied and yanked from him in one quick pull. The smell of rot and death struck him like a slap to the face. Amelia had unceremoniously reclaimed the cloth so that she might be saved by the god-awful stench.

Joe holstered his firearm and jumped back out of the room while covering his nose and mouth with his gloved hand. John was hot on his heels.

Amelia tied the cloth round her face, then took the helmet from Joe's head and flicked on the lantern light before proceeding alone. As the framework had shown him, the room was small. The light from her helmet lantern illuminated much of the room as the spotlight was broad.

On the far wall, opposite the iron door, sat a metal-framed cot. Upon the cot was the golden-eyed man, dead.

~ ~

Doctor Broom confirmed what they had all already known based on the pale body and the horrific stench. "Decomposition, color, and smell suggests he's been dead a day or two. I'll know a great deal more once I get the body back to the station for a full examination."

The doc had his own face cloth that did the same thing as Amelia's handkerchief, except it had ear loops, like most surgeons' masks Joe had seen as a Green Coat. He presumed the man was also used to the smell of corpses.

Someone had found a lantern hanging above a work desk that was set adjacent to the iron door and flicked it on so that they could all see without the need of individual helmet lanterns.

Petals paced about the room, seemingly undisturbed by the smell with his lack of cloth. He looked around at everything and absorbed it all with a scrutinizing gaze. "There's a great deal of evidence here, but none of the missing gems."

Joe had noted a similar issue with everything he had examined prior to his superior's descent into the hideout. There were city maps, storm tunnel maps, and notes for dates and times of deliveries and store hours for various jewelry shops, but nothing else.

The doctor proceeded to open a large black cloth canvas and set it beside the body on the cot.

Something was irritating Joe from the deepest depths of his core. "Wait." He stepped toward the doc and pointed to the dead Eagle Eyes. "Open his eyelids?"

Petals piped up, "What is it, my boy?"

Joe started shaking his head. "Something doesn't add up about any of this."

The lot of them turned and raised their eyebrows at Joe.

"Seriously, rook?"

"I agree with Amelia; this hasn't exactly been an easy first case for you." John had a valid point, but something was still bothering him.

Petals took the longest to say anything as he narrowed his eyes at Joe, as if he were looking for some deeper thought within. "Check the eyes, Mr. Broom."

Joe thanked his superior and turned to watch.

Mr. Broom shook his head, sighed, and used his gloved hand to open an eyelid.

The eye was undeniably a golden eagle's eye. The shape and coloring made it unnervingly clear that they were not normal.

The man's frame, clothing, and even the powder burnishing the vest suggested it was the exact same person that Joe had shot the night earlier. Yet something still felt off to him.

Not wanting to delay the doctor any longer or irritate the kindly man that had patched him up twice, he apologized, and stepped out of the way.

The others shook their heads and went back to cataloguing everything and writing in their notepads.

Not wanting to fall behind on paperwork, Joe reached for his notepad. It was then that a question bubbled to the surface. "How did he get in?"

Everyone stopped and turned to look at him as though he'd just asked why the sky was up.

He shook his head to rid himself of their glares and pointed to the door. "He had the key, but how did he get through the water?"

That was when they all stopped taking notes and stood a bit straighter with looks of bewilderment.

Amelia chimed in with the same thought that had just struck him. "He's right. That night, the rain was coming down, and the storm tunnels should have been full. How did he get through without flooding his hideout?"

Petals stood in the center of the room with a self-satisfied grin on his face.

Joe had spent enough days working alongside the trickster menace to know that there was something they weren't seeing. Instead of grabbing the notepad, he pulled out the violet-shaded magnifying glass and began scanning the room.

The floor beneath Petals' feet lit up with circular runes of residual energy. It didn't take long to recognize the pattern either. He lowered the magnifying glass and looked to the others. "It's a destination circle."

They all threw up their arms in an 'of course' gesture. Destination circles were the designated arrival points for Recall spells. It perfectly explained how Eagle Eyes had managed to escape and leave no trace. Unlike any other Teleportation spell, the Recall spell didn't require two designated points. It simply snapped you back to the one you had designated earlier. Such spell-work was also referred to as Hearth spells in the ancient days.

I'm still not satisfied.

There was nothing he could put his finger on, so he decided to go about filling in his notes.

The remainder of the day was spent clearing the scene and bagging up evidence for removal and delivery to the precinct. Once done, the lot of them said their farewells to the city workers and headed back to fill out their reports.

Despite that Eagle Eyes was dead, there was still a requirement for all detectives to pair up, as it was looking more and more likely that the shooter was unidentified.

Joe rode back to the station with Amelia, and their conversation mostly covered logistics and reporting procedures. It was mostly business, but she did finally toss him a hint and suggested he speak with Doctor Broom on how to craft a smell and gag-proof mask. As much as he loved the idea of not choking on the smell of death, the creation of such a mask was an expenditure he simply couldn't afford.

The daylight hours were burning away as they kept themselves busy with filling out their reports. Partway through the afternoon, another case was thrown at him. Seeing as how he was the rookie, he was likely to get thrown cases the other detectives didn't want or couldn't handle on top of their already existing caseload.

Apparently, an elderly woman had started experiencing chaotic malfunctions with her kitchen appliances. She also complained of odd cackling noises and feared she was being watched and stalked inside of her own home. Based on the written testimony provided within the file, it looked like some form of chaotic creatures such as gremlins were the likely culprits, though nothing could be confirmed until the completion of a full examination. He questioned why an extermination team hadn't been contacted to handle the issue, but he had a more pressing case to work on.

Long hours were spent sitting beside the steam-belching radiator while tapping the rune keys of his typesetter. Eventually, the multi-page report was ready for examination. He left out the letter from Mr. Marcano for obvious reasons. Every instinct told him not to file it, that the report was unfinished, but he couldn't for the life of him figure out what was missing.

While waiting for the ink on the reports to dry, he wrote up a letter for a messenger boy and sent the young man running. There was no point in having Ms. Bellcreaux rebuke him for tardiness when he wasn't going to be home for dinner.

He proceeded to type up a formal request for an infestation inspection to be completed upon the old gremlin lady's behalf. Hopefully it would resolve the issue without him needing to get involved.

He set that request aside and collected the dried report papers. Joe shuffled them together, organized them, clipped them, and took them to Petals for approval.

"Well done, my boy." Petals shuffled the papers back into order and handed them back to Joe once he had stamped them as approved.

He reluctantly took back the report and sat in silence across from Petals.

"Something is still bothering you."

Joe shook his head. "Didn't need to read my head for that one."

The little man chuckled. "Quite right! You've been voicing it quite loudly since we found the body."

His head shakes changed to nods. "We found bloodied bandages and an empty vial, suggesting he tried to patch himself back up. I guess his efforts failed... but why?"

"We'll know come the morning when the doctor provides us with his report."

His nods returned to shakes. "It doesn't feel right."

"Too bad you can't put rhyme or reason to the feeling."

Joe looked to his superior to find the trickster gnome supplying him with a half-hearted and tight-lipped smile. "The first case always feels off. You'll get used to it."

It's more than that.

"Come," his superior put on a hearty smile, "We've done all we can for today, and my lovely wife has made a delightful dinner."

Despite everything, Joe couldn't help but feel a bit better.

The little man scrunched his nose after taking a sniff of the air. "You might want to change first. The storm tunnels and the radiator have conspired against you."

Joe frowned and dared to tilt his head down slightly and take an experimental whiff.

Whew!

He jerked his head back and agreed whole-heartedly, "Yep! I think I'll take a quick bath as well."

"Good plan."

~~

The Pettlebottoms' residence was on the edge of the precinct's district and nestled in a group of gnome homes. He'd been there before, but it was nice to be invited instead of showing up unconscious and waking in a child's bed.

Pink lilies were painted across the white door leading to their residence, located on the third floor of a larger complex. The neighborhood looked to be quiet and peaceful, and the grounds were well-kept with abundant and colorful foliage.

He felt a sudden desire to settle into a gnome home. It seemed so much greener and livelier than the dingy and dark domicile that Ms. Bellcreaux kept. Sadly, his first pay deposit wouldn't come for another day yet.

Petals snapped his fingers and stepped through the freshly unlocked door while throwing his hat up into the air. It landed perfectly upon the coat and hat rack. The trickster then snapped the fingers of his other hand and spontaneously produced a bouquet of white and pink flowers of varying species and fauna. It was momentarily surprising.

"I have returned home, my lovely dear!"

Flair for dramatic entrances… that's so you.

Ms. Pettlebottom absolutely beamed as she hurried from the kitchen to the entrance to hug her husband, kiss his cheek, and claim the flowers as the delightful present that they were.

The motherly and elderly crafter gnome waved Joe inside. "Come in, Joseph! Come in, dinner is almost ready!"

If she hadn't said anything, he was almost certain the intoxicating smell of whatever she was making would have bewitched his feet into doing so anyway. He shuffled inside and hung up his hat and coat before taking the seat offered to him by Petals. Strangely, there were only three settings. "What about the children?"

Ms. Pettlebottom perked up and answered over her shoulder, "Oh! The lovelies went home to the fey realm. They only visited the other day to bake cookies with me."

Joe shook his head and looked to Petals. "Wait, you can come back from the fey realm? I thought the doors were all closed?"

He waved it off as though it were nonsense. "Only the primary doors that we bothered to share the existence of."

Huh.

That realization opened a great many new possibilities, and partially explained how the fairies were able to pass through to the mortal realm when called.

"Dinner's ready!" Ms. Pettlebottom returned to the table with a steaming platter upon her oven mitts.

Fantastic!

The meal was as reinvigorating as it was delicious. The tiny woman somehow managed to pack a great deal of heartwarming weight within such a tiny plate of food. She had made butter-sautéed carrots with spiced peas, served up beside baked and breaded chicken.

When offered, Joe had to refuse a second serving. "Oh no, Ms. Pettlebottom. While absolutely tempted, I fear I won't fit in the gnome cart if I have another bite." He then had to stifle a burp.

She smiled proudly and set about clearing the table with a few waves of her hands and simple gestures. Cabinetry opened and released glass bowls and little parchment parcels. Food was divided in a matter of moments. Then the chilling cabinet opened, received the containers, and shut. It was a glorious dance that Joe couldn't help but compare to Petals' performance of moving the shelving about the basement of Runelore's Refuse. Plates and utensils glided over to the countertop and lowered into a sink full of bubbly water. In less time than it would have taken to walk one plate to the countertop, the kitchen table had been cleared.

Despite the fact that there were decades of experience separating them, Joe couldn't help but feel a bit underwhelming in comparison to the two gnomes. They made everything look easy.

"Now, my boy, about this letter."

Joe turned his attention to Petals with a look of some surprise and silently gestured to Ms. Pettlebottom.

He waved it off as unimportant. "She's quieted her ears. She won't hear anything."

"I– uh– all right." Joe wasn't sure if his superior was joking or serious. With all attention on him, he proceeded to reiterate the letter, verbatim. No detail was left behind. The observations and deductions he had made were included.

"Hmmm." Petals sat back and stroked his long white beard.

"I didn't bother trying to work out why he wanted me to go alone. I simply figured he wouldn't want a grand audience, and Amelia didn't exactly come across as 'solid' during our first encounter." Joe didn't want to put down Detective Iceheart, but her handling of the situation wasn't exactly a textbook definition of 'keeping one's cool'.

The elderly gnome looked to Joe and nodded while smiling. "Not to worry, I'll go with you."

"What? Wait, no. You can't. He said, 'come alone'." The thought of losing out on potentially vital information didn't appeal to him in the slightest. "If you come with me, any miniscule amount of trust I have garnered will be forever lost."

Petals shrugged. "If you wish. I will stay back a few buildings and wait a total of ten minutes, no more."

Joe contemplated his options and raised a concern. "What if they see you following me?"

That was when his superior said the most unsettling thing. "My boy, when a trickster gnome chooses not to be seen, they give the gods themselves the slip." The most frightening part about that simple statement was that Joe believed it to be true.

Once their plan had been established, Joe said his farewells to Ms. Pettlebottom and set out with fare in hand and a meal for the next day's lunch. There was still enough time left in the evening that he could make it home to get a few hours' rest before having to get back up and make his way to the meeting spot.

His only hope was that whatever information the graying werebear had wasn't already old news.

Fates, please be kind to me tonight.

Chapter 25

.

Despite the messenger boy he had sent earlier in the afternoon, The Crow had been waiting for him. She stood in the doorway to the brownstone walk-up like any other day that he'd been late.

"Ms. Bellcreaux?"

"Joseph." She said it with a cool detachment.

"May I enter and head to bed?"

Surprisingly, the old woman stepped aside and gave him no fuss or grievance over the hour upon which he returned. She even accepted the wrapped meal so it might be stored in the chill cupboard. Not wanting to test the Fates any further, he stepped inside and headed for the stairs.

With one foot on the first step and his hand on the railing, he paused and asked as she shut and locked the front door, "Why do you always wait at the door for me to return?"

Her answer was a bit chilly. "You have a dangerous job. I like to know when and if your room might suddenly become vacant."

Glad to know you care.

"Of course, Ms. Bellcreaux." Joe headed up to his room. The first thing on the list was to go about the regular routine as though he were preparing for bed, which he was, if only for a short nap.

The second thing was to set out his street clothes. He wasn't supposed to walk about in uniform when off-duty. To that end, he had a jacket and a pocketed vest he typically wore when out and about his regular day.

Once cleaned and dressed in pajamas, he quickly set himself to bed with a partition set to the specified hour. There was no point in startling the others with the bedside alarm clock. The goal was to sneak out, not wake the whole house.

A focused will sent him into a deep sleep.

~~

His eyes popped open and a quick glance at his watch informed him it was the appropriate hour. With care and ease, he slowly shifted weight and slipped out of bed to tip-toe about the room. He quickly gathered and changed into the street clothes that were set and ready.

The old jacket was beaten and discolored in several places and patched in many others. It would hopefully produce the look of an unsavory fellow, as opposed to a strait-laced detective. While much shorter than the standard-issue trench coat, it was long enough and still had enough padding to hide his holster and firearm.

His wand just barely fit into one of the vest pockets. It was then he wished he could have worn his detective's vest, as it had been enchanted with deeper pockets than typical civilian's clothes, and also helped stop bullets. Unfortunately, that would have meant walking about with a giant 'I'm a detective' sign strapped to his chest. The less he wore the greater the risk of injury, but the easier he'd blend in as a civilian.

Another check of the watch told him he had to get going soon if he wanted to be there in a timely manner. Joe turned and tip-toed to the boarded-up window and was about to pull the wood out of the frame when something tickled in the back of his mind.

Joe pulled his wand, released it into a staff, and side-stepped out of the window frame. A shallow scrying dip into the cosmic pool informed him that there were eyes on his window.

Back for another round, shooter?

He didn't feel like testing the Fates and decided on utilizing the front door. Tip-toeing back to the door, he touched the head of the staff to the lock and muffled it before turning the key. Similarly, he muffled the hinges and the door itself as he slipped through and shut it behind him.

The floorboards in the hall were a bit older and creaked and groaned a bit louder than inside the room. Another gentle muffling helped him to step his way past the snore-rumbling doors of the other residence, and slowly descend the steps without waking the household or setting anyone at alarm.

His staff was able to quiet the front door just as easily. A brief and shallow scrying dip into the cosmic pool informed that nobody was watching the front. Joe reached out with the staff, pointed it at the lantern light above the door, and gave it a brief jinx to stifle the flow of energy and snuff it out. Once under the cover of some much-needed darkness, he slipped out and turned to lock the door again.

A partition in his mind was set to keep an eye out for any peering eyes or alarming hostilities. His staff was compressed back into a wand and he stuffed most of it up his sleeve.

Nobody was out at such a late hour of the night. The street was silent. Joe didn't want to take any chances and muffled his shoes before heading down the steps and turning to head toward the intended meeting spot. Once he was a few doors down, he flicked his arm and wand behind him and un-jinxed the lantern, allowing it to flicker back to life.

A glance at his watch told him he'd just be able to make it with a minute to spare if he didn't have any hold-ups. The possibility of being followed concerned him and forced him to take appropriate measures. The partition would only be able to help him so much. It didn't prevent someone from simply following his tracks, presuming they had the ability to track.

In addition to the muffling of his shoes, another twist of the wrist made it so that any footprints he made were immediately scuffed up and weathered enough to hide his trail.

While it cost him a few seconds, Joe took odd and unnecessary turns while heading directly toward the meeting point. It wasn't long before he entered the commercial district of their precinct and the warehouse came into view.

He didn't know where Petals was, but he hoped the little gnome was close enough to jump in and help at the moment he started yelling for it.

The good thing about the commercial district was there were no workers out during the night. The bad thing was all the undesirable ruffians tended to congregate here for their black market deals. Joe couldn't see them, but he felt the odd set of eyes turn on him, then turn away. He wasn't the one they were looking for, and neither was he a Blue Coat on patrol.

The warehouse was across the street, and it looked to be unoccupied, as the lights were off. Joe shut his eyes and muttered a prayer the sisters had taught him. Once his pleas were made, he headed across the cobblestone road and around the side to the kicked-in entrance.

Pausing to steady himself, Joe moved his wand from his right sleeve to his left, then reached under his jacket to put his hand on the handle of his firearm in case he needed to draw it.

Backing up against the wall and shuffling to the doorframe, he glanced inside and noted that nobody had arrived yet. At least, nobody was visible in the pitch of the abandoned warehouse.

I don't like this.

Joe took a deep breath and steadied his hammering heart before sliding in through the door and sticking to the wall. Didn't exactly feel like being jumped from behind.

"Mr. Marcano?" he whispered into the shadows.

"Not quite." The voice rang through the building in an odd all- consuming echo, as if the source was everywhere at once.

The entirety of his mind screamed to run. But the sudden pinch of an insect sting against his left leg was immediately followed by a jolt of white-hot light. Every muscle and fiber of his being clenched and held as pain ripped through him.

While momentary, it was enough to leave him feeling like he'd just been dumped into a hot bath after having every bit of his body beaten with a club. His flesh was even steaming, and his muscles were twitching. The shock left him weak in the legs and nothing stopped him as he fell to his knees and dropped his hands to the floor for steadiness and balance.

Confusingly, the floor wasn't dirt or dust but hard stone. A few moments of blinking brought his vision back to normal and cleared the spots. He began lifting his head to look around when he felt something long, hard, and hollow poke him in the back of the head.

"Don't. Move." The voice was identical to the hideout owner's.

Joe didn't have the strength or wherewithal to attempt to resist. His tongue felt numb and thick in his mouth. Despite that, he tried to speak, "Wh–"

The tip of the long barrel – what he guessed was pressed against his skull – poked him once more. "Be quiet. Listen, don't do anything stupid, and you will be allowed to walk away."

He didn't have the strength to resist, even if he wanted to. He wasn't even sure he could bring himself to throw together much of a sentence. Instead of trying, he simply nodded his head.

"Good." The voice had the same depth, reverberation, and eloquence to it as he felt when he had crafted the 'mind key'. "As insignificant as I find them, I'll answer the questions that are undoubtedly swimming about inside your thick skull."

Eagle Eyes, or so he thought it to be, reached down and yanked free the dart from Joe's leg. It pinched, briefly. "I shot you with an electric dart. You're recovering from its effects as we speak. You'll fully recover within the matter of an hour. I'll need you at your best."

What?

"We are in the hideout that I sacrificed to your precinct so that I might 'die' in the eyes of the law."

Joe shook his head and did his best to squint into the darkness and focus his vision. The man was right. They had somehow been transported to the hideout beneath Sprocketweaver's shop.

"I utilized one of the many Recall spells at my disposal to bring us here." There was a brief pause as the end of the long-barrel eased off the back of his head and rested on his shoulder. "You're undoubtedly wondering why I would go through so much trouble to stage my death only to reveal myself to you."

Yep, was thinking that.

"The answer is simple. Because I can."

That's a dumb answer.

"Now before you go getting any flippant ideas…"

Too late.

"Let me explain what I mean. I have not only the means, but the resources to fake my death and toss away a well-designed hideout on a whim. I'd like for you to take a moment and contemplate what that means and how easily I could crush something if I gave it my undivided attention."

All right… not so dumb of an answer.

Joe managed to shake off enough of the numbness to feel his tongue working again, "So—"

The long-barrel moved to poke him in the back of the jaw. "I'm not finished, Joseph." The threat felt very real, and the man took great care to enunciate his words so that he was undeniably clear.

Joe lifted a hand in apology and immediately put it back down. The spinning and dizziness wasn't done with him yet, it seemed.

"I told you I would answer your questions, and I am still in the process of doing so."

Petals, I really could use you right now.

"You and I have a common enemy. Timothy Grimthorn," that name definitely got his attention, "is out to avenge the death of his father, Nathaniel Grimthorn."

Joe tilted his head to the side so that he might hear a bit better.

"Ah… I see the gears and cogs are finally at work. Good to see that you're playing along." The long-barrel eased off his jaw and rested back upon his shoulder. He wished he could glance back and identify where the man was standing, but he doubted he'd be given that chance.

"Timothy grew up thinking the world of his father and investigated the public records of his death. He too noted the mention of a man with golden eyes. Utilizing what remained of his father's wealth, he established a name for himself in the criminal underworld and began seeking out the one mentioned."

The long-barrel switched from his left shoulder to his right, and he could hear the man step accordingly to the other side. "A moon ago, I was contacted and requisitioned to plan a jewelry heist. Being the professional I am, I took partial payment up front and began investigating the stores in the area. Then, half a moon ago, I was told to focus on one store in particular…"

Holy fireballs.

"Billburn's Brass and Gold."

"It wasn't fate that I happened across the break-in that morning, was it?"

"Correct." The man almost sounded pleased by the question. He then sounded irritated and sternly rebuked him, "Don't interrupt me again."

Joe lifted his other hand, only to again drop it.

"Timothy invested a great deal of time and effort into manipulating events to his liking, but he was inexperienced and sloppy." Eagle Eyes moved the barrel from Joe's shoulder, stepped out in front, and began pacing the room.

It was indeed the very same man. He was identical to the corpse they had found… but how?

"The first stage of his plan was to get caught and leave behind enough evidence to suggest a third party was involved in the heist; a third party with eagles' eyes. He even went so far as to exactly duplicate my shoes."

That answers a few questions

"He also paid off a well-to-do private advocate to remove Blackfinger from the precinct. He wanted to be the only one to provide a testimony of the events in question. He undoubtedly made it sound like he was the victim, when in truth, he was the mastermind."

Joe clenched his fists as he felt the proverbial knife dig deeper.

"As I understand it, he put on quite the performance of an innocent and skittish juvenile."

Manipulative little mimic, I will strangle you when I find you.

"The only point at which I underestimated the little bastard was when I received word that he was at Billburn's. I took it upon myself to steal the shock barrel that Timothy had provided to Blackfinger to make it look like a simple quarrel of riches gone wrong."

You didn't expect me to be there.

"I wasn't expecting detectives. I presume that Timothy was hoping you'd kill me. Despite your lucky shot, it was a sloppy setup at best."

Joe couldn't deny that logic.

"Fortunately, I used that incident to cover my trail and create a scenario in which you would find my body. I cleared this hideout of any valuables and adjusted the illusion so that the brick was discolored from the rest."

Seriously?

"I also adjusted the fuses and deactivated several other traps to make it easier for you."

SERIOUSLY?

"Even if you had failed, I set the incendiary spells to their lowest settings; at most, there would have been some flashes and smoke and plenty of evidence to rifle through."

…I hate you.

"A hired gunman shot at you the first night. The one to kill Travok and graze your leg was undeniably Timothy. I have made no attempts on your life and I'd rather not begin to do so. Your instincts are serviceable at best, but you do have quite the skill with barriers." The man turned toward Joe and leaned closer to ask, "How many bullets did you stop that day?"

Joe cleared his throat and answered, not wanting to incur the man's anger or another electric dart, "I stopped a regular long shot and one arcane-powered long shot. The second arcane-powered long shot pierced the barrier and grazed my leg."

"Ha!" Eagle Eyes threw his head back and barked aloud. Joe had clearly made an impression upon the man. "I'd like it if you didn't sniff my tail. I'd hate to have to turn and kill you." He placed great emphasis on the last two words.

In that moment, with how easily Joe had been duped, he didn't doubt the man capable of it. "I'd really like to keep living."

His tone lightened slightly. "I'm certain you would. To that end, I suggest you listen closely, as I'm about to tell you where to find that traitorous little bastard so that you can finish him before he finishes you."

Joe let out a deep sigh and nodded his head. "I'm listening."

Chapter 26

Joe suddenly appeared in the middle of the warehouse with a nauseating sense of dizziness. Teleportation events weren't always smooth, and the lightning dart likely had interrupted some of the flow of his body's natural energies. Light, if there was any nearby, was too bright. The sound of footsteps on gravel was like nails scratching against his brain.

"JOSEPH RUNEWALL!" He'd never heard Petals so angry.

Dropping to his knees and covering his ears failed to halt the unsettling flip his stomach decided to engage in.

Oh, gods! Don't yell!

"Where have you been?"

His stomach churned and the certainty of something bubbling up doubled. The threat of vomiting was suddenly interrupted as something was waved in front of his nose by a vaporous hand.

"Take a whiff of that, mate. It'll sort you out."

The only means to imaginably describe the onslaught to the senses would be to take a bag full of the hottest spices and cram it up your nose and down the throat, with some of it spilling out your ears and infusing your tears.

Joe shouted until his throat went hoarse from the effort. It was the only acceptable response to such an olfactory assault. Rolling about the dirt-covered floor while screaming and pulling at his hair also seemed to be the only means by which to vent the painful existence. Propriety be damned. Thankfully, the assault only lasted for a few agonizing moments, and the pain quickly ebbed away into nothingness.

Fireballs. I hate you, William!

Panting and blowing up dust and dirt, he lay on the ground, trying to collect his thoughts. He likely looked like a copperless mess. Snot dribbled down his face and cheek along with a long stream of tears.

Petals' feet appeared beside him a moment afterwards.

Joe turned his head to see the trickster gnome looming over him. The little man's foot wasn't tapping, and his face was twisted in rage. "I was worried sick!"

He let out a long deep sigh, then grunted and slowly drew his body up into a seated position with his legs sprawled out before him. "I got it."

The little man scowled and narrowed his eyes. The tiny button nose continued to flare with each rage-fueled breath. "What *exactly* did you get?"

"Everything."

"You were gone for an *hour*!"

Joe nodded and lifted his left hand to show his superior the luminescent red rune mark burned there. "I had to negotiate for it." In days long past, important agreements were sealed with magic. Rune marks burned into the palm of the hand were often the result of such handshakes.

Petals' eyes grew wider with each passing second as they flicked between Joe's face and his marked hand.

Uh oh.

The saying 'they never saw it coming' was often associated with individuals that were struck so violently and so quickly, that they honestly couldn't remember upon waking what it was that struck them. Joe never saw it coming.

~~

He stood at full attention with his hands clasped behind his back as the dragon kin captain eyeballed him with an electric gaze and an aura of intimidation that would scare the hair off a hare.

Petals stood on the captain's desk, delivering the meanest of stink eyes he'd ever seen delivered by a rosy-cheeked gnome.

He had no explanation or recollection of what the little trickster had done to him, but he had awakened the next morning in bed, with all his clothes neatly tucked away and not an inch of his skin blemished, bruised, or broken in any way. Despite that, he hurt. Everything hurt. His hair hurt, and he'd never been able to feel his hair before.

Breakfast had been consumed with a pit in his stomach, and the walk to work had felt a great deal longer than it actually was.

As much as he wanted the approval of his superiors, he knew that he'd done the right thing.

"Explain it to me, *slowly*." The captain's voice shook everything in the room, despite the audible level of his question being completely within a tolerable range. The monstrous captain breathed power.

Joe swallowed hard and chose his words carefully. He was bound by a rune mark and didn't want to suffer the agreed-upon consequences "I was contacted by someone that believed they had credible intelligence concerning my case."

"Someone?" The lumbering dragon kin slowly stepped around Joe, examining him and dressing him down as any Academy drill master had done in the past.

The quickest answer was usually the best, so he lifted his hand for visual inspection. "Yes, sir, 'someone'." He had already revealed to Petals that it wasn't Gino. "Part of the agreement was that I not reveal who they are or pursue charges against them for any crime *I* perceived that they had committed." Petals seemed to twitch upon the emphasis that Joe had placed upon the single 'I'.

The electric blue eyes darted to his hand and a snarling growl followed. It caused Joe to flinch and shut his eyes. He didn't want to be eaten. He knew that the captain would never do such a thing, but the fact that a dragon kin was standing before him and snarling caused the less civilized portion of his mind to panic and think it anyway.

Captain Bolt turned on Petals. "And where were you during this arrangement?"

"The rookie had been spelled away to a remote location. Attempts to discover that location were blocked and hampered by the sophistication of the spell utilized… that was when I called dispatch for backup."

Thundering fireballs, it's on record.

His heart started galloping at an even greater pace. His career was teetering on a precipice.

Rounding back on Joe, the captain pressed further. "What exactly did you gain?"

Joe didn't lower his hand. The hand remained upright as though he was being sworn to speak the truth. He kept his thoughts and his words specifically vague. "Everything, sir."

"Everything?"

Joe nodded. "I can't reveal those details until you accept the conditions, sir."

"I?"

"Yes, captain. The individual in question was very specific. They said that the captain of my precinct had to accept the conditions I was empowered with communicating."

I'm either going to be eaten, or the Fates will smile on me.

His voice lowered to a near inaudible rumble, "Continue."

"The arrangement is sealed with the shaking of my hand and that of the captain of my precinct. *I* cannot reveal their identity, nor can *I* pursue charges against them for any perceived crimes *I* believed they had committed at the time of the handshake." He was wholly uncertain with his attention fixed on the captain, but Joe thought he saw a tug of a smirk trying to escape from the depths of Petals' soul. The man hadn't missed the emphasis of 'I' that Joe had placed on each line of the agreement.

The captain stood, holding Joe's gaze for a long minute. His scaly face was completely unreadable. "Do you think this exchange, this agreement, was worth it?"

"I'd bet my career on it, sir."

Petals flinched and squeezed shut his eyes.

Uh oh...

The captain let loose a deep grunt. "Done." The massive draconic hand gripped his and squeezed.

Searing heat filled his hand. It set the arcane mark to burning anew. "HAAAA!" Joe yanked his hand away only to see a new mark overlapping the old one.

He looked to his captain with horror, "What? I– did you!?"

The snarling teeth drew closer to him as the electric gaze narrowed, "Tell us *everything* and hope it keeps you your job. If there are no convictions from this, you'll be off the force, *permanently.*"

...Oh fireballs, what did I do?

~~

He'd never led anything before as a Blue Coat, let alone a raid. Such things had always been left to the detectives, and never a rookie. The captain had clearly chosen to put everything on Joe's shoulders. As the saying went, it was time to sink or swim.

While Petals had been understandably upset about the whole secrecy and rune mark agreement, he had shown some sympathy for Joe and offered him the best of luck.

Joe didn't believe in luck and trusted that the Fates would get him through it all. Eagle Eyes had provided him with a treasure trove of intelligence.

The assembled detectives and Blue Coats had gathered around a central desk in the bullpen where Joe had lain out a section of the city map.

There was a great deal of murmurs and glances to the captain and Petals. The dragon kin and senior detective were standing in the doorway to the captain's office and observing silently. Figuring there was enough chatter about it, he got to work.

"Ahem!" All chatter halted and eyes turned to him in both curiosity and a touch of surprise. "I know I haven't been here long," he glanced at the captain out of the corner of his eye, "and might not be here for much longer, but if we're going to put a stop to this partner system and get back to a regular caseload, then you all need to listen in."

Appealing to their desired need for personal space and comfort seemed to do the trick, as all the detectives assembled leaned closer in. "Our target is Timothy Grimthorn."

That name tuned in more than a few ears. Many of the detectives assembled had heard about the Noble Killings or had been around when they happened and recognized the name immediately. Amelia, in particular, shook her head in an 'of course' manner and shut her eyes in frustration.

Joe proceeded to explain the grudge that Timothy, or Tim, as they knew him, had against the man with the golden eyes and the manipulations that followed. After getting everyone caught up to speed, he turned to one of the

Blue Coats that had gathered around with them. "Mr. Tannen?"

The young man was a little older and slightly shorter than Joe and had broad shoulders and an athletic frame. He had graduated from the Academy when Joe was first arriving as a cadet. Despite being older, the man didn't seem to hold any grudge about taking orders and stood a bit taller, as though ready for any order given.

Joe sighed and nodded to the stairs. "I need you to go detain Ms. Rosewater."

The entire bullpen burst into hysterics as the men threw a stink about arresting a beautiful dame while Amelia crossed her arms with a serious scowl. There was arm waving, papers tossed into the air, and a few curses thrown at him as well.

A look over his shoulder gave him a glimpse of a less than impressed captain, and a slightly worried Petals. The thought of being thrown from the force caused him to momentarily panic.

Rule one: don't panic.

He focused on what he did have control over, the detectives and Blue Coats before him. Captain Bolt had given him a conditional command to prove his worth.

Sink or swim.

Joe whipped his wand from his pocket, released it into a staff, and slammed the butt end into the ground with every ounce of intimidation magic he could muster. While his decision had been spur of the moment, his absolute frustration from the days leading up to that moment boiled over and fueled it into something he thought was rather impressive.

An audible thunderous strike ripped through the wood floorboards, shook the desks and rippled the coats of those assembled, and tossed a few hats. It sounded as though someone had struck a wooden mallet against a solid iron door. The reverberation hung in the air for several moments as silence encompassed them all.

All the attention on him was neither out of fear nor surprise. They simply looked to be ready to shout again. The last thing he wanted was another shouting match or some sort of contest of who could throw the heartier fist.

John would win that contest.

Instead of yelling or showing his frustration or anger, he opted for giving them the plain and simple facts. "Ms. Rosewater is Timothy Grimthorn's half-sister."

Faces shifted from confrontational agitation to immediate confusion. He doubted any of them expected him to say such a thing. Their faces shifted again from confusion, to shocked betrayal, then anger.

Once the outrage set in, he continued, "She has been feeding her half-brother information for the past three moons."

Amelia turned out to be the most vocal in the ensuing outburst of justifiable anger. "That wench!"

Joe slammed the butt of his staff into the ground again. It was less powerful than the first time and only charged with a bit of energy to replicate the sound from the first outburst. No intimidation magic had been implemented the second time. It did as he intended and brought the room back to order.

"Mr. Tannen."

The young man had been one of the less-vocal opponents of locking up the young woman and stood at attention again.

"I believe I gave you an order." He hated to pull rank, but he needed to show them that he meant business and wasn't going to be a pushover.

Tannen grimly accepted his orders and headed for the stairs.

Joe turned back to the rest of the bullpen and raised one hand into the air as a show of non-threat. "Ms. Rosewater is just as much a victim as we have been. Her brother promised to cut her in on some of her late father's fortune in exchange for information. He lied. He spent that fortune on building up his criminal contacts."

Looks were exchanged amongst the men, and Amelia turned her back on the group. She'd obviously been touched by the betrayal a bit more personally.

John was the first to speak up. "How do you know all this?"

Joe put his staff away and leaned forward, putting both hands on the desk. "I bet my career for the intel."

Several heads snapped to attention, including Amelia's. Joe stood straight again, then pulled off the silk gloves he had been wearing to try and hide the rune mark burned there.

Gasps filled the room and John stood up straight while rubbing his face with his hands. Amelia jumped around the corner of the table and gripped his hand to see it closer.

She looked up at him in a very unnerving and probing way. "You did this to catch one criminal?"

His decision to take the agreement provided by Eagle Eyes was wrought with doubt. Not that the information was bad, as he had already negated that possibility by stating that any information provided in bad faith would result in repercussions for Eagle Eyes. His only doubts were whether the captain and Petals would believe him. Otherwise, he had been ready to accept the consequences.

Joe leaned closer to her and spoke with a bit of grit behind it. "I. Protect. The people."

Amelia seemed a bit surprised by his intensity, and even stepped back a bit before nodding her acceptance. "All right, I'm with you, rook. Keep going."

John didn't look as convinced, but he eventually threw up his arms and shrugged. "Why not?"

The rest of the gathered detectives and Blue Coats looked to the others and then threw in their lot.

Thank the gods.

Having rallied the forces, Joe pulled out a red pin that had been stuck in the cuff of his shirt and pinned it to the map. "Our target is here, in the dead center of Red Lightning Boulevard. They're hiding in the basement of the dark dwarf-run bank, The Bloodvault."

John Stonehand stood upright again and breathed out a deep sigh while scratching the back of his head. "That's a lot of bloodlings and dark dwarves between us and them. They'll see us coming from down the road. And they're in the basement of a dwarf bank. That thing will be a fortress."

Joe nodded in understanding and answered, "It won't be easy, but I have a plan for getting in." He pulled three white pins and placed them at marks surrounding the red pin. "These are potential escape routes that Timothy may teleport to. He's shown us that he has the resources to purchase such spells."

One of the white pins covered an empty warehouse on the seaside docks. The day that Timothy shot Travok, he had teleported away. That warehouse had been the traced location of his escape. The dock wardens were the designated authorities in the area and had discovered runes etched into the floor there.

Eagle Eyes didn't disregard the possibility that the young and inexperienced crime-lord wannabe would utilize the same exit twice.

"I've discussed this with the captain and Petals. They will take these two," Joe pointed to the two pins other than the docks. "The dock wardens already know about this one and will cover it in a coordinated effort to prevent Timothy's escape."

John lifted one of his meaty hands. "What if he has more escape routes?"

Joe nodded and sighed in frustration. "That's the most difficult part about this entire raid. We have to make sure he doesn't have the chance to teleport, as he may have another exit already set up since he gave away his exit at the docks."

Amelia raised an eyebrow. "How do you plan to do that?"

Joe shrugged. "Jump him."

"Ha!" She barked and shook her head.

He defended his answer with sound reasoning. "Short of detonating an anti-magic incendiary, physical contact is the only means by which to prevent him from escaping. He also has the uncut gems stored at this location, and may be ready to bolt with them at any moment if he so much as smells us coming."

Several men stood staring at the map, shaking their heads. John pinched his nose, then rubbed his eyes with his finger and thumb. Amelia crossed her arms and scrunched her nose as she stared at the map as well.

Joe didn't want to add to the pile, but he had to. If they were to follow him on the raid, they needed to know all the facts... almost all the facts. "He's an expert marksman. If he draws a long-barrel on you, don't hesitate." He hated to do it, but he threw on more, "There's also an unknown gunman that may still be in his employ."

Amelia stood a bit straighter and worked her jaw. He could tell she wanted a swing at the treacherous little roach as well.

John eventually piped up with the question Joe had been waiting for. "All right. We clearly can't walk down the street and up to the front door because the dark dwarves and bloodlings have likely been paid off, and they don't exactly like us all that much either. So what's your crazy plan?"

"We're going to make a deposit."

Chapter 27

Grimbomb led the way. It was undeniably the most unstable portion of his plan, but it was the best one he had. The man was a dwarf, so his accent was spot on.

Joe, naturally, couldn't stop grinning, as he had finally gotten his ultimate revenge on Amelia.

"This is stupid! And it's itchy! I hate it!" Amelia furiously scratched at the wisps of ebony hair that covered her face.

Joe lifted his staff, hidden as a Blackwood cane, and swatted her hand. "No scratching, you'll give us away."

She turned a vicious, red-eyed scowl on him and clenched her hands while fuming and breathing heavily through her nose. It caused the wisps of her beard to flutter, making her look more deranged, as it likely tickled her.

Petals had pulled his greatest 'prank' yet and performed a bit of transformative magic upon each of them. Despite the fact that Amelia had been transformed into a dark dwarf woman, she had a beard. It was common for them to have beards. The beards were thinner than that of their male counterparts, but they had beards nonetheless.

John turned and thumped Joe in the arm with a meaty fist and barked aloud, "Don't hit your sister, or I'll break that cane over your head!"

Way to get into character!

Joe quickly glanced around while rubbing his arm. Nobody seemed to notice or care about four dark dwarves having a family squabble while walking down the street. He muttered under his breath for the three of them to hear, "Mind your accent, or you'll raise suspicion."

Amelia shot proverbial fireballs with her eyes over her shoulder. She wasn't in any mood to check anything about her behavior. "Do I *have* to wear *this*?" She pointed to her chest and the corset that accentuated it.

Petals had done an amazingly accurate job of transforming them to appear as dark dwarf nobles. Amelia in particular was wearing a black leather corset and wool skirts done up with silk embroidery.

Joe didn't dare let his eyes sink to the bosom she was blatantly pointing at. Instead, he hurried a few steps ahead to walk beside her and shushed her. "Shhh! Yes! It's traditional fashion for a dark dwarf noble woman right now."

"Shush me again, rook, and I'll freeze your head and smash it!"

Grimbomb threw explosives into the mix. "I think ye look smashing!"

You really do enjoy dancing with death.

Amelia fumed and screamed internally until she started making a noise typically reserved for boiling kettles.

"We're almost there... Princess." Joe couldn't contain his smile. He had specifically chosen her undercover name: Princess Bloodstone. Dark dwarves often gave ostentatious names to their daughters.

"DON'T CALL ME PRINCESS!"

That one got everyone's attention. The entire street ground to a halt, except the carts. Thankfully, it also caused the bloodlings and dark dwarves that were near to divert and walk further away from them.

The bloodlings far outnumbered the dark dwarves and often kept their distance unless in greater numbers. The pointy-toothed pale menaces were as tall as gnomes but were far thinner and bore a far more sinister appearance.

Amelia kept fuming as she stood clenching her fists and breathing heavily. Joe threw up his hands in a show of backing off.

John, as ever the voice of reason, didn't break stride and pushed Amelia ahead while Joe took up the rear. He only hoped that the others were ready for when the chaos erupted.

The Bloodvault stood out among the dingy red brick buildings of Red Lightning Boulevard. It was staked out by red marble pillars and had a great deal of its architecture modeled after the gothic and grotesque. Figures were smashing each other with hammers or dismembering or piercing each other with spears, swords, and axes.

Heavily-padded dark dwarves stood guard at either side of the entrance. Their coats reached their thick and heavy boots, and they had helmets and long-barrels at the ready. They were undoubtedly private security. The bearded men had their heads on swivels and largely ignored Joe's group. The coloring of their armor was black, gray, and roughly-polished iron. They also had a crest over their left chest, a red hammer crossing a long-barrel. He didn't recognize it, but figured it belonged to a private company.

They would have pressed through the narrow set of doors unbothered had it not been for Grimbomb.

"Oi! What kind of stocks them bangers have?" The overly curious quartermaster got right up close to the guards and started eyeballing their firearms like it wasn't a highly suspicious thing to do.

Joe bolted for the quartermaster in a moment of panic and gripped him by the beard and the coat at the same time. "Grimly!" He had chosen an easy-to-remember name for Grimbomb in case his explosive-addled brain couldn't remember.

"AH! NOT THE BEARD!" Grimbomb flailed his arms as he was spun about to face Joe, then growled as he tried to pry Joe's hands off his coat and singed locks of wiry hair.

Joe gave it his best shot and snarled back, "Keep yer eyes off the bangers! You got plenty of boom-sticks of yer own to play with!"

Grimbomb must have forgotten what Joe looked like, because he swung with his full fist. "Get yer hands off me, ye dirty dark excuse—"

Years of Academy training had given him a slight edge on the stout dwarf, and his right hand came quicker than Grimbomb's. He managed to catch the man before he said something potentially damning to all of them. Thankfully, he had also spent a great deal of time sparring with his classmates and knew how to throw a kiss of a punch.

Grimbomb was so stunned by the quick touch to the cheek that he remembered what he was supposed to be doing.

The guard that Grimbomb had been getting far too close to stepped forward with his long-barrel pulled up and at the ready, like some great pike or halberd. "What was he about to say?"

Oh fireballs... damn you, Grimbomb!

John was quick to jump to the recovery. "Dark excuse for a brother! I can't get these ungrateful children to stop fightin' each other." He swatted Joe upside the back of the head, then gripped him by the arm and shoved him to the entrance. "Get goin', or I'll forget about setting up your accounts all together!"

The guard seemed to accept the answer and allowed them all to pass.

The interior of the bank was modeled in the same fashion as the exterior. The floor tiles were a checkered pattern of red and black marble. Red pillars seemed to form the majority of the support structure and dark dwarves and bloodlings sat behind large red-oak desks, stamping forms and counting coins.

Black and red seem to be favored colors of criminals.

There were a great many more guards – *many* more guards. Joe counted twelve that he could see, and he bet there were more he couldn't. The plan was looking a bit hairier than he had originally thought, but it was so far progressing as intended.

John pressed Amelia ahead as she continued to furiously scratch at her face. Joe kept a grip on Grimbomb as the bomb-brained dwarf kept eyeballing the guards and their armaments.

They followed the designated crimson rope barriers until they were standing in the appropriate line, awaiting their turn. There was only one other in front of them, thankfully.

He felt an odd sense of calm, as the plan seemed to be working. They hadn't been hit with any anti-magic, and they weren't especially acting out of character.

Two loud pops echoed from the outside, and turning to look back, Joe spotted a small gang of bloodlings storming the front door with miniature firearms drawn. The guards that had been standing at the door slumped to the ground and fell over, presumably dead.

The half-sized menaces were dressed in black leather and wore red cloths over their mouths while their heads were covered by the typical blood-red cap that was associated with every bloodling.

More black and red, must be a fashion trend.

The leader of the group lifted his weapon and fired off a shot into the ceiling. "This is a bank robbery! Everyone get on the ground!"

You have to be kidding me.

Gunfire erupted immediately after the pronouncement. The armed guards either dropped to a knee to steady the shots of their long-barrels or they took up cover behind one of the many pillars that lined the grand hall.

The bloodlings began jumping about the entryway in a chaotic mess of red blurs. Being creatures of magic, they were known to utilize a variant of teleportation that allowed them to cover short distances in the blink of an eye, with the only indication that they'd moved being a red streak of light.

Long-barrels thundered and took great chunks of stone and marble out of the floor and walls as the dark dwarf bank guards opened fire on the gang of bloodlings.

The bank robbers peppered the pillars and the guards with a hail of much smaller bullets and at a much higher rate. Thankfully, the bloodlings were only capable of carrying much smaller ammunition and firearms.

Joe had been struck by the smaller rounds before and could say from experience that they hurt a great deal less than the larger ones. However, they were no less deadly. A single shot to the head was all it took to kill, just like any other bullet.

Many things took place over the first few moments of the gunfight. Joe grabbed Grimbomb and dove behind a bench. The wooden box-frame bench had been set up for banking customers so that they could wait their turn. Naturally, the explosive-happy dwarf barked in defiance of being yanked away from watching the chaos unfold.

John and Amelia managed to make it to a nearby pillar. The bank guards advanced past the both of them with their long-barrels at eye level.

Bank clerks slammed closed their books, slapped bells on their desks, and ducked out of sight. The bells must have been laced with trigger spells; as soon as they were struck, great metal sheets rose up to fill the windows the clerks had been speaking through a moment before.

Customers yelled, screamed, fainted, and dove to the ground, covering their ears and heads.

As much as Joe wanted to get his man, he was also a man of the law. He felt a deep-seeded obligation to protect the innocent.

I wonder how innocent they are, banking in such a place?

The thought struck him and was just as quickly abolished by the thought that the people in this part of town likely had no other choice.

Before he could act on instinct, the bank guards did their duty and stepped into the line of fire. One stepped out from behind a pillar while carrying a massive iron shield that covered the dwarf from head to toe. He stood out and deflected the odd bullet or ricochet so other guards could guide the customers to safety.

As much as he distrusted dark dwarves, he couldn't fault these ones. They were doing as he would have, and in an effective fashion.

Of the dozen or so bank robbers that had initially entered and began firing, four were limp and surrounded by puddles of blood. Only one bank guard had fallen, and he looked to be writhing in pain.

"GET UP!"

The gruff and muffled voice caught Joe by surprise. Looking to his right, he spotted a similarly-shielded guard offering his hand. Grimbomb was already over by Amelia and John. Joe took the hand and was immediately yanked across the floor, where he slid across the polished marble with ease.

"Now stay here!" The guard deposited Joe with the others he had entered with, turned back to the chaos at the entrance, and advanced.

John grabbed Joe by the back of his coat and hauled him to his feet as they all huddled behind the pillar. "This is going swell!"

"Better than I hoped!"

Amelia turned a shocked glare upon him. "Are you mad?"

"Maybe." He turned his attention to the truly mad one among them. "Grimbomb?"

The crazed lunatic was fully leaning around the pillar while bullets whizzed about. "Aye?"

"Make the deposit!"

The mad dwarf didn't even bother acknowledging. He simply reached into his long coat and pulled free an iron-caged cylinder full of fuse string and fireworks wax caps of various colors, then tossed it. Once air-born, the king of pyrotechnic chaos bolted from the pillar with two modified short-barrels in hand and let loose a maniacal cackle.

Joe turned to Amelia and John and yelled, "NOW!" before turning and running toward the back stairs. The stairs, like the layout of most banks, lead toward the basement and the vault. It also led toward his intended target.

They hadn't made it ten steps when the mysterious contraption that Grimbomb had lobbed into the lobby erupted. Screaming lights of color shot out in every direction and exploded in a rapid succession that he'd never imagined hearing in his lifetime.

Joe was certain that fireworks were not meant to be released inside of a confined space that could echo the explosions. It was thunderously deafening, and he was wearing his detective's hat. Streams of light shot over head, causing him to duck as he ran. The lights struck walls and left colored powder burns.

As expected, Timothy emerged from the basement. The young and scrawny man that Joe had tried comforting in the Blue Coat bullpen was wearing an all-black ensemble. His trousers were well-cut and cleanly trimmed. His vest was akin to Joe's, with its own arcane runes of violet and red. His hair was blond instead of ruddy, and it was combed and neatly trimmed.

The thoroughly confused and shocked man stood at the top of the steps with his hands covering his ears. He was screaming something that Joe couldn't hear as he looked about at the chaos unfolding.

Joe decided to pay him an unkind visit, barreled forward, and threw himself head and shoulders first into Timothy's gut. Wrapping his arms tight around the waist of his perp, Joe yelled the release word that would undo the transformative magic Petals had placed upon him, "JELLY ROLLS!" He felt a jarring – but non-painful – pop in his joints as he returned to regular size. His clothing, skin, and hair reverted to its normal coloring, size, and shape.

The moment after his body reverted to normal, they struck the marble stairs. Timothy grunted as they landed, and Joe barked out in pain as his elbow hit hard. Pain shot up his arm, into his shoulder, and numbed his fingers. He only hoped his arm wasn't broken.

Timothy and Joe began sliding and rolling down the marble steps. Every single bump on the stairs was jarringly violent and painful. Thankfully, Joe easily overpowered the scrawny assassin and thief and rode the man down the last few steps while gripping his vest in both hands.

Surprisingly, Timothy had plenty of fight in him and managed to throw Joe off but not break his grip.

Being the bigger of the two of them, Joe used the leverage from being thrown to roll and haul the smaller man with him. Timothy let out a yelp of surprise as he was yanked from the ground and tossed at the office door.

Joe regretted many decisions he had made in his life. Few he regretted as much as when he attempted to throttle the smaller man by throwing him at a door.

The vault of the bank was seated beneath the main lobby and to the left of the bottom of the stairs. The manager's office – as the painted lettering on the glass of the door proclaimed – was directly in front of the descending stairs. Joe had thrown Timothy at the manager's office door, unaware as to what was beyond it.

The shattering of the glass was insignificant to the dwindling, yet still ongoing, cacophony taking place in the lobby. Despite that, it was hard for the small horde of bloodlings that were crammed into the manager's office to not notice a man being thrown through the glass.

Ah, fireballs.

Timothy groaned and mumbled something to the small horde of sharp-toothed wretches as they started snarling and advancing through the hole in the door. Each one of them pulled an appropriately-sized blade from their pocket or belt.

Joe reached out to the left for his staff, only to flinch and yell out in excruciating pain. A red streak of light had shot forth and a bloodling jumped him and stabbed him in the back of the hand while stepping on his staff.

Thundering fireballs!

The bloodling yanked his dagger free and lifted it above his head as he prepared to plunge it into Joe's head. At the peak of his arc, the entirety of his being was suddenly walloped and thrown against the wall as a tenderized and peppered mess of bloody holes.

Joe peered over his shoulder to see John, still in his dark dwarf disguise, standing at the ready with a smoking shock barrel in hand.

Amelia descended the steps to stand beside John. Her six-shooter was leveled and at the ready. "Iced cream." With her release word spoken aloud, she suddenly popped back into her regular apparel and appearance with a cloud of blue sparkles evaporating around her.

Oh good, she chose food too.

John glanced up at Amelia, rolled his eyes and sighed under his breath, "Chocolate cream pie." Like Amelia, the man popped back into his regular size and appearance, and he looked to the gathered bloodlings and barked, "On your knees!"

Yay! We all went with food words!

Joe turned his attention back to the bloodlings and Timothy, then shifted and rolled to grip his staff with the hand that didn't have a bleeding hole in it.

"You all right there, rook?"

Joe grunted and managed to get to one knee. "I'll live."

With the opportunity to get his bearings a bit better, Joe could finally see that the manager's office had been transformed into a gem-cutter's shop. There were glittering stones all over the desk and cutter's tools strewn about. It was just as Eagle Eyes had said.

Timothy – despite being a glass-cut, bruised, and beaten mess upon the floor of the office – was grinning. He lifted a long and thin rectangular rune stone from his pocket and pressed his thumb against it to snap it with one hand. He managed to bark out, "Maleficence."

The word must have been a trigger for a spell, similar to the release word that Joe, Amelia, and John had used to drop their disguises. The instant after it had been spoken, a black handbag suddenly jumped from the desk to land in Timothy's other uplifted hand. While the bag was airborn, every visible ruby, emerald, and sapphire leaped off the desk and into the bag.

"No!" Joe threw himself toward Timothy with his staff leading the way.

Time seemed to crawl to a stop as the chaos intensified. The rune stone that Timothy had in his grip and was proceeding to snap in half was likely charged with some form of escape spell. Teleportation, Recall – it didn't matter.

The bloodlings began slashing their fingertips, undoubtedly to begin drawing blood spells. Bloodlings were named for such abominable magic practices. Another thunderous blast erupted from Joe's left, likely from the shock barrel that John had brought along.

The rune stone in Timothy's hand snapped. The physical form of the young, scrawny, and pulverized man began to warp and swirl upon a point in space and time. His grin, despite the warping of reality, remained.

Fate, as it would have it, wished Joe to succeed. His staff managed to connect with Timothy's foot, just as the spell was about to pull him fully into the void. A twist of his wrist and a thorough push of his will made a solid connection between the two of them.

It was thankfully, perfectly timed. Several bloodlings had been in the process of jumping to Joe with their knives drawn, and he had little, if any, chance of defending himself against that many knives in such close quarters.

That thought made him concerned for John and Amelia. He was leaving them to handle a good dozen bloodlings by themselves. Blue Coat backup was at the end of the street and awaiting the 'package' to be delivered. They would likely have already begun charging to the rescue upon the noisy deployment, thanks to Grimbomb. However, there was no telling what sort of damage the little monstrosities could cause between the onset of the onslaught and backup arriving. It was all well and possible that he had just doomed Amelia and John to a gruesome fate.

Gods be with you.

The spell that Timothy had initiated grabbed hold of Joe and yanked him from the air into the nothingness between realities, just shy of being slashed to bits by a handful of bloodling knives.

Chapter 28

The professors at the Arcanum had discussed at great length the dangers and disastrous effects of interrupting or jumping in on an outgoing teleportation event. It could result in death, dismemberment, permanent discombobulation, spontaneous relocation, blindness, deafness, and any other myriad of unknown side effects.

To that end, it wasn't a surprise to Joe when he was violently hurled into the air and Timothy was shot out sideways as they both exited the destination vortex. The Fates had been kind enough to merely throttle them instead of whatever other horrible ending they could have been given.

Joe grunted and attempted to utilize what little memory and skill he had of levitation magic to right himself and ease his descent to the ground. That didn't happen.

Instead of tumbling through the air in a clockwise rotation, he instead started spinning counter clockwise. He managed to cushion his fall, but not enough that he didn't feel it in every fiber of his being when he landed on a book-laden tabletop of the local library. It broke in half.

Timothy was lucky he only knocked over a few half-shelves in the children's section. It slowed his momentum in a far less painful fashion. At least, Joe presumed, it was far less painful than breaking an oak table in half.

Children and patrons screamed at the sudden appearance of people being thrown about, not to mention the destruction. It only took a few seconds for a librarian to appear and began screaming obscenities.

"What in the holy gods is going on here?"

Any attempts to speak were stifled by the wind that had been knocked out of him.

Some of the slightly older children began pointing at his hat and clothes. "Look, he's a detective!"

"He's bleeding! Look at his hand!"

Someone muttered near the back of the growing circle, "I have a book on first aid and bandages."

A wailing scream broke through the crowd. It originated from where Timothy had been ejected.

Joe fumbled and struggled to sit upright.

"Sir! No! You must stay down!" The librarian was dressed in the standard brown robe with white stripes. She bent down to try and stop him from moving.

"Mommy!" A little girl had been the source of the wail. "Bad man has my mommy!"

Grunting with the effort, Joe pushed passed the pain and sat upright. He then partitioned his mind and forced the pain to the side. Using the staff for support, he hauled to his feet and steadied himself. Warmth ran down the side of his head.

"Sir! You can't go on! You're severely wounded! Let the Blue Coats outside handle this!" The librarian tried to hold him back.

Joe yanked his arm free and nearly collapsed from the piercing pain that shot through it; it was definitely broken. After a second of quick, sharp breaths, he managed to steady and control the dizzying need to give in and pass out.

Assessing the situation, he needed to mend his arm and get back after his target. With a deep breath, Joe lifted his staff, pointed the head at his broken arm, and released a bit of magic.

There was an audible meaty crack as the bone set. Joe nearly blacked out from the sudden sharp pain. He roared incomprehensibly and twisted the staff to dig in deeper and set a binding barrier around the bone. It should hold for a few minutes.

Not wanting to lose any time, Joe kicked aside the rubble of books around his feet, turned, and set out in the direction the little girl was jumping up and down and pointing at. The librarian followed, "You'll collapse if you keep doing this to yourself!"

A glance at the librarian made him realize where he was. He had visited the library hundreds of times before while studying at the Arcanum. It was one of the few city-run libraries that had a restricted section for Arcanum students. The librarian was Ms. Watts, if he recalled correctly.

He slowly pulled away and headed to the exit the little girl was bawling in front of. Joe found his stride as he limped along and thumped his staff as he reached the doors. They swung wide as he used a bit of magic to throw them open.

Timothy hadn't gotten far. Folks were standing about, shouting and calling for a Blue Coat as they pointed down the road. They were close to the central district and in a busy part of town. Many of the buildings were at minimum three stories tall and cast long shadows.

Joe wasted no time in throwing himself across the street with his staff held high. Gnome cart and city cart drivers shouted out their windows and rang their bells as he darted out in front of them.

The pain from earlier was starting to subside as the rush overtook him. He picked up the pace and started to sprint as pedestrians pointed the direction they saw Timothy drag his hostage.

"Save that poor woman!"

"Get that madman!"

"He was carrying a six-shooter!"

The last few shouts were encouraging and helpful.

Upon rounding the corner, he spotted the limping, scrawny man dragging a hysterically screaming young woman along with him.

Joe gained a few more paces before stopping to store his staff and draw his firearm, roaring, "TIMOTHY GRIMTHORN!"

The scrawny blond-haired man spun on the spot and struggled to stay on two feet as he dragged the woman close and stuck the barrel of the gun to her head.

The young lady must have been little more than Joe's age. The child he'd seen wailing in the library was likely no older than four or five. Her blonde curls and pleated skirts acted as a sufficient screen for Timothy to hide behind as he wrapped one arm around her neck and held her tight against him. There was no clean shot. He couldn't graze him without the risk of hitting the hostage.

Timothy yelled out from around her as he held a snub-nosed six-shooter to the side of her head, "Detective Runewall! How? How did you know where I was hiding?"

Joe kept his firearm level and steadied it with a small secondary partition. He couldn't hold it for long as the pain was starting to seep in again. "I'm a detective, *Tim*."

The crazed man breathed heavily as he grinned wickedly and shook his head. "No! No! You're not that good! I paid off every single one of those moronic and disgusting creatures to keep their mouths shut!"

He couldn't disclose the fact that Eagle Eyes was alive, so he decided to play off the wretch's distaste for anything non-human. "Treating partners-in-crime as moronic and disgusting creatures might be the very reason that paying them to keep their mouths shut didn't work!"

Timothy turned spiteful and sneered while shaking the hostage and sticking the barrel tighter against her head. It caused her to scream out and beg, "Please! No!"

A local Blue Coat arrived on the scene on the other side of the street and drew their firearm, leveling it at Timothy from behind a network booth.

Stupid!

Timothy noted the direction of Joe's attention, spun about, looking behind and around him as he stepped closer to an alleyway. "Get back!"

Joe roared at the Blue Coat while waving him off with his broken arm, "Get back!"

The mustached man seemed confused by the order but complied and slowly retreated.

The woman started wailing to not be left alone and for someone to please save her. Timothy only got angrier and shook her more. "SHUT IT!" He turned his attention on Joe and pulled back the hammer on his six-shooter. "If so much as one more of your friends show up or if you follow me, I'll make another orphan friend for you to play with!"

"What did you just say to me?"

"You heard me, Joseph!"

Only once before in his life had he ever felt so utterly and completely certain of the need for violence. Morality and law suddenly became secondary in his mind. Timothy was going to suffer.

The terrified woman that was begging him with her tear-stained, snot-bubbled, quivering-lipped face made him feel like a little boy again. It made him feel like the little boy that stood before a group of bullies torturing a poor fairy. He felt like the little boy that swatted a bunch of bullies and threw them like ragdolls.

There was suddenly no more pain in his broken arm, and the blood stopped dripping from the knife wound in his hand. Joe eased the partition in his mind and withdrew his firearm, holstering it. He eased up out of his firing stance and stood tall, with a look of grim determination.

A maniacal and tooth-filled grin spread across Timothy's face, as he presumed that Joe was reluctantly giving in. The hostage in his arms seemed to have the same idea in mind, as she started to whimper while reaching out for Joe.

He wasn't throwing in the towel; he was focusing his rage. Unlike that moment in his youth, Joe knew what it was he could do and how to accurately strike instead of acting like a hammer and treating everything like a nail.

Timothy turned his hand to aim the firearm at Joe.

That's right… point it at me, you smug little goblin shite!

The woman threw out both her arms, reaching for Joe while screaming for him not to give in.

Time slowed yet again. The energy that had built up within him was likely going to leave him drained if he released it all, so he flipped the partition and squirrelled away some power just in case his first attempt failed.

Joe waited for the appropriate moment. He could nearly count each thump of his heart as the barrel of Timothy's firearm steadied.

Now.

A brief release of energy made his wand jump from his vest pocket and expand to full staff. Joe caught it mid-air and released the remainder of the energy untouched by the partition.

Timothy pulled the trigger and screamed, as Joe had packed the barrel with as solid of a barrier as he could conjure. He had also surrounded the barrel and Timothy's hand to prevent any explosion from affecting the poor wailing hostage.

The world seemed to jolt back to life as Timothy's arm and hand recoiled away. The young woman ripped herself free to run towards Joe.

Joe staggered on his feet as he was suddenly drained of energy and the throbbing in his arm and searing hot pain in his hand returned as quickly as it had vanished.

Timothy gripped his wrist and screamed. His hand was gone. The explosive blowback had taken his hand clean off. He turned to Joe and screamed in rage, he then tucked his stump under his armpit while bolting down the alleyway.

Joe righted himself and took a step toward following, only to be detained by the hysterics of the woman. She felt to her knees, gripping his vest as she fell, thanking him over and over while sobbing.

"Blue Coat!"

The mustached officer appeared nearly as quickly as he had vanished. He ran across the street with his firearm at the ready and grabbed the young woman by the arm, heaving her to her feet. "Come along, ma'am. let's get you somewhere safe."

Joe released the partition holding back the reserves and felt partially reinvigorated. Once steady, he took off down the street and noted the bits of metal and human flesh on the curb that had once been Timothy's hand and firearm.

Joe didn't need to be a detective to follow that messy trail. The blood led down the alley and over a short fence smeared with blood at the top. He didn't feel like climbing, so he thumped his staff, blasting the boards in half and making a decent-sized hole to step through.

Sadly, he hadn't been paying enough attention, and stepped halfway through only to be struck upside the head by a bit of wood that Timothy swung like a bat.

Joe grunted and stumbled through the fence. Unfortunately, he dropped his staff, leaving it on the other side and out of reach. His head swam as he reeled from the well-placed hit. His hat had even flown off from the sudden jolt.

The blows rained down on Joe in an unrelenting assault. "You! Took! My! HAND!" First his back and shoulders, then the back of his leg, and finally his broken arm. The barrier didn't hold in his weakened state, and his forearm bent at the wrong angle.

During his twisted fall, Joe was just able to see that Timothy had hastily wrapped up his arm and cinched it off with his belt. The man was pale and sweating, but still able to put up a fight.

How are you still standing?

"Now... I'll *finally* kill you, just like how your precious law enforcement killed my father." Timothy raised his stick once more to bring it down on Joe's head.

"Not today." Joe swung his leg around and caught Timothy in the side of his right knee, causing him to buckle and scream out in pain as he crumpled to the trash-littered cobblestones of the alley.

He wished he had the strength to immediately jump up and clasp irons on the man, but he didn't. Timothy didn't appear to have energy anymore either.

Joe took the moment to gather and steady his swimming vision. With great pain and effort, he slowly stood up and looked to the one-handed human stain. He was desperately trying to use his stump to reach into his right trouser pocket; undoubtedly attempting to grab another rune stone to escape. The goblin shite was sobbing in frustration.

With an outstretched right hand, Joe called to his staff. It blasted through the fence like a battering ram and didn't seem to be slowed by the remnants of the standing wood. The hard metal and wood staff clapped into his hand, and it immediately made him feel safer.

Timothy jolted to life, lunged with a knife in hand, and buried it in the side of Joe's right leg. He screamed and tried to pull away, but Timothy pressed in and twisted the knife. The partition in his mind that had been holding back what little pain it could, broke.

Joe released his grip on the staff, grabbed the psychotically grinning Timothy, and hauled him up so they were face to face. He took in a deep breath, pushed Timothy away by the collar, then jerked him back in while tilting his forehead into it.

The sickening crunch of bone and splattering of blood was all Joe needed to know that his head-butt had landed as intended. Timothy lost his grip on the knife, and a small portion of the pain that inundated Joe in sickening waves eased slightly. Amazing how the pain was slightly less when the knife was no longer being twisted.

Knowing better than to remove the knife without medical attendance, Joe left it in. He whimpered and felt tears stream down his face; he could no longer hold any of it back.

Keep breathing, we can do this. Just keep breathing.

Joe reached under his coat and pulled a set of irons from the back of his belt while Timothy choked on blood through a broken nose and missing teeth. His eyes were already starting to swell shut, and his face looked slightly sunken.

"You... are under... arrest." He could barely get the words out through the ungodly pain.

Timothy made one last attempt and gave a sobbing roar of defiance as he threw himself blindly at Joe.

Not caring anymore for the well-being of his perpetrator, Joe whipped the irons at him and struck the man in the side of the head. Timothy fell limp on his face.

With Timothy unconscious, Joe took the time to slap on the irons before picking through his pockets. It wasn't until he got to the back of Timothy's vest that he finally found what he was looking for. The handle to the black handbag peered out from under the back of the black magical vest. Joe yanked it free, and the bag suddenly appeared from under the vest. There was no way the bag itself could have fit under the vest comfortably had it not been spelled for space-saving pockets, much like Joe's vest.

A quick unsnapping of the clasps and opening of the folds revealed a small treasure trove of uncut gems.

Thank the gods.

His head nearly tilted forward as the blood ebbed from the wounds in his leg and hand. Medical attention was necessary, or he wouldn't survive for long.

Reaching into Timothy's right trouser pocket, Joe found a small collection of rune stones. Each one had its own destination. Joe felt each of the four remaining stones until he singled out the one that would get him to the hideout that the captain was guarding.

Joe picked up his staff and hat, struggled to stand on one foot, and stuck the butt of the staff through one of Timothy's belt loops. Once ready, he wrapped his good arm around the staff and used his thumb and good hand to snap the rune stone.

In less than two shakes of a stiff drink, Joe found himself standing in the basement of an empty rental. The dust from lack of use kicked up a cloud from the floor around them. There was a small basement window behind him, providing little light.

"Hello?" The effort of speaking felt like enough to knock him over. He needed help, fast.

There was a giant thundering step above his head, followed by another, and another.

Thank the gods.

Captain Bolt – or at least he hoped the thundering footfalls belonged to the captain – made way across the room above, then the stairwell lantern light flicked on, nearly blinding Joe. Nausea swam over him. The head injury was taking its toll and would soon have him unconscious, so long as the blood loss didn't take him first.

The thundering dragon kin soon appeared as he made his way down each creaking step. Blue Coats were hot on the captain's tail.

Please let there be a doctor nearby.

Thankfully, the captain picked up his pace when he spotted the condition Joe was in. Once at the bottom of the stairs and in front of Joe, he reached out and placed a steadying clawed and scaled hand upon his shoulder.

"Steady, soldier." He looked down at Timothy. "Is he still alive?"

Joe turned and kicked the man in the ribs, causing a wheezing and whimpering whine to rise from him. "Yes, sir." Unfortunately, it was all he had left and dropped under the weight of his injuries.

The captain surprisingly cradled him as he fell. It turned out that the imposing, intimidating, and legendary beast could be quite gentle when necessary.

"Permission—" He couldn't finish making his request, and blackness took him.

Chapter 29

Echoes surrounded him. Everything had been a haze and memories faded as quickly as they appeared. At first, he thought the god of death had claimed his soul, but he started becoming aware of his surroundings; the opposite proved to be true.

Pain was his first recollection, then sounds, smells, and finally sights. He wasn't sure how long it took him to regain consciousness, but he regretted it as soon as he gained it. Everything hurt. The hum of the lantern light above his head was too loud. It was also too bright.

Joe couldn't move, but he could groan in the hopes that someone would hear him, understand his thoughts, and turn off the lantern light in answer.

"Hnnggh."

"Oi! Mate! You awake?"

Oh, fireballs, anyone but you!

"Captain! I think he's awake!"

STOP YELLING!

He whimpered more and shook a little when his leg, arm, hand, and head all started to cry out in agony. Joe lifted his one good arm to cover his eyes and let out a painful sigh.

"Mate, I got something that will fix you right."

He whined, "Noooo…" then dropped his good arm and managed to bump the oncoming hand of William's. He didn't know what was being offered to him, but he didn't want it.

"All right, mate." He heard William get up and out of what sounded like a cushioned chair with rusted springs. The man was to the left. His steps moved off around the bed and to the right. "I'll go see about getting you a nurse and find the captain."

You do that… please do that.

Joe lay there for a time, listening, and eventually lifted his arm to cover his eyes again. He peered out from the cover of his arm. William was gone, and he had no clue as to how long ago he had left. The man was far too silent.

Based on the general noise coming from the hallway, Joe figured he was in a medical ward. There was the odd noise of groaning and complaining. The sudden appearance of a nurse at his door confirmed it.

The woman wore the typical white gown, and her curly brown hair was pulled back with a white cloth bearing the symbol of the medical corp. Her apron had many pockets, all of which had some sort of instrument poking out of them.

"Glad to see you're up, Mr. Runewall. It was a little touch-and-go there for a bit with your head wound and blood loss." She reached over and turned a knob that lowered the light in the room. "The doctor said you'd likely be a bit sensitive to the light for a day or two. Head wounds tend to do that."

She walked over to him, lifted his arm away from his head, and began unwrapping bandages that had been wrapped around his skull. He hadn't even noticed they were there until she started touching them. The pain was sickening and caused his stomach to lurch. Thankfully, he hadn't eaten in some time and there was nothing to heave. Her hands were gentle and soft.

She flinched as Joe did, then apologized as she fully removed the bandaging and examined him. He hadn't looked in a mirror for a while, so had no idea how bad he looked or how much he'd already healed.

The nurse gave him a tight-lipped smile and nodded. "You're healing well. A few more days and you'll be right as rain."

Good to know, nothing permanent.

"They say you're quite the hero, saved a woman from being a hostage... saved a little girl from losing her mother." The nurse caressed his cheek in a very affectionate way, one that he hadn't been expecting at all.

A guttural and deep clearing of the throat rumbled from the doorway. The nurse jumped and turned to spot a massive body filling the doorway. "OH! Oh, I'm sorry, sir, I – " She stopped speaking, picked up the bloodied bandages, and hurried to the door to squeeze past.

Captain Bolt slowly entered and thumped his way across the room to stand at the foot of Joe's bed. He was a towering and frightful figure that would give any child nightmares if it were spotted at the foot of their beds.

Fireballs, the man could scare grown men if he stood at the foot of their beds.

Joe did his best to clear his throat and used his one good arm to salute. "Captain."

The massive dragon kin lifted a hand to wave off the salute and placed it behind his back again. He was wearing a massive brown trench coat with a gold badge pinned over the left breast and gold bands on either arm. It denoted his rank as captain. Joe hadn't noted it earlier, as he had been busy bleeding to death.

"Sounds like you will recover."

He struggled to clear his throat and answer, "Yes, sir."

Again, the dragon kin lifted his hand and waved it off. "Don't try to answer, soldier. I'll simply speak for a little and then let you rest. You can answer questions later."

Fantastic idea.

Thankfully, he started with the agreement the two of them had made. Joe would keep his job.

Thank. The. Gods.

Captain Bolt then proceeded with a brief summary of the events following Joe's loss of consciousness. After collapsing, the captain had pulled out a trusty healing potion and poured it down Joe's gullet. It had done the job of clotting his bleeding wounds and stabilized him. The doctors commended the captain for his work, for without it, Joe would surely have been dead.

Timothy had survived, thanks to the doctors that had managed to get a hold of him. His broken nose had been repaired, and his amputated wrist was properly cared for. His teeth *could* be fixed, but he was a criminal on a city budget. He would only get what was necessary to keep him alive.

Joe couldn't recall what else had been discussed, as he lost consciousness again. The relief of knowing that he'd keep his job and that he'd managed to capture and not kill his first criminal was overwhelming.

~~

It was Petals' turn to tell Joe the good news, as upon his re-awakening, the old gnome was lounging in the nearby chair. The sun was out, and the drapes were pulled open along with the window to let in some fresh air. Thankfully, his eyes didn't scream at him, and the light seemed rejuvenating.

"Amelia and John are absolutely fine." He waved the question off as though it had never been anything to worry about at all. "She froze all the bloodlings after John turned a few into meat confetti with his shock barrel. They walked away with minor bruises and scratches at the worst."

"What about Grimbomb?"

Petals raised an eyebrow. "Seriously? You must have really hit your head if you're worried about that one."

The ensuing chuckles caused him all kinds of pain. His body had stiffened during his many unconscious hours. "Oh! Oh! Don't make me laugh. It hurts."

After several hearty exponential bouts of laughter, they both eventually settled. Petals hopped off the chair, tenderly patted Joe's cast, and told him, "Good job, my boy, good job."

Petals headed for the door and paused to turn and tell him, "I'll have my wife make you a few meals while you recover. You'll need the strength."

Joe rested back against the pillows and simply smiled while breathing deeply. He thought he could already smell her cooking. He passed out again and started dreaming of Ms. Pettlebottom's basket of goods.

A sickly sweet smell pulled him from his dream, and he woke in the same position he had fallen asleep. It was night outside, and the street lanterns were lighting.

He turned his head and spotted someone sitting in a chair just beyond the foot of his bed. Joe didn't recognize the man. His trousers, coat, vest, shirt, shoes, and hat were all black. A blue badge hung from his coat pocket. One leg was crossed over the other, and his head and hat were tilted down, as though sleeping... or wishing to remain anonymous.

"Good morning, Mr. Runewall." Puffs of white smoke followed the words. The voice was that of a smoker, grizzled and full of phlegm. "Or should I say, good evening?"

The head slowly lifted, but only enough for Joe to spot the hand-rolled paper smoke poking out the side of the mouth. Red light burned within the ashes of the tip as the man took another deep breath and released another sickly sweet smelling puff.

Joe recognized the smoke as sweet leaf. No wonder the man's lungs sounded like they were rattling with each breath.

One black-gloved hand lifted, and a single finger tapped the blue badge. "Do you know what this is?"

He didn't. Joe had never heard of or seen such a badge before, so he slowly shook his head in reply. His head still hurt and spun a bit if he moved too quickly.

Another puff of smoke, then the hand lowered and picked up a stylus as the other hand held a notepad. "It means I'm with Internal Investigations."

Uh oh.

"You mind telling me what all happened the other day?"

Something felt off to Joe. "Don't you want to wait until I write up my report, once I return to duty?" He cleared his throat and glanced about. "Can I have some water?"

The man sat still for a moment, then slowly stood. Joe used it to check the man's height. The man stepped over to a stand near the corner, picked up a pitcher and mug, and poured out some water for Joe.

It was too dark to see, but Joe guessed the man to be a bit shorter than himself, and his hair was graying and thinning. All of it suggested the man might be telling the truth; Joe doubted young men were experienced enough to be involved in something like investigating detectives for potential wrongdoings.

Eventually, he stepped up to Joe's side and offered the cup. Joe daringly forced himself to sit up straighter and take the cup in one swift, nauseating movement. It was brief, as the man immediately stepped back, but Joe managed to get a good look at the man's face. Surprisingly, it wasn't Eagle Eyes. He had piercing blue eyes and a face of leather and scars.

After a gulp of water, he was able to better clear his throat and rest back against the pillows again. "Sorry, thought you might be someone else." He put the cup on his beside table.

"Your informant?" Another puff of smoke curled out from around his hat as he slowly walked back to his chair, then turned and sat in it.

Figured you were here for that.

"Yes." There was no point in lying about it.

"Why would you think I was them?"

"Checking to see if I kept my end of the deal."

A slight smirk tugged at the corner of the smoke-puffing mouth. "Smart kid." He settled back in and began writing notes into his notepad. "Who was it?"

Joe sighed. "Can't say; repercussions, that was part of the deal." He settled back into the bed and closed his eyes. He still felt exhausted and doubted that would change anytime soon.

"A magical agreement, I understand?"

"Yes." He didn't bother opening his eyes, as he just hoped sleep would take him soon and save him from the probing.

"What if someone were to peek into your head?"

Frustration infused its way into his breathing. "I took precautions against that."

"Oh?" There were more scribbles.

"You're not going away until I answer, are you?"

There was a slight pause before the gravel-voiced investigator answered, "No, you won't fall asleep unless I let you."

Joe opened his eyes, then closed them to feel about with what little magic he had. There was a slight aura in the room, but he couldn't tell what it was. Exhaustion wouldn't allow him to utilize any more of his will.

Figuring the aura was designed to keep him awake and conscious, it was best to answer all the questions as soon as he could so that he could get back to resting. "The agreement covered that as well. I would lock away that information so no prying minds could scry it."

More scribbles. "How?"

"I'm good with barriers; do the rune-work in your head."

More scribbles. "You seem awfully defensive."

Joe opened his eyes and slowly lifted his head to glower at him. "How about you do an investigator's job and look into my file, just like *Timothy* did... with his half-sister's help! The half-sister hired to work in a precinct! Where were your grand investigative abilities then?"

A puff of smoke curled out from around the brim of the hat again. "She was cleared by the city; her half-brother had yet to commit any crimes."

Fireballs.

Joe couldn't deny that answer was reasonable.

"What about Timothy? What did he say to you when you were both alone?" The man scribbled more notes and never once looked up or broke his monotonous assault of questions.

Let me sleep already!

He rattled off the details as quickly as he could. "Made threats, demanded he be allowed to escape, swore at me from blowing up his hand, and griped about how law enforcement failed to protect his father, the end. Satisfied?"

The man slowly raised his head to peer out under his hat at Joe, then released another long puff of smoke that curled out from under the brim. He looked back down and took several moments to scribble into the notepad. "Good enough."

He seemed to be finished, as he flipped closed his notepad, then stood and headed for the door. "Get your rest, detective."

Joe fell asleep instantly. All he could recall was the figure in the doorway, then his eyes shutting.

~~

Unsurprisingly, Petals pranked him. Joe woke with a giant pink flopping fish for a cast. Its mouth gummed his arm as the tail flailed about, slapping everything and anything near it.

Naturally, Joe screamed at the sudden absurdity of it. He'd thought he was hallucinating from whatever pills the nurses had been feeding him, but the barking jovial laughter from Petals suggested it was real.

Nurses had run into the room only to scream in turn. After the trickster gnome had his roaring fit of laughter, he turned the cast back to normal and was promptly kicked from the room for a whole ten minutes. He managed to sneak back in without being noticed by the staff.

Joe threw his pillow at the little man and swore at him under his breath. He didn't want Petals to be kicked out either, but he also felt he deserved some pillow retribution. He wanted to discuss with his superior the odd late-night visit and learn more about what had happened while he'd been out.

"Internal Investigations, you say... well I'd say you're safe. If they even had the slightest thought that you were guilty of something, they would have dragged you away in irons."

It was only slightly relieving, as Joe was holding on to the secret of Eagle Eyes' faked death.

"While your actions were a bit reckless, you got your man, and you lived. The captain said once you've filed your report, he'll shake your hand and take that mark from you." Petals pointed to Joe's casted arm and bandaged stab-scarred hand.

The bright pink line of a scar was unavoidable, but he figured it would make for a good story. His arm would take another day or two to fully heal, based on the runes set into the plaster of his cast and the notes made by the nurses. His leg was already mended, but his head needed a few more days before it stopped randomly spinning.

"Anything else I should know?"

Petals tapped his chin in thought as he sat upon the doctor's wooden stool beside Joe's bed. "Now that you mention it, Doctor Broom wanted me to tell you that your theory was correct."

Joe's brow furrowed in thought. "What theory?"

"Your theory about the underground experimental surgeries. Turns out that the man we named Eagle Eyes had his eyes replaced with the eyes of an eagle. The examination confirmed it. There were also several broken ribs piercing the lungs on the left side, right where you shot him. It explains the failed patch-up attempt."

"Were they able to identify the body?"

Petals shook his head.

Everything seemed to be tied up so neatly, yet he knew that Eagle Eyes was still out there.

"Joseph?"

He turned to look at his superior. "Yes?"

"You don't look satisfied." Petals narrowed his eyes at him.

Joe had placed a barrier inside his mind, preventing certain thoughts that would suggest Eagle Eyes was still alive and had been the source of information. "I guess I'm mad at myself."

"For what? You got all the gems back, caught the criminal, and killed Eagle Eyes." Petals looked to him with a wide grin and a raised eyebrow.

"I was duped from the start, and I can't talk about the informant. You happy I said it out loud now?"

Petals feigned ignorance. "I have no idea what you're talking about, my boy. I simply wished for you to be honest with me."

Joe nodded and apologized to his superior. "I promise I'll always be honest with you, especially since you're the one that helped me discover what I am." He said the last in hushed tones.

Petals smiled appreciatively. "My job as your training officer is to turn you into the finest detective you can be. I can't do my job very well if you've got blinders on, my boy."

"I suppose not."

The old gnome grinned, then turned and hopped off the stool. "Get your rest. Mrs. Pettlebottom prepared you a few pies. I'm sure they'll be better than the slop they serve here."

She could bake a shoe and make it taste good.

Petals barked out another hearty laugh as he headed out the door.

Chapter 30

Joe emerged from the hospital the next day without a cast. The next two days were spent resting at home in bed. Mrs. Pettlebottom had shown up at every meal to make sure he was fed and resting. The boys had visited after each dinner and chatted with him about how he had made the letter of news as the 'hero detective'.

He'd known about it through Nurse Bell. She'd shown him more than was an appropriate amount of care in thanks.

Joe doubted that the library would see him as a hero. He'd done quite a bit of damage and had terrorized a few people in the process. Word was, one of the kids had fainted while holding a first aid textbook. Coin was on the kid not becoming a doctor.

His first day back at the precinct was spent finishing his report. Sadly, four more cases had suddenly appeared on his intake pile. Amelia and John looked completely untouched.

The new joke was to suggest tackling every problem with a 'jelly roll in hand'. In hindsight, he should have handled his anger with Timothy in a much more civilized manner. His zealotry resulted in collateral damage and emotionally scarred children.

Grimbomb was apparently the king of the hour. His distraction bomb was the talk of the precinct, and so were his gum bullets. The maniac had somehow figured out how to mix metal chemical canisters and gunpowder to create a bubble-firing short-barrel that hit targets with expanding gelatin. He had managed to single-handedly incapacitate all the bank guards and remaining bank robbers with gummy green gelatin before the Blue Coats had arrived as backup. Zero casualties.

Show off.

However, the idiot somehow managed to incinerate his trousers and create an obscene incident and was written up for indecent exposure. Joe shuddered at the thought of a hairy dwarf rear.

The only thing that they had failed to find was the second gunman that had initially shot Joe in the arm. There was no indication that he'd been at the bank and Eagle Eyes hadn't provided any information either. He placed the notation in his reports and hoped that they would catch them at a later date.

In all, it had been a difficult first case, and he managed to keep his job, just as the captain had promised. The rune mark on his hand was fading, with a glaring line of a scar for a reminder on top of it.

~~

Due to his success, there was a Blue Whiskey Grill voucher waiting for him on his desk. Petals took him there after his first day back from recovering at the hospital.

It was a short walk south of the precinct, happily nestled between a flower shop and a grocer. The sign on the red brick structure was identical to the calling card Marcus had left behind after his 'first bullet' meal.

Hard to miss.

Surprisingly, an old tavern sign hung out from above the door on an old metal hinge sign post. He'd never seen any still in use. Petals shooed Joe and pushed him through the door.

The door was situated with a bell that rung, like any other storefront. Upon his musically-announced arrival, the entire establishment glanced up to see who had arrived. It was an unnerving experience, until his eyes adjusted to the dim lighting, and he realized all the patrons were Blue Coats and detectives. Nearly every last one of them was in law enforcement. There was the odd patron that looked like they were a civilian, based on their attire, but overall, it was a tavern made for law enforcement.

The whole room cheered once they saw he had arrived. Most of the cheering consisted of lifting a glass or tankard into the air, yelling "Hey!" and then taking a swig.

As a Blue Coat, he had visited a few establishments with some of his colleagues, but none of them specifically catered to that crowd. The walls were littered with framed letters of news clippings of events surrounding the neighborhood precinct. High up on the wall above the bar was memorabilia from cases past. There was even an old model of long-barrel almost bent at a square angle.

Petals looked to where Joe was looking, then let out a soft and delighted laugh. "That was the working of our captain."

Joe glanced down and back up again. "He smashed a long-barrel?"

"Bent it… with one hand."

What?

Joe shook his head and looked to the elderly gnome. "I'm sorry, what was that?"

Petals gave him a pleasant and calming smile. "Don't worry, he was in the midst of a dragon rage."

It sounded like such a simple answer, yet it left Joe in a state of bewilderment. How did one respond to such an absurdly legendary feat of strength? The captain had bent an iron tube with one hand. The sheer force required for such a thing to happen was beyond his reasoning.

"Calm yourself, my boy. There are plenty of stories to be told here and plenty of lessons to be learned." He pushed Joe toward the bar and hopped up onto a stool, pointing to the one next to him.

Joe mindlessly sat as he tried to work his head around the bent long-barrel and what other amazing tales he'd hear that night.

Marcus, as Petals introduced, was the owner and barkeep. He had short silver hair and a stubbly shave. His blue eyes were the intelligent penetrating type. He stood a bit shorter than most men Joe had met, but by the looks of the pale scars that covered his face and arms, he wasn't one to be taken lightly. The man bled blue; he was law through and through. His shirt was even the same blue as a Blue Coat's trench.

"Welcome, lad." Surprisingly, he spoke with a touch of a dwarven accent.

Joe thanked him for the 'first bullet' meal, and told him how much he had enjoyed and desperately needed it at that moment. It turned out to be the first mistake he would make that night. Not only did he get appreciative thanks in return for the compliment, but also a long-winded story about the first time that Marcus had been shot. That, in turn, spurred the Blue Coat sitting next to him to start in with the first time he'd been shot, which started a line of stories.

Despite the ale-fueled storytelling session, Joe managed to get Marcus' attention long enough to call in that voucher for his 'first case meal'.

Within half an hour, a perfectly seasoned and bourbon-basted steak arrived, along with a spiced and buttered baked potato. All in all, it had been a good night. Many of the detectives clapped him on the back for having done a good job without getting anyone killed, including himself. The Bloodlings shooting the bank guards didn't count.

Blue Coats gave him a bit more praise and cheer, even going so far as to raise their glasses and drunkenly sing the Stormbay Anthem. That eventually led to sea shanties, which devolved into incoherent caterwauling.

Joe wisely consumed only one tankard of orange peel cider. Petals was a bit more jovial and consumed two drinks of something called ambrosia cream and thoroughly enjoyed his time. He went as far as pranking every single patron within the Grill. They'd counted; he'd got them all.

At the end of the long night, Joe paid for his cider, which sadly didn't come with the meal, and waved them all a good night as the caterwauling intensified.

Joe turned to head north to home, and Petals turned to head south. They waved, wished each other a good night, and said they'd see each other in the morning at the precinct. Only a few minutes into his walk, someone stepped out from an alley and directly into his path.

Despite the fact that he just left a bar, he had his wits about him and wasn't a drunken target anyone could simply jump. Joe reached for his holster when the shadowed figure raised an empty hand. "Don't bother." The voice wasn't familiar, and it sounded a bit rough around the edges.

He still didn't trust the stranger or know their motive, so he kept his hand near his firearm. The man swore up a storm, stepped into the lantern light, and pulled off his hat to reveal his face, "I'm a damn detective, you numbskull". He was thinning on top with gray hair and bags under his eyes. The eyes were the most unsettling, as they were a deeply burnt shade of orange.

Joe still didn't recognize him or understand his intentions. "I doubt that, seeing as how I've never seen you at the precinct."

"Have you met all the night shift detectives?" He put his hat back on his head and stuffed his hands into his brown trench coat, which didn't look like a detective's trench coat.

Still don't believe you.

It was possible, but the man wasn't in uniform. It didn't add up, so he still didn't move his hand. "Where's your coat?"

"I'm off duty."

Plausible, still don't believe you yet.

"I want to know who your informant was… 'cause I know that body the doc examined isn't him."

Uh oh.

Joe panicked and tried to play dumb. "What do you mean it isn't him? I also shook on an arcane agreement, I can't reveal the informant."

The man shook his head, stepped closer, and pointed a finger accusingly. "I've met the golden-eyed man. I know how smart he is. I also know he'd never be so unlucky to get killed at the hands of a rookie like you." He pointed at Joe's chest and made it sound like an insult to be caught by someone as lowly as him.

"Hey!"

"Don't feed me that goblin shite that he's dead! I *know* the intel you got was from him. The arcane agreement is exactly his style, and I'll prove it!" The man turned and stormed off down the alleyway he'd come from.

Joe stepped toward the entrance and watched as the unidentified 'detective' shrugged his coat tighter about his body and continued walking off into the dark.

"That was Kane."

Joe would usually jump, but he had heard Petals approaching from behind. "So he actually is a detective?"

Petals stopped and wobbled a little at Joe's side. "He is… currently on suspension for unlawful use of force against a suspect."

'Off duty', huh?

"I have a feeling he has an anger issue."

"Good feeling – *Hic!*"

Joe turned and looked down at his superior with a raised eyebrow. The elderly gnome was wobbling on his feet. "You should really head home and sleep that off."

Petals turned and looked up with bright red cheeks. "You should really avoid having conversations with Julian 'The Fireball' Kane. That man is manipulatively destructive. There's a reason he only works the night shift, never has rookies assigned to him, and is constantly getting suspended."

Noted.

"All right, I'll make sure to avoid having discussions with him, but you need to get to bed."

Petals began waving off the suggestion when he accidentally plastered a rainbow of colors onto a nearby stray cat with a puff of blue sparkly smoke. It caused the poor creature to raise its hackles, hiss, throw a fit, then dart in a dozen different directions before dashing down an alley.

They both stood in silence for a while before turning and nodding in agreement. "Yep! Time for bed!" The two of them turned their respective directions and made mad dashes for home, hoping nobody would notice what they'd done.

~~

After all that Joe had been through, it was only appropriate to visit his sick friend Jacobs. Following the next day of work, he decided to visit and climbed the steps to the residence above Runelore's Refuse.

Once at the top, he slowly pushed open the white-washed door to the flat above the store. A city nurse turned to see him come in, then smiled as she continued packing up her things at the foot of Jacobs' bed. The nurse had been informed that Joe would eventually visit.

The nurse picked up her bag, swung it over her shoulder, and informed him in soft whispers, "He needs rest; try not to wake him or keep him up too long." She offered a sad smile before heading for the door and bidding him a good evening.

Joe waited for the young lady to leave before daring to step further into his old friend's domicile. He'd been invited up many times before. They'd sit and have tea and discuss all things magical. By arcane law, Joe was technically not allowed to teach Jacobs any magic, so he didn't. They mostly discussed naturally-occurring magic and the history of magical items: crystals, metals, relics, and the sort.

The room hadn't changed since those long nights. The wallpaper was peeling off the wall, but it was the same pink-flowered vine pattern. Sky blue paint was flaking off the trim and cabinetry. The floorboards creaked in all the same places, plus a few new ones.

Everything was as it had been all those years ago. Jacobs' bed was set above the storefront and his kitchen over the back. The water closet was opposite the door he'd entered through. The only thing that had changed was the age of everything. All of it was much older and worn down. It also seemed smaller, but that was merely because he had grown.

Joe stepped to the kitchen and picked up one of the wooden chairs before making his way over to Jacobs. The man was covered up to his neck in a heavy blanket, and his pillows were starting to yellow with use and sweat.

His good friend, who had always seemed so lively, was deteriorating before his eyes. The man was pale, and his face was sunken and hollow. If Joe couldn't have heard Jacobs' rattling breath, he'd think the man had already passed.

Setting the chair to the right of his old friend's bed, he sat and listened for a time. Each breath sounded frighteningly like it would be the last. His breathing was so laborious it seemed like each one was a struggle.

Eventually, Joe reached into his coat pocket and pulled free a hefty brown envelope. It bore an advocate's seal. "You chose me." He didn't know if his sickly friend could hear him, but he spoke anyway. It felt necessary to speak it aloud.

Joe slowly shook his head. "You chose me to take care of your store after you were gone… but I'm a detective now."

The man kept breathing, slowly and laboriously.

He didn't know what to do with the store. Running it simply wasn't an option. Selling it seemed like the only logical choice, but that also felt like a betrayal to everything Jacobs had wanted to build and give to the neighborhood.

Joe reached into his other coat pocket and pulled out another brown envelope, also bearing an advocate's seal. "Looks like you had an estranged uncle that left you a few coins in his passing."

In all the conversations he'd had with Jacobs over the years, never once was an estranged uncle mentioned. He couldn't help but think the uncle was a fictional concoction, created by Eagle Eyes as a form of 'thank you'.

Jacobs remained unmoving, except for his long deep breaths.

Joe watched for a time longer, before he finally decided it was time. He reached into his vest pocket and pulled out his coin bag. From it, he drew a single copper penny. The coin barely covered his thumbnail and was stamped with the Stormbay city mark.

Closing his eyes, Joe spoke the necessary words and flicked the coin into the air. It disappeared in the air in a trail of copper sparks. From those sparks descended a tiny woman, no larger than his thumb. Little insect wings fluttered behind her back as she slowly landed atop his outstretched hand.

She had white hair that was styled and puffed straight up to resemble a bright white molar. Her knee-length dress sparkled with white sequins, and she had a little wooden pick in her hand like some grand staff. "Hi, Toothy."

The tiny fairy pouted, tilted her chin up, and crossed her arms while turning away.

Joe sighed and apologized, "I know, Toothy. It's been too long." He looked to the tiny line of a scar that marked one of her wings and felt even guiltier. "I should have called you long before now."

She looked over her shoulder at him with a little less of a pout.

"I promise to call on you at least once a week, especially since now I can afford it."

Toothy turned on the spot and clapped excitedly with her wooden toothpick stuffed under her arm. Her claps made her wings flutter, and she floated into the air with a trail of glittering white dust falling beneath her.

It was when Jacobs rattled out from the bed that Toothy suddenly noticed the man was there, then bolted to fly and hide behind Joe's hat. She left a trail of fairy dust in her wake.

Joe sighed, and awaited the onslaught.

Toothy crawled to the edge of his hat and peered at him from the top of it. The sight of it made him think of Amelia, and that caused him to laugh despite her fuming red face.

"I'm sorry, Toothy, but I was hoping maybe you'd say hello to my old friend." He'd asked her in the past, and she'd outright refused to meet any other humans after her first encounter. This time felt different. Joe gestured to Jacobs and added, "He doesn't have long."

Toothy's little head turned to look at the sickly gray man lying helplessly in the bed. Her frown didn't seem to budge.

Joe lowered his hand and looked at the floor. "It's all right. I just thought it would be nice for him to meet a fairy. He's so fascinated by wondrous things." His own breathing felt a bit difficult and heavy in that moment.

Toothy slowly slipped from the top of his hat and fluttered down to land on his open palm. She looked up at Joe with a tilted head and a tiny furrowed brow.

He took in a deep breath and steadied himself. "I once tried to draw a picture of you for him after telling him about you. But don't worry, I never told him how to summon you. That's between you and me." Joe looked off to the kitchen table in memory of that day. "He thought you were probably the most beautiful thing he'd ever heard of."

He sniffed back tears, swallowed hard, and cleared his throat before looking back to his life-long fairy companion.

Her little wings had wilted. She was clutching her little wooden toothpick and had a look of absolute and abject sorrow on her tiny face. Some fairies tended to have flighty emotions, especially the silent ones. Toothy looked over to Jacobs, then nodded.

Oh, thank you, Fates.

Joe nodded and shifted a little closer so that he might reach out and try to wake his old friend. "Hey... Jacobs? I'd like you to meet someone."

To Be Continued...

Author Bio

B.T. Frost is an avid fantasy writer and a fan of Dungeons & Dragons. Their writing credentials include an Applied Bachelor's Degree in Communications in Professional Writing from Grant MacEwan University and a seat as a Dungeon Master at the gaming table. They grew up in Edmonton Alberta Canada, devoured books of the fantasy genre and spent countless hours absorbing crime dramas and movies.

Made in the USA
Middletown, DE
08 June 2021

41234979R00195